Colin Langley is a former college lecture[r in?] the ancient land of Cornwall in the far sou[th of the] Kingdom. As well as writing he is inters[ted in] medieval history, cooking, European fore[ign?] travel. He has travelled extensively in Eu[rope, United] States and Canada.
This is his first work of fiction.

Thank you so much for your support. Best wishes

Colin W. Langley

GRAVE CONSEQUENCES

A NOVEL

BY

COLIN LANGLEY

**TREMENNEK PUBLICATIONS
PO BOX 662, CHACEWATER,
TRURO TR4 8WE
UNITED KINGDOM**

First published in approved form in 2008 by: Tremennek Publications, PO Box 662, Chacewater, Truro, TR4 8WE, United Kingdom

ISBN 978-0-9558539-0-6

Copyright © Colin Langley 2007

The right of Colin Langley to be identified as the author of this work has been asserted by him in accordance with sections 77 and 78 of the Copyright, Designs and Patents Act 1988.

In this work of fiction the characters, living or dead, places, organizations and events are either the product of the author's imagination or they are used entirely fictitiously.

All rights reserved. No part of this publication may be reproduced, stored in a retrieval system, or transmitted, in any form or by any means, electronic, mechanical, photocopying, recording or otherwise, without the prior written permission of the publisher.

Cover Design and Layout by: Colin Langley

Conditions of Sale: This book is sold subject to the condition that it shall not, by way of trade or otherwise, be lent, re-sold, hired out or otherwise circulated without the publisher's prior consent in any form of binding or cover other than that in which it is published and without a similar condition including this condition being imposed on the subsequent purchaser

Printed and bound in the United Kingdom of Great Britain and Northern Ireland or elsewhere under arrangements made by Lulu.com.

"Say nothing of my religion. It is known to God and myself alone. Its evidence before the world is to be sought in my life: if it has been honest and dutiful to society the religion which has regulated it cannot be a bad one."
(Thomas Jefferson 3rd President of the USA 1743-1826 in a letter to John Adams 11th January 1817)

AUTHOR'S NOTES AND ACKNOWLEDGMENTS

The inspiration for this novel came from a mix of legends circulating in West Cornwall with regard to a medieval castle that was, supposedly, once located near Praa Sands. Suffice to say that nothing of this castle remains today.

Amongst these legends was one that claimed that the castle had belonged to a knight who had taken part in the Fifth Crusade and brought home a Saracen princess to Cornwall. This, in itself, would have been enough to send shockwaves running through local society in thirteenth century England.

However, the knight in question was reputed to have added to his problems by getting himself excommunicated by the Church for attacking two priests.

This novel is a total work of fiction based on pure conjecture as to what events might have led to such a knight's fall from grace in those days. It is not about any person or persons, who are, or ever have been, connected with any other castle.

Most of the historical characters in the novel are fictional. Some characters had a place in history but the activities ascribed to them, which have not been documented outside of this novel, are totally fictional. All the modern characters in the novel are fictional and any resemblance to any person or persons, alive or dead, is entirely coincidental.

I am enormously grateful to many friends and family who read parts of the manuscript drafts and/or offered enthusiastic encouragement. I am particularly grateful to my wife, Carole, who came up with the title and undertook some basic proofreading and Lesley Chandler who proofread the final printed copy of the book before its release and made some insightful editorial comments.

CONTENTS

Chapter One	*A Castle Is Destroyed*	1
Chapter Two	*A Grave Discovery In Granada*	9
Chapter Three	*The Fifth Crusade*	17
Chapter Four	*The Search For A Castle*	34
Chapter Five	*Victory, Defeat And Capture*	46
Chapter Six	*The Tunnel*	66
Chapter Seven	*Escape From The Nile*	73
Chapter Eight	*Crisis In St. Albans*	84
Chapter Nine	*A Knight's Tale*	91
Chapter Ten	*Serious Discussions*	105
Chapter Eleven	*More Of The Knight's Tale*	109
Chapter Twelve	*Danger Below*	115
Chapter Thirteen	*Granada*	125
Chapter Fourteen	*A Letter From America*	146
Chapter Fifteen	*The Knight's Dilemma*	150
Chapter Sixteen	*More Mysteries Unfold*	161
Chapter Seventeen	*Kidnap, Ransom And Rescue*	170
Chapter Eighteen	*The Chalice*	188
Chapter Nineteen	*The Search For The Holy Grail*	196
Chapter Twenty	*Problems With Relations*	204
Chapter Twenty-One	*The Return Of The Knight*	215
Chapter Twenty-Two	*Shock And Confusion*	228
Chapter Twenty-Three	*The Evil Knight*	239
Chapter Twenty-Four	*The Desire For Retribution*	246
Chapter Twenty-Five	*A Problem Of Two Chalices*	251
Chapter Twenty-Six	*Knight Errant*	264
Chapter Twenty-Seven	*The Theft Of The Chalice*	272
Chapter Twenty-Eight	*The Marriage*	280
Chapter Twenty-Nine	*Serious Injuries*	286

Chapter Thirty	*Excommunication*	289
Chapter Thirty-One	*Surprises, Fact And Speculation*	292
Chapter Thirty-Two	*The Attack On The Castle*	299
Chapter Thirty-Three	*A Twist In The Tale*	304
Chapter Thirty-Four	*The Escape*	308
Chapter Thirty-Five	*Trials And Tribulations*	313
Chapter Thirty-Six	*Lost And Found*	325

CHAPTER ONE

A Castle Is Destroyed

It was in the year 1228, shortly before the Feast of the Ascension, that they came for the disgraced Templar Knight, Sir Elvin le Gard.

Night had cast a blanket, black as pitch, across all the land. Sir Elvin had not slept well, tossing and turning. But now he was suddenly awake. He sat bolt upright, breathless. He tried to gather his wits. The sweat was pouring off him. He thought he had had a nightmare. But he knew it was no nightmare. He had definitely heard something. He remembered that he had slept fitfully, his mind full of worries over what was about to happen. Would they come that night? He slipped back into a drowsy slumber. But then he was wide-awake again.

The events, which were about to unfold, were hardly unexpected but nevertheless made him very uneasy. The Church and the Templar Brotherhood had a reputation for being merciless with those who strayed from the flock.

He pushed back the woollen blankets and got out of the bed that he shared with his bride of just a few days, Tayri. He was a tall man with thick dark hair and smouldering black eyes. His swarthy good looks betrayed his Breton ancestry. There was no doubting the fear that was churning around inside him at that moment.

Elvin pulled on his boots and stumbled across the freshly strewn rushes that covered the stone floor. He peered through a narrow window and strained to gaze out into the blackness beyond. Then, as the moon drifted from behind a dark cloud, he was sure that he had caught a glimpse in the distance of moonlight reflecting off the hilt of a sword or the tip of a lance. Quickly he hurried past the still smouldering fire, and went out onto the staircase. The smoky atmosphere made him cough and he hawked up a large globule of phlegm, which he directed to one side and ground into the stone step.

Tayri moaned drowsily, barely half awake. He turned and looked towards her, her long, reddish brown hair spread across the pillow. She was asleep again. He marvelled at how beautiful she looked in the depths of peaceful slumber and he remembered the first time he had set eyes on her in the sunshine of the courtyard in Granada. Peaceful as she now looked he knew that this apparent calm hid a deep-seated fear of what might soon happen. She murmured in her sleep and her forehead betrayed a frown, perhaps showing signs of the disturbing dreams besetting her.

Elvin ran up the staircase to the top of the keep and stared out over the battlements. Yestin, his steward, was already there. They nodded to one another, both aware of the perils about to beset them. Elvin had been sure he had heard the sound of voices.

Gazing through the cool night air both men could not make out anything at first. Then they heard it again. It was the sound of low voices. Elvin's eyes strained to identify from where the voices were coming. He peered down along the path that led up the hill. Both men heard the creak of leather, the muffled jingle of bridles and the snort of a horse. As their eyes became more accustomed to the darkness they saw them.

Advancing up the hill from the village was a group of heavily armoured knights accompanied by a small band of foot soldiers and retainers. They were all in full armour and some of the knights were distinctive in their white mantles, decorated with large red crosses. The group was treading very purposefully and in almost complete silence.

"They're here, my liege," whispered Yestin. "I'll raise the others."

* * *

Piran, the miller, had also been awakened that night. He left his bed in the mill in the village below the castle and walked into the next room, past the big grinding stone, and over towards the open doorway of the mill. Sacks of threshed corn were stacked up against the far wall ready to be ground into flour. On his way through he picked up a shovel in case he had need to defend himself and his family, whom he had left cowering in the bed in the room next door.

Outside he heard the relentless rush of the water from the stream as it turned the groaning mill wheel and then sped away, over the rocks and stones, down towards the sea.

He stationed himself by the low doorframe, bent his body slightly and peeked out. He peered along the path that led up the hill and saw what Elvin and Yestin had already seen.

He had, in common with all the villagers, an ingrained suspicion and dislike of strangers. They all resented the fact that people whom they regarded as outlanders or foreigners had occupied their land and imposed a ruthless will upon them all. All villagers kept sickles, scythes and pitchforks close at hand in case of attack in what were very uncertain times.

The miller stood at his door watching the armed men heading up the hill towards the headland and the castle. There was no danger to the village itself. Piran realised immediately what the objective was and who the men were. He thought it advisable not be seen so he returned to bed.

"What was that?" asked his wife, only just barely awake.

"T'was up at the castle like Father Trystan did say."

"Oh," she said and turned over and went back to sleep.

Piran found it difficult to get back to sleep. He struggled with his conscience about what was happening at the castle and whether he owed any duty to his lord. But he persuaded himself that there was little he could do to influence events and he gradually dozed off.

* * *

"Holy Mother of God, the castle's ablaze!" somebody yelled out.

Piran and his wife were rudely awakened from their all too short slumbers.

All the inhabitants of the Cornish village of Tremennek were up. They began rushing out of their roughly thatched, cob-walled cottages to see what was happening. There was a tremendous hubbub. Some people ran down along the side of the stream to the beach and were quickly followed by others.

The tide was out and the sea was unusually calm. The waves lapped the shore in a gentle, therapeutic manner. But nobody was interested in or could even hear the waves. The villagers gathered in small groups on the sand talking excitedly to one another and gazing up at the headland at the western end of the beach. All they could hear was the sound of the blazing inferno on top of the shadowy cliffs.

The castle on the headland was burning fiercely. In the moonlight the blaze added an orange glow that could be seen all over the western tip of Cornwall. The roaring flames were licking the heavens and great showers of sparks burst into the skies each time a piece of the timbers collapsed. The snap of the breaking beams and the crackling sound of the fire, consuming everything, could be clearly heard on the beach below.

The villagers chattered amongst themselves in their native Cornish.

"The Breton bastard is getting what's owin' to'n. I'ope he d'rot in hell – and his Saracen whore with'n," growled Myghal, the blacksmith, nursing the stump at the end of his left arm.

Myghal had never liked Sir Elvin and felt no regret that the castle was now burning. Some years before, Myghal had had his hand cut off because he had made a bad shoe for Elvin's father. The faulty shoe had caused the tetchy knight to fall from his horse. The elder Le Gard had hacked off the blacksmith's hand with a war axe in a fit of bad temper and Myghal's hand had been nailed to the forge door as an example to the entire village. It had remained there until it had rotted. Myghal had nearly died and had been forced to accelerate the teaching of his trade to his elder son so that he could take over the brunt of the work. Myghal bore a fierce hatred of the whole Le Gard family as a result.

"I'm like all of ee, see," said Piran, the miller. "I can't abide the Bretons. I can't forgive'm for siding with the Normans all them years afore." He was referring to the fact that Sir Elvin, who was the Lord of the Manor of Tremennek, was descended from Bretons who had aided William the Conqueror at the Battle of Hastings.

"I don' really see why we should be forced to swear homage to such bastards," said Myghal.

"Be careful, boy," said Piran, "you don' want'm hear ee say things like that. You'll be in real trouble, for sure. Any'ow Sir Elvin weren't as bad as his father. He were harsh in punishin' anybody who broke the law but he always gave'm a fair hearing. He never used his right to take our daughters to bed the first night of their marriage like his father always did." A number of the villagers nodded their heads in agreement.

The Le Gard clan had been Lords of the Manor ever since the castle had been constructed some thirty years before. Being from Brittany originally, they could speak the same Cornish language as the villagers and were basically from the same original stock. But they were regarded as traitors for having taken up the Norman cause even though that had happened nearly two hundred years before. They were regarded quite simply as foreign intruders.

"I d'often wonder what Sir Elvin was really doin' in the East," Piran said. "They d'say there's been some strange goin's on up at the castle."

"Es," grunted Myghal, "some d'say magic and sorcery goes on up there. I've been told that Sir Elvin d'have lots of magical books, all written in a strange foreign hand. And more'n that, he d'keep weird liquids and powders up there in big earthenware pots. He's s'posed t'ave brought'm with'n from the lands of the East. He d'spend hours in the keep, on his own, mixin'm all together, concoctin' evil potions."

"It all d'seem very strange to me," nodded Piran.

"I knew somethin' was wrong when he arrived with that Saracen whore," Myghal went on. "She were a witch if ever ee saw one. Although she appeared t'be a pretty maid, I'm sure she used her good looks to trap unwary lads for Sir Elvin's disgusting experiments. She did have the evil eye, that's for sure."

The flames were still burning brightly but, from time to time, the acrid smoke swirled around the headland and even drifted down to the beach area. The smell of burning wood was intense and the smoke was the type that got right to the back of the throat and began to make some villagers cough and spit.

Suddenly the crowd of villagers on the beach parted and Father Trystan, appeared. Father Trystan was the parish priest, a man who wielded enormous influence and power in the area. Apart from Sir Elvin he was probably the most feared man the villagers knew. To cross him invited eternal damnation and he ruled his village with an iron will.

"You should all go'ome now, my children," he said. "There is nothin' for ee here. What I warned ee about in Church has come to pass. Sir Elvin has refused to submit to the orders of the Sheriff and so the Sheriff and his men, together with Knights Templar, have attacked the castle to rid our parish of this evil man. T'is God's will. You should get your sleep, for there are fields to tend tomorrow and much work to be done." Father Trystan clapped his hands in an insistent gesture.

It was no secret that their liege lord had not got on with the village priest at all.

Father Trystan had been a clever boy and his father had been able to afford to pay a fee to the previous lord to allow him to leave the village to become a novice in the monastery on St. Michael's Mount. For a country boy he had progressed well enough to avoid a life of toil in the fields and streams and to return as the priest for the village. Priests who could speak Cornish were in very short supply anyway and Father Trystan took full advantage of his position.

He was not a wealthy man but he had a holding in the fields, which was larger than any other villager and he was relieved of the normal feudal dues that had to be made to the Lord of the Manor. The villagers worked his land for him and he received a tithe of one tenth of the corn produced by his flock on their own land together with gifts from time to time and fees, usually in kind, for weddings and such like.

No one liked leaving his own land to tend either that of Sir Elvin or the priest very much, especially at busy harvest times. But Father Trystan possessed considerable status and the villagers looked upon him for guidance in all things, albeit more out of fear of damnation than respect.

No lord normally dared to interfere with the rights of the Church. But the Lord of Tremennek had apparently grievously offended against the Church.

Things appeared to have come to a head between Father Trystan and Sir Elvin on the day that the priest together with a visiting abbot from a place called Glaston, or Glastonbury as it later became known, had gone up to the castle to collect tithes for the Abbey there. The villagers had little idea where Glaston lay but what they did know was that some altercation between the Lord and the two clerics had taken place. Sir Elvin had set about the priest and gravely wounded him – and he had cast both of them out. Such a thing was unheard of and it was thought that Sir Elvin would surely risk excommunication for such an offence.

The villagers had continued to exercise their duties to the lord of their domain until one Sunday, a few weeks previously, Father Trystan had spoken to his congregation in very sombre terms:

"I have to announce to ee all that Sir Elvin Le Gard, the lord of this domain, has gravely offended our Holy Mother Church and will shortly be excommunicated by papal bull and his soul damned for ever. He has also offended against the Rule of the Poor Knighthood of the Temple of Solomon, of which he was previously a brother, and will pay dearly for his transgressions. There will come a time in the near future when the Sheriff of Cornwall and certain Knights Templar will arrive in the village to take'n away to answer for his crimes. You are all henceforth absolved of any duties to this man and any man who comes to his aid will be regarded as an outlaw."

The villagers gasped at this announcement. " What does he mean by an outlaw?" Piran's wife enquired.

"He d'mean that he will be cast out of the village and any man has the right to kill'n just as if he were a wolf," whispered the miller in reply.

"The sins of the Lord Elvin must have been very grave indeed," sighed his wife.

And so here they were some weeks later witnessing the destruction of the castle.

The castle itself was not really a castle in the proper sense of the word but more like a fortified manor house. The outer walls were of solid granite and difficult to scale. The great hall, and the living quarters attached to one end of it, was also constructed of stone, as was the small keep, which was attached to the other end of it. The rest of the buildings inside the bailey were wooden and this is why they had been so easy to set ablaze.

As the villagers returned to their homes they could hear the shouts of the knights setting about their slaughter amongst the leaping flames. Few servants and retainers had remained at the castle but it sounded as if those who had were being quickly put to the sword or consumed by the flames. Their agonised yells and screams could be heard echoing around the cliffs of the bay and down in the valley below.

By the next morning all was quiet. It was a dark, dank day and there was a slight drizzle. A huge plume of smoke lingered in the sky above the headland, trapped by the low clouds. Nothing remained of the wooden buildings but piles of ash and men were now in the process of demolishing what was left of the stone buildings and walls. Carts had been brought up to take away some of the granite whilst the rest was being tipped over the cliff onto the rocks below.

The villagers in their fields occasionally glanced up at the headland but then got on with their work with a sullen resolution. Many were apprehensive as to what would happen to them now.

The following Sunday Father Trystan told them "The evil Crusader and his Saracen whore are no longer. They have been plunged into the oblivion of hell. The castle has been razed to the ground and soon no trace of it will remain. The lands that belonged to this evil man will become part of the lands of the Bishop of Exeter again and you will owe your duties to him. Let us be thankful to God that we have been saved from the influence of this evil man. Let no man ever speak of him again."

And so the village was rid of its lord in the castle on the hill. Just on the odd occasion did the more curious of its inhabitants give a thought to the strange events, which had taken place there. But the peasant villagers of Tremennek neither understood nor cared to think too much about them, and continued with their never ending struggle for survival in a brutal world.

The empty headland went back to nature and all was consigned to legend and folklore.

It took another eight centuries for anybody to question again what had happened there.

CHAPTER TWO

A Grave Discovery in Granada

Dr. Peter Verity booked into the Tremennek Bay Hotel. He gave an address in St. Albans, Hertfordshire. He entered his occupation as a Research Fellow at the University of London. After he had registered he went up to his room.

He came down again about 7.30 p.m. He had dinner and then retired to the bar.

"Good evening, sir. What would you like?" asked the barman.

"I'll have a pint of your best, " said Verity, gazing at the collection of old-fashioned drinking vessels, which were displayed on shelves all around the lounge bar area. The hotel, if you could call it that, was an eighteenth century public house with a number of rooms to let.

Peter sat quietly drinking his beer. The bar was not very full because there was still some way to go before the holiday season began. The barman busied himself cleaning glasses and sorting out his stock of bottles.

"I take it from your accent that you're not from these parts then," commented the barman after a while.

"No, I'm down from St. Albans on a job here," said Peter.

"What kind of work do you do?" asked the nosey barman.

"I work at the University of London's School of Oriental Studies. I do research into medieval armour," said Peter, who was sure that he was going to get the same bemused reaction as he always did.

"Is there much call for that sort of thing?" The question had been predictable.

"Well, I don't earn a fortune but I get to travel. I suppose it keeps me off the streets," quipped Peter. "Tell me," he continued, "Do you know much about the history of this area?"

"No, not really. I'm not really sure there is much history apart from the tin mining. More legend really," was the reply.

"Do you know anything about a castle once being on the headland above here?" asked Peter.

"I have heard something about it but you need to talk to Old Tom.

He'll be in shortly. He knows all the local tales," the barman assured him.

Sure enough about ten minutes later, in came Old Tom. He was a man who could have been of any age between about sixty and eighty years old. He wore a greasy flat cap, which gave the impression that it was pretty well a permanent fixture. He had on a navy blue blazer, which had seen better days but his trousers were sharply creased. The badge of the Royal National Lifeboat Institution was proudly displayed on the breast of the blazer.

It was not long before Peter had engaged him in conversation and offered him the customary bribe of a pint of beer in exchange for some local information.

Old Tom was used to visitors pumping him for information about the area and in the summer he did quite well out of it, seldom having to buy a drink for himself.

Peter posed the question again.

"Well, see," said Tom, "people d'say that, once upon a time, there was a castle up there but nobody can ever remember there being any ruins. There is a story that an evil knight lived there and, after fighting away in the Crusades, brought home a Saracen wife. He delved into all kinds of evil sorcery and in the end God put an end to his satanic practices by destroying the castle. They d'say that you can sometimes see his ghost riding across the headland."

"That's very interesting," said Peter.

"We've got a number of other people arriving tomorrow from London," observed the barman. "Are they anything to do with you?"

"Yes, they are," said Peter. "We're all part of an archaeological team who've come down to survey the headland to see if there are any remains up there of an old castle."

"You'd better watch out for the ghosts, then," commented Old Tom wryly.

After a bit more gossip and a few more beers Peter retired to bed. In his room he began to reflect on the reason why he had come down to Cornwall.

A few months before he had received an e-mail from a colleague in Spain, Dr. Anya Naziri, asking if he could possibly come out to Granada, as she needed his help with an archaeological dig. The problem had been that an unmarked grave had been discovered with a badly weathered stone bearing what appeared to be a highly unusual form of grave decoration. Within the grave had been the remains of a body dressed in armour and a number of artefacts that just did not add up. She had been sure that Peter would be able to help with his expertise in armour.

Peter had duly flown out and had been taken to the site on a new housing development in the old part of the city on the other side of the valley from the Alhambra Palace.

It was part of a gentrification scheme for the area and developers were converting ancient gypsy houses into ochre coloured modern holiday apartments. At the site Peter examined and advised on the armour and artefacts that had been discovered under the floor. Fortunately the city authorities were very sensitive to Granada's historical past and immediately called a halt to the development for an archaeological investigation to be undertaken.

It had been a strange find, for the armour, as far as Peter could tell, was medieval, probably from the beginning of the thirteenth century. Clearly the owner of the armour had been no peasant but it was difficult to establish exactly who he had been. The armour showed certain Islamic traits but certainly was not Berber or Arab in design. It was typical of European Crusader armour, which would not have been totally unusual, as the region would have changed hands during the medieval period. However, the Christians had not reconquered this region until the late fifteenth century and the style of the armour predated that by some two or three centuries. The style was that of an English or French knight of the thirteenth century and this seemed a strange place to discover it.

Even more mysterious, however, was a brooch, of the type used to secure a cloak, which had been found in the grave. This was a tin or bronze artefact decorated with the twists and swirls reminiscent of the "Celtic knots" found on Irish jewellery.

The man's sword had also been found nearby and was of typical North European, probably English, design. It could be quite feasible that a Moor might have come into possession of such a sword whilst fighting against Christian Crusaders in Spain. But this one had a particularly intricately designed hilt. Whilst it had not been in good condition it was still possible for an expert to make out the painstakingly fashioned swirls and loops of further "Celtic knots."

However, the man was not alone. There was another grave next to his, which probably contained his wife. Here were the remains of a woman who had been dressed in the typical style of a highborn Berber of the age, an opinion that was reinforced by the discovery of gold and silver jewellery of Islamic design around the body. But it was not the discovery of her remains that had prompted the call for Peter to visit the site. The man's body was clearly a bit of a mystery.

In consultation with Anya and others at the site, Peter had decided to make some drawings of the designs on the brooch and the sword, and send them to a colleague at the University of London who knew a lot more about Celtic designs than he did. They also successfully extracted a DNA sample from the bone marrow of the knight and sent it for analysis to University College, London. Peter then returned home.

A few days later he received a telephone call from his colleague, Bill Alexander, the expert on Celtic designs.

"I've had a good look at the drawings you've sent me and consulted with a colleague in Wales. We're both pretty sure now that these designs are of Cornish origin. They're definitely not Welsh or Irish. So our bet would be Cornwall," he advised.

"Many thanks, Bill. Grateful for that, buy you a pint sometime," said Peter. He phoned Anya in Granada right away to give her the news.

The analysis of the small sample of DNA they had painstakingly managed to extract took somewhat longer.

About a fortnight later Peter heard by telephone from a colleague in the UCL genetics team. A genetics survey had recently been undertaken to discover how far genetic traces of the Normans had remained in the British Isles and was, therefore, a good source for the information on the DNA from the remains discovered in Andalusia.

"Since we were dealing with a male, our investigations into the Y chromosome, which is carried only by men and passed on from generation to generation, was relevant," it was explained. "We took samples of DNA from modern Normans and Bretons who were very local to their areas and whose families had been there for generations, and compared them with men currently living in Britain.

"As a result we were able to draw up a genetic map of the U.K., showing the effects of the Norman invasion. In this respect the results were disappointing, because they were not very conclusive at all. When we compared your sample with those from Cornwall we could not find much link at all. The Norman influence on Cornwall was small and the DNA did not compare. However, we did find that there were striking similarities between your sample and samples we had taken in Brittany.

Therefore our conclusion is that you should be looking there."

"OK," said Peter. "Many thanks for your help. Can you send us your report as soon as possible?" Peter had been a touch disappointed as he now had slightly conflicting clues to the origins of the body in the grave. Was it from Cornwall or was it from Brittany? He had phoned Anya and told her of his disappointment and they left it at that for the moment.

A few days later however, Anya had rung him to say that a further discovery had been made. Pieces of a shield had been found and students at the site had been painstakingly trying to fit them together. What they had discovered, when they had cleaned everything up and got all the available pieces together, was that faint traces of a crest could be discerned, which they thought might give clues to the family from which the man had originated.

"Can you get some drawings to me via the Internet?" Peter had asked Anya. "I will consult some texts on heraldry to see if I can come up with anything."

When the drawings had arrived from Spain, Peter spent some time in the British Library pouring over books on heraldry to see if he could identify anything like the crest. He spent several days wading his way through great tomes on heraldic designs trying to match the drawings with known medieval crests.

He had almost given up hope of finding any kind of match when he turned a page and there it was. He had been looking through a large volume filled with the crests of knights who had taken part in the Battle of Hastings and there before his eyes lay the almost perfect match. It was the crest of one Steven Le Gard, who had been one of William the Conqueror's personal bodyguards at the Battle of Hastings and had fought with distinction. Even more interesting, however, was the fact that Steven Le Gard had been a Breton. Could he have been an ancestor of the man in the grave?

Very excited with his find Peter contacted Anya again.

"I think I've found the origin of the crest," he told her. He explained about Steven Le Gard and they both agreed that here was the probable Breton connection. But Peter added, "It's quite feasible in my mind that a Breton coming to England at the time of the Conquest might well have ended up somewhere like Cornwall. There would be racial and linguistic connections with the Cornish anyway at that time. He was probably sent down there because he would understand the local language. The only problem is I don't seem to be able to find out much more than that so it's not conclusive."

"It's extremely interesting," said Anya. "Thanks very much for your help. I just wonder how one of his possible descendants came to find himself in Muslim Granada."

"Have you found any more artefacts of interest?" asked Peter.

"No," she replied. "I'm still a bit intrigued by the actual gravestone. It's strange that there are no markings on it except for some odd shapes that I haven't really figured out as yet. It was probably because there were not many decorative markings that the grave remained untouched for so long."

"Yes, it is strange," said Peter. "It seems neither an Islamic practice nor a Christian one to bury somebody of the status of a knight anonymously like that. Can you send me some drawings of how you see the designs and if I get any bright ideas about them, I'll let you know?"

When he received the drawings Peter tried to recall where he had seen similar designs before. He had a good knowledge of sites in the Middle East and he recalled visiting the site of a castle at Athlit in Israel, which the Israelis had excavated.

There had been a lot of gravestones. They had been very weathered but some of the more deeply chiselled designs were still discernible. He looked at his notes taken on this visit and was surprised at what he found.

The castle at Athlit had been built in the thirteenth century about the same date that had been assigned to the grave in Andalusia. This had been a Templar castle and some of the gravestones, where the designs could still be discerned, had contained similar designs to those associated with the Freemasons of today.

As he looked at the drawings from Spain he could just make out what looked like a Templar Cross. That was the only grave decoration. He was convinced, therefore, that the grave must have a Templar connection of some sort. But then he thought again. This just did not make sense. What was a Templar knight doing buried in a grave in the midst of what could be considered enemy territory in the Moorish stronghold of Al Andalus, as Andalusia had then been known?

The whole thing remained an enigma for some time afterwards and the remains in Spain were forgotten for a while.

In the meantime Peter took his family on holiday to Cornwall. Mary and the two girls, Emma and Martha, aged thirteen and eleven, had looked forward to the break. The marriage was on slightly rocky foundations, perhaps, because of the long periods Peter spent away from home as part of his researches. The idea was to get some quality time together and, at first, it was a success.

However, it was whilst spending that time in the Penwith area of Cornwall that Peter had first come across the legend of the Evil Knight of Tremennek. It was said that the Knight had taken part in the Crusades and had brought home a Saracen bride to the castle that had once stood on the headland above Tremennek Bay. The castle no longer existed and not a trace of it remained. But the Knight's ghost was reputed to haunt the headland above Tremennek Bay. This was precisely the same legend that Old Tom had just repeated in the bar of the Tremennek Bay Hotel.

Peter's children had been very excited, at the time, about the prospect of meeting a ghost. Peter had scoured libraries and bookshops for any further information on the legend but found nothing. He was convinced that there might have been a connection between the legend and the findings in Southern Spain.

He had got into contact with Anya again and told her of his thoughts. She was sympathetic and supportive. They both came to the same conclusion. If there was any truth in the legend they would have to excavate the headland to see if there had, indeed, been a castle there.

Mary, however, was far from supportive. She had come down to Cornwall with her family to have a pleasant break and to repair some of the damage done to the marriage in recent years. Yet again her husband was deserting them to pursue some fantasy about a ghost from the Middle Ages.

"It's a local legend," she said disparagingly. " It's been dreamt up by the locals as a tale to tell the tourists. I don't know how you could fall for it." And, indeed, she had her supporters. There were people in Tremennek Bay itself who gave the legend very scant respect and had said that it was all a lot of pub talk for the visitors. To be fair these were mainly "emmets," incomers from outside of Cornwall, who were inclined to be sceptical about some of the things they were told. The local Cornish, almost without exception, did not doubt the possible truth of the story, which they claimed had been handed down by word of mouth over centuries.

Peter had a feeling about the legend. He could not explain it. But one thing he was convinced about. The headland had to be excavated to see if a castle had once been there. He told Anya in Granada what he proposed to do and she was very enthusiastic. "Let me know when you get funding," she said, "I'd love to be involved."

Peter returned to London before the holiday fortnight had been completed in order to put the wheels in motion to seek funding for the project. Mary was left in Cornwall with the two children to see out the rest of the holiday in their rented cottage. Peter wondered continually about the Templar knight in the grave in Andalusia. Mary wondered continually about the state of their marriage.

CHAPTER THREE

The Fifth Crusade

Ten years before the destruction of the castle at Tremennek, in the year 1218, the people of the Nile Delta in Egypt had been just as fearful of a sudden visit by armed strangers from afar, as the peasant villagers of West Cornwall.

On the day that it happened, the sun was baking down on the rolling dunes above a long sandbar, which protected the Delta from the sea. The temperature was in the mid eighties and the dunes reflected back the heat of the mid-day sun.

It was humid. A dirty, shoeless urchin boy, dressed in a scruffy gallabaya, the traditional floor length garment of Egyptian males, was puffing hard and beads of sweat were pouring down his face. He could taste their saltiness on his lips. He had lost some of the goats that he was tending and had had to scramble over the sandbar down to the seashore to retrieve two strays.

The sea was calm and the waves gently lapped the shore. His younger brother was looking after the main herd some way away down at the edge of the dunes beside the great lake where the fertile greenness of the Delta began.

Fortunately the sandbar was only very narrow here and the sea had stopped the goats from going too far. The boy dared not lose any of them for fear of his father beating him severely if he did so.

He gathered up the strays and began clambering up over the dunes again giving the goats an encouraging smack on the rump every so often to concentrate their minds on the direction in which they ought to be going. He reached the top of the dunes and looked down on the greenness of the land below.

Stretching as far as the eye could see into the distance were the bountiful crops of an enormous oasis. All around the young boy could see the immensity of the desert and the arid mountains, which stretched away to the west and east of the Delta. The richness of the vegetation had sustained animal and human life in the area for thousands of years.

Abdul, for such was his name, stared down at a tributary of the river, which flowed down from the mouth of the Nile on the Mediterranean Sea to the fortified trading city of Doumyat.

The city was perched on a headland overlooking the river and was protected on its east and west sides by water, and by the huge Lake Manzaleh behind it. It was, to all intents and purposes, built on an island.

On the banks below the walls of the city was where Abdul lived. His family occupied a small mud house next to the river and his mother and sisters drew water from the river in buckets. The house had steps leading down to the river and their sheep and goats were allowed to pasture at liberty, day and night, which was why they sometimes strayed - as on this day.

A saying went of Doumyat that "its walls are sweetmeats and its dogs are sheep" because of its prosperity and because of the number of sheep and goats roaming free.

Unlike the Cornish village this was a flourishing city and its residents seldom went hungry. They were kept well fed with an abundance of seabirds and fish, mutton and kid, and buffalo milk famed for its sweetness.

The young goatherd loved to stop occasionally and gaze at the sea eagles swooping down and snatching fish out of the water. But he knew that it was not wise to dally on the banks of the river. Crocodiles were common here. It was not unknown for them to attack careless passers-by, who were not paying sufficient attention, and they would frequently take sheep and goats as well.

These enormous beasts could grow up to fifteen feet long. They had a long narrow snout with razor sharp teeth and very tough, horny skin. They would often group into several dozen animals and were to be avoided at all costs especially if the females had young to protect.

Wiping his sweat filled brow Abdul caught a flash of something white out to sea and turned his head. At first, he thought that it had been a diving sea bird but now he realised it was a ship just visible on the horizon. Perhaps it was another vessel bound for the port laden with trade goods? Then he spied another, and another. And soon the horizon was filled with sails. How could so many be approaching at the same time?

Then he saw something, which filled him with absolute dread. The sweat from the heat turned to sweat from fear. Several of the mainsails carried red crosses and he knew at once what was happening. He scurried down the dune as fast as he could and met up with his brother.

"We must return to the city as speedily as possible and warn them," he said. "The infidels are coming."

The two young boys drove the goats as fast as they could back to the city, which lay some two miles distant.

They made immediately for the fortified inner city, which was going about its daily business behind its tall, orange, sandstone walls overlooking the river.

Built on the headland, so that all traffic up and down the river could be controlled, its high walls were flanked by square watchtowers, which faced every direction.

Ochre coloured houses spilled down the slopes from the city walls to the river's edge interspersed by date palms and leafy shrubs. A thick savannah formed a lush carpet underfoot. Along the banks, on either side of the river, beans, corn, cotton, rice and wheat grew in abundance kept irrigated by donkey-powered shadoofs raising water from specially constructed canals.

In between the banks of the river, feluccas, the traditional sailing vessels of the River Nile, were crisscrossing all the time, carrying people and goods, their tall triangular sails bending in the breeze.

Running all the time, the boys cried to anyone they could see, warning them of the impending danger. Leaving the goats below, they scrambled up the hill to the main city gate manned by the Governor's guards.

"The Franks are coming," they cried gesturing towards the sea. An officer of the guard was called for and interrogated them closely. He called up to one of the watchtowers requesting news of what could be seen.

"Many Frankish sails," was the reply.

"Sound the alarm," cried the officer and all around the city walls men began to appear with long curved buffalo horns and they blew them to warn all soldiers to return to the fortress and all citizens to take shelter in their houses or to come within the walls of the city for refuge.

Then all there was to do was to wait.

* * *

Sir Elvin Le Gard stood on the deck of the Templar vessel "Le Chevalier de la Croix Rouge" and gazed at the land ahead.

The fleet approaching the shore was made up of a mixed bunch of vessels of varying nationalities. Quite a number of vessels had been left behind in the Holy Land, becalmed by a sudden drop in the wind. They would have to wait for these to catch up before they could risk any excursion ashore.

The ships, bulging with men, horses and equipment, were embarking on the Fifth Crusade against the Saracens, instigated by the new Pope, Honorius III, and Egypt was thought to be a key capture in the struggle.

Ahead of them lay the vast delta of the River Nile. On either side a narrow, green, fertile line cut through the desert to the west and arid mountains to the east. Riding the swell created by the many cross currents the ships were making for the Damietta Mouth with the aim of landing close to the fortified city of Damietta, as the Christians called Doumyat.

Elvin could already see the magnificent fortress perched on a hill above the city some two miles inland. As they got nearer Elvin spied the young boy, Abdul, gathering up his goats, scrambling along the top of the dunes and fleeing towards the city. He realised that the alarm was about to be given but there was little they could do to prevent it. It would be unwise to land and so the vessels stood off the Damietta Mouth and waited for reinforcements to arrive.

Within a few days the other vessels turned up with the leader of the Crusade, John de Brienne, the elderly King of Jerusalem. King John had lost his kingdom to the Saracens some time before and was seeking to regain it on this Fifth Crusade against "the heathen."

Elvin knew little of this man. The mood was tense and everybody felt ill at ease. Expeditions such as this were usually plagued with leadership squabbles and this one would be no different and had had the usual shambles of a start.

Apparently, King John had been a popular choice for leader because he had a reputation for dealing with all the different nationalities involved in a Crusade with diplomacy and tact in what was not an easy task considering the number of strong-willed barons and knights he had under his command.

A shantytown was already under construction on the western bank of the river, so that there could be immediate protection from the scorching sun. All kinds of temporary structures were being hastily knocked together from wood and other materials, which had been brought on the ships in order to get the huge army and its supplies quickly under cover.

Timber began to litter the beach to be used later for the construction of catapults and battering rams.

King John held an immediate council of war.

He began in the universal French tongue. " Let us remind ourselves, my lords, as to why we are here. We have come to repel the foes of the Cross of Christ and, in the course of time, to return Jerusalem to us as its rightful Christian king.

"We must remember that it matters little whether we live or die on this Crusade. We are in the service of the Lord. What greater glory could there be than in gaining victory in the coming fight? But we must never forget that it is also exceedingly blessed to die as a martyr for the Lord!

"At Acre, in the Holy Land, a council of your leaders decided that it would be in the best interests of Our Lord's work to attack Egypt first and defeat the Sultan's heathen hordes. To attempt to retrieve Jerusalem whilst Egypt was so strong was considered unwise.

"Our aim here will be to render Egypt and the Sultan impotent in the struggle against us. The ultimate objective will be to capture Cairo, the Sultan's capital. The immediate objective is to take the nearby city of Damietta, because it guards the way up the river.

"After gaining the fall of Damietta, we will then move on to capture Cairo and then the rest of Egypt will fall. Be sure of this - to capture Damietta will open the way to Cairo!

"With these objectives in mind we have, today, ordered a small group of the Knights of Christ to spy upon the city this night and counsel us as to its situation. They are brave servants of the Lord and we are confident that they will report well."

The Knights of Christ were the Knights Templar. These famous warrior monks had a fearsome military reputation and were the most highly trained warriors on the Crusade.

An hour later, when dusk had fallen, Sir Elvin Le Gard rode out with six knights who were all members of a special cavalry unit of the Templars, skilled in scouting operations.

He had been put in charge of them with the task of reconnoitring the enemy's position. One of the knights had served a long time in the Holy Land and spoke Arabic, so that if they were able to capture any prisoners, they would be able to interrogate them.

At that time Elvin was aged about twenty-four years old and was a tall, handsome young man with smouldering black eyes, which had entranced many a fair maiden. He wore a thin beard and his jet-black hair was cut short, just like his colleagues.

For this expedition the knights had abandoned their distinctive white mantles and armour and wore only padded thick leather jerkins and breeches and carried a single sword each. They were mounted on swift, light horses, whose hooves had been covered in sacking to deaden their sound. Their orders had been clear — ascertain the chances of a successful attack upon the city and return quickly to report.

Being on the west side of the river they were on the opposite bank to the city and they hoped, therefore, not to meet the enemy in any force.

As they approached closer in the moonlight Elvin fingered the lucky talisman, which he always wore round his neck. It had accompanied him all the way from his home land of Cornwall. It was made of hammered Cornish tin mixed with copper for strength. It had an intricate Celtic design and a large black opal in the centre. It was called a Cross of St. Piran, and, according to the Cornish, was named after the patron saint of all tin miners.

Finding themselves in a good position, the group of knights was able see the city on the opposite bank and could make out the glow of the fires in the courtyards within the walls. In the light of the moon the huge red sandstone walls looked magnificent. Below them houses spilled down to the river's edge but these were in darkness.

Elvin guessed that their inhabitants had retreated within the fortified walls of the inner city, if they possessed any sense. The battlements appeared to be fully manned and it was obvious that the Crusader army had been expected.

They cantered further along the riverbank and then they drew up quickly. In the distance before them, there lay a fortified tower on their side of the river. It was situated on an island close to the bank and this fortress, too, appeared to be fully guarded. This they had not anticipated. It was, therefore, vital that they found out more about it.

Leaving two of the squires behind to tend the horses, Elvin and the others crept on foot towards the tower concealing themselves as far as possible amongst the palms Down by the river there were several large trees like weeping willows. They used these for cover whilst they entered the shallows and swam their way round to the tower. Then, they realised its importance.

A huge chain stretched from the tower all the way across the river to the city opposite making navigation down the river impossible. Behind the chain was a bridge constructed on boats giving access to the other bank. It was obvious that this chain would have to be broken and the bridge destroyed if the Crusaders' ships were to be able to get down the river. With this information in mind the knights began to swim and wade their way back through the water to the horses.

Just as they reached the safety of the west bank again there was the sound of something speeding through the water and the most ungodly scream.

"What in God's name was that?" whispered the startled Elvin, looking around at the others.

In the light of the moon Elvin caught a glimpse of a long, narrow snout full of the most vicious teeth he had ever seen, the glistening water dripping from it. As the crocodile raised its head in the air and began thrashing from side to side he realised that Rodrigo, one of his companion knights, was struggling between the creature's jaws his half severed body pumping out blood like a fountain.

Confused, Elvin attacked the animal with his sword. Rodrigo continued to scream and struggle in his intense agony. The animal sped off back into the water taking its prize with it. Others joined it and a bloody feeding frenzy began. The life of Rodrigo was brought to a terrifying and agonising end. The moonlit waters ran red with the poor knight's blood.

Rodrigo's screams alerted the guards on the tower who were now sounding the alarm. A shower of arrows flew through the night air with a gigantic whoosh.

"We will have to get back quickly if we are not to be discovered," cried Elvin desperately.

They all ran as fast as they could up the bank and along to their waiting horses. It was clear that the tower was heavily guarded and soon the gates to it had opened and turbaned men with flaming torches began searching for the intruders. Spears were thrown vainly into the water and then, realising that the intruders had escaped, several of the men mounted horses and began a pursuit.

Fortunately, with their relatively light clothing, the knights were able to regroup quickly with their horses and to speed off into the darkness. The Saracens gave up their pursuit as soon as they felt they were within uncomfortable proximity to the Crusader army.

Elvin reported back to the overall leader of the Templars, Peter de Montaigu.

He was a very experienced knight from the Auvergne, who, like Elvin, was a veteran of the campaigns against the Moors in Spain. He was a commanding man of well over six feet who bore the scars of many a victory. He hoped soon to be elected the Grand Master of the whole Templar Order and was keen to assert his authority. He closely interrogated the returning knights:

"Well, what did you discover, Brother Elvin?" he asked.

"We were only just able to escape. There is a fully guarded tower on a small island on this side of the river. From it is suspended a huge chain, which stretches all the way across the river to the city thus preventing navigation upstream. Behind the chain is a bridge of boats, which enables those in the tower to reach the other side. There is no way our ships will be able to sail up the river unless the tower and the chain are destroyed."

Peter de Montaigu reported what Elvin had seen to a further council of war and it was agreed that the only way they were going to take the fortified city of Damietta was to capture the Chain Tower first, cut the chain, and then, with the river open to them, mount a full assault on the city with their ships. But the big question was how to gain the Tower.

Elvin described the fortress to the assembled barons.

"It consists of a single tower much like the keep of a castle. It is between fifty and a hundred feet high with very thick walls, perhaps fifteen feet in thickness, which will make them almost impenetrable to battering rams or smaller siege engines. The Tower is round in design and difficult to scale. There are fortified walkways at two stages up the tower, which go all the way round it and will be heavily defended."

Further tactical discussions took place and it was agreed that the only serious way that the Tower could be attacked was from the water as well as the land. Asked for his opinion on the terrain Elvin described it thus:

"The land along the river is fraught with difficulties and much different from anything that I have experienced in Spain or elsewhere. The network of waterways, which makes up the Delta, calls for our serious consideration. The handling of horses in the mud and swamps could be a real problem and fierce crocodiles lurk everywhere on the banks."

In the following days there were several unsuccessful attempts at trying to take the Chain Tower. Even the use of eight stone throwing engines had been to no avail. Then one of the German barons came up with an idea.

"My lords," he asked at yet another meeting of the barons, " would it not be possible to lash two of our ships together and construct upon them a wooden tower, from which we could use our scaling ladders to gain access to the lower battlements and thereby take the Saracen fortress? I have seen such a contraption used on land at Constantinople some years ago."

Master carpenters were called to discuss the feasibility of the plan. It took five days to actually build the tower and another day to test it out to see if it was likely to work. It was a construction consisting of four masts and two cogs lashed together. A wooden fort was built on the top together with two drawbridges, which could be lowered down and operated by a pulley system. Everything was covered in leather to make the construction less vulnerable to catching fire.

On the seventh day several ships of the Crusader fleet, together with the newly constructed fort on the two ships, moved into the Damietta Mouth and upstream towards the Chain Tower. The ships carried archers to provide covering fire as well as the foot soldiers who were going to make the assault over the drawbridges from the wooden fort.

The task of the Templars was to take the Tower on the landward side. Peter de Montaigu led the Templars out on this important mission. Peter had become a respected leader and all the Brothers agreed that he was very likely to be elected the new Grand Master.

Elvin Le Gard rode out in full battle gear on his heavily armoured warhorse. This was reserved for special use in big battle charges. He was one of a large group of knights sent forward on the mission.

After the blessing and after each knight had kissed the chunk of wood, which was reputed to be part of the True Cross, they had been divided into three squadrons. They were reminded that no Brother was allowed to leave his squadron unless he had strict permission, even if he was wounded. He could go to the rescue of a fallen comrade but had to return to the squadron as quickly as possible.

An Aragonese nobleman, Enrique de Larraga, was in charge of the battle tactics of the Templars. He carried the black and white banner, which was vital to the battle order and it was forbidden to leave the field whilst the banner could still be seen.

Elvin had first come across him in Aragon, where he had been originally recruited, but that was another story. Elvin had fought with him ever since.

Each knight wore extensive armour, the weight of which meant that he had to be assisted onto his mount by his squire and an assistant. One had to hold the horse steady whilst the other held the stirrup down on the other side to prevent the saddle slipping as he mounted.

Over their armour the Templar knights wore their white smocks with the famous red cross. Over the smock each knight wore a white mantle with yet another of the distinctive red crosses sewn onto the left shoulder. This uniform struck fear into many an enemy, for the reputation of these knights with their heavy horses was second to none throughout Europe and the Middle East.

Their mission was to create a diversion and engage any of the enemy who might try to thwart the naval attack from the landward side of the Chain Tower. They had no idea what to expect when they arrived at their destination.

As the ships moved down the river the knights trotted slowly down the west bank in support accompanied by several hundred foot soldiers. They had to weave their way around the various waterways and canals, which interspersed the land, and take care to avoid the swamps which could be so treacherous to man and beast.

In spite of the early hour the sun was already very hot and Elvin, encased in his heavy armour, felt stifled. But it was something to which he had become accustomed as a reasonably seasoned warrior and he knew this would be forgotten in the heat of the battle. Underneath the armour he felt again the comfort of the tin cross hanging round his neck. He felt that it had always brought him good fortune and he had every trust in it to protect him.

Elvin was the heir to land and a small castle close by the Mount of St. Michael in the West of Cornwall. His father had been given the land as a reward for his loyalty to King Richard some years before.

Like all young boys of his class he had been taught the knightly skills from a very early age. He had been able to ride and use a sword with some skill before the age of twelve years and he remembered well the first time he had donned the traditional armour of the knight.

His father had been a hard taskmaster and determined he was not going to be a wimp nor was he going to be over-conceited. On that day, all puffed up with pride in his shining armour, Elvin's father had suddenly pushed him over and left him on the ground unable to rise because of the weight of the armour. His father and the grooms and squires had stood round laughing at his feeble attempts to get up. His father had always been a bit of a bastard, he thought to himself. The master-at-arms had taken a more kindly approach and had whispered afterwards:

"Never fear, my young Lord, when we get you really fit you will be able to rise in that armour with no trouble at all."

And indeed it was so. Long hours of training in his youth and skills honed at tournaments in England and France had meant that by the time he had reached sixteen or seventeen years of age he was a fit, lithe fighting machine who was skilled with sword and lance.

As they approached the Tower it was clear that there were more soldiers manning it than had previously been the case. The Crusaders had brought with them a number of boats, which had been recently constructed by the carpenters so that the heavily armoured knights could get across the short stretch of water between the Tower and the land. The Tower would thus be attacked from both the river and the landside. They did not expect to be able to do this without considerable opposition and, in spite of the extra numbers occupying the Tower, the knights were surprised by the seeming lack of opposition on the ground when they came before the Tower.

Drawn up along the bank between the Crusaders and the Tower was a small force of mounted warriors and considerably fewer foot soldiers than they had anticipated. The Crusaders heavily outnumbered them.

"Hold...hold steady there," ordered Enrique de Larraga. This was where Enrique's hard training tactics would hopefully pay off. He brought the throng to a halt a few hundred yards off and carefully surveyed the scene.

"Allahu-akbar!" ("God is great!") cried the Saracen host in

traditional fashion, raising their weapons in the air and beating their shields.

Elvin could see that the mounted warriors consisted of some very heavily armoured men with their customary spiked helmets carrying lances and javelins and a majority of warriors with only very light armour on smaller horses who were armed with the dreaded Turkish bow. This specially shaped bow was made of layers of horn and sinew. It was a deadly weapon used from horseback and probably about a meter in length when unstrung. Like the English longbow it needed special training and strength to pull it.

Added to these men were a handful of auxiliaries armed with lighter bows and foot soldiers carrying javelins and spears.

The horses' hooves scuffed the ground. They snorted and neighed as their heads tossed from side to side straining at their jingling bridles. There was the creak of leather and the clash of shields against armour as the knights endeavoured to hold their heavy horses back, waiting for the order.

De Larraga knew that it was the enemy horsemen who posed the biggest threat to the Crusaders taking the Tower. All his wits would be necessary to undertake their rout.

He ordered one squadron of knights to make ready to charge the enemy. He then called up his longbow men to station themselves on each side of the cavalry in two rows, one kneeling, one standing. Finally he ordered the knights to commence their advance urging them:

"Remember - God wills that you slaughter the heathen and all your sins will be absolved." The familiar war cry "Deus le volt (God wills it)" was the signal to attack.

As the knights cantered forward the archers raised their bows into the air and let off a salvo of arrows in the direction of the enemy. For a moment, the sky ahead went dark with their number. The Saracens immediately raised their shields to protect themselves from the hail of arrows raining down on them.

As the knights stepped up to a full gallop there was a further whoosh of arrows over their heads and then yet another one. The cavalry was in full charge now with lances horizontal ready to deal a crunching blow to the enemy crouching under their shields.

As they were about to clash with their opponents, the Saracens suddenly scattered taking the knights completely by surprise.

There was disarray for a moment as the Templars wheeled around looking for an enemy to charge. Before they knew what was happening the Saracen horsemen were weaving in and out of the melee of knights with their lighter and much speedier horses, delivering shots from their strange bows of much deadlier accuracy and more penetrating power than the longbow.

Although the Templars were fully armoured their horses were much less protected. Knights began to tumble everywhere as their horses were targeted. As soon as they fell to the ground the foot soldiers leapt upon them stabbing them with their spears and slicing at them with their swords. Limbs and heads were hacked off and blood seemed to be spurting everywhere. A number of knights managed to get to their feet and put up a brave fight, only to be bowled over again by the mounted Saracens.

It was clear that a change of strategy was needed. De Larraga cursed and called forward his crossbow men and ordered them to seek out the offending horsemen. Although they could not deliver shots at the speed of their comrades with longbows, the bolts that they used had a much greater penetrating power. The crossbows delivered their deadly strike with considerable accuracy and soon the armoured cavalry and the Turkish bowmen were falling all around as well.

De Larraga ordered the other squadrons to divide into two and to prepare to mount an attack upon each side of the struggling mass of fighters to prevent the Saracens scattering as they had done before.

Having been given their orders, the second and larger group of knights began their charge. Elvin was full of anticipation. The thrill of the charge had always excited him and now, bent forward in his saddle with his lance at the ready he set forth lusting for the blood of the enemy. The thunder of hooves was deafening. They rode hard at the melee and hemmed in what was left of the Saracen cavalry.

The crash as each knight clashed with a mounted opponent must have been heard on the other side of the river. Elvin brought down a heavily armoured warrior with his lance and then wheeled round to deal him a stunning blow with his Turkish mace. With the Saracen on the ground, his helmet split and blood pouring from a gaping wound in his head, Elvin lent down and sliced off his head with his sword. The blood spurted out of the gaping neck wound like a scarlet coloured fountain.

As Elvin straightened himself up again he was set upon by a group of foot soldiers, who attempted to pull him from his mount. This was the one action that made him go cold with fear. He slashed desperately at them with his sword and left one with an arm hanging by but a few tendons. He drove his sword through the chest of another and then urged his fully trained horse forward to rear up, knock the only remaining man down and crush his skull under its hooves.

As Elvin charged towards another mounted Saracen he felt a searing pain in his lower left shoulder and realised that an arrow from a Turkish bow had penetrated his mail. Unperturbed by this, in the adrenalin flow of the battle, he knocked the Saracen off his horse. A brain-shattering blow from the mace to the unfortunate man's head sent him to his maker.

There were few of the mounted enemy left by now. So Elvin whirled his horse around and began setting about the foot soldiers, stunning them and hacking at them with vicious ferocity.

By now the Crusader foot soldiers were advancing in some numbers and the Egyptians had clearly had enough. Those, that were able, ran off along the riverbank pursued by the Crusader knights who continued the relentless slaughter. Where once had been a proud host of martyrs for Islam lay heaps of bodies and limbs. The sand and the riverbank were stained and greasy with blood. The now dismounted Crusaders despatched any soldiers, who lay moaning, dreadfully wounded, on the ground. All was done without an ounce of mercy.

The knights had done their work. Enrique de Larraga checked on casualties and ordered a Brother to break off the shaft of the arrow buried in Elvin's shoulder and to stuff a piece of cloth around the wound to stem the bleeding.

The foot soldiers were now bringing up the boats and the ladders ready for the assault upon the Tower.

On the other side of the Chain Tower the two Crusader ships with the strange wooden fort astride them were attempting to lower wooden drawbridges onto the battlements. The Christian archers were trying to provide cover. The attack from the landward side of the Tower had been designed to keep the Saracens fully occupied. This was to give the sea-borne attack a chance to establish itself as well as creating another option for taking the Tower.

Every time the ships got anywhere near the Tower arrows dipped in flaming pitch were being fired down onto the wooden tower construction in an attempt to set it alight. A large part of it had been covered in leather. The bloody hides of unwanted slaughtered animals had been draped over the planking along with damp cloth to try and deter these attempts at setting fire to it and whilst the odd small fire did break out it quickly fizzled out or was easily put out by those on board.

With a great crash, like a tree being felled, the drawbridges were successfully lowered onto the battlements. Men began immediately scrambling across them. Arrows rained down on them, along with boulders, boiling water, boiling oil and anything else to hand. The first man across had his skull crushed by a large boulder and fell to his death below but he was immediately followed by others who began to lay into the defenders with sword and axe.

Once on the battlements the Crusaders began fighting their way through the clamour. The aim was to find a door to open to let in their colleagues, who would be arriving in the boats on the other side.

The Saracens continued to use any means to repulse the attack. All manner of missiles rained down on the attackers. Having seen what had happened to their colleagues below at the hands of the Templar Knights, the Saracens knew it was a fight to the death and they steadfastly refused to surrender.

Suddenly they were successful in virtually demolishing one of the drawbridges with several enormous boulders and it collapsed into the river with its badly injured occupants tumbling from it.

Below, a battering ram, brought over on one of the boats from the west bank, was now doing its work trying to demolish the thick wooden door at the base of the tower.

Wave upon wave of soldiers from the ships was pouring across the remaining drawbridge, as the enemy ran out of missiles to hurl at them. It became almost impossible to repulse them.

Fierce hand-to-hand fighting on the ramparts took place. The leather armour of the defenders was no real defence against the mail clad soldiers who scrambled across the ladder and they were hacked down in the onslaught.

Elvin came across full of reticence on one of the boats. Not only did he feel uncomfortable about the materials being thrown down on the attackers by the Saracens but also the screams of Rodrigo still rang in his ears. He was fearful that a crocodile might suddenly lurch up out of the red-brown water and grab him with its vicious jaws. He comforted himself by thinking that his heavy armour would more than protect him this time but he would probably drown from the weight of it anyway. In any event, all the commotion of the attack had long scared off any groups of crocodiles. They had moved off further down the river.

The end came eventually when Elvin and the others literally pushed their way through the door at the foot of the Tower to finish the slaughter. Bodies and limbs were strewn everywhere and by the time the flag was raised barely a hundred Saracens survived to surrender.

When victory had been assured Elvin and the other Templar knights knelt down amongst the blood and the gore and sang, in chorus, the Psalm of Peter "Not unto us, O Lord," as was their custom.

Later in the day, having rounded up all the prisoners and taken them away, the Crusaders began scouring the fort for booty. Down below, the soldiers were already constructing a pontoon from the Chain Tower to the riverbank with the object of carrying any booty away. They found a quantity of food, armaments, cooking pots and other items, but no treasure.

Whilst at the Tower Elvin got treatment for his arrow wound which was in danger of festering if something was not done speedily.

Elvin stretched himself out, face downwards, on a wooden table and gripped the sides. He had a leather belt stuffed in his mouth.

The Infirmarer pulled through the remaining shaft and head of the arrow with a pair of surgical pliers. Then he applied the tip of a sword, which had been left in a brazier of burning wood for a while, to the wounds to cauterise them before binding them up. Elvin had been given a cup of wine to drink immediately beforehand but still he had been acutely conscious of the intense agony of the red-hot sword point being applied to the wounds. But he tried not to flinch and knew this was the only way to avoid further problems with it.

Immediately after the treatment Elvin did pass out for a short while but then, with a shake of his head, he crossed himself and raised himself carefully off the table. He took a deep breath, swung round and went on his way.

In the meantime the chain and the bridge behind it had to be destroyed. It took some time to hack through the chain and when it was finally broken and slid into the water there was a huge cheer from the men watching from the battlements.

The destruction of the bridge of boats was easier as it was simply set alight and burned on into the evening, a timely message to those on the other side that the assault on the main city was about to begin.

Leaving a small detachment at the Chain Tower the main body of the Crusaders returned to their encampment to plan the next stage of their campaign – the seizure of the city of Damietta.

CHAPTER FOUR

The Search For A Castle

The day after Peter Verity had spoken to Old Tom in the pub, the others began to arrive and by evening they were meeting in an upstairs room in the Tremennek Bay Hotel.

The leader of the "dig" was Professor Bernard Harper of the University of Reading, who was an expert in medieval castle remains. There was Brian, a land specialist, Tim, a finds expert, and Richard and a small team of student diggers. Mr. John Trehane, a local historian, had also joined them.

Professor Harper opened the proceedings and got everybody to introduce himself or herself.

"I am sure you all have a good idea as to why we are gathered here but I will pass you over to Peter Verity to give you an overview of the project."

"Thank you, Bernard," said Peter. "This all started when my colleague, Dr.Anya Naziri, the renowned Spanish archaeologist, contacted me regarding a grave discovered in the old part of Granada in Southern Spain. It appeared to contain the remains of an English knight, possibly with Templar connections, originating from the thirteenth century - a strange find indeed in the middle of Moorish Spain! Furthermore, a number of artefacts discovered in the grave provided links with Cornwall and questions began to be asked about the origins of this man.

"It was almost more by luck rather than judgment that I happened to be holidaying in the area when I heard of a legend regarding a knight, who had fought in the Crusades and returned with a Saracen princess.

"The knight had apparently fallen foul of the Church and had been excommunicated. He had been killed and his castle destroyed when he resisted efforts to capture him and take him for inquisition and trial.

"It is said that his ghost still haunts the headland above Tremennek Bay where the castle was reputed to have been located.

"Our job is to try and discover whether there was, in fact, a castle on the headland or not. I'm very grateful to you all for coming and I hope our efforts are fruitful.

"I want to introduce you, first, to John Trehane, who is a local historian and who will tell us something about the feasibility of a castle having been on the headland."

John Trehane stood up. He was a middle-aged, bespectacled, fellow with a studious air who spoke with a broad Cornish accent.

"Well," he said, "I can tell you now that there are absolutely no records of a castle for this site held in the archives at County Hall or anywhere else. In medieval times the land was held by the Bishop of Exeter and was grazing land. In more modern times it has been owned by a variety of people up to the time that Fred Tregenna, the farmer who currently owns it, bought it some thirty odd years ago.

"Having said that," he continued, "the legend regarding the knight has persisted here for centuries and there are people in the village to this day who swear they have seen the ghostly figure of a knight on horseback riding across the headland.

"My own view is that the ghost story was invented by people in the past to scare their fellow villagers off the headland and the cliffs so that they wouldn't see too much of the smuggling that was rife here – particularly in the eighteenth century.

"Whether there was a castle up there I am very doubtful without the records but I shall be very interested if you find anything."

"Thank you both," said Professor Harper, puffing on an ancient Peterson pipe, which wasn't to everybody's liking. It caused rather pointed coughing to break out amongst the students from time to time, but this did not perturb the professor in the least

"Now, the work will start in earnest tomorrow morning. We have very limited time so we've got to get on with it. As a result of the recent foot and mouth crisis Mr. Tregenna has been forced to review his use of the land and has decided to turn it into a golf course. He was about to start work when we came along. He has given us a week to carry out our investigations. It's not a lot of time but we ought to be able to come to some kind of conclusion in that time. A geophysics survey was, therefore, imperative in my opinion and John Trehane agreed. We hope to get the results of that by tomorrow morning. Now I suggest that we carry out some modest research into the real ales of the county, then get a good night and be ready for some serious business tomorrow morning."

The next morning the team gathered in the meeting room again, after breakfast, to examine the geophysical survey. There were several interesting features revealed by the survey.

"There definitely looks to be a ditch or something right round the site," said Professor Harper. "There are also a number of other possible places where we might lay down trenches. I would suggest that we agree on the positioning of the trenches and start work right away."

Having selected where the trenches were to be dug the excavator got to work cutting them out. When the basic trenches had been dug, the student diggers got to work on the painstaking business of examining the contents of each trench. Two of the trenches were positioned on what the geophysical survey had indicated was a surrounding ditch.

During the afternoon Professor Harper, John Trehane and Peter were called over to one of the trenches on the boundary. Professor Harper jumped excitedly down into the trench to examine the pieces of a wall, which had been discovered.

"It looks very definitely like the foundations of a thick outer defensive wall with a ditch below it," he said. It was not long afterwards that a similar feature was discovered in the other trench on the boundary, which appeared to fit in with the general oval shape of the boundary ditch indicated by the geophysical survey.

That evening Bernard Harper could hardly contain his excitement.

"I think there is no doubt," he said, "that we have found the foundations of a medieval castle. We need some artefacts to support it but it is looking extremely promising. It is beginning to look as if the legend about the castle, at least, is beginning to be substantiated."

That evening Anya Naziri arrived. She had flown over from Malaga to Bristol and taken the train down to Penzance. Peter picked her up from the station. They embraced affectionately when they met. They had known one another ever since they had been postgraduate students doing research together some years before. It was in the days before Peter had met his wife and there was no doubt there was a strong bond between them.

Peter took her back to the Tremennek Bay Hotel where she freshened up and changed and then they went for a meal together at a new Italian restaurant in Penzance.

Peter thought she looked stunning. Although she was a Muslim by faith, Anya normally wore western clothes. On this occasion she wore a lilac suit, which perfectly complemented her coffee coloured skin. She had shortish, jet-black hair and captivating deep blue eyes – a most unusual combination for a Moroccan Spaniard but known to be found occasionally amongst people of Berber descent.

He fell in love with her almost as soon as they had met at university. She was pretty, vivacious and seemed to like his quiet, self-assured manner even though he was nine years older than her. They spent a lot of time together to the extent that most of their fellow students thought they were an item. That, however, was far from the truth.

One evening, when they had been out together, a few weeks after they had begun their course, he had made a rather clumsy attempt to kiss her. She resisted his advances and said:

"I am sorry Peter. I like you very much but I am betrothed to another. I am going to marry a Moroccan lawyer called Yuba at the end of the year. We were sweethearts together at the University of Granada and our parents expect us to tie the knot before the year is out. In any event my parents are very devout and would not permit me to marry a non-Muslim. I have to honour their wish."

Peter had been immensely disappointed and, in normal circumstances, that would have been the end of the relationship. Indeed, he did give up seeing her for a few days. But he found that he was lost without her. He just needed her company. He was, to some degree, a lonely person and enjoyed chatting into the early hours about all sorts of aspects of both their lives. They came to rely upon one another, voicing many of their innermost thoughts, fears and feelings to one another, and helping one another with the rigours of their course.

Yuba had been undertaking a Masters Degree in European Law in London. This meant that Anya went away to see him at the weekends and during vacations. These periods were complete agony for Peter, who could not get her out of his mind. He was intensely jealous of this man he did not know. He usually resorted to binge drinking sessions with other male students, at these times, to try and forget.

On one occasion Anya invited Peter to London to meet Yuba and had even fixed him up with a blind date with a Danish girl whom she knew. Peter took an instant dislike to Yuba. He seemed quick-tempered and rather arrogant. The Danish girl was very pleasant but was rather uninspiring in both looks and personality. Peter was also acutely aware that Yuba was far from happy about the time Anya and he spent together although it was clear that she had explained the situation carefully to him.

Peter lived in hope that things would change. It was quite apparent that Anya and Yuba had an up and down relationship and that arguments were common. He hoped that perhaps the relationship would collapse and leave him free to try to woo Anya. He had even considered converting to Islam but it was debateable as to how serious he was about that. In any event it didn't happen.

On one vacation he had travelled back home to Kenilworth to visit his mother. He had been in a particularly depressed state and rather foolishly told his mother about the situation.

"Don't worry," she had said, trying to reassure him, "you will find someone. A handsome young man like you won't have any difficulty finding a nice girl of your own age and your own faith. Besides it's probably all for the best. Mixed marriages never work. I certainly wouldn't be happy leaving my money to you if I thought your children were going to be brought up as Mohammedans."

It had been just as well that he had neglected to tell his mother about his thoughts of conversion to Islam. Anyhow, if her remarks were designed to console him, they had quite the opposite effect.

Inevitably the course had to come to an end. Peter escorted Anya to the final ball, because Yuba was doing some exams. He felt proud to have her on his arm. But all the time he knew that the close relationship they had had was bound to come to an end.

On the last day he made a bumbling attempt at telling her how much he loved her and to beg her to share her life with him.

"But Peter," she had replied, "you must not continue like this. There is no future in it. Our cultures are very different and we can't be together. I am going to marry Yuba and you must resign yourself to that. I like you very much and I don't think I would have got through this year without you."

He had detected a tear in her eye as she had said this and he knew that she had valued her relationship with him, even if platonic. The platonic nature of it had been convenient for her but agony for him.

And so they had parted. He was invited to her wedding but he did not attend, making some excuse or other. From time to time they met professionally at international conferences and always spent time together. She said little about her marriage but it seemed that it did not completely fulfil her. Peter thought that it was probably difficult for a highly educated, intelligent and westernised woman to accept the constraints of the traditional Islamic role destined for her. Besides that the marriage had, so far, remained childless because of a tendency for Anya to miscarry.

In the meantime Peter had himself married Mary, an English girl, who had worked as a secretary in the administrative department at the University. For the first few years the marriage had been a happy one producing two fine children who Peter dearly loved.

"How are things at home?" Anya enquired during the course of their meal in the Italian restaurant.

"Oh, I don't know really," said Peter in a rather vague way.

"What do you mean you don't know?" replied Anya. "What kind of an answer is that?"

"Well there have been problems recently," said Peter.

"What kind of problems?" urged Anya.

"Well," continued Peter, "Mary has never shown much interest in my work. Come to that, nor do we share much in the way of pastimes or talk a great deal to one another about how we feel about life. She does her thing and I do mine. I find it difficult to talk to her at times. I am not great at expressing my feelings and when I do it generally ends in a row. I found it much easier to talk to you when we were at university."

"But that was a long time ago and in the past," said Anya. "You have got to move on."

"It's not always easy," said Peter. "There are times when I have gaps between contracts, as you know. I then have to go on the dole, which Mary doesn't appreciate very much. And, then, when we were on a weekend break on one occasion I made the great mistake of telling her about how I had felt about you when we were students and how I still fancied you to some degree. Then she had a bout of tears and it was very difficult to console her. I told her that I loved her, and the kids, and that any kind of relationship I might have had with you was all in the past. But from then on things began to change."

"Oh, Peter," said Anya, "no woman likes to hear that her husband fancies somebody else. Didn't you think about that?"

"No," replied Peter. "I was just telling the truth. Men do fancy other women. That's a fact of life. But in a normal relationship that's all it is

– in the mind."

"But, if you really understood women," she said, "you should know that it is not something that you openly admit to. Women don't want hear that you fancy anybody else but them."

"Well, I think I understand that now," he said. "But, anyhow, it didn't seem to make any difference after that what I said. Then Mary began to complain about my being away from home or working long hours on research projects and she seemed to be particularly sensitive when I attended conferences and she knew that you would be there as well. Needless to say she is not very happy about the current project."

"Oh dear," said Anya. "Do you think I had better talk to her?"

"No, I don't think it would make any difference. It might even make it worse."

They left the restaurant and returned to Tremennek Bay.

The next morning the diggers working on the trenches along the line of the ditch discovered several pieces of pottery. Richard called Bernard Harper and Peter across and pointed out the interesting finds.

"There are several shards of pottery that people have dumped out here at some time including some quite modern stuff. But look at these," he said, indicating a number of small pieces.

"They are part of a wheel thrown spouted pitcher and are definitely twelfth or thirteenth century. When Tim gets them back to base he will be able to confirm that pretty easily. It wasn't unusual for the people of those days to chuck broken pots and such like into the moat or ditch surrounding a place like this. We may find more."

Later in the day they were called to another of the trenches where Professor Harper was consulted for his opinion.

"Hmm, this looks interesting," he said. "You may well have got the foundations of the main stone hall here. I'd like to open another trench on the other side just to see if we can find the corner of the building as indicated by geophysics."

As the day went on footings of various other buildings were being discovered but the principal discovery that excited everybody was that of the Hall. They were all in absolutely no doubt now that a major fortification had been sited on the headland in medieval times and it looked as if, to some degree or other, the legend about the castle was being borne out.

During that evening Anya received a telephone call from Yuba in

Granada. Peter could hear snatches of Anya's end of the conversation from where he was sitting in the hotel lounge bar. There appeared to be quite an argument going on. After a while Anya slammed down the receiver and returned to the bar with the trace of a tear in her eye.

"You'll have to excuse me," she said. "I'm going up to my room." With that she dashed out of the bar.

Peter was quite taken aback and, after a short while, he thought he had better go up and check that she was all right.

He knocked on her door. "Who's that?" she replied.

"It's Peter. Are you OK?"

"Oh, Peter. Come in."

She had obviously been crying. He sat down on the bed beside her.

"What's wrong?" he asked. "It's unlike you to be so down."

"It's Yuba," she said. "He's become very jealous of my being here with you. He's demanding that I return to Granada"

"I only wish there was something for him to be jealous about," mumbled Peter.

"He really got angry and called me a whore — more exactly — that Christian's whore," she said, the tears welling up in her eyes again.

"The son of a bitch," Peter thought to himself. "He was always a spoiled brat who could act up."

Anya was really sobbing again now. Peter put his arm round her and began to try and calm her down. He stroked her hair and ran his index finger and his forefinger down the side of her face and over her eyes to try and soothe away the tears. He found her a tissue.

"Come on. Don't distress yourself. He'll get over it," Peter told her. "He always does."

"I suppose that's true," she said softly, becoming a little more reassured.

"It's more than I ever will," said Peter quickly. "I've always loved you. You know that. I could never treat you like that."

"Oh, Peter," she said softly, snuggling into his arms. He continued to stroke her face with his fingers and to give her soothing little pecks on the cheek. These progressed gently to her eyes and the side of her nose. Then he turned her head towards him and kissed her full on the lips.

To his surprise there was no resistance. She responded with a degree of passion that was quite unexpected. Soon they were engaged in the most passionate embrace he had experienced for a very long time.

He began to nibble gently at the lobe of her ear and then to kiss her seductively and slowly down the side of her neck. She was now entering into the spirit of the embrace, squirming and moving to him.

He began to move his hand over her breast, but then there was a slight intake of breath. As he began to explore further, she suddenly went rigid.

"No, Peter, no. I can't," she said softly, looking at him straight in the eyes. "This is not the answer. You are married and I am married. I do feel a great deal of affection for you, Peter. Had things been different and had I been a Christian English girl I might well have fallen in love with you all those years ago. But I am a Muslim and adultery is a grievous sin in my faith. I owe my duty to my husband no matter what the circumstances are. I think you had better go now before something awful happens."

"Would it be that awful?" Peter said and put his head in his hands.

"It cannot be, Peter. Yuba is my husband and I owe love to no one else," she said emphatically.

"But the guy's a complete bastard," he had wanted to say but somehow restrained himself. He slowly got to his feet. He looked completely dejected.

"We can still be friends, can't we?" he asked.

She grasped his hand tightly. "Of course, we can. We have always been friends and you mean a great deal to me, Peter."

With that Peter left her and went down to the bar for a spot of alcoholic consolation.

Early next day Professor Harper called a progress meeting and reviewed the state of play to date.

"Well, there doesn't seem any doubt that we have a major medieval site here," he began.

"It's almost certain that this was the site of a thirteenth century castle or fortified manor house although I would like a few more artefacts to confirm dating.

"So far, we have found evidence of the outer fortifications with shards of pottery in the ditch or moat indicating medieval occupation. We have also located what we think is the great hall of the castle. The rest of the buildings would have been wooden and have not survived.

"One other thing should be mentioned. There are more and more signs within the outer boundary that there was a major fire here, which was probably responsible, in part, for the destruction of the castle. At all the levels we are digging within the walls there are signs of considerable charcoal deposits. Our valiant diggers" —here there was a loud cheer from the students — " have also come up with some human bones with signs of major injuries. They do seem consistent with some kind of skirmish or battle having taken place even if it was not a major one involving hundreds of people. I think our job now is to see if we can come up with a few further artefacts, which will confirm the medieval origins of the site."

"The one thing that concerns me is that we are running out of time," interjected Peter.

"Yes, I am aware of that," said Bernard Harper. "I have, therefore, been in contact with a friend of mine from South Devon, who is a detectorist. I know you will all say that these people shouldn't be let lose on an archaeological site but we are strapped for time. This chap I know very well and I know that he will be very careful. The important thing is that he has some sophisticated and very expensive equipment, which could outdo even the efforts of the geophysics team. Are we all agreed that we use him?"

There was agreement to this move and Bernard Harper's friend arrived with his metal detectors that afternoon. Richard, the leader of the team of diggers, was put in charge of the operation and pointed out exactly those areas, which needed to be searched. It took about two hours for anything significant to be found. A strong signal indicated that there were several metal objects in one of the trenches at the site of the hall.

Brian, the detectorist, said, "It is very similar to the signal I usually get for medals or coins." The diggers got to work and soon came up with a couple of coins. Students immediately began the painstaking task of cleaning up the discoveries. When they had done this, Bernard Harper and Peter were quickly called across.

"Bingo," said Richard. "We've got two medieval coins. They're hammered silver pennies. They're both short cross pennies, which means the cross on the obverse side does not extend across the full face of the coin. This is typical of the coins of the Plantaganet era. One is a Richard the First coin which would put it between 1189 and 1199 and the other is a King John, 1199 to 1216."

"Good work, people," said Bernard. "Keep on looking. See if you can find any more."

"Well, there's all the indications," said Brian. "I am getting lots of very strong signals."

Over the next hour several more coins were dug up and all seemed to point to the same Plantagenet period. Then Bernard and Peter were called back to examine a brooch which had been found.

"I don't know what we've got here," said Richard. "It's a most strange thing. I haven't seen anything quite like it before. One of the girls has cleaned it up and it really looks to be a bit of a find."

Bernard and Peter examined the brooch carefully. It was really quite a beautiful object. It was made of intricately worked filigreed silver formed into the shape of a hand and with a floral design of gems mounted in the palm of that hand.

Just then Anya appeared and Bernard said, "What do you think of this, Anya?"

"Good heavens," she cried. "It's a Hand of Fatima."

"A what?" queried the two men almost at the same time.

"A Hand of Fatima," she replied. "They have been made in Morocco and Andalusia for hundreds of years and you can still buy them today. In fact, they are produced in thousands for the tourist market. But you can also find ancient specimens in Andalusia from the days when the Moors were there. This one looks very old. How unusual to find it here! If you will let me do some work on it I can probably date it for you."

"Sure," said Bernard and handed over the brooch.

Work went on and at the evening meeting Anya confirmed that the broach was from the medieval era like the coins.

"Fantastic!" exclaimed Bernard. "So, in summary," he continued "it looks as if we've got enough to confirm the existence of a medieval castle here during the Plantagenet period, which was the scene of some kind of battle, as a result of which it was razed to the ground.

"It looks as if the local legend is gradually being borne out. The broach, however, is the icing on the cake. If our knight really did bring home a Saracen princess she almost certainly would have been the owner of a piece of jewellery like this. I've never seen anything like it this old in this country before and Anya has confirmed that it is of typical medieval Islamic design from Morocco. It could have found its way to medieval Spain and, then, to Cornwall.

"It's early days but it looks as if we now have a possible connection with the site in Granada. Good work everybody." Bernard gave two enormous puffs on his Peterson and rubbed his hands gleefully. He was obviously very pleased with progress. With that, everybody retired to the bar.

Anya and Peter sat together in the bar enthusiastically discussing the day's events. All their hard work appeared to be paying off. Whilst they were talking Peter got a text message from Mary to ring her at home. He disappeared outside to ring her.

He returned some minutes later looking extremely glum.

"What's the matter?" enquired Anya.

"It's Mary," said Peter. "One of the kids has contracted chicken pox. She said that she thought that I ought to come home to help out. I explained to her that work here has reached an important phase and I cannot just drop things like that. She replied to the effect that the real reason was that I did not wish to leave whilst you were still here and then another row started. There were some harsh words said and the upshot of it all was that she said that if I did not return home by tomorrow I might as well not bother at all as she was going to leave me anyway."

"Oh, Peter. You'll have to go," said Anya. "I know," sighed Peter.

The next morning he left for London.

CHAPTER FIVE

Victory, Defeat And Capture

"When, in the name of God, are we going to take this city?" Elvin thought to himself.

It had been over a year since they had landed in Egypt and still the resistance was as strong as ever. Quarrels about how to capture Damietta rumbled on.

Then the Holy Father took action and sent a Cardinal to take charge. Cardinal Pelagius was a Spaniard with a reputation for energy and industry. But he was no diplomat and was soon upsetting everybody.

Elvin took an instant dislike to him. Pelagius seldom listened to the opinions of the more militarily experienced barons around him and thought the lack of success on the Crusade was down to poor discipline in the ragbag army. He became obsessive about stamping it out.

The soldiers had become bored with waiting around for their leaders to make decisions and were deserting in droves. The Cardinal was determined to act.

Elvin had little time for priests. He always remembered the times when an envoy of the local bishop had visited his father at the castle in Cornwall. The envoy was an overweight, pompous man, full of his own importance, dressed in a manner, which suggested he was a long way from living the simple life of the Saviour. He ate too much and drank copious amounts of his father's best wine. But it was not wise to cross such people.

Elvin Le Gard had more respect for the more dedicated of his comrades in the Templar Order. All had taken strict vows as warrior monks and all had to undergo the deprivations imposed by the Templar Rule. They lived under a strict religious code, obeyed humbly, had no private property, ate sparingly and dressed in the meanest of clothes. Because of this they could proudly wear the famous white mantle with its distinctive red cross when they went to battle.

Most Templars were completely conscientious with regard to the Order's Rule. But there was a small clique of Brothers, that he had noticed, friends of Enrique de Larraga, who paid scant respect to the

Rule, especially under battlefield conditions. They fought hard and thought to play hard. They drank alcohol to excess, associated with women and collected loot. All these activities were totally contrary to the Templar Rule.

Elvin had found it very hard, sometimes, to see how these men could claim to be Templars. He was perfectly prepared to admit that he found it difficult himself to comply with all of the monastic requirements. Perhaps he was not really cut out for a cloistered life but he certainly was not as lax as some.

One morning the whole camp was summoned together to witness the punishment of six soldiers who had got themselves hopelessly drunk the night before and had attempted to desert.

Guillermo de Veruela stood before the host. He was a Spanish bishop, who was one of Pelagius' assistants. He was often delegated to deal out punishments. Some said he took an uncommon pleasure in the task.

Bishop Guillermo addressed the throng of soldiers and said:

"These worthless wretches have besmirched the good name of the army and refused to do their duty before God. They are not worthy to be soldiers in Christ's name and they shall be an example for all of you to bear in mind." He then turned to one of the barons and said, "Hang them!"

This must have been a pre-arranged exercise because a baron would seldom take orders from a cleric, but on this occasion there was no hesitation. The baron gave a cursory nod to one of his soldiers and the six were taken, struggling to some hastily constructed gallows where six nooses had been prepared.

Then aghast, Elvin realised that one of the men was his squire, Petroc, who had been with him ever since he had left Cornwall. He had been a faithful servant and companion throughout travels in Cornwall, France and Aragon. He was now frantically calling out to Elvin to speak on his behalf.

"My liege, I beg you. Don't let them hang me," he pleaded in the Cornish language,

"I got a bit drunk, tha's all. You know I wouldn't desert. I just wan'ed to find a few extra bits of loot for me wife and children afore I goes 'ome."

Elvin was sympathetic, for he liked the man, who had served him well as his squire. He had first met him at a Templar refuge on the moors above Bodmin. He, too, came from the West of Cornwall and had served him faithfully over several years. They had been through a number of adventures together. These were hardly the first desertions either. Some of the Germans, in particular, had been leaving in hundreds of late.

"Your Grace," Elvin cried, "I must protest. This man is not a common foot soldier but a squire in my service and in the service of the Temple. He has served God well for several years and to lose him would be a grave loss to our cause. We have already lost many soldiers and we cannot afford to lose more."

"You know full well that, just because he serves a Templar Knight, it does not make him a member of the Order. In any event it matters not who the vile wretch is," fumed Guillermo. "He is a deserter and will get his just reward before God along with the others — and they will be an example for the rest of this rabble. It will serve to persuade them of the wisdom of continuing God's work rather than scampering away like frightened vermin."

"Your Grace, I must appeal to you to rethink your judgment in this case. He is a good servant of God and to our endeavours," cried Elvin desperately and conscious of Petroc's blubbering as he was being lifted onto a horse and the noose put round his neck.

"Sir Elvin, are you questioning the judgement of Our Holy Mother Church?" snapped Guillermo testily, looking him straight in the eye. Elvin knew better than to argue.

With a smack on the hindquarters of each horse the six were hanged there and then, their bodies performing a macabre dance before each shuddered into death. The bodies were left unburied and hanging from the gallows, for several days, as a warning to all that discipline was paramount.

Elvin felt very disgruntled at the harsh action of the bishop, whom he really felt should not be meddling in matters of the discipline of the soldiers anyway. But the Cardinal to whom he was responsible was the leader of the Crusade and it was unwise to complain too vociferously. What displeased Elvin most was the fact that he had lost a very efficient and faithful squire.

Desertions were far from uncommon. It was not unusual for men to leave a Crusade especially if there was a period of inactivity like there had been at that moment. The only difference on this occasion was that the drunken fools had been caught and Guillermo had been looking to make an example of somebody. A sound flogging would have been a sufficient punishment. Elvin felt that it had been a wrong decision in an already demoralised army.

Over the next few months came other disasters. The worst was an epidemic. Many Crusaders started to feel ill. Soon they had a high fever and their skin turned black. They started dying in thousands and nobody seemed to know what to do.

Elvin was fortunate. He managed to survive but he was left feeling very tired and depressed. The mood was not one of an army filled with the fervour of their cause. More and more desertions took place.

Before they lost all their army, the leaders agreed they had to make their move. They brought up a number of siege engines, which had been constructed by the carpenters, and landed them on the slopes below Damietta.

All the houses were deserted. A ceaseless bombardment took place upon the walls of the city. Huge boulders were hurled at the walls to try to break them down. The rotting carcasses of animals and the dead corpses of diseased humans were hurled over the walls. An epidemic inside was inevitable.

The Crusaders made a number of attempts to undermine the walls. But they had not reckoned against the Saracen's fearsome weapon, Greek Fire. Nobody had yet discovered the secret behind this weapon used by the Muslims to repel attacks both on land and at sea. Liquid fire was hurled at the Crusader engines from siphons on the walls. It set them alight immediately on contact. It caused panic and dread because the fire was generally regarded as inextinguishable. It seemed impossible to put the fires out even when copious amounts of water, wine and even acid were thrown onto them.

Any soldier caught in the stream of fire from one of these weapons had no chance of survival. They ran around screaming, engulfed in burning pitch or whatever the deadly fuel consisted of. They rolled around on the ground in a desperate attempt to put out the flames but to no avail. The flames were relentless in their destruction of the carcass and little was left but teeth and charred bones.

As a result the Cardinal became even more enraged and raved at the attacking masses:

"Come on, men. Greek Fire is the Devil's creation. We must strive harder to defeat the Forces of Darkness. Once more, charge upon them, slay the heathen unbelievers and save Damietta for the Lord!"

But still the city remained elusive and the quarrels continued. The Saracens even offered a treaty, which would have given King John Jerusalem back but the Cardinal would have none of it.

"It is absolutely out of the question that we should treat with these unbelievers," he said. "The aim of this Crusade should be nothing less than the completion of God's work by the absolute elimination of the evil of Islam in Egypt – and beyond. What better cause is there than to die for the Lord?"

In the end it was the inevitable plague that defeated Damietta. One day a scouting party returned to report that one of the towers on the outer walls of the city appeared to be unmanned. A squadron of Templars led by Elvin stormed unchallenged up the slopes to investigate. They climbed a ladder and found the watchtower empty. Inside the once prosperous trading city of Damietta all seemed deadly quiet.

The next day the Crusader army swept over the walls in force with little opposition.

The city was in a dire state. The Crusader siege had, after all, been successful. As Elvin and the Templars entered they found almost the whole garrison sick. The stench of death and decay was awful.

Only three thousand citizens had survived out of some eighty thousand inhabitants. Bodies lay everywhere, for the survivors had been too feeble to bury the dead. Dogs growled at one another and bared their blood soaked fangs in the competition to tear at the corpses.

Everybody covered their faces with pieces of cloth to keep out the fearful smell of death and to try and stem the onset of any further disease.

Food and treasure were there in abundance, for the rich city had never been short of these. It had been the epidemics, which had destroyed the population and its will to continue defending the city.

The army set about the systematic looting of the town's empty houses. All treasure had to be handed in and there were severe penalties for those that did not do so. It was then divided amongst the Crusaders according to rank.

The Templars could take no part in the distribution of loot because they had to abide by their vow of poverty. Elvin sometimes wondered whether every Brother was as scrupulous about this as they should have been. He knew full well that Enrique de Larraga and a few others were probably filling their saddlebags as they willed

Disease had taken a dreadful toll and amongst the bodies that still lay unburied was that of the young goatherd, Abdul, who had first warned the city of the Crusader invasion. The skin of the once fresh-faced boy had been blackened and bloated by disease and he had obviously died very unpleasantly.

Rape was considered as one of the rewards for victory over the heathens and neither Church nor knights could or would do very much to prevent it. Indeed it was often seen as the way to bring a city to submission. The few fit women, and even some of those still unwell, were repeatedly raped, as were their young daughters. Many did not survive this awful experience.

Elvin did not regard himself as an angel, but he found the antics of some of the men highly distasteful. There was little he could do to intervene. It was part of the spoils of war and the animal instincts of the peasantry had to be appeased. Elvin just shrugged his shoulders and decided that this was the penalty, perhaps, for those who denied the True Faith.

But Elvin was not inclined to share the brutish habits of Enrique de Larraga and friends. He had little liking for the noisy, drunken and abandoned carousals, which followed every victory or the barbarous treatment of civilians, which took place. He felt somehow uncomfortable with this side of war, especially where women and children were concerned.

This was not to say that he was not confident as to why he was fighting the war in the first place. He had been taught to regard Islam as a threat to Christianity and it was the duty of a Christian knight to help to preserve the holy places of Christendom, especially Jerusalem. They had a duty to drive out the infidel.

When Damietta was fully secured three hundred of its leading citizens were set aside as hostages. The very young children were handed over to the priests for baptism and for the service in the Church and the rest of the population was sold as slaves. Life looked as if it would never be the same for those citizens who had managed to survive.

This triumph and the arrival of reinforcements a few months later raised morale still further. With fresh confidence Pelagius insisted on an attack on the Sultan of Egypt's main army. This had taken up a position behind a tributary, which ran from the great lake behind Damietta into the Nile.

With lightning speed, the Crusaders marched right in behind the Egyptians and set up camp. What they did not foresee was that it was a potential death trap and would lead to ultimate disaster.

En route to taking up their position the Crusaders crossed a dry canal. Once more the barons warned the Cardinal of the potential danger of this position but he chose to ignore all advice. Divine providence would carry the day, so he thought.

The Christian army had brought little in the way of supplies with it, as the leaders were counting on capturing those from the enemy, so that the army could then travel light and make speedy progress.

As the days went by the river rose and began to fill the dry canal. As predicted by the barons it soon became navigable. The Egyptians sent ships down it and totally cut the Crusader force off. Now they had no way of escape and no source of fresh supplies. They could do nothing but retreat.

The army was ordered to leave behind what supplies they had. As was their usual custom, the common soldiers had brought with them large supplies of wine to fire them up before the fight. They were not about to leave this behind. So they drank it. The result was inevitable. When the order to move out was given many of them were hardly capable of going anywhere. The order was given to burn all supplies so they did not fall into the hands of the enemy and the Templars and others were left to arrange this. Then they realised the folly of this order.

The enemy spotted the flames and the pall of smoke and, realising that the Crusaders were about to retreat, the Sultan ordered the banks of the canal to be breached. Water flooded into the area through which the Crusaders were attempting to move. Soldiers found themselves suddenly wading through mud or falling into gullies quickly filling with water.

Elvin found it extremely difficult to manoeuvre his horse in the boggy ground.

Then the Egyptians attacked.

The foot soldiers fell like flies. They were no match for a

determined enemy when they were bogged down in the mud and staggering around in a drunken haze. The Turkish bows wrought absolute havoc. The Templars tried valiantly to protect the retreat but to little avail. There was nowhere to go. A meaningful charge was impossible. The horses were bogged down.

Elvin was thrown from his horse into the quagmire. Assisted to his feet he hacked and slashed desperately with his sword but his armour weighed him down and his feet were fast sinking into the mud. The dead were piling up all around and soon there was hardly room to move amongst them. He looked round desperately for the black and white standard but could not see it anywhere and there appeared to be very few survivors by this time. Suddenly he was overwhelmed by Muslim soldiers and quickly disarmed and dragged out of the mud. He found himself encircled by dozens of soldiers. They waved their swords in the air and shouted victoriously. He prepared himself for a martyr's end. He crossed himself and waited for the onslaught he thought bound to come. He was determined to go down fighting even if only with his bare hands.

Then the throng parted and a magnificently clad Saracen general mounted on a superb white charger confronted him. At first he thought that he was being reserved for the final kill at the hand of this man. But this was not to be. The general dismounted and approached him and spoke in good French:

"You soldiers have defended your Cross bravely this day. You will find that the sons of Islam are not wanting in their compassion towards their enemies. You will see the measure of that benevolence in celebration of our great victory. Your life will be spared but you will remain a prisoner until a ransom is paid." He then barked an order and Elvin was grabbed from behind and his arms tied.

He was escorted to an area where a few other knights were being kept — the only survivors on this disastrous day — and then they were marched away to the Egyptian encampment.

The next day they were transported in an open cart to Damietta, which was now, back in the hands of the Egyptians. It was a very different scene that greeted them as they entered the city once again compared with when the Crusader army had taken it all those months previously. It had come back to life and was full of the hustle and bustle of a town going about its daily commercial business.

As soon as the crowds saw the cart bringing the Crusader prisoners there were howls of derision and hate and they were soon being pelted with rotten fruit and vegetables, stones, animal dung and almost anything that came to hand. The Saracen guards made a cursory attempt to keep order but missiles continued to rain down on them all the way along the route. A sharp edged stone struck Elvin on the forehead and drew blood.

One citizen, armed with a large cudgel, escaped the clutches of the guards and attempted to get onto the cart with the idea of beating the prisoners but was roughly hauled down and was left lying on the ground with a disgruntled look on his face.

They were taken to the inner city and to a watchtower set into the walls. They entered the tower and immediately began to descend a winding stone staircase. They arrived at a chamber set deep in the foundations of the tower and there in the centre of the room was a thickly studded wooden trapdoor with a small iron grill in it. It was opened and the prisoners were prodded down a staircase into a very unpleasant looking dungeon.

It was dark and dank. Soiled straw covered the floor. As his eyes became more accustomed to the dark Elvin could make out the pathetic bodies chained to the walls. Two of these were kicked to one side to make room for Elvin. He was pushed to the ground and then chained to the wall along with all the others. The gaolers disappeared again up the stairs and the trapdoor was closed behind them with a heavy crash. Elvin had never felt so low.

His days in the dungeon did not persuade Elvin that his life had really been spared at all. The outlook was far from bright. From time to time the trapdoor opened and the gaolers would descend to check on the health of the prisoners — or more correctly to see if anybody had died or not. The dead body was bundled up the stairs and the trapdoor shut, leaving them all in the dark again.

The only relief from the darkness was when the trapdoor was opened once a day and loaves of bread and few leather bags of water were tossed into the dungeon. The prisoners were just about able to reach these from where they were chained and it seemed like some evil game was being played. The articles were always thrown into the middle so that it was a real strain to get at them. There was no doubt that on some days certain prisoners would go without because they were unable to get at the food and drink.

The one comfort Elvin retained was his St. Piran Cross, which somehow the guards had missed and he had managed to conceal in one of his boots, which, strangely, he had been allowed to keep. He had always felt that this gift many years before from Tryfena, the lady he knew as his "second mother" in Cornwall, had always brought him luck and protection.

He was very proud of the doubly encircled cross, designed with intricate Celtic knot work. In particular, his greatest pride was the polished black opal set inside the second, smaller circle between the two intersecting pieces of the cross. It gave off a full spectrum of colours depending on the light. The cross itself was only about four or five inches long. It was simple and yet of great beauty — the work of a peasant. A lot of work had gone into painstakingly designing the knot work.

Tryfena had told him: " It was made by my father, who was a miner of tin. He fashioned it out of waste tin and copper from the mine. He found the gemstone when he was a young man working in the mine. It had always been his secret, for he risked terrible punishment if he had been discovered with it. He had always said that he would keep it for a special day but he did not live to enjoy its fruits. I want you to have it because I know that it will protect you on your travels to far off lands." Elvin had made to protest but she had insisted. She had said it would protect him and he had always believed it.

One grim night Elvin awoke with a start. He felt something crawling over him. He could not see a great deal in the darkness but the sound of creatures scuttling about, the occasional squeak and the frantic gnawing left him in no doubt. There were rats in the dungeon.

He felt yet another creature run across his legs and kicked out with his feet in disgust. He lived with a nightmare of rotting away in the dungeon and of rats gnawing away at him whilst he was still alive.

Elvin's startled cry and the thrashing of his legs had awakened the prisoner next to him. He yelled something in a language, which Elvin did not understand. It was not French or Occitan or Catalan. In fact it sounded more like Arabic, which surprised Elvin. He did not expect any Saracens to be amongst the prisoners here.

After a while all went quiet again and Elvin realised that the rats had disappeared. He heaved a sigh of immense relief and began to relax again.

He sank into drowsiness and found himself dreaming of his native land and the place where he had been born. He had been absent from there for many years and began wondering whether it had changed in any way from how he remembered it. Was his father alive or dead? How fared Tryfena and his boyhood friend, Yestin? It seemed such a long time since he had left the shores of Cornwall.

Tremennek Castle lay on a headland overlooking the sea in the West of Cornwall. Down from the walls and ditch dropped boggy, grassy slopes interspersed with blackthorn, brambles, elder scrub and gorse bushes – home to rabbits and badgers. All kinds of birds hovered and skimmed over the water, gorging themselves on the abundant fish. Now and then he remembered spotting a stonechat perched on the gorse bushes puffing out its little orange breast. It's sharp cry sounded almost like the clinking of pebbles on the shore below. When it was stormy out to sea you could often see dolphins and porpoises leaping along the waves.

The weather could be dark, dank and cold but the climate was mild and frosts were not common. There were days when the sun showed its full splendour and there was a light, the like of which could not be equalled anywhere else in Europe. In spring the slopes of the headlands were covered in carpets of yellow ling and pink thrift.

The sea crashing onto the rocks below produced a constant roar. To the east swept a sandy bay and, beyond, further headlands. In the distance you could just make out the long arm of the Lizard where those unfortunate beings, who had contracted leprosy in the Holy Land, were exiled. To the west lay the Mount of St. Michael and a glimpse of the beginning of the land's end.

The castle was perched on grassy slopes above sheer cliffs, below which dangerous rocks littered the frothy sea. No vessel could easily approach from the seaward side unless the crew was as knowledgeable as the locals were about the rocks. The cliffs were composed of a mixture of sandstone and granite. The sandy soil easily became boggy and wet and the granite slippery. Prickly gorse bushes grew all the way up the cliff. All in all scaling the cliffs would be particularly difficult for any intending invader.

The land around had not been particularly good for growing other than a few root crops and was used mainly for grazing animals. Apart from this the main product of the land was the tin, out of which his cross had been fashioned and for which this part of Britain had long been famous. It was used to make bronze implements and weapons in the main. Although there were some underground mines, the tin was largely won from the beds of streams where it was deposited in the form of sand and gravel and washed down from the granite hills around.

One such stream ran out into the sandy bay below the castle on the eastern side. The ore was taken by packhorse to Marhas-gow or Market Jew as the English called it. This was a small settlement, which lay below St. Michael's Mount. There the tin ore was sold to ships anchored in the bay, which came from many parts of Southern Europe and North Africa. It could be a very lucrative trade.

He always strained to remember his mother but she had died when he was very young and he had been weaned and cared for in his first few years by his "second mother" the village woman, Tryfena, the wife of the castle butcher. Elvin always regarded her with the greatest affection.

Elvin awoke again with a start. He was not sure what had awakened him. Perhaps there had been the thought at the back of his mind that the rats might return. As he lay pondering it suddenly occurred to him that the rats must have got into the dungeon by some means. Perhaps there was a hole in the wall somewhere nearby, which could be exploited. Elvin had often watched the men working under the cat, the machine used for trying to undermine the outer walls of a castle. He thought he had a fairly good idea of how to construct a tunnel through masonry if he ever got the chance. But chained to the wall in the darkness and without an implement of any sort it would be virtually impossible.

However, Elvin began, as far he could in the darkness, to seek out any weaknesses in the stonework. Whilst he had found the darkness disquieting when he had first arrived, his eyes were now reasonably accustomed to it. He ran his hands over as much of the wall as he could reach searching frantically for any imperfection. He thought it was most likely that any hole made by the rats was likely to be along the line of the wall with the floor of the dungeon.

He ran his hands along it but discovered nothing. Then he brushed back some of the stinking straw and discovered it. There was a small slit in the stonework about eight inches wide. He was amazed how a creature the size of a rat could squeeze through such a narrow opening.

He pushed the straw back to hide the opening and settled down to reflect.

It was obvious that, chained to the wall, and without any implement, he was not going to get very far but at least he could make a start whilst he had further thoughts about what the possibilities were.

The next day, after the guards had delivered the bread and water, he turned himself round, drew back the straw and began scratching away at the hole with his bare hands. His hands were soon sore and chapped and he appeared to be making little progress. As he scratched away he was suddenly aware of his neighbour whispering to him:

"What are you doing, knight?" the stranger asked in surprisingly good French.

Elvin whipped his hand quickly away from the slit in the wall and said, "That is none of your business, stranger."

"I, too, have thought, in my mind, that the rats must come in from somewhere," said the other, "and if the hole could be found, it might provide a means of escape."

"I have found nothing," lied Elvin.

"I think you have." replied Elvin's neighbour, "and, if an escape is to be made, two heads are better than one. Is this not true?"

"What possible kind of help can you be to me, foreigner?" questioned Elvin crustily, straining to make out the features of the stranger in the darkness.

"I am versed in some of the magical arts and could provide you with a tool to aid your digging," was the reply.

"Do not try to tempt me with the ways of the Devil. Magic is a tool of Satan and his sorcerers," retorted Elvin.

"That is not true. I am a servant of Allah and would have no truck with the Devil," said the stranger.

"Allah?" questioned Elvin. "If you serve Allah, you are an unbeliever and a heretic. I will have nothing more to do with you. If I were free I would kill you and send your damned soul into the fiery furnace where it belongs."

The stranger attempted to say more but Elvin cried, " Enough! I wish to hear no more of your infidel tongue." Elvin then turned and faced the other way.

The stranger remained quiet and the two did not converse again for over two days.

Elvin continued to scratch away at the rat hole but it was a frustrating task and his fingers were becoming chapped and bloody with his efforts. He was quite simply getting nowhere.

Rats invaded the dungeon again the next night. Elvin felt nervous and uncomfortable with them running around in the darkness. He had the same nightmarish feeling that he was going to be eaten alive by these disgusting vermin.

"If we work together we can get out of this hell," came a voice in the darkness. It was the stranger again.

Elvin ignored him at first. Prayer would provide the answer, he thought. But he had prayed before. Perhaps the Lord was answering by willing the stranger to assist him. The will of God worked in wondrous ways and perhaps he could even make this unworthy infidel serve his purposes, if he so willed it.

"And how do you propose that we can do that, heretic?" questioned Elvin with a sneer.

"As I have said, I have developed special skills. With your help I can get a tool to help with the digging," he said quickly.

"How?" asked Elvin.

"That would be my business," replied the stranger.

"Why would you do such a thing?" asked Elvin.

"Because, if you are able to find a way out, you can take me with you," came the reply.

"You are going nowhere with me, dog. I am just as likely to kill you for your sinful unbelief as to allow you to escape with me," Elvin growled.

"You need me, Christian. You cannot get out of here without my help and, like it or not, we are going to have to co-operate and help one another if we are going to be able to rid ourselves of this poisonous hole."

"How do I know that I can trust you, foreigner?" pleaded Elvin.

"You don't, but I am your only possibility of help. We can help one another," stressed the stranger.

"All right. What do you propose to do?" asked Elvin.

"Tomorrow when the guards open the trapdoor to throw in the bread and water, tell them that you think I am dead. Leave the rest to me," said the stranger.

"How can I do that? I do not speak the language."

"Yet another reason why you need me," came the speedy reply.

Elvin then received a painstaking lesson in the Arabic he would need to get the guards' attention.

The next day the door burst open and the sudden light blinded the prisoners. The bread and the containers of water were thrown down and just before the guard was about to close the trapdoor Elvin cried out in his faltering, broken Arabic:

"This prisoner – I think he is dead!"

The guard hesitated and then began to descend the stone steps into the dungeon followed by his colleague.

"You had better not be wasting my time, infidel," he muttered.

He approached the stranger who lay prostrate on the straw looking for all the world as if he were dead. The light streaming in through door brought Elvin his first clear glance of the stranger. He was a handsome man of good physique with a longish black beard.

Both guards kicked the stranger several times and the body rolled over lifelessly. Then, when the guards tried to pick up the body, the stranger began to moan and groan to indicate that he was, indeed, alive.

"You stupid bastard," the guard cried and both guards set about beating the unfortunate Elvin for his mistake.

Just then the sergeant of the guard presumably called down for them to hurry up because they let Elvin go and briskly ran up the steps and closed the trapdoor.

"Are you all right?" Elvin enquired of his neighbour. "Fine. Just a few bruises," he replied. "What about you?"

Elvin told him he was as good as could be expected.

"I have a little present for you," said Elvin's newfound ally. And he handed Elvin a small knife, curved in the Saracen style.

"By the love of Christ, where did you get that?" questioned Elvin.

"I noticed the other day that the guard always carries that knife in the top of his boot. Whilst they were kicking me about I took the opportunity of removing it from him. It is a skill I have perfected. He will not miss it for some time. But you will have to keep it concealed when you are not using it, because he may just think he has dropped it down here and come searching for it."

"I am in awe of you," said Elvin. "Not only have you produced a digging implement but we may also be able to remove our chains."

"Quite so," said the stranger.

The first task that the two men set one another was to rid themselves of their chains at their own convenience. It turned out that amongst his other talents the stranger could pick locks with consummate ease. They were soon free of their chains. The idea was to work on the tunnelling at times when the guards would not be expected to appear. They would be free from the chains and then lock themselves up at other times in case there was a surprise visit of the guards for whatever reason.

Progress on the tunnelling was painfully slow. A big problem was what to do with any earth dug out. They hoped perhaps to come across a drainage conduit, which might offer them a way out but after several days there seemed little chance of this.

The hole in the wall got ever bigger. They decided that the stones had to be replaced after each session and straw used to conceal the work. In one of their periods of rest from the digging Elvin asked of the stranger:

"Tell me, who are you and from where do you come?"

"My name is Uzmir ibn Aderbal of Granada. I come from the land of Al Andalus across the sea in the peninsular of Spain. I am a Berber and, originally, my ancestors came from the Atlas Mountains of Morocco but established themselves in Spain when it came under Moorish influence."

"I know the area," said Elvin, "I helped to carry our Christian Cross to Al Andalus and fought in many battles there. We sent you Moorish dogs running for the sea. But what are you doing here in Egypt?"

"That is a long story," said the stranger. "My family are of the Islamic faith but our tribe follows a path which has not always been acceptable to very orthodox Muslims."

"I do not understand," said Elvin, "I am of the Christian faith. We believe in Jesus Christ, who is the Son of God and who died on the Cross to save our sins. We are all sinners and we can only obtain forgiveness if we find Christ through the Church and the Head of that Church, the Pope, God's representative on Earth. There is no different path. Anybody who follows a different path is a heretic"

"Muslims believe in only one god too, called Allah, just like you Christians. Unlike Christians we do not believe God can be three persons. God cannot be Father, Son and Holy Ghost all at the same time. The Prophet Mohammed revealed Islam to humanity. Unlike your Jesus, the Prophet Mohammed was a human being, not a god and

Mohammed was the last prophet of God."

"Why do you not believe in Jesus Christ?" queried Elvin.

"We do. The difference is that we do not believe Jesus was a god. He was a prophet of God just like Mohammed and we believe Mohamed was the last of the prophets."

Elvin listened intently. He was outraged that anybody would question the divinity of Jesus or the Holy Trinity.

"How did you get to know about Islam?" asked Elvin.

"We learned about it as children, just like you learned about Christianity in your church, by visiting the mosque for communal worship and by hearing from our scripture called the Holy Qur'an just like you hear stories from the Bible. Many of the stories are exactly the same as those of your Old Testament and some of the stories from your New Testament are there as well."

"Then what is this path, of which you speak?" enquired Elvin.

"We try to find divine love and knowledge through direct personal experience of God. Man gets closer to truth and knowledge if he can shorten the distance between him and God. Our people have adopted various rituals, which help them to extend their souls beyond their carnal bodies to get closer to God. Even if you never get the whole way, the closer you get to God the greater your knowledge and insight will be."

"And why has this not been acceptable to other Muslims?" asked Elvin, slightly lost.

"Because, first of all, we accept the validity of all religions. All men have their own way of finding God — even Christians. The teachings of all religions appear to be basically the same. They all preach that love, kindness, patience, generosity and social responsibility are the basis of ethics and improving man's condition and all preach that there is some form of God. There is a great danger in restricting yourself to one religion and disbelieving in anything else. Allah or God is too great to be retained by one belief to the exclusion of others. This is difficult for some Muslims to accept as is, indeed, our drinking of wine, our practice of magic and our use of music in our rituals."

"You can believe in one religion if it is the true faith revealed by the teachings of Jesus Christ," said Elvin curtly. "All others are the invention of the Devil."

"You disregard, then, the beliefs of many, many people in the world, who are not necessarily as evil as you brand them," said Uzmir. "They believe in many of the things that you do."

"Then why are they killing my brother Christians all over these lands?" asked Elvin sharply.

"Because in wars people do kill one another even though their religion may forbid it," replied Uzmir. "They often use their religious texts to justify what they are doing even though the writings may not have meant literally what is written. Unfortunately greed for power and land often lead to religious principles being pushed to one side."

"Are you saying that the Bible is telling lies, heretic?" snapped Elvin.

"No, no, not necessarily. I am only saying that religious texts, like the Bible, are often just a collection of writings by different people that may be open to interpretation."

"The word of God is not open to interpretation," said Elvin coldly.

"The word of your God or my God?" Uzmir asked.

Silence ensued. The arguments of the heretical Berber were frustrating Elvin. He deserved to rot in the stinking dungeon as far as Elvin was concerned. If it were not for the fact that the Berber was assisting in his own efforts to escape he would probably kill him before he left. That would be one less heathen in the world. But he was in for a surprise.

"You asked how I came to be here in a dungeon in Egypt," said Uzmir. "It is because, although I am a Muslim, I am also a baptised Christian."

"Do not mock me, infidel. You talk like a Muslim dog," said Elvin.

"It is true. The Berbers, who rule in Al Andalus, tolerate our beliefs and when they appealed to us all to defend Islam we felt we could not ignore them. I took part in the bloody battle, which you will know of. It took place on the field that the Spaniards call Las Navas de Tolosa."

"I was there," declared Elvin. "It was a great victory for Christ."

"No quarter was given," continued Uzmir. "I was one of only a thousand left out of the many, many thousands who fought on that disastrous day. The Crusaders offered every prisoner a choice – baptism into the Christian faith and join the Crusader army or be executed as a Muslim heretic. What do you think I chose?"

"I would rather die than betray my faith," said Elvin. " I cannot see how you could ever do such a thing."

"Perhaps I am weaker than you. Or perhaps I knew that no one on earth could truly take my religion away from me. Whatever I swore before those Crusaders meant nothing. I believe that every man finds God in his own way and in my own heart I knew that I would always seek to get closer to God. Anyway I was not too sure that my basic beliefs were very far removed from those of the genuine Christians anyway."

"So did not the Crusaders find out how you felt?"

"No, I was enlisted in the army and became a scout. I came across to Damietta with the main force and was captured on a scouting mission not far from the city. It is strange that we have not met before but I know you Templars tend to be a very tight community and probably mistrustful of Arabic and Berber speaking scouts."

Elvin was aghast at the news and shocked in a way. He really did not know what to think. Was this man a Christian or was he a Muslim or was he neither or was he both? It was all very confusing.

However, he did not have time to think more on the subject for the hatch to the dungeon was flung open and a number of soldiers rushed down the steps and grabbed hold of several of the prisoners including Elvin and Uzmir. They were bundled up the steps into the light, which almost blinded them.

Elvin was fearful. He felt sure that they were going to be executed at last and the promise of the Saracen general had been just another vain heathen lie. They were pushed into a courtyard, lined up and told to wait. He found himself standing next to Uzmir.

"What in hell's name is going on?" he asked. "Are they going to kill us?"

"No," replied Uzmir. "Apparently they are going to take us to Cairo and keep us there to offer us for ransom."

"Where in God's name is the knife?" whispered Elvin.

"Don't worry. I have it and it is well concealed. They will never find it."

Elvin felt his St. Piran Cross under his toes in his left-hand shoe. He dearly hoped that it would protect him now.

A cart drawn by mules was brought into the courtyard and the half dozen or so prisoners, including Elvin and Uzmir, were roughly and hurriedly bundled into it. They trundled over the cobbles towards the narrow, bustling streets of the city. They passed through the gatehouse and descended steadily towards the river.

Once again their appearance in the city drew shouts of derision from the many passers-by. Missiles of all kinds showered down upon them from houses and roadway alike, but few of the nasty objects found their mark.

To Elvin it was just such a relief to be out in the fresh air again, away from the stench of the vile hole where they had been incarcerated. What was more, there was always the lingering hope that they might be able to extricate themselves from their seemingly hopeless situation and make their escape to wherever might present itself.

CHAPTER SIX

The Tunnel

Peter returned to Cornwall a few days later. This time it was Anya who picked him up at Penzance Station.

"How were things at home?" she enquired.

"Oh, I'll tell you later," Peter replied in a somewhat dismissive manner. Anya knew that he would probably tell her in his own time. So she left it.

"How's the dig going?" Peter asked.

"Good," said Anya. "There are indications that quite a fight went on there. There are a lot of charcoal deposits indicating a sizeable fire. We have also dug out quite a number of medieval iron nails which indicates that there must have been wooden buildings on the site in those days which were obviously destroyed in the fire."

During the course of the next day a number of further artefacts were discovered which pointed to some kind of battle having taken place. Medieval arrowheads and part of the blade of a sword were amongst the haul.

Later, at the evening meeting, the various artefacts were displayed so that everybody could get a look. Bernard Harper spent some time closely examining the various arrowheads. Suddenly he called Tim, the finds expert, over.

"Where did the diggers find these two?" he asked.

"In the trench at the far end of where they think the Hall was," Tim replied.

"But that would have been inside the building?" said Harper.

"Yes, it would," said Tim. "They found them scattered on the ground with the remains of a leather pouch of some sort."

"Do you know," Bernard Harper said, half thinking out loud, "I don't think these are arrow heads at all. Look at this one. It's completely blunt on one edge and sharp on the other and the other one is a different shape altogether. Give me your brush a moment."

Bernard brushed away some more of the deposits on one of the supposed arrowheads, which had been left behind by the initial cleaning that the students had undertaken.

"Look there's some writing on this one." Sure enough the cleaning had revealed part of an inscription on it. "Good heavens," said Bernard, "it looks like Arabic script."

He called Anya and Peter over to have a look and both agreed with his view that these artefacts were not what they had, at first, thought they were.

"I don't think they are arrowheads at all. I think we need further advice on these. Any ideas?"

"Well, I do have an idea what they might be," said Anya. "I have seen similar artefacts in Spain from the Moorish period. It seems highly unlikely, I know, in a medieval castle in Cornwall, but they look a bit like some medical instruments I've seen in the past. They almost look like part of a set of crude scalpels. I'd certainly like to have them checked out in Spain."

"Well, well, well," said Bernard, "we'll certainly send some photos right away to the expert who you think can enlighten us."

The following day there was a further interesting discovery. Professor Harper and Peter were called across to one of the trenches to look at a discovery, which was rather perplexing to the student diggers.

"It looks as if we've got a cannon ball," Richard, the leader of the diggers, said excitedly. "Does that mean that the site is a little older than we thought – perhaps fourteenth or fifteenth century?"

"No, not necessarily," said Bernard Harper. "It may be that it is simply from a different era. Let's have a look." He examined the metal ball very carefully and noticed a protrusion on the outside of the metal ball on one side of it.

"This isn't a cannon ball," he said. "It's part of the ball and chain from a quintaine. It was used in practices for jousts. It puts it firmly in the same sort of period as the rest of the artefacts we've got."

At the evening meeting Professor Harper seemed extremely pleased with the progress being made.

"There is no doubt that we have a major medieval site of some importance here," he said. "So much so that I'm pleased to announce that the developers have given us a little extra time to finish our examination of the area. Not much time but hopefully it will be enough.

"Today we've found some artefacts, which look as if they might be very ancient medical instruments and possibly Moorish in origin. We're not sure what they are doing in Cornwall well before such things would have been used in this part of the world, but we are having them checked out by an expert in Spain.

"We've also discovered part of the ball and chain from a thirteenth century quintaine together with one or two pieces of broken mailed armour of the period. Sally" — and he pointed to a fresh-faced teenage digger, who seemed a little self-conscious and embarrassed by the attention directed towards her — "has also found a rather interesting clasp for a cloak which we think is also from the same period.

"So, well done, everybody. We seem to have established beyond any doubt that there was a castle here in the thirteenth century and that, for some reason or other, it was destroyed completely. It may, therefore, suggest that there are elements of historical truth in the legend surrounding the knight who lived in a castle on this site.

"Now, there is one area of the site that I think we ought to examine more closely. The aerial shots of the lumps and bumps have indicated that there is a place where there might have been a burial site. It could be a well, or something of that sort, of course. But I feel we ought to have a look. So I'm getting the GPR machine back in so that we can get a radar scan of it. It will give us literally a slice through the earth and the radio waves reflected back should indicate what's underground. We may sink a trench there as well if we think it would be worthwhile."

As everybody repaired to the bar after the meeting Peter took Anya to one side and said: "Look, do you fancy going up to the pub on the main road for a drink? I want a chat."

"Yes, of course," said Anya. They drove up the long, windy and narrow lane from Tremennek Bay to the main road to Penzance and ensconced themselves in an old coaching inn. It was mid-week and there weren't many customers in the bar that evening.

They sat down with their drinks in a corner away from the bar. Peter looked slightly uncomfortable and a little uneasy.

" I think it's a bit better to talk here than down at the hotel with all the others looking on," he said.

"Yes, I'm sure that's so," said Anya, not really pushing him to say anything he did not want to.

"Well, it was an interesting day or two," he said. " Mary and I did a lot of plain talking. I think we've sorted things out now."

"I'm so glad to hear that, Peter," said Anya.

"It was very touch and go at first," he said. "I think she was relieved that I had turned up. I looked after Martha, who was the one with the chicken pox, whilst she was at work. It was difficult keeping her entertained and in bed, but I managed. In the evening, when Mary returned home, the atmosphere could be a bit taut. We had obviously reached a crisis in our marriage and we really needed to talk but somehow found it difficult.

"Actually it was Mary's mother who came to the rescue. She's a woman I haven't always respected. She's a bit snooty and has given the impression over the years that she doesn't think I'm good enough for her daughter but she has a way of reducing things to the absolute bare essentials and calls a spade a spade.

"To be fair she was very good. She sat us down together and made us talk to one another and really analyse what was wrong. She was better than any professional counsellor and was a wealth of wisdom. And she did it in a way that was, for a change, not interfering but genuinely aimed at helping if help was to be accepted. She told her own daughter that she was much too sensitive and jealous and she told me that I had to stop living in the past and face up to my responsibilities to her daughter and to her two lovely grandchildren. What she said, I suppose, needed saying. Mary and I were then able to talk over things in a much more sensible way afterwards and come to a number of important agreements."

"Oh, I'm so glad, Peter," said Anya. "I really was worried when you left. I did not want to feel that I had somehow been the cause of any problems between you and Mary."

"No, it wasn't you, Anya. It's all down to me really. But it does affect you in a sense."

"How is that?" enquired Anya.

"I had to promise Mary that I would no longer have anything but a professional relationship with you. No more going out to dinners together or, indeed, being alone together at all. If it wasn't for the job, I think she would have banned me from seeing you again. But even she realises that we are bound to meet professionally from time to time and she is OK about that so long as that is it."

Anya mused for a short period. "It is all probably for the best," she said.

"I shall always hold a very special place for you in my heart," said Peter taking her hand.

Anya looked into Peter's eyes and said, "I know, but your mother-in-law is right. You have to move on. We must never speak of this matter again. I appreciate your feelings for me and I have regarded you as a very good friend. But this is for the best – for both of us."

They embraced one another affectionately and then returned to the hotel.

The next day the geophysics team came back with their Ground Penetrating Radar equipment and examined the area requested by Bernard Harper. Later, looking at the printout, all agreed that further investigation would be necessary. The printout indicated something rather deeper than a burial chamber and the obvious conclusion was that it must be a well or something of that sort.

A JCB was called in to excavate the area. It was not long afterwards that there was nearly a nasty accident. As the JCB was painstakingly digging out a trench in the area concerned, the ground in front of it suddenly collapsed nearly taking one of the young diggers with it as well as the excavator. Professor Harper and Peter and the others were immediately called over.

"Good God. What is it?" asked Harper. The driver looked slightly puzzled but said, "It definitely looks like a well or something but I'm not sure how deep it is."

Peter picked up a small rock and tossed it down into the chasm that had appeared. It hit what appeared to be the bottom after a very short while which should have indicated that it was not very deep at all. But then the rock appeared to bounce its way further down and the clattering sound could be heard for some time afterwards.

"Hmm. It sounds as if it is vertical for a short way and then slopes downwards at an angle for goodness knows how far," said Bernard Harper. "I think it is time to dig out the caving gear. I haven't done any of that since I was an undergraduate."

Later that afternoon Peter and Bernard Harper drove into Penzance to hire the caving gear from a specialist outlet near the station. They were informed that if they needed a winch they would have to go to another firm in Pool near Camborne.

By the next morning they had managed to get together all the necessary equipment. It was decided also to contact the Caving Society at the Camborne School of Mines to see if they could send somebody out on a consultancy basis. About mid-day a lecturer at the School of Mines arrived on the site. He was also a leading light in the Caving Society.

"What do you think it is?" enquired Bernard Harper.

"It could be an old mine shaft. The area is honeycombed with them," said Bill Tregenza, the caving expert.

"But according to our observations this was possibly inside the main building of the castle," observed Peter.

"Well, there could have been an old building constructed on the site later that housed the headgear for a mine," said Bill. "But it's rather strange that there are no industrial remains of any sort. Well, we'd better go down and have a look."

It was decided that Bill Tregenza, and Peter, would make the descent together to investigate. Bernard Harper felt that his caving days were best left in the past and was happier for the younger man to go down. So suitably kitted out, the two men were winched down to the bottom of the vertical shaft. They were in touch by walky-talky with the surface.

"What can you see? Over." asked Bernard Harper, when they had reached the bottom of the shaft.

"Well, it certainly looks as if it is man-made. There's not a lot of room but room enough for people to get down here one at a time. Over."

"Any sign of when it was last used? Over."

"Not yet. But there are a lot of bits of wood at the bottom of the shaft so it looks as if there was a modern trap door or something disguising the entrance that the digger must have destroyed. The rest of it looks much older. It's very muddy and there's a lot of rubble about. Some efforts have been made to shore the roof up. There appears to be a sloping tunnel dug out at the bottom of the shaft so we're going to investigate where that goes. Over."

"OK, we'll await reports. Take care. I'll speak to you later," replied Harper. "Over and out."

The whole team stood about, intrigued, and waiting for further news as to what lay down in the tunnel.

"Bernard?" About twenty minutes later the walky talky crackled back into life.

"Hello, Peter. Where are you?" said Bernard Harper. "Over."

"If you go to the cliff edge, you'll see us," said Peter.

Everybody gathered at the cliff edge and looked down and there on the rocks below stood the mud-caked Peter, and Bill, waving.

"We're coming back up," said Peter. "Over and out."

When Bill and Peter had returned to the surface everybody gathered round to hear what had been discovered.

"It's a tunnel and cave, which, lead right down to the sea," said Peter. "The age of the tunnel is difficult to judge. But we have some problems. First of all the tunnel appears to have been used recently. We found bits and pieces of wooden barrels down there and a small stone quay has been constructed at some time in the past, probably in the eighteenth century. I suspect that it was used for smuggling then and that this has continued until the present day. There are a number of modern crates stored down there. We haven't looked inside them but our suspicion is that they probably contain illegal goods. No wonder the story of the ghost of the Evil Knight was spread around the district. They obviously did not want too many people wandering around up here."

"Well, I'd like to try and find out exactly how old the tunnel is," said Bernard Harper. "It would be interesting to establish whether it was here in medieval times."

"Yes. That could put a wholly different complexion on the fate of the Knight and his Saracen bride," added Peter. "But we have a problem. We are going to have to report our find to the police and you know what will happen then. The whole place will become a crime scene and there will be the inevitable delay.

"Damn," was Bernard's only remark.

"There's also another problem. Although the tunnel has been used it is far from stable. There appear to have been other tunnels off to the side in the past and some of those have been blocked off or have simply collapsed. The whole place is full of rock fall rubble and really gooey mud. It won't be easy going and we'll have to be extremely careful."

"Damn, damn, damn," repeated Bernard to himself, "it could be weeks before we get back down there."

CHAPTER SEVEN

Escape From The Nile

Elvin and Uzmir found themselves being transported on a sailing vessel down the Nile towards Cairo. Both of them knew that, if they were going to escape, they would have to take their opportunity on this journey. The vessel was a traditional felucca but a bit larger than average. A large canvas canopy kept most of the vessel shaded from the fierce sun.

The vessel criss-crossed slowly from bank to bank of the river, stopping to pick up further prisoners. All the prisoners were knights and nobles and presumably thought worth keeping alive for their ransom value.

They had two guards, who kept a very close eye on them. One wrong move and they knew they would be cut down with the wicked looking curved sword, which each guard carried. They would then be tossed overboard to feed the crocodiles and a report submitted that they had tried to escape.

Now, in the daylight, Elvin was able to observe his fellow prisoner. Uzmir was a tall, handsome man with deep brown eyes and distinguished by a full black beard. For all their arguments there was a gentle look about him, to which, had he not been on his guard, Elvin might have warmed.

Uzmir still had the small knife he had stolen from the guard in the dungeon at Damietta. He seemed to be adept at concealing things and, even if a search had been made of his person, he would have been able to palm the object and turn his hand in such a way, that it could never be seen.

Their plan was simple. Uzmir would work on picking the lock to the new chains, in which he had been shackled. His skills permitted him to do this even if a guard appeared to be looking straight at him.

At the rate that they were travelling it would take them a few days to get to Cairo. That night, when they moored up at a jetty the guards took it in turns to go ashore so that there was only one guard overseeing the sleeping prisoners.

Sometimes that guard would either be looking in the opposite direction or nodding off in a half slumber. It was then that Uzmir was able to work on the lock of Elvin's shackles.

They planned to attack the one guard on duty the next night and disappear over the side to make their escape. It would not be easy because the Nile was a busy river with thousands of boats plying their way upstream and downstream. However, at night, most of them moored up to jetties on the bank and it would be easier then.

They had not found it easy to discuss this plan of action because the guards did not like the prisoners whispering to one another and were always very alert during the day. It was altogether easier for them to discuss their plans at night.

The following night not everything went according to plan. It was a rather brighter night than they had anticipated. It was almost a full moon. The guard steadfastly refused to be anything other than totally alert and awake. The two prisoners waited several hours before the guard turned his back on them to look across the river from the bow of the boat.

Uzmir went to work and, within a few minutes and with occasional stops for fear of being discovered, he had managed to release Elvin from his chains. However, just at that moment, the second guard returned. Why he had done so they would never know. He flopped into the boat, kicked out at a prisoner, swearing in Arabic, and then collapsed in a heap to sleep off his indulgences. The other guard remained awake and it seemed like hours before he nodded off at last.

Elvin and Uzmir delayed for a while to be quite sure. Uzmir went first, leaving Elvin to try and reduce the rocking of the boat as Uzmir quietly slipped into the water.

He left the knife with Elvin as insurance against one of the guards suddenly waking up. A guard snorted and started and Elvin thought his chance had gone. But the guard turned over and resumed his dreams.

Elvin, boots around his neck, very carefully slipped into the water. It was colder than he had anticipated but he began gently pulling away from the boat and, when he found himself at a sufficient distance, struck out for the opposite shore. There was no sign of Uzmir.

The river was very close to its full flood and running quite fast. The water was reddish brown in colour — the source of all the nutrients, which made the Nile Delta so fertile.

Elvin was soon struggling and felt himself sinking. He held his breath. Bubbles surged upwards and there was a roaring in his ears. The desire for survival made him kick for the surface and a few seconds later he broke through the water gasping for air.

Elvin's one phobia remained with him — crocodiles. He was fearful that massive jaws would suddenly grab him from the deep and drag him to the bottom or that he would be tossed from side to side in the beast's fearsome snout before being snapped in two just like it had happened to his fellow knight, Rodrigo, on their expedition to the Tower.

He forced himself to remain alert and suddenly his heart stopped. Slowly floating towards him was a long thick dark object that looked in the darkness every bit like a big male crocodile. He was very conscious of the St. Piran Cross, which had been hidden in his boot. He did not want to lose it and he trusted in its power to protect him from misfortune.

He froze in sheer terror as the dark object touched him. But it was only the broken branch of a tree. Elvin let out a huge sigh of relief and used the branch to give himself a rest from his exertions for a short while.

Eventually he reached the other shore and fell exhausted onto the bank. He checked his boot for the St. Piran Cross. Almost by some miracle it was still there in spite of the water that had filled his boots. When he had got his bearings he looked around to see where he was. His eyes had got used to the darkness and the moon was quite bright.

They had chosen the long swim to the other shore because it was less populated and they had felt they would have a better opportunity to make their getaway.

Elvin crawled up the bank and peered over the top of it to find himself staring straight into the eyes of a scrawny goat that was just as surprised to see him, as he was to see it. The goat took off in fright probably thinking that Elvin was a hungry crocodile seeking a nourishing meal.

Not far away he could make out a village but all was quiet apart from the odd dog barking.

Elvin stood up and began skirting the village in an effort to avoid being seen. He had no clear idea what he was going to do or where he was going. He felt his first duty was to try and return to the Crusader forces but he knew that would be an extremely hazardous venture. The Nile Delta was quite well populated and there would be Saracen patrols everywhere.

He was quietly walking along when a lone figure leapt out of the darkness, grabbed him from behind, imprisoned his arms and placed a hand across his mouth.

"Don't make a noise and I'll remove my hand," said the figure in French and he knew that it was Uzmir.

Elvin nodded and Uzmir let him go. "So you are not yet crocodile meat!" whispered Uzmir.

"God chose to spare me," uttered Elvin pointedly.

"What do you propose to do now?" asked Uzmir.

"I shall try and return to the Crusader forces, if I can," replied Elvin.

"They will accuse you of treachery without any doubt. Not only have you not died as a martyr in the cause of Christ but also you have allowed yourself to be captured by the enemy. And now you have entered into an accord with a Christian who was formerly of the Islamic Faith and whose loyalty will now also be in question," said Uzmir.

Elvin knew full well there could be a problem. Templar life was enforced by a series of penances for wrong-doing, of which deserting the banner in a battle or desertion to the Saracens were deemed amongst the worst and could carry a sentence of perpetual imprisonment. Although he was innocent of such crimes he might well find it difficult to explain what had happened. However, he felt that he was under oath to return to the Christian lines.

"I am obliged by oath to find my way back to the Crusader forces," he said.

"You will find that difficult," said Uzmir. "Even if you manage to avoid the Egyptian patrols you could be killed by brigands. Even if you are lucky enough to avoid that you are unused to the type of terrain to be experienced in the Delta. It can be very treacherous with all the tributaries and canals. You would have to travel by night and it would be difficult to see where you are going. You could easily drown in one of the thousands of water filled gullies. Even if you were to overcome all those problems you still could not be sure of the reception you would receive if you were successful in reaching the Christian lines."

"Nevertheless I must try," said Elvin emphatically. He brushed his hand across his brow. He was feeling distinctly hot and not a little dizzy.

"All right," sighed Uzmir. "it is my intention to try and find my way home to my family. I am weary of battle and of living a lie. After the Christian victory, where I was captured, they all fled to Granada, which lies in the part of Al Andalus still in Moorish hands. I hope to find them there."

"My God, I don't know how you think you are going to find your way there. It must be hundreds of leagues from here and then you have to cross the sea," observed Elvin.

"I know. It will be difficult but I will get there," said Uzmir optimistically.

"I will begin my journey tomorrow," said Elvin. "I am feeling tired now and need to rest."

"You would be wise to rest up for the whole day tomorrow," said Uzmir. "It is best to travel by night in spite of the difficulties. It is cooler and you have less chance of being discovered. I have found an outhouse where we can rest up for now."

They made their way to a small stone building and Elvin collapsed on the ground. He drifted off into a feverish sleep.

He was racked by dreams of being attacked by crocodiles. He imagined being recaptured and of having some terrible revenge imposed on him by the Saracens. He was plagued with fear of the consequences of the Brotherhood's wrath at his disappearance and how they would react should he return to them.. They must surely know of his capture by now and possibly of his escape with Uzmir. He drifted in and out of one scene after another and was conscious of being very hot and had difficulty in breathing. Then all seemed to go blank.

Elvin awoke with a start. The world around him seemed to be moving and he was conscious of being slumped over something that was buffeting him backwards and forwards. His eyes were now wide open and he was straining to see in the darkness. He sat up and tried to rub his eyes but realised his hands were tied.

As he gathered his thoughts he realised that he was sat astride a horse and that his hands were tied to the saddle with a piece of cloth or some such thing. A deep depression descended upon him as it dawned on him that the Saracens had recaptured him. But then Elvin realised that only one other mounted person accompanied him and that person was leading his horse.

He was dressed in a white gallabaya and wearing a white turban.

"Who are you and where are you taking me?" asked Elvin in a croaky voice.

"It is I, Uzmir. So you are returned to us. I was beginning to worry."

"What do you mean?" questioned Elvin.

"You have been ill of the fever these past three days and I was concerned that you might not recover."

"Why are my hands tied so?" asked Elvin.

"So that you would not fall from your horse," replied Uzmir

"Where are we and how did you come by these horses?"

"Even though you were ill, I felt it would be wise to move on. I could not leave you where you were, as you would have surely been captured. There are many, many Egyptian patrols.

"I managed to acquire these horses last night together with some more appropriate clothing. The owner will probably have a sore head for a day or two. We will attract less attention dressed so."

Elvin glanced down and realised that he was wearing a similar white gallabaya and turban to Uzmir.

"Incidentally this dropped out of your shoe as I was changing your clothing." Uzmir handed the St. Piran Cross to Elvin. "I would keep that out of sight if I were you. It will not be appreciated in this part of the world. I don't know how you have managed to conceal it thus far"

"Thanks," said Elvin. "It is of great personal importance to me."

"Where are we now?" he enquired of Uzmir.

"We are close to the city of Alexandria and the coast. We are on the other side of a lake that lies just over there"

"But this is taking us away from the Crusader lines and any chance of my rejoining them," protested Elvin.

"I had no choice. You were ill. I could not leave you where you were. I had to take you with me," responded Uzmir.

Elvin fell silent, pondering on his position. Deserting the Order was a serious offence and escaping and failing to return to the Crusader forces would probably be deemed desertion. On the other hand having been captured by the enemy and failing to fight to a martyr's death could also be construed as an offence and his reception, if he did return, might be equally uncertain. He was much troubled in his mind.

Dawn was breaking and the two travellers sought to find shelter from the heat of the day. They were very much on the edge of the Nile Delta now, seeking to avoid concentrations of population but needing to rest up in the day.

They took shelter under some palms by a stream, ate some dates and took some water, and agreed to take turns on watch. Elvin was still very tired and weak and Uzmir suggested that he should take the first watch. Elvin prayed to God for guidance as to what he ought to do and then fell into a deep slumber.

He dreamed that that he was on the wing of some great bird that was flying over deserts and mountains, and the sea, ever westwards. He finally landed by a river bordered by poplar trees. The river wound its way across a vast plain towards a huge hill in the distance. On the hill lay a magnificent fortress. Behind the hill he could see snow-capped mountains. As he approached the hill, he felt somehow that this was where he should be. He awoke with a start as Uzmir roused him for his turn on watch.

"Everything seems to be in order," he said and settled down to sleep himself. The day passed without incident but Elvin was confused by his dream. Towards the evening when Uzmir awoke again, he spoke to him of his dream.

"It's a sign," said Uzmir. "You are destined to come with me to Al Andalus for what you have described is the Valley of the River Genil in Al Andalus and the great Kadima fortress at Granada."

Elvin was far from convinced by the truth of that contention but at least the Berber had not stolen his valued Cross. Perhaps God was suggesting that his destiny lay in remaining with Uzmir for the moment at least.

"Once we get away from the Nile Delta and reach the coast, there will be less danger and we will be able to travel in the cooler parts of the day and make better progress," explained Uzmir.

It was not long before they knew that they had left the great city of Alexandria behind them and had begun following the coast road towards the open desert lands beyond Egypt. The two companions felt fortunate in having evaded recapture but the dangers were far from over.

A few days later they found themselves travelling through a pleasant land, which made a change from the vastness of the desert. The air seemed fresher here and it was almost as fertile as the Nile Delta. The way ran through outcrops of white rock, scattered woods of pine, areas of scrub and gorse and patches of soft springy grass. Every so often they came across refreshing streams running between reedy banks. It was a welcome relief from the vast seas of sand.

But they were not happy. They had company. For some hours they had been conscious of being trailed by a small group of heavily armed Arabs, about six in number, whose intentions looked far from honourable. Their leader was a particularly unsavoury looking character with a huge scar across his face and hardly a tooth in his head.

" I don't like it," said Uzmir. "I think they are brigands. They will kill us for our horses and anything else they think we might have. It will be dark soon. We must try and lose them."

As the sun set Uzmir motioned to Elvin to follow him and galloped off at high speed along the trail. The time taken for the brigands to react to what was happening enabled the two men to put some distance between themselves and their trackers. Rounding a bend they noticed to the left of the road some rocks interspersed with groups of scattered pine trees. They dismounted quickly and concealed themselves behind the rocks. They waited, keeping an eye on the road. A few minutes later the band of brigands galloped, at full speed past them in the darkness, unaware of their hiding place.

They waited behind the rocks for several hours but the brigands did not return. They decided to camp there for the night. The next morning they departed very early before the sun had reached its full intensity.

"There is always safety in numbers," Uzmir said, "I feel that we would be better placed if we were to join up with others travelling the same way. If you could pass as one of us, we would be all right. What you are wearing now will do. But you must never reveal your short hair. You will need to let it grow. Whatever happens you must not speak whilst we are in the company of others. I will say that you are from Doumyat and that your whole family died in the siege there. Consequently you have not spoken or comprehended anything since. Hopefully nobody will suspect. We will find somewhere safe for you to hide whilst I ride on to the next town to see if I can arrange for us to travel with a group from now on."

A little while later they came upon the ruins of a city built during the time of the Romans. It's setting was beautiful, for it overlooked an almost turquoise sea. The coast was littered with these old ruins of a by-gone age. But this one was far grander than most.

The ruins were deserted and a bit overgrown. A lofty gateway of honey-coloured sandstone beckoned and they rode through into a vast forum. Broken down arches and columns were visible as far as the eye could see. Paved roadways stretched out in an orderly grid fashion from the centre. The remains of pools, patios, gymnasia and temples were everywhere. As well as these buildings there were the simple homes of citizens, who had lived there some seven or eight hundred years before. It must have been a city of some importance, but it had suddenly become deserted, perhaps when the Romans left.

Most amazing of all, there was a well-preserved semi-circular theatre under which they found the changing rooms the actors had used all those centuries before - the perfect hiding place.

Uzmir left Elvin well concealed in the underground ruins and made off for the nearest town. Elvin had his doubts as to whether the Berber would return but had little alternative than to trust him.

There was an eerie silence about the place. It was quite warm although it was considerably cooler below ground than it was outside. It was warm enough, however, for Elvin to begin to nod off after not having slept very much the night before.

Elvin was not sure how long he had been sleeping but he was awakened by the sound of voices chatting in the guttural Arabic tongue. At first he thought that Uzmir had returned with others but, acting cautiously, he crept carefully up the steps to an entrance onto the terraces so that he could observe the people concerned.

It was not Uzmir but, to his horror, Elvin recognised the scar faced Arab and his band of brigands who were now sitting around a camp fire, laughing and chatting, only some fifty paces distant from where he was hidden.

Elvin kept himself hidden. He could not afford to be discovered. On his own he would not stand any chance against the six bandits. But he was worried. Uzmir, if he were to return, would walk straight into a trap and there would be no way he could warn him.

He considered what he ought to do and wrestled with his conscience over what seemed like hours. Should he just stay where he was, let the brigands deal with Uzmir, as they surely would, and then wait for them to depart on further murderous expeditions? Uzmir was a heathen after all. What was the life of another heathen dog, anyway? Or should he wait for Uzmir to get back and then rush to his aid when the two of them might stand a better chance than one on his own?

Elvin knew in his heart that he needed Uzmir. Although he was afraid to trust the Berber overly, he had developed a healthy respect for him. He prayed to God for guidance once more.

A commotion stirred Elvin from his thoughts and he peered out from his hiding place. Uzmir had returned and had ridden right into the trap. The Arabs had grabbed the reins of his horse and forced him to dismount and the toothless leader was now teasing him with a sword blade slicing pieces out of his gallabaya whilst the others stood round with murderous grins on their faces. Elvin fully expected them to murder him at any moment to obtain his horse and rob him of anything they might find. He had no doubt as to what he had to do.

Fortunately all had their backs to where Elvin was and he would have the element of surprise. So he crept round quietly to the entrance onto the terraces that was closest to where the group was. He had the advantage of being above them

As Scar Face lifted his sword to smite off Uzmir's head Elvin launched his attack down onto the brigands, shrieking at the top of his voice to give them the idea that he was more than one. He went for the nearest bandit and grabbed him in an arm lock swiftly breaking his neck.

The element of surprise distracted Scar Face from beheading Uzmir as he turned his attention towards Elvin.

Armed with the first bandit's sword Elvin used all his training and guile to set about the other shocked bandits, who had now all turned their attention towards him. With a swift downward thrust of his sword he knocked a second Arab to the ground and threw his sword to Uzmir. But the fallen brigand grabbed his leg and tried to pull him to the ground, pinning his arms to his side.

Templar training paid dividends. Elvin struggled with the brigand for an instant but he had no intention of yielding the sword. Having got his arm free again Elvin ran the sword across the Arab's throat and, with a horrible gurgling sound, he went to the fiery furnace where he belonged.

Uzmir, with reflexes like lighting, had sliced the leader in two from his collarbone almost down to his breastbone with a massive and perfectly aimed blow.

Moving with great agility Elvin turned his bloody sword just in time to fend off a blow from another of the bandits. One or two clever thrusts and feints and Elvin had dealt with him as well.

Uzmir had pinned yet another brigand to the ground with his sword. A fountain of blood spurted from the man's stomach as Uzmir withdrew the blade.

The last brigand did not wait. He rushed off, grabbed a horse and galloped away in full retreat.

Both men collapsed on the terracing exhausted.

"I owe you my life," gasped Uzmir, still breathing heavily from his exertions.

"No, I think I owe you mine. I am so glad you returned, my friend," said Elvin, almost without thinking. He knew then that he had made an almost unconscious choice. He and Uzmir were destined to travel together and a strong friendship was developing between them.

The two men put their arms around one another and Elvin knew that things would never be as they had been before. No longer did he regard this man as his enemy, despite his different religion. He had a growing feeling their lives had now become inextricably entwined.

"We are in luck," said Uzmir. "I have found a party of pilgrims in the next town who are on the way along this coast after returning from making a pilgrimage to Medina and Mecca. They have agreed that we can travel with them as far as they are going. They will wait for us until tomorrow morning. But remember you must say nothing when we are in their company."

That evening they washed their blood soaked clothes and bathed in one of the pools nearby. It was clear from that day on that a new and unbreakable bond had been forged between them.

CHAPTER EIGHT

Crisis In St. Albans

Bernard Harper brought all the members of the team together on the Thursday evening.

"Do you want the good news or the bad news?" he said.

"First of all — the good news," he went on. " I'm pleased to tell you that we have had the report back from Spain with regard to the artefacts, which we thought, initially, were arrowheads.

"It has been confirmed that they are part of a set of medical scalpels, of Moorish origin, dating from the thirteenth century. This is an absolutely fabulous find because it's very doubtful whether precision instruments of this type were in any kind of general use in the England of the time. So it's a very definite first. Very well done, everybody."

Peter and Anya smiled at one another and the whole room erupted into applause.

"Now the bad news. We have a problem, folks," he said. "As you know we discovered the tunnel running down to the seashore. Unfortunately it appears to be a tunnel, which has been used, for some centuries, as a means of landing contraband goods. It has now become a crime scene and we have been asked to move off the site for the foreseeable future.

"You can only imagine what I feel about 'Mr. Plod' going up and down the tunnel searching for evidence. We can only hope that he doesn't totally destroy our chances of adding to the substantial archaeological finds that we have made already. I don't know whether we will be able to continue with this project, or not, at the moment.

"I understand that the farmer, Fred Tregenna, is now assisting the police with their enquiries so where that puts the land in terms of its legal position I really don't know.

"What I am going to suggest is that we all take a week's break and then see what the position is after that. I just hope that all our work has not been ruined at the last moment by this incident."

And so they all dispersed from the meeting and it was clear that several of the members of the team were rather at a loss as to what to do. Anya, in particular, did not know whether to return to Granada or not.

"There is not a lot of point for just a week," she told Peter. "No sooner will I have arrived than I will have to come back again," she added. "I think I will have to remain here in the hotel. The trouble is that it is very expensive here in England and I am not sure the people funding me will wear it without a dig going on."

"Oh, you can't do that," said Peter. "Why don't you come home with me? You'd be very welcome."

"I can't do that. What is Mary going to say?"

"Well, I don't know yet. But, I can only ask," said Peter.

He tried to ring Mary but she was out. So he sent her a text to say that he and Anya were on their way and that there had been a postponement of the dig for a week.

They left it till lunchtime and there was still no reply from Mary.

"Well, it's no good," said Peter, "we might as well set off and hope we can contact her on the way."

They set off up the A30 towards London and St.Albans, where Peter lived. They arrived in St.Albans about five hours later having failed to make any contact with Mary at all.

They drove up to the house in Chiswell Green and found nobody in.

"I'll ask over the road," said Peter and went across to speak to a neighbour, who he knew to be quite friendly with Mary.

The neighbour opened the door and looked quite surprised to see him.

"Oh, Peter," she said, "we didn't expect to see you."

"No," said Peter, "there's been a hold up at the dig in Cornwall and so I've decided to come home. I've got a colleague with me. Do you know where Mary is?"

"Well, she's gone out for the evening and may not be back until later," said Jean.

"Hello, Daddy," said a little voice, which was that of Martha, "we didn't know you were coming home today."

"Mary asked me to baby-sit the two children until she comes back home," explained Jean.

"Well, that's very good of you," said Peter. "They might as well come with me now."

So he collected up Martha and Emma. Emma was the most reluctant to come because she was involved in discussing a new mobile phone with Sam, Jean's daughter of the same age. She came under protest, however, and they returned to Peter's house.

"Do you know where Mummy is?" enquired Peter.

"I expect she's out with Uncle Alex," said Emma with a rather cynical thirteen-year-old edge to her voice. "She's been seeing quite a lot of him lately."

Peter knew exactly whom she meant.

Alex Crosby was a colleague at the University. He had always appeared to take a bit of a shine to Mary and at social gatherings at the University he had frequently spent a lot of time talking to her and dancing with her. It had led to more than one argument in the past.

It was not till about eleven thirty in the evening that Mary arrived home. She had clearly been drinking and professed surprise that Peter was there, although she had been across to Jean's first and had obviously been informed that he was home.

"Hi," she said with her speech slightly slurred. "I didn't expect to see you."

"No," said Peter. "We've got a problem with the dig so we've all been given the week off. Didn't you get my text?"

"No, I didn't check today," said Mary with a shrug. She went into the lounge and immediately spotted Anya.

"Oh," she said with a rather disapproving look, "I didn't realise you were here. I hope Peter has offered you a drink."

"Hello Mary," said Anya. "No, I'm OK, thank you. I don't drink alcohol."

"Oh yes," said Mary, "I forgot. It's against your religion. Well, I think I'm going to have one."

"Don't you think you've had enough?" said Peter.

"No, I haven't as a matter of fact," said Mary dismissively and she made for the drinks cabinet. She poured herself a large whisky and added ice and some dry ginger.

"So what hotel are you staying in Anya?" asked Mary.

Anya looked a little embarrassed and Peter chipped in:

"I thought that Anya could stay here with us," he said.

"Oh, you did, did you?" said Mary rather rudely. "Well, I haven't made up a bed or anything. I'm afraid you're going to have to do that.

I'm going to bed and I don't want to be disturbed. I've got to be up sharp for work in the morning. You can sleep in the spare room." Then glancing at Anya she added, "or wherever you like."

With that, Mary swept out of the room with her whisky and disappeared upstairs.

"Look, I'm going to have to find a hotel," said Anya. "I can't stay here. It's clearly the cause of some grief and the last thing I want to do is to cause friction between you and your wife."

"I think that's there already," said Peter with a shrug. "OK, there's a good hotel near the Abbey. I'll give them a ring to see if they've got a room."

The hotel had a vacancy and so Peter took Anya into St.Albans.

The next morning Mary came down looking slightly the worse for wear. Peter had already prepared some cereal, tea and toast. Mary began searching through a cupboard.

"What are you after?" enquired Peter.

"The bloody paracetomols," grunted Mary.

"I'm not surprised," said Peter.

"Look, Peter, don't start preaching. I'm not in the mood. Where's your woman?"

"What do you mean - my woman?"

"You know very well what I mean," came the reply.

"Look, Mary," said Peter, "there is nothing going on between Anya and I. I explained our previous agreement to her and she understands fully the situation. I just thought that, since there is a week's break from the site and she would be on her own, she might as well come and stay with us."

"Well, you thought wrong. I don't want that woman in the house," said Mary, her voice at a higher pitch.

"She is not in the damned house," shouted Peter. "She's gone to stay in that hotel near the Abbey. Why don't you get it into your stupid head? There is nothing going on."

"Well, maybe there isn't. But I know bloody well that if it were offered, you'd be there like a shot."

Peter shrugged.

"You bastard," said Mary, "you haven't even got the decency to deny it. I'm going to work. You can take the kids to school. I'll pick them up and I don't expect you to be here when I get back."

"Oh, you don't, do you? I might just go and change all the locks whilst you're out," said Peter.

"Don't be sarcastic, Peter," said Mary, "it doesn't suit you. If you're still here when I get back, I'm taking the children and I'm going to Mother's and you can do what you like."

With that Mary stormed out of the house. She reversed the car off the drive at a furious speed and shot off.

"Fuck it," said Peter and threw the spoon he was holding across the kitchen breaking a coffee cup in the process.

He telephoned Anya and told her what had happened and said he would book into the hotel with her.

"I don't think that's going to be a good idea at all," said Anya. "It will only compound the difficulties that Mary and you have at the moment. And I am sure, if Yuba knew, there would be even more trouble for me as well. I'm going back down to Tremennek Bay. I think you'd better try and do what you can to rescue your relationship."

"I don't think there appears to be much chance of that," said Peter glumly.

That evening he waited for Mary to return. She came in, threw her keys on the kitchen counter, barked some orders at the children, who disappeared, and said:

"I thought I told you I didn't expect you to be here," she said sharply.

"I've every right to be here," replied Peter. "It's my house as well as yours and you don't dictate whether I go or not."

"Well, then, I'm going to telephone Alex to come and collect me and the children and take us to Mother's."

"You can do what you fucking like as far as I am concerned," said Peter, standing his ground. "Give my regards to Alex," he said with a sneer, "and to the old bat," he added, referring to Mary's mother.

Mary began packing and told the children that they were going to stay at Grandma's for a few days. Alex Crosby picked them up later in the evening, but by that time Peter had decided to walk down to the local pub for a drink and to be out of the way.

In the pub he sat with his pint and mused on his disastrous marriage, which now seemed well and truly on the rocks.

It had all been very good at first. They had got on well and he had found Mary attractive. Before the children had arrived they had had several good holidays together.

Neither of them was perfect. Mary could be irritatingly overbearing at times. He got very annoyed with her for ringing him at work, especially when he was on site. It was often about things, which seemed to be quite inconsequential compared to the importance of his work.

Mary did not feel that he pushed himself enough. After the arrival of the children and when money got tighter, the put down jokes about his work began. They would be at a party and she would say:

"Well, of course, my husband is an expert in medieval armour. As you can imagine our phone doesn't stop ringing." Peter would laugh it off by saying something like:

"But, then, of course, we've got the cheapest phone bill in the street." But there was no doubt that it hurt.

Peter, in his turn, could sometimes be disparaging about what he regarded as her inferior academic qualifications or her work. She would arrive home from work and he would say:

"I suppose your brain has been suitably exercised by deep discussions about nail extensions?" he would say. It was meant to be a joke but somehow didn't sound like one.

There would be rows and then they would make up and, perhaps, spend a weekend away.

Then there were problems with regard to the in-laws. Peter's widowed mother lived in Kenilworth. His mother and Mary did not get on very well. Mary saw very little of her. But Peter saw plenty of Mary's mother.

Mary's mother made no secret of the fact that she considered Peter's work to be something less than a proper job. She would have preferred her daughter to marry a high flyer in the city, earning proper money, and made little secret of her opinion on the matter.

Things really started to get worse when Peter made the mistake of telling Mary about Anya. Her growing jealousy caused a considerable rift between them. Mary's calls to the site, especially if he was working with Anya, became more frequent and could only be interpreted as check up calls on a lot of occasions. Colleagues were hardly discreet either. If he and Anya had gone for a meal together, they would say so and this would make their relationship seem to Mary to be far worse than it actually was.

It had all been a bit of a disaster really and Peter knew that it was over. He sat there a bit longer, then drained his drink and set off purposefully home.

At home Peter packed up all the stuff that he regarded as his and stacked it in the study/bedroom, where he did his work when he was at home. He closed and locked the door to it, went downstairs and strode out of the house without a second look.

CHAPTER NINE

The Knight's Tale

Some time after leaving Egypt, Uzmir and Elvin found themselves close by the city known to the Crusaders as Algiers.

Their journey across Northern Africa had been a long and arduous one but, apart from the clash with the brigands, it had passed largely without incident. They had stuck to the coast, travelled with groups of returning pilgrims from Mecca and Medina, and had arrived eventually within sight of the flourishing seaport which lay a reasonable distance across the sea from Al Andalus, the homeland of Uzmir.

They had had to rely largely on the charity of pilgrims to survive. They kept up the pretence of Elvin's misfortune in Damietta successfully and the pilgrims were generous towards them. They were kept supplied with dried fruit and dates, mutton and goat, camel's milk and flat bread and were even given some money to help them on their way.

They had to contend with scorching sun at times and drenching, incessant rain at others. They had crossed vast sand seas interspersed, very occasionally, with tracts of fertile land and, sometimes, rugged, brown mountains.

The desert had been like no other experience for Elvin with the great bowl of the sky always above them. He had been very conscious, at times, of the great solitude and vulnerability of the pilgrim caravan with not a soul around for hundreds of miles. It was a feeling the like of which he had not experienced anywhere else.

Then one evening they found themselves, alone again, camped on a hillside among trees overlooking a waterfall, which provided the clearest air they had experienced for some time. Green forests covered the mountainside and giant cedars were all around. It could almost have been somewhere in Europe apart from the noise of the Barbary macaques, who were leaping and screeching amongst the branches quite inquisitive as to their presence.

The next day it was their intention to sell the horses in Algiers and haggle for a passage by boat to the Spanish Peninsular and Al Andalus.

For the moment, however, they were seated around their fire having just finished the remains of some pressed dates and a quantity of hard cheese given to them by the pilgrims, before they had said their goodbyes. Uzmir broached the question:

"Elvin, how did you come to be a Templar? I know you have been in Spain as well as Egypt but how did it all start?"

"Well," said Elvin, "it's a long story really. Some years ago my father wanted me to marry the daughter of a nobleman from another part of Cornwall. She was called Alis de Trevarno. But I had no liking for her at all. She was not bad looking in her way but she was older than me and could be a hellish mare at times. She was conniving, foul-tempered and overbearing and her evil tongue was not to my liking at all. But she convinced many people that she was of a different nature and always attended church and so the local priest, Father Trystan, was happy.

"I was not interested in her at all and pursued my liking for hunting, wrestling and sailing with my boyhood friend, Yestin. He was the true son of the woman who had raised me in my early years.

"My father could not understand my attitude and, since a sizeable dowry was involved and he was a widower, he began to court Alis himself. My mother had died when I was but a young baby. As a result he ended up marrying Alis and she became my stepmother."

"Did that not prove a little awkward?" asked Uzmir.

"As it turned out, it became very awkward," replied Elvin.

"Alis' marriage to the old man was not a success and she produced no offspring. It was apparent right from the beginning that she secretly desired me. She desperately wanted a son because, if anything happened to me, she would inherit the castle and lands when the old man died. My suspicion was that this had been her motive in marrying the old man."

"So, what did she do?"

"Alis seemed beside herself with frustration at not being able to seduce me. She made efforts to tempt me but it was to no avail because I preferred riding wild horses around the hills to mounting her."

At that Uzmir gave a little chuckle.

"So what happened?" he asked.

"Well, I was more interested in one of the ladies-in-waiting that Alis had brought with her to the castle.

"She was a wench surely made for love and, the more I saw of her, the more I wanted her. In a haze of lust, one evening, I took her in front of the fire in the great hall. I mistakenly thought that my stepmother had taken to her bed.

"As we made love, my stepmother appeared. What feelings she might have had for me disappeared just like that. Being the ill-tempered soul she was, she began to plan her revenge."

"So, what did she do?" Uzmir enquired.

"The next morning Alis told my father falsely that I was continually pestering her and that he must do something. Upon enquiring further my father established from her that I had a passionate love for her such as which had not been the case before her marriage to my father. Alis implied that I simply would not leave her alone even though it was a scandalous lie."

"So what was your father's reaction?" asked Uzmir.

"Well, he was beside himself with rage. When he had calmed down a little he promised her that he would send me away so that I could not bother her again.

"A few days later he confronted me with the village priest, Father Trystan, and told me what the evil woman had said. Of course, I protested but it was completely in vain. Neither of them believed me. My father told me that, on the advice of the priest, he was sending me off on a pilgrimage to a place in Spain called Santiago de Compostela. It was the site of the shrine of St. James, the brother of Jesus, and I was being sent there as atonement for my sins. I was left in no doubt that it was going to be sooner rather than later."

"Were you not able to persuade your father of your innocence?"

"No, there was no way that he would listen to me," Elvin explained.

"A few weeks later I found myself riding out of the castle, alone, bound for Fowey and a boat to Bordeaux. My father had arranged passage with a sea captain in Mousehole who had a licence to take a cargo of sixty pilgrims from Fowey down to Bordeaux. Before my departure, Tryfena, the woman, who had brought me up as a child, gave me the cross, which you found in my boot in Egypt. She said it would protect me and so I believe it has.

"The next day I rode down into an isolated, wooded valley on the moors above Bodmin and approached Temple Abbey, which is a place of hospitality for pilgrims and travellers run by the Knights Templar. It was a damp, dark day and the Abbey was shrouded in fog giving it a rather eerie appearance.

"It is set in a clearing amongst trees, scrub, gorse and bracken. Next to it is a tiny church dedicated to Our Sacred Martyr, Saint Catherine, who was so cruelly condemned by the Romans to be torn to pieces by four spiked wheels. Do you know the legend?"

"No, I don't," replied Uzmir.

"Well, the story goes that a flash of lightning shattered the wheels and killed her captors — a truly miraculous event.

"Anyhow," continued Elvin, "the refuge, attached to the Abbey on the moors, is a tiny place and rather gloomy inside. It serves not only pilgrims from my part of Cornwall but also those, who brave the sea crossing from other places like Ireland and who prefer to risk that very treacherous, short sea route to Cornwall rather than face the uncertainties of a bandit infested and much longer land route.

"At the refuge I met up with an assortment of other people going on the same pilgrimage and we travelled together from then on. One of them, Petroc, I took as my squire.

"The pilgrims were a motley lot. Petroc had accidentally killed a fellow villager in a fight and had been forced to undergo the pilgrimage as a penance. There were those from Wales and Ireland and others just doing the pilgrimage as thanks for surviving a nasty disease.

"Later we were to meet up with merchants with goods to sell including the scallop shells, which every pilgrim to Santiago is expected to wear. There were also performers, dancers and minstrels who hoped to earn a little money from the others."

"Were the pilgrims as kindly as the ones we have met on our journey?" asked Uzmir.

"Far from it," replied Elvin. "There were some quite unsavoury looking characters that I would not have let out of my sight at any cost.

"The sea voyage, upon which we embarked, was long and dangerous. We were beset by storms and nearly everybody went down with seasickness. I am good sailor so that it did not bother me. I had been warned on boarding, by one friendly soul, that it was unwise to be anywhere near the ship's pump and catching a whiff of its foul stench, I quickly realised why.

"We arrived in Bordeaux in early summer, which was a good thing, because the passes into Spain were clear.

"We crossed over the Pyrenees Mountains through the tortuous pass known as Roncevalles and attended a thanksgiving mass at a large pilgrim hostel there.

"From the pass we descended down into the country of the Basques. Few people choose to go that way because it is a land of very unfriendly people with an outlandish language that nobody can understand.

"They seem to owe allegiance, in practice, neither to the nobility in France nor to the nobility in Spain although the country of the Basques is all now part of the Kingdom of Aragon.

"We followed the pilgrims' way through forested hills and small villages. Beech and oak trees lined the way along with holly and hazel trees. There was a mass of blackberry bushes to provide sweet berries for refreshment."

"So how long did it take you to reach the holy place you were seeking?" asked Uzmir.

"Well, this is exactly it. We never made it," said Elvin.

"All seemed to be going well when a feeling came over us that we had, perhaps, taken the wrong turning. Towards dusk we were expecting to have site of the beautiful city of Pamplona with its magnificent cathedral. But it appeared to be nowhere in sight. Where we should have reached the foothills of the Pyrenees the mountains seemed to be getting higher and, as the sun was setting, we realised that, far from moving in a westerly direction, our path was taking us towards the southeast. We decided to camp up for the night and review the situation in the morning.

"The next day we decided that there was no point in going back and that we might as well proceed in a southerly direction and hope to pick up the other route to Santiago which passed through the town of Jaca.

"The countryside all around has been won back from the Moors gradually over many years but there are still marauding bands, which attack villages from time to time. The Knights of Santiago — a military order rather like the Templars — has been created for the purpose of protecting the pilgrim route. But it is a long route of many, many leagues, which is difficult to protect all of the time. At the southern end of a river valley Moorish bandits attacked us and escaped with a number of our horses and pack animals."

"So, what did you do?"

"We decided to follow them in order to retrieve our prized animals," replied Elvin.

"We crossed a major river and went on for what seemed many leagues. They disappeared eventually into a region of high, craggy mountains where doubtless lay their hideout. We were not familiar with the area and knew that we were in perilous danger of ambush.

"It was not long before superior numbers of Moors attacked us in a rocky ravine and most of our small party were killed. I, and my squire, Petroc, managed to survive but our horses took off. We were alone and not very sure where we were."

"How did you think you were going to find your way out of there?"

"We had an idea that the pilgrim route from the east, which we had been seeking, was somewhere nearby. So we started out on foot to try and locate it. But we were soon hopelessly lost in a valley deep in the mountains. Dark green, forested slopes surrounded us. Ahead we could see the distant snow-capped peaks of the High Pyrenees. Out of the pine clad slopes extended cliffs and buttresses from which, from time to time, an eagle would glide seeking an unsuspecting hare or some such other small animal. We were beginning to feel very isolated and worried as to whether we were going to find the right way.

"Just as we felt at our lowest ebb we stumbled through a clearing and there, tucked away under the brow of an enormous cliff, was a fortified structure isolated and hidden from any pathway. It was an impressive place and immediately we thought it must be the castle of some local warlord. It was our only source of help and we made towards it as swiftly as we could.

"Suddenly there was a sound like distant thunder. The birds in the forest began to scatter skywards screeching in panic. Out of the forest, coming straight at us, rode a group of heavily armoured knights with their swords drawn. Their white mantles flapped behind them as they sped towards us. I recognised, at once, the red cross sewn over the left shoulder. I had seen it before in England and France. They were Knights Templar and they were bearing down on us in a very threatening manner. Their horses were pulled up and we were surrounded. The knights slowly moved their horses closer and closer in a circle around us until we could hardly move. The leading knight was a tough-looking, dark-skinned man with a huge scar running from his right eyebrow down over his right cheek. He drew his sword and leant down with it placed at my throat. Petroc found himself in a similar position."

"And what are you two beauties doing here? Don't you know that it is forbidden to come anywhere near the monastery?" he sneered in the Aragonese language, with which I was not familiar.

"I replied in French. I tried to explain our predicament and how we had pursued the Moorish bandits, been ambushed and then left without horses. Somehow I don't think he believed me. He just spat on the ground and, before long, we were being prodded and pushed towards the castle-like building.

The place was constructed right out of the rock face and it looked as if part of the building actually consisted of the mountain itself.

We were taken into the building, which was, as it turned out, a monastery. We were then taken down to a subterranean area and separated. I was locked in a small cell to await my fate."

"Were you fearful?" asked Uzmir

"I wouldn't say fearful," replied Elvin. "A bit apprehensive, perhaps. We had done no wrong, after all. Nevertheless I clutched my St. Piran Cross for protection.

"What seemed like several hours passed and then the door to the cell opened. I was roughly dragged to my feet and taken up into the light, which made my eyes blink at first.

"I was escorted along a cloister, which was full of both monks proceeding to and from their devotions and an unusually large number of soldiers. We arrived at a large room at the end.

"There seated at a table was the leader of the knights, who had captured me, together with another very tall, commanding man, who, by his manner of dress appeared to be a Templar as well, but I had the feeling he was of higher rank.

"My captor introduced himself as Enrique de Larraga."

"Was he not the man who was in charge of the training of the Templars in Egypt?" Uzmir suddenly enquired.

"Yes, that's the fellow," replied Elvin. "He's a tall, dark skinned man with a scarred face, a very experienced warrior. He did not introduce the other man, who appeared to be there just as an observer.

"My captor began to interrogate me in good French but with a bit of an evil sneer."

"Now, my good fellow, I want you to tell us the truth as to why you are here," he said.

"I repeated my story but, once again, I felt that it was being received with a great deal of scepticism."

"Come now, my friend, we know why you are here. You have come to steal the relic. You may as well tell us the truth."

"What relic?" I replied. "I know nothing of any relic here."

"Don't be clever with us, sir knight, we followed you some way through the forest and it was quite clear you were making for this monastery."

"What we were trying to do was to get back onto one of the pilgrim routes to Santiago," I replied.

"Tell us the truth. You know full well that we have ways of dragging it out of you," came the threatening statement, uttered almost with a sense of impending pleasure.

"I am telling you the truth," I insisted. My captor consulted with the other man and it was clear that they were not satisfied.

"Pablo, take him away and see if you can loosen his tongue," was the sharp order given to the sergeant of my escort.

"I was dragged along the cloister again and then down to a part of the monastery obviously occupied by the military. It was surprising how many soldiers appeared to be garrisoned in what was supposedly a religious building. The monks were of a different order to the Knights Templar and I recognised the monks in this building as being of the Order of St. Benedict.

"We were down once more in quite a wide underground tunnel. Torches, placed at various intervals, dimly lit it. Off to each side were cells, which were presumably those of the monks, but currently occupied by soldiers.

"Pablo, the sergeant, disappeared. He returned with some rope. A number of soldiers had now gathered round in anticipation of some entertainment at my expense. I was stripped to the waist and my cross was taken from me despite my protests.

"The soldiers had already started to work on Petroc, for the most horrendous screams of agony were coming from further down the corridor where the poor lad was being questioned. Whatever devilish torture was being concocted could only be guessed at.

"My arms were tied behind my back and, then, a further longer piece of rope was looped through the rope binding my wrists together. This rope was then slung over a beam and two soldiers grabbed the other end of it and began pulling hard on it. The agony was intense as my arms were pulled upwards behind my back. I felt like yelling out but gritted my teeth and made no sound.

"The sergeant stuck his face almost into mine as I was doubled over and said:

"Now then, compadre, we can dispense with the unpleasantness if only you will tell us the truth."

"I have told you the truth," said I.

"The soldiers wrenched the rope up another few notches and my toes were only just touching the ground. The agony in my shoulders was excruciating.

"I can't tell you any more than the truth. We are pilgrims who have got lost," I tried to explain.

"The sergeant motioned to the soldiers and the rope was pulled higher. My feet were now off the ground and I could feel the pressure on my shoulders and arms. I gasped with the most severe pain, as my right shoulder was dislocated out of its socket."

"Come on, amigo, tell us the real reason why you are here," Pablo said, taunting me.

"I've told you," I stuttered, the pain almost unbearable.

"Bastard," he shouted and lifted his mailed foot to kick me in the genitals as hard as he could. "Don't play games with us. We are not in the mood."

"I still had not cried out and restrained myself from so doing. But I could not avoid gasping from time to time as such blows winded me."

"I'm going to ask you once more. Why are you here?"

"I was beginning to lose patience myself by this time and made a silly mistake.

"I keep on telling you, you poxy son of a whore, we got lost," came my reply.

"This was just the excuse he needed to make me suffer further. He grabbed one of the torches from the wall and came towards me with it. He ran the flames over my body about an inch from the skin. It was enough to scorch the skin black and was incredibly painful.

"So you like that do you, you worthless bastard?" Pablo said with an insane grin on his face. Some of the soldiers sniggered. "Then see if you like this." With that he pushed the brand right into my stomach. "Aaah," I gasped, trying hard not to betray my fear and pain.

"There was a stench of burning flesh and a huge blister appeared on my stomach. He then took great delight in taking his sword and puncturing the blister. That was when I blacked out.

"I was awakened by water being thrown over me. Just at that moment Enrique de Larraga appeared and spoke quietly with the sergeant.

"I was taken down and escorted to a cell and dropped into it unceremoniously. I was in agony with my dislocated shoulder and seriously burned skin.

"Not long afterwards a monk came to my cell with a cloth bag slung over his shoulder.

"He chatted to me in a soft, reassuring manner but I could understand little of his Aragonese.

"He examined me and then gave me something to drink to ease the pain. He treated the burn first by continually pouring cold water from a pitcher over it until it had cooled down.

"Then he disappeared and came back with some honey, some marigolds and various other herbs. He spread the honey over the blister and then proceeded to make up a tincture using the flowers and leaves of the marigolds, which he applied to the rest of the burned area. He then covered it with a sort of poultice."

"You must have been in great pain," declared Uzmir sympathetically.

"Yes, I was, " said Elvin, "but the liquid he had given me began to take affect and I felt less pain. He then examined the shoulder. This was still extremely painful, as it appeared to have come out of its socket. He got me to place my hand on my waist with my arm sticking out to the side and then placed one hand below my forearm and the other firmly on my upper arm and then with an almighty thrust pushed the shoulder back in. This time I did let out a roar of pain but I was somehow conscious that the shoulder had successfully engaged back in the socket. The monk then made up a sling with a piece of cloth to support my arm.

"A few hours went by and the cell door opened. Soldiers entered again and lifted me to my feet. This time they seemed to be treating me very gently and escorted me along to the room, in which Enrique and the other stranger were waiting."

"This is Peter de Montaigu, the deputy Grand Master of the Templar Order, who is on a visit to the monastery," de Larraga said, motioning towards the stranger. "I am sorry we have had to use such unseemly methods but, believe you me, it is necessary. We are inclined to believe your story and, in fact, we have managed to substantiate that some pilgrims, who were subsequently ambushed and killed, pursued Moorish bandits into the Sierra. It is a gang that we have been after for some time but they have always alluded us. We had no idea that there had been any survivors of the massacre.

"My sergeant says that you behaved with immense bravery under torture. You are a strong and fit man with the courage of a knight. Naturally the same could not be said of your squire, who appeared, between his screaming like a stuck pig, only to be able to answer in some devilish language that nobody could understand."

"It would be Cornish, his native language," I explained haltingly, for I was still in considerable pain from my torture. "It's much the same as Breton. He speaks only English and a little French besides that."

"Right. Anyhow, we accept your story and must apologise for our treatment of you both. We want you to be our guests whilst you recover. From here you will be taken to the Infirmary. Your injuries will be watched over and, hopefully, you will make a full recovery. Apart from the injuries I am told that you are a young man in prime condition so that there is every chance of a full recovery within a few weeks. When it is appropriate we will give you the opportunity to bathe. One of the things that convinced us in the end that you might be pilgrims was that you both stank like men, who had been travelling the roads for some weeks." If this was a jest it was lost on me at the time.

"I hope that, if the Infirmarer can fix you up well, you will be as good as new," continued Enrique. "When you have recovered we have much to discuss."

"You must have been quite severely hurt," said Uzmir. "The marks of the burns on your body were very noticeable when I changed your clothes during your fever in Egypt."

"I know, they still sting and itch to a certain degree." Elvin said.

"It took a few days" Elvin continued, "and then I was invited to dine with Enrique. I complained that my St. Piran Cross had been stolen from me and he promised to investigate"

"I am glad to see you have been making a good recovery," he said. "That pleases me greatly because I have a job for you. Peter de Montaigu and I are of one mind. We feel your arrival here was no accident."

"I began to get nervous again but I need not have worried."

"We are convinced that God has brought you to us," he continued. "Worthy though a pilgrimage is, He has brought you here for another purpose as part of His Divine Plan.

"As you know, we are in the process of pushing the heathen Moors back across the sea to their African lands. We are having some success but it needs one last push. A large Christian army is now gathering and training for the final thrust.

"We know that you wanted to go on a pilgrimage to show your love of God. But what better way of doing that than fighting in the cause of the Lord? You are a brave knight and when you are fully fit we want you to prepare for entry into our Order to carry the Cross against the heathen Muslims. But, enough of all this, you need feeding up, so let's eat."

"At that moment he clapped his hands and monks brought venison, beans, cabbage, cheese and good red wine and I ate heartily on the health-giving fare. No more was mentioned of my entry into the Templar Order but I had the distinct feeling that little choice in the matter was being offered.

"Some days later my cross was returned to me without comment. Later on I was told that jewellery was not normally permitted in the Templar Order. However, I explained its importance to me. Enrique de Larraga then told me that, since it was a religious symbol, and, if I kept it discreetly hidden, I could keep it. For this I was thankful.

"When I was on the road to recovery, I was invited to attend a special Mass in the chapel of the monastery. It was obviously an important occasion because all the Benedictine monks of the monastery were there as well as the Knights Templar dressed in their own white monk's habits, as was the requirement of their Order.

"The chapel consisted of a single nave and three vaulted semi-circular recesses. The rock of the mountain itself formed part of the roof of the nave. I had discovered earlier that this was an extremely important place because several Aragonese monarchs had been buried here.

"I thought that this was the reason that the place was so heavily guarded but in that I was wrong.

"During the Mass a most amazing thing happened. A priest entered, preceded by two Benedictine brothers carrying large wax candles. The priest was carrying an ornate jewelled chalice, consisting of a reddish bowl supported by a beautifully worked gold structure with two handles. I gasped in awe. All the brothers fell to their knees and Enrique motioned to me to do the same."

"Show respect for the Sacred Chalice of the Last Supper," he whispered to me.

"The Chalice shone out in the gloom of the nave as if it had a light of its own. The flames of the torches on the walls appeared to dim as it passed by and it was a wondrous sight to see. I found myself in much awe of such a thing."

"Was it really the Chalice of the Last Supper?" asked Uzmir.

"So it was said," replied Elvin. "I asked Enrique later and he told me that King Ramiro the First had entrusted the Chalice to the monks of this remote, castle-like place for safe keeping and that it is piously guarded by the Knights Templar. He said that the monastery had been chosen not only because it is the traditional burial place of the Kings of Aragon, but also because it is an elusive and inaccessible place. 'Those who seek it find it not,' he had said. 'It can only be found unsought, if God decrees it.'

"I had heard tales in France of a distant castle perched on a wild mountain where the Holy Grail could be found guarded by knights but had never ever expected to stumble upon it like this.

"Some days later I was declared fit. I broached the matter of our return to the pilgrim route with Enrique de Larraga."

"Return?" he questioned, seeming somewhat irritated. "There is no question of any return. You have seen what no other man besides the monks here and the Templars have seen. That would only have been possible if God had decreed it. And God's purpose is that you join with us in the Templar Order and carry the Cross against the infidel. That is the end of the affair."

"Later in the day I noticed that a guard had been put on my cell. When I enquired as to why this was the case, I was simply told that it was for my protection although against what I was not completely sure. I knew now that there was no way in which the Templars would let me leave of my own free will.

"Not long afterwards Enrique told me that I would be moved to the castle of Monzon, the Templar headquarters in the region. The question of whether I was to join the Order or not did not come up again and it was assumed, as if decreed by God, that I would be admitted to the Order. I made a request that Petroc should accompany me as my squire and this was granted."

"Were you both really fully recovered by then?" Uzmir asked.

"Oh yes," replied Elvin, "the monks had done well in returning us to full fitness."

"Anyhow, some weeks after our arrival at the Monastery of San Juan de La Peña, as I found the place to have been called, we rode out with an escort of Knights Templar bound for the fortress of Monzon. It was a few days journey to the southeast. We descended through the woods from the mountains and skirted grey-gold, dark green-forested foothills. The horses picked their way down the rock strewn paths taking care not to stumble. Waterfalls cascaded down the mountainside, the clear inviting water rushing down over rocks, pebbles and boulders.

"Eventually we skirted the town of Huesca and descended onto a vast, sandy plain with the sun relentless in its intensity. The change in temperature from the cooler uplands was most noticeable and was not unlike that of the deserts you and I have lately crossed.

"Was it really as hot as that?" exclaimed Uzmir with some surprise.

"Well, it was not far from it," said Elvin.

"It took us two days in that heat to ride across the plain to Monzon. The castle stood on a rugged escarpment atop sheer, sandstone cliffs, which seemed almost impossible to scale. We approached it along a path, which twisted through thinly spaced trees and tall grass and then along a dusty, sandy track around the base of the hill. We had been conscious of being spied upon from for some miles. The Muslims had built its massively high walls, dominating all around, over two hundred years before. It was seemingly impenetrable. When finally conquered by the Christian Kings it had been given to the Templars as one of their main settlements in Aragon. We rode up a huge stone staircase set into the cliff below the walls and passed through the main gate. We had arrived at the castle of Monzon."

CHAPTER TEN

Serious Discussions

It was three weeks before the archaeological team was allowed back on the site at Tremennek Bay. Even then they were not allowed to continue their investigations into the tunnel and had to be content with further work on the surface. Fred Tregenna, the farmer, had been released without charge but several other arrests had been made.

Anya had returned to Spain, as the University of Granada had been unwilling to give her further leave of absence.

A colleague of Peter, knowing of his predicament, had suggested that he looked after his house in Welwyn Garden City, whilst he was away on holiday in the Canary Islands. It was mutually satisfactory because it gave Peter a chance to sort things out with Mary and to find alternative accommodation and it suited Richard because his house would be more secure whilst he and his family were away.

Peter rang Mary at her mother's and made arrangements to meet up with her to discuss the future. The atmosphere was very strained and Mary had requested that Alex Cropley accompany her but Peter had put his foot down at that.

"I couldn't care a fuck about the house as long as you don't accuse me of deserting you and the children," he told her. "I've put all my stuff in the study and you can continue to live in the house as long as you take over the mortgage. That will give me the opportunity to find alternative accommodation."

"But I can't afford to pay the mortgage," she said angrily. "I just don't earn enough. You know that."

"Then get your boyfriend to help you out," said Peter with a bit of a sneer.

She shrugged her shoulders at this suggestion. "There's no need to be nasty about all of this," she remarked. "I know you've never loved me. It's always been that Spanish cow."

"You know that's not true and she's not a cow. You've just been insanely jealous about my friendship with another woman – and that's all it is!

"Do you think we ought to get divorced?" she asked tentatively.

"Are you thinking of marrying Alex then?"

"No," she said quickly. "I've had enough of marriage for quite some time — if not for ever."

"I don't think it would be in either of our financial interests to get divorced," he said. "Solicitors would take us to the cleaners. I think as long as we can come to some sensible arrangement, we can do without all that. You need a home for you and the children. I'm quite happy for you to stay in the house."

"And what do you want?" she asked.

"I want to be sure that I get my share of the funds from any future sale of the house and, also, that I can see the children on a regular basis."

"It's a bit much to expect me to pay the mortgage and yet you retain a half share of the house," she said sarcastically.

"But I've contributed more than half to the purchase and the maintenance of the place," he protested. "I'm entitled to a good share."

"But I just can't afford it!" she shouted in desperation.

Peter thought for a bit and then said: "OK, what we'll do is this. I'll pay an agreed percentage of the mortgage for the moment. I've no wish to see you or the kids out in the cold, cold snow. But it can't be too high a percentage or else I'll not be able to afford accommodation for myself."

Mary agreed to this and they parted on reasonably good terms.

Peter spent the next weekend searching for a suitable flat. He did not want to pay too much for it, as he was frequently away during the week. Prices were rather higher in St. Albans than when he had last been looking and it came as a bit of a shock to him. Eventually he found an agent who directed him towards a small house in Marshallswick.

The owner agreed to lease half the house to him at a reasonable rate provided he kept an eye on the place. His landlord was an engineer in the oil industry and was frequently abroad for lengthy periods. It was a satisfactory situation and Peter felt quite pleased with himself.

He set off back to Chiswell Green to collect some of his belongings. As he unlatched the front door he realised that things had changed to some degree but he could not put his finger on it at first. Then he realised.

"You fool," he thought to himself. "You've spent all that time listening to her sob story and the bastard has already moved in." All around the house was evidence that Alex was already living there. He even recognised some of the furniture. Peter was furious.

In his anger he collected up the furniture, which he knew belonged to Alex, and took it out into the garden. Still fuming he got some paraffin from the garage and poured it over the small pile and set light to it. It was soon burning furiously.

Feeling very pleased with himself he wrote a note to Mary suggesting that, with Alex's help, she could afford the mortgage payments and didn't really need his help. He then collected those belongings, of which he had immediate need, and left the house.

On the Sunday he returned to Cornwall to join the rest of the team.

Bernard Harper had shown interest in an area of the site outside of the main hall where aerial pictures had indicated that there had been some disturbance sometime in the past. They already knew from the aerial photographs where the fields lay and where the main crops, which had sustained the castle, had been grown but this was different. It was within the castle walls just behind the main hall and might have been a kitchen garden or something of that sort. But it seemed a bit strange and consequently he had ordered a trench to be laid.

When Peter arrived the student diggers were hard at work in the trench. Bernard explained the objective and they both visited the trench.

"Found anything yet?" enquired Bernard.

"We've found the remains of a wall," said Richard, " and, clearly, something was grown here so we think that it was possibly a kitchen garden or something of that sort. There are some charcoal deposits so we think there might have been a bonfire at the site and that's our best bet for finding deposits of plants and seeds that might give us further clues. There are also a few shards of green-glazed pots, which have presumably been used to collect the produce. They're definitely from the right period. It's typical lead glazing."

"OK, well, let us know when you find anything else."

Later that evening Peter had a drink with Bernard Harper. Bernard innocently enquired about Mary and Peter felt disposed, after having had a couple of real ales, to tell him the whole sad story including the bit about the burning of Alex Cropley's furniture.

Bernard Harper chuckled. "Well, I've heard of people being tempted before, but you're the first I've come across who's actually done it. Have there been any repercussions?"

"No," replied Peter with a grin, "I've not heard a thing from either one of them."

The next day Richard called them across to the 'kitchen garden'

"We've found a number of charred seeds and pollen samples which we can't readily identify. I don't know whether you can throw any light on them."

Bernard looked at them carefully. "They don't look like any food crops that I've seen before," he said. I think we're going to have to refer these to someone else. There's a colleague I know in the Institute of Archaeology, who knows just about all there is to know about medieval seed finds. She specialises in archaeobotany, so we'll send some samples to her and see what she comes up with."

"Well," said Bernard as they walked away from the trench, "I don't know whether those discoveries are going to take us any further or not. I wish we could get down into the tunnel again although I'm not very confident that is going to reveal a great deal. What with the police having been all over it, the activities of the smugglers in the past and the rainwater washing down through it, there can't be a great deal left to find." Both he and Peter had to confess that they were a little despondent – Peter for more reasons than Bernard because of his marital relations, or lack of them. The situation at home was not helping at all.

He spoke to Mary on the phone that evening in order to let her know where he was. She made no mention of the burned furniture and, indeed, was quite tolerable in her dealings with him. She knew now that he knew the truth about Alex and, indeed, Alex had answered the phone.

After speaking to her he reflected that he was now becoming more accustomed to the reality of the situation. He was annoyed. There had been an assault on his pride. At the end of the day, however, he probably deserved it. "Sod it," he muttered to himself and took comfort, yet again, at the bar.

CHAPTER ELEVEN

More Of The Knight's Tale

"So what happened when you arrived at the castle of Monzon," continued Uzmir, as they sat on the hill overlooking the waterfall.

"Well," said Elvin, "the castle was packed with troops training hard for a major operation to be launched for the Reconquest of Spain for the Faith.

"It was not long before I was initiated into the Templar Order in a secret ceremony, about which I have sworn, on my life, to reveal nothing. I was already trained as a knight in Cornwall and consequently my entry into the Order as a warrior monk was relatively speedy.

"How did they know you were who you said you were?" asked Uzmir.

"To enter the Order my status as a knight had to be checked," replied Elvin. There happened to be two other Templar Knights from Cornwall at Monzon and it was Henry de Doublebois who confirmed my identity.

"I did not find the training hard from the physical point of view, because, as a knight, I was already trained in individual fighting skills. What was different was the need to learn to engage in disciplined joint action with others.

"That training started even with the setting up of a camp. We had to learn to pitch our tents in relation to the chapel, which acted as the assembly point if the alarm was raised. Everything we did from loading up to actual cavalry charges was strictly organized. Enrique de Larraga was in charge of all the training and a figure of some prominence."

"I know. I've seen him in action. He looks like a hard task master."

"He is, but it wasn't the military training that bothered me so much. It was life as a monk that was hard. There were a lot of chapel services everyday starting at daybreak with matins and finishing with compline at dusk.

"But the food was good. We ate beef, mutton, veal, goat, trout, eels, cheese and vegetables. There were lots of lentils, beans and cabbage too

— all designed to build up our strength."

"Trout and eels I have not heard of," remarked Uzmir.

"A trout is a fish and the eel is another creature found in rivers in Europe," explained Elvin.

"Anyhow, apart from all that, we were obliged to pay close attention to our equipment and horses and every day after matins and compline I would consult with Petroc, my squire, and check these.

"Even our spare time, such as it was, was expected to be filled with meaningful tasks like making tent pegs or repairing equipment.

'Idleness is the tool of the Devil', Peter de Montaigu often said. Our guide was the Templar Rule, which suggests that Satan troubles a lazy man with evil desires and vain thoughts much more than he does one whom he finds himself busy in good work.

"It all sounds like a very strict regime," commented Uzmir with a shrug.

"Yes, it was really," said Elvin. "I can't say I enjoyed the life but there was a certain camaraderie. You hadn't much choice but to obey the rules. Life was governed by a whole series of penances for those who failed in their duty as laid down by the Rule and vows once taken could not be undone. But there did seem to be one rule for some and another rule for Enrique de Larraga and friends.

"One day we were ordered to prepare to move out and found ourselves joined up with whole hosts of other knights, squires and serving men from all over Europe bound for Toledo. The road was crowded with wagons, troops, knights on horseback, and equipment all bound for that illustrious city and it was there that we all assembled.

"Where were they all bound for eventually?" asked Uzmir.

"They were destined for Al Andalus to crush the Moorish army and send it scuttling back to Africa," emphasized Elvin. "That was the idea, anyway."

"The campaign launched by our massive army was mightily successful at first. That was until we reached a vast mountain range, which seemed almost impossible to cross.

"We found ourselves at the foot of a range with the Moors on the crest. We battled hard to take a fort on the top, which had been built specially by them to block our way. After that the mountain was ours.

"It was a treacherous place because of the lack of water and the barrenness of the land. As a result of our victory the enemy retreated down the other side of the mountain and blocked the only pass, which was extremely narrow and difficult to get through.

"Dissent broke out again amongst the Crusade leaders because the Moors kept mounting isolated raids on our camp to undermine our morale. We were left in a bit of a quandary as to what to do.

"One day I was out on patrol with a small group of knights when we came across a local shepherd, so I asked him if he had seen any Moors.

"He volunteered the information that they were camped on the other side of the mountain in a pass down below the fort. I replied that we knew that, but that it was going to be exceedingly difficult for us to get down there. They would almost certainly set up an ambush for us.

"The shepherd said that there was another way down, along the ridge, that only local people knew. He explained that it was steep and quite narrow but he had taken sheep and mules over that way without too much difficulty.

"And so the shepherd showed us the alternative, almost unknown, pass through the range. We were much strengthened in our resolve by this. The information from the shepherd must have come from God, we thought. Anyhow, he was rewarded handsomely.

"The alternative pass through the mountains came out very close to the enemy camp. The Moors knew nothing of this route. We took them completely by surprise."

"I am only painfully aware of that because I was part of the main Moorish force gathered there," said Uzmir. "We had no idea."

"The next day, we set out in God's name down the mountain to do battle for our beliefs with those we regarded as infidels.

"The terrain was difficult, very steep in places, with deep gorges cut by streams, all of which were a major impediment. By the time we reached the bottom a huge army faced us on the plain below.

"Our resolve, after our endeavours in crossing the mountain range, was never stronger. Our standard cavalry charge, with the famed black and white flag, created an absolute rout."

"That I know full well," said Uzmir, "because I was one of only a thousand survivors of that dreadful battle and the penalty I paid was to have my religion taken from me. At the end of it all I was baptised a Christian, or a Morisco as the Castillian Spanish call us. In my own mind, though, I always knew what I wanted to believe and the Islamic way is still my path to salvation."

"Hmm," pondered Elvin. "It was certainly a defeat on a grand scale. Do you know, we did not even have to collect wood for our fires for cooking and baking bread? Such were the numbers of enemy dead that we used their arrows and spears for firewood and still only used about half of them. We were able to replenish our supplies from the battlefield alone such was the abundance of food and weapons, warhorses and beasts of burden available to us."

"Yes, I know," said Uzmir. "The slaughter was terrible."

"What happened to you after that?" enquired Elvin.

"Those of us spared and willing to be baptised went on with the army as scouts and participated in the capture a number of fortresses. Then we were temporarily put to work repairing monasteries along the border," he said. "The slaughter continued to be terrible. If the Crusaders could not settle a city, they razed it to the ground. Sixty thousand perished in one city alone."

"Such are the fortunes of war," commented Elvin philosophically, although, privately, he sometimes felt uncomfortable about the Crusaders' over exuberance in banishing the taint of Islam. He felt it unnecessary to indulge in the wholesale slaughter of women and children. But many men, when their blood lust was up, just went crazy.

After a good night's rest Elvin and Uzmir packed up their camp and descended from the forested mountains to a fertile plain behind Algiers. They entered the city through the main gate later that day.

Algiers was one of the principle ports and strongholds of the Berber dynasty, which ruled most of North Africa. The city consisted of a complex labyrinth of narrow alleyways that ran down to the port, which was built into a large bay dotted with islands. Above the walled city, as in many such places, stood the reassuring presence of an imposing fortress surveying all around.

Once again Elvin had to keep up the pretence of having been struck speechless by the events in Egypt so that he could avoid detection as a foreigner. It was even more difficult here than it had been on the open road from Egypt. But Uzmir was diligent in his protection of him and he had grown to trust him completely.

If they were to sell the horses they had to attend the daily market, which took place on the hot and dusty open expanse in front of the city walls. Here local peasants from surrounding villages spread out fruit and vegetables and other trade goods on blankets and appealed to the public with a shrill, whining cry to purchase their wares.

In one specialised portion of the market camels and horses were traded and this is where Uzmir took them.

In spite of their long journey the horses were fit and of good stock and Uzmir was confident they would command a good price.

The area stank with camel and horse dung. In the heat, the flies were unbearable. The horses swished their tails back and forth in an unsuccessful effort to rid themselves of the irritation of the insects buzzing round them. Everywhere their frustrated owners were beating cantankerous camels because they would suddenly try to take off or rise up when they were supposed to be sitting. Elvin was well aware from his travels of their nasty habit of spitting and biting if they were not kept in order. A good horse he could appreciate but the so-called ships of the desert did not appeal to him at all.

The hubbub in the market place was unbelievable. Traders gesticulated and yelled at one another as they tried to make a trade. Every so often there was a resounding slap of hand upon hand as one or other of the traders tried to persuade the other to agree a price. But a price was only agreed when finally the hands of both men were linked in agreement.

Uzmir tried several traders before one showed real interest in the horses. He examined their teeth, prodded and pushed them and then the high-pitched bargaining began. A small crowd gathered.

After some hand slapping the trader suddenly started looking at Elvin.

"Your friend does not have much to say," he said.

"No," said Uzmir. "He lost his whole family in the siege of a city in Egypt by the Franks and has been speechless ever since."

"He cannot utter even a word?"

"No," confirmed Uzmir.

"He seems to take an distinct interest in everything that is going on even though he is shocked and speechless," declared the trader. A number of people in the crowd were now turning their attention to Elvin. Uzmir was now visibly uncomfortable at the attention that Elvin was getting and motioned to him to move away.

"Do you want to buy these horses or not?" asked Uzmir short temperedly and the haggling continued.

Shortly afterwards the agreement was concluded and the money changed hands.

Uzmir moved away and motioned Elvin to follow quickly.

"That was close," he said. "I thought they were getting a little suspicious about who you were. I had to agree a lower price than might have been the case but I thought that it was best for us to depart before they got too inquisitive."

Suddenly there was a shout and the trader and a number of other people came rushing after them. Uzmir and Elvin were about to make a run for it when a gabbling crowd surrounded them, filling them full of apprehension.

"You have left some food in the saddlebags," said the trader. "You may need it."

"Many thanks, my friend," said Uzmir. "We have much travelling yet to do."

With that the crowd dispersed much to the relief of the two.

So they returned to the city and made their way down through the narrow, meandering streets to the port. There were quite a number of ships in the port. Amidst the hustle and bustle of the loading and unloading of cargos, Uzmir haggled with several ship's captains over a passage to Al Andalus for the two of them.

At last he was successful in getting passage for them on a ship bound for Almeria with a cargo of silks and spices from the East. It would be leaving the next day. The captain agreed that they could spend the night on board in exchange for keeping watch over it whilst he and his men indulged themselves in those delights in the city, which took their fancy. The night passed without incident.

CHAPTER TWELVE
Danger Below

The seed and pollen samples were returned from the Institute of Archaeology a few days later along with a report on them. Having sifted through the report Bernard Harper was able to announce to the evening meeting:

"It appears that the small garden we have discovered was not a kitchen garden at all but a garden where ingredients for medicines of various sorts were grown and it has been confirmed that our samples were indeed from around the twelfth or thirteenth centuries and perhaps somewhat ahead of their time.

"There were carbonised samples of poppy seeds, hemlock, deadly nightshade and lettuce seed, all of which could have been used as narcotics or possibly as a mixture for anaesthetics. Now this, so our expert informs us, is fairly unique because there is very little evidence for the use of opium extracts for anaesthetics in Europe before about the sixteenth century. Before that time patients would have been stupefied with alcohol rather than anything else. And that probably would only have been if the patient was someone of importance and if the medics considered the operation serious enough. Hacking off a few minor limbs here and there probably wouldn't have counted," he added rather flippantly.

"We do know now, however, that soporific sponges, containing opium extracts, were used as anaesthetics in the Muslim world, which would have included Southern Spain, in the thirteenth century. So, with these, and the medical instruments, that we have already found, we are establishing a very definite connection with that part of the world."

"Perhaps our knight was experimenting in medical knowledge he had picked up as a Crusader abroad," observed Peter. "If he was, I can't imagine what the locals would have thought. They would have been very suspicious of him, if they knew about it, and some of them might even have thought he was some kind of sorcerer."

"Well, anyway, another good result," said Bernard. "Now I've also got some further news. We have been given clearance to work on the tunnel again from tomorrow."

Peter was clearly pleased at this and the students greeted the news with a resounding cheer.

"Once again," said Bernard, "time is of the essence. We'll have to get a move on."

The next morning the weather was atrocious. The rain was lashing down and there was quite a wind blowing. The weather had turned bad the previous evening and it had been raining most of the night. It was decided to postpone the exploration of the tunnel until the weather improved. There was no chance of utilising any heavy equipment on the boggy ground in any event.

By the afternoon the rain had eased off and the sun had come out and so it was decided to send Bill Tregenza, the caving expert, down to see what the state of the tunnel was.

He came back up after a while and said: "It doesn't appear too bad. It's still quite wet down there so you'll have to check your footwear to see that it grips well in the wet. I think it will be all right but we need to approach it with caution because there's been a lot of rain and the ground around will be absolutely sodden. There are a lot of old mine workings in the area and there's no real way of knowing where all the water's going, but I suspect some of it is finding it's way into our tunnel because it is so muddy and unpleasant down there."

"Well, we're perilously short of time so I think we'd better make an attempt," said Bernard looking at Peter. "Would you like to go down with Bill again and see what you can find? You had better take our detectorist friend as well to see what he can turn up. But for heaven's sake be careful!"

"OK," said Peter and the three men began preparing for their descent. It was a dullish, dank day although there was now some evidence of a weak, watery sun. As Peter looked out across to the southwest a big bank of black, threatening clouds was building up over the Scilly Isles.

"It certainly is wet," thought Peter as he climbed down the ladder that the police had constructed. The walls were extremely damp and there was a bit of a noxious stench coming from the slime and sodden plant life that covered the walls of the shaft. At the bottom of the shaft an oozy concoction of water and mud was trickling down the slope towards the sea at a steady rate.

Each man had a lamp attached to his hardhat and, in addition, carried a large hand torch. For safety's sake they were roped together.

Brian, the detectorist, scoured the floor of the cave with his apparatus for signs of metallic objects but did not come up with anything other than a few modern coins.

Bill concentrated on examining the features of the cave workings.

Peter examined the walls for any graffiti of interest and there was certainly plenty of that. Every smuggler for several centuries seemed to have been disposed to leave his signature on the walls.

After a while Bill called the others over to look at a discovery he had made. Off to the side, part way down the tunnel, there appeared originally to have been another tunnel.

"I don't know what this is," said Bill, "but I suspect it may have been a drainage tunnel from mine workings over on the other side of the headland. It's been capped off in the usual eighteenth, early nineteenth century style with mine rubble and soil." He prodded the wall with a stick in one or two places and water began very slowly trickling through.

"I don't much like the look of this," he said. "This sort of cap is OK normally but if there is a big build up of water on the other side caused by exceptionally heavy rainfall there could be a problem. As I said before, there's no knowing where all the water is going. We had better get a move on."

Peter continued with his work of examining the walls for any evidence of use before the eighteenth century.

"Surface to tunnel," crackled his walky-talky.

"Tunnel here," he replied.

"It's Bernard here, Peter," came a voice. "Just to let you know that it's started to rain heavily again. So don't delay down there. Over."

"OK," replied Peter, " we're working as speedily as we can. We'll be up before long. Over and out."

They were all continuing with their tasks when there was a loud crash, and then the sound of falling rubble followed by a roaring sound. Before they knew what was happening a huge surge of water came rushing down the tunnel accompanied by rocks and soil.

Peter felt his feet taken from under him. As he fell he tried to use his hand to break his fall and felt a jolt to his arm and an ominous crack as he hit the floor of the tunnel. One leg was taken one way and the other was impeded by a piece of rock jutting out from the cave wall. He felt the most excruciating pain. The force of the water released him and his fear now was of drowning. He managed to keep his head just above water and then came to a rest in a sitting position on a slight ledge. But this respite was only temporary for the ledge was slippery and the water was still plunging down the tunnel at a real rate of knots. He felt his feet taken from him again and fell with yet another crash. He was whirled round and then he felt his head hit by either the wall or an oncoming rock. He raised his arm to his head and felt the stickiness of the blood oozing from a large gash on his forehead. Then he seemed to come to a halt. That was when he blacked out.

"Peter, reply please." The voice on his walky-talky crackled as he recovered consciousness.

"It's Peter here," he replied, wondering how the walky-talky had managed to survive the flood. "There's been an accident down here. Water has broken through into the tunnel and I've been injured. I think I've broken a few bones. I don't know what's happened to the others. Can you telephone for help? Over."

"Copy, Peter. Stay where you are and don't move. We'll get help as soon as we can. Richard, the guy in charge of the students, is a qualified first aider. He 's coming down to suss out the problem and gather some information for the rescue authorities. Over."

"OK, Bernard. Please hurry. I'm in agony down here and I'm a bit concerned about the others. Over and out."

Peter had somehow lost his hardhat and that was how he had got the gash on his head. He considered himself fortunate he had not been even more seriously injured or even killed.

He sat in the dark for a while and then began to fumble around for the hand torch. Eventually he located it and, to his surprise, it was still functional. He began surveying the scene. The tunnel was strewn with rocks and debris. There was no sign of the other two. He yelled out for them and heard a distant cry. It was Bill. But there was no sign of Brian.

Peter flashed the torch around the immediate area although any kind of movement was painful and he was beginning to feel nauseous. Suddenly something caught his eye. It was a piece of graffiti on the wall opposite. It was different from the scrawling of smugglers he had observed previously. Large letters, of which only a few were visible, had been painstakingly carved into the rock. He was sure he had not seen them before. The rush of water had possibly washed plant material protecting it away from the rock face and revealed the lettering for the first time. He longed to be able to move over and examine the inscription in more detail but he could not move. Of one thing he was sure. What letters he could see were characteristically medieval and possibly in Latin. He could not imagine any smuggler taking the time to compose a Latin tag and carve it on the wall of the tunnel even if he had been capable.

"Peter, can you hear me?" crackled the walky-talky again.

"Yes, Bernard," replied Peter excitedly. "Look, I think I've discovered something. There's what looks like a medieval inscription down here. We've got to locate it again and examine it properly."

"Yes, yes, my dear chap," replied Bernard, "but our first job is to get you and the others to hospital, if necessary. There are some paramedics coming down to examine you. They say on no account must you move. So keep still and they'll be with you shortly."

"But,........." Peter began, but was quickly interrupted.

"No buts," said Bernard, "The first priority is to get you to hospital."

Peter was desperate. He did not want to lose sight of the inscription. He had to mark the place somehow so that he could find it again. He looked round for a sharp piece of rock and painfully carved his initials on the wall against which he was leaning so that, hopefully, he could identify the inscription opposite when he came back down again. Archaeologists would hardly have approved of his leaving his own personal graffiti at a site but it was the only way he could think of identifying the spot. Then he felt giddy again and passed out.

He awoke again to find himself surrounded by paramedics, who were strapping him to a stretcher.

"Good man," said one, "we were beginning to worry about you. You're going for a ride in a helicopter. How about that? We've just got to pick you up and take you to the rocks below the cliff. It may hurt a little."

As they emerged from the entrance to the cave the cold of the rain on his face was a shock. At first he thought a gale had blown up as well but then he realised that this was the draught created by the rotor blades of the helicopter. The red helicopter was hovering above the rocks and the roar of its engines was almost deafening. There was another stretcher about to be attached to the helicopter's winch and a hand waved weakly at him. It was Bill. He was then raised up into the helicopter with the assistance of one of the crew. There was no sign of Brian.

Peter was lifted up into the helicopter a few minutes later. The helicopter moved swiftly away from the cliff and soared away above the headland to start to make its way towards Truro and Treliske Hospital. Through the open door of the helicopter Peter could see the excavations on the headland and a number of somewhat bemused archaeologists, gathered in little groups, gazing up and waving to the helicopter as it swung out over Tremennek Bay.

Peter had been in hospital only a couple of days when a nurse informed him one afternoon that he had visitors. To his surprise Mary and the two children were ushered in.

The two children rushed to his bedside, gave him kisses, and were eager to show him what they had brought him. Emma had brought him a book of puzzles and Martha a little bunch of flowers.

Mary was more reticent and let the children and their father chat at first. She then moved forward and placed some fruit on the bedside cabinet.

"You do look a mess," she said with a weak smile.

"How did you know I was here?" asked Peter.

"Alex told us. Apparently Bernard Harper informed the University and Alex heard it from a colleague. How bad is it?"

"Not as bad as I feared at first," replied Peter. "I've broken my right leg, bruised some ribs and badly sprained my hand. I'll be out of action for a day or two."

"Rather longer than that I should think," said Mary. "How are you going to manage?"

"Well, I'll just have to go back to the house in Marshallswick and lie low for a bit," he replied.

"Well, look," she said without meeting his eyes, "I've spoken to Alex and we're both agreed that you can come and stay with us until you're fit and well again."

Peter was somewhat surprised but said: "Well, that's very kind of you both. We'll see how it goes. I may be able to manage."

The next day Peter learned that Brian, the detectorist, had come out of the tunnel completely unscathed. He had been trailing behind the other two and had not quite reached the breached side tunnel that had been responsible for all the water rushing in from the old mine. Somehow his rope had become detached from the others and that had probably saved him from serious injury.

Later in the afternoon he had another surprise visitor, Anya. Because Peter was out of action Bernard had requested that she be allowed to return to the site and the University of Granada had sanctioned it.

"I'm sorry to return to England under such circumstances," she said. "It seems that you and Bill had a pretty lucky escape."

"Yeah, we've both been knocked about a bit but fortunately we're both on the mend," said Peter. "I'm ever so glad to see you back again. I'm sorry about Mary's attitude towards you in St. Albans."

"Oh, don't worry," said Anya. "It was probably all for the best anyway."

"Anya, there's something I want you to do as a matter of urgency," said Peter. "As I was lying injured in the tunnel I spotted what looked like a possible medieval inscription in Latin. I've had a word with Bernard about it but he doesn't seem to have taken a lot of notice. Can you get down into the tunnel and check it out for me? I've carved my initials on the wall exactly opposite to where the inscription can be found. It's about seventy or eighty meters beyond where the water burst through from the side tunnel. You should be able to find it fairly easily."

Anya left, promising to check out the inscription as soon as she could.

A couple of days later Peter received a phone call from Anya.

"I talked to Bernard about the inscription and we both went down to have a look. He was quite pleased because, in fact, it was the first time he had been down into the tunnel. I was pleased to see that the police had put a ladder there."

"Yes, yes," said Peter a little impatiently, "did you find anything?"

"Yes, we did. According to Bernard it's almost certainly from the thirteenth century and looks as if it's in Latin. We've got to do a little more work cleaning up the letters on it but we hope to be able to decipher it in the not too distant future. The rush of the water probably cleaned off the wall to some degree and revealed it. We're busy brushing and sponging off all the muck to see what we can make of it.

It was a very lucky break. I'll get back to you as soon as we have something concrete."

Peter thanked her and could hardly contain his excitement. There had been all kinds of artefacts discovered on the headland but to find a piece of writing, maybe from the knight himself, was a real find and he could not wait to discover the outcome.

A couple of days later Anya phoned him to say she was coming across to the hospital to discuss the inscription with him and would be there that afternoon.

He watched out for her full of anticipation. She arrived about three and approached his bed.

"Don't get excited," she said. "I don't think it will take us much further forward."

"Well come on, what did it say?" urged Peter.

"This is what I made of it. To be honest, it was written in a rough kind of Celtic script, which was difficult to make out. But there is no doubt that it is Latin."

She handed him a piece of paper with some Latin words on it.

It read: *'Pugna adversa est. Tr marem reviviscemus.'*

"The battle is adverse," he translated aloud haltingly. "I suppose it means the battle is lost," he concluded from his schoolboy Latin. "Then it's something sea. I don't know really," he said.

"Apparently Tr is short for 'trans'. So it's 'across the sea' and then the next bit apparently means, 'we will come to life again', said Anya.

"Hmm, it's not telling us a lot really," remarked Peter. "I suppose it tells us that our friend escaped. That much we can conclude. But the whole point is – where to?"

"Well that we don't know," said Anya. "It would be lovely if we could find a stronger connection with the site in Granada."

"Yes, it would. But it looks a bit remote at the moment," said Peter. "I'll give it some thought. After all I've got little else to do at the moment."

Anya stayed a while chatting, mainly about the work in hand, and then she left.

Peter thought about the problem. They had an undoubtedly medieval site and some cataclysmic event had taken place there, which history did not seem to have recorded. There did seem to be a connection with the grave in Granada but it had not been satisfactorily established. Most of what they knew about what had taken place at the castle came from the legend about the Evil Knight. And then Peter suddenly thought of an idea. Why not go back to the legend? After all, the Knight was supposed to have returned home from the Crusades with a Saracen bride. Where did she come from?

He decided that the best thing to do was to ask someone who knew a good deal about the legend to see if they could throw some light on the matter. The first person to spring to mind was John Trehane, the local historian.

He got hold of Anya on his mobile and arranged for John Trehane to visit him. John worked out of County Hall, anyway, and was based only a short distance from the hospital.

He arrived the next afternoon and they soon got chatting about the legend of the Evil Knight.

"I've been most impressed and somewhat mystified about what you archaeologists have found up there. I can't understand why there are no records," Trehane said. "It may mean that there is some substance in the legend after all."

"Well, I think that's possibly so," said Peter. "Tell me, John, does the legend say anything about where the Saracen bride came from?"

"Well, let me think. No, I don't think there is any direct reference in it to a country we know of. That's why it's always been regarded as partly fantasy. As far as I can remember all it says is that she came from "a charitable land" across the sea. Doesn't really tell us very much, does it?"

"It's a bit of a strange description," said Peter. Then a thought occurred to him.

"Of course," he said, "the original legend would have been transmitted orally, and in Cornish, so there were bound to have been changes, embellishments and misunderstandings. Perhaps "a charitable land" is some kind of mistranslation or something of that order. I take it you have studied Cornish?"

"Yes, of course, I have," said Trehane, who was intensely proud of his heritage.

"Well," asked Peter, "what is 'a charitable land' in Cornish?"

"Well, I think it would be something like 'tir an alüsen', replied Trehane. "That means a 'charitable' or 'bountiful land' as far as I can recall."

"Hmm, that doesn't seem to have got us very far," said Peter rather despondently.

Later that evening Peter was thinking the whole thing over again. 'Tir an alüsen,' he thought. "That doesn't sound like any country I know of in the Middle Ages."

He ran it over in his mind again. It could be a corruption of something the local peasants had heard. 'An Alüsen.... Analüs.... Andalus. That's it! Andalus,' he cried out in his excitement. It was 'Al Andalus', the Moorish name for modern day Andalusia in Southern Spain.

When asked what land his bride had come from the Knight had probably replied something like 'tir an andalus' and it had been misunderstood as 'tir an alüsen', the 'charitable' or 'bountiful' land.

Peter went to sleep that night very pleased with himself. At last they had a connection with Granada, for the historical city lay, indeed, in the heart of what had been in medieval times 'Al Andalus.'

CHAPTER THIRTEEN

Granada

Elvin and Uzmir set sail late the next afternoon on a fine day and soon left Algiers and the coast of North Africa behind them.

They made slow progress because of the lack of wind and it was not until the next morning that they sighted the coast of Spain and Al Andalus or Andalusia as the Christians called it.

As they approached the coast the wind got up. The Mediterranean began to show its unpredictability as, in no time at all, a heavy swell began to develop and the small ship began to rise and fall and sway from side to side pushed on by a strong wind from the west.

Elvin was eager to catch the occasional glimpse of the coastline ahead and was excited at the prospect of returning to Europe once more, albeit in a region still part of the Muslim Empire of the North African Berbers.

He could sense the wind beating behind him, making his gallabaya billow out like a sail, and he felt the sting of the salty air on the back of his neck. It reminded him of glorious days spent sailing with Yestin off the coast of Cornwall when he was a boy and he tried to think how long it had been since he had been in his homeland.

A big red sun had risen earlier in the east and that was when they could see high, snow covered peaks inland. At least they thought it was snow, but it could well have been the sun reflecting on the bare mountain walls, for this part of Al Andalus was not dissimilar from the Africa they had left behind.

They hugged the coast for a while to get some shelter from the relentless weather. But then suddenly it seemed as if they had come in too close to the shore. They were in a cauldron of swirling, churning water with the waves crashing against the shore and then retreating back into the maelstrom of the inshore waters. The wind and the spray were relentless. At times the swell rose above the vessel and it seemed to fall into a deep trough and then just as suddenly the ship was thrown up onto the peak of the waves only to be tossed on to the next watery hazard. The pitching of the vessel from side to side stirred up the insides of all but the hardiest of mariners.

Soon they could spy the approaches to the harbour of Almeria. The high winds and the rolling seas made it very difficult to negotiate the harbour entrance. Elvin caught glimpses of the impressive fortress, which looked out over the whole harbour and bay.

They made several attempts to negotiate the harbour entrance but did not seem able to get onto the appropriate wave that would carry them through. But at last they succeeded. And once they were in the lee of the breakwater wall, the water became calmer and much more comfortable. They knew they had arrived safely.

Just as suddenly as it had arrived the wind died down later in the day and the full force of the heat of the sun became evident. Whilst the weather out to sea could be very unpredictable the weather inland in this part of the world was very equable. They were thankful that the ship was now safely secured to the inner harbour wall.

The city was not a lot different to what could be found on the other side of the Mediterranean in North Africa. The obligatory sandstone fortress, set on a hill above it, dominated the whole port.

The importance of Almeria to the Berbers was indicated by the huge size of this fortification. Down the slopes below it spread the narrow winding alleyways so typical of the towns of the whole Empire.

There was little money from the sale of their horses in Algiers left over after the passage to Almeria had been paid.. Only one horse could be afforded to take them on to their ultimate destination. They had, therefore, to share. This did not concern Elvin at all as Templar tradition dictated that, where necessary, two knights might be forced to share the same beast to achieve their goal. It emphasised to him as well that, far from being an inferior, he now regarded Uzmir as his equal, something not conceivable when they had first met all that time before.

The cargo was unloaded at the port and Uzmir negotiated with a merchant on the quayside that they could travel in the company of his mule train to the city of Granada where he would be selling his wares in the markets there.

And so, rather meagrely equipped, the two companions set out, mounted on their locally purchased horse, not much better than a nag. They rode steadily across the sun-baked plain of Almeria towards their destination in the hinterland.

It was warm inland with the mountain ranges blocking the cold northerly winds. In the past the local peasants had been well acquainted with hardship and hunger in their desert like environment but it appeared that the Moors had taught them new and more successful methods of growing crops, shown them how to carry water long distances through pipes made of lead and introduced novel varieties of fruit and vegetables from Africa and the East.

The Moors seemed to be far from the savages that Elvin had been led to believe they were and he felt that there was a lot that could be learned from them.

They shared the road with donkeys and mules, flocks of sheep and herds of goats. There was a fertility and prosperity about the region that Cornwall could not match in spite of its more temperate climate and the riches derived from its tin.

Many parts of Almeria were not dissimilar from areas of North Africa. There were vast plains, totally devoid of trees. Once in a while one could spy a vulture or an eagle, taking advantage of air currents in the distance and gliding above the arid plains but that was all.

The journey to Granada was not that far but it took them several days. Here and there they would cross rich agricultural lands and then desert-like plains again. Their greatest challenge was to scale the high mountains in between. These really were snow covered and they had to keep below the snow line. Some of the paths were very treacherous and winding but the mules seemed to know the way and, apart from stumbling from time to time, the merchant muleteers got through with all their cargo intact.

The man, with whom Uzmir had negotiated, was a tough, sinewy individual well used to the dangers of the road. Like his companions he was well armed and ready to protect his cargo to the death. His skin was like brown leather and his black eyes portrayed a tough resolve to get his goods safely to market. He would shout at his mules to urge them down a craggy defile and then tap them sharply on the rear end to encourage them up the other side.

"How does the city of Granada fare these days?" Uzmir enquired of him on one occasion.

"There are problems now throughout all Al Andalus," the muleteer replied. "Since we lost that last great battle more and more towns have fallen to the Christians. From time to time now they even make raids almost up to the gates of the city. Everybody lives in fear of an impending siege. Many refugees are living on the slopes below the Kadima fortress and all around it is very chaotic. There is constant strife between the rulers of the different cities and I fear it is only a matter of time before Al Andalus falls to the Christian Kings."

"It would be a sorrowful time indeed," commented Uzmir.

"Yes, it is difficult enough to make this journey at times without being harassed by the Christians on top of it all."

In spite of his problems the man always seemed to keep cheerful and Uzmir and Elvin quite took to him and enjoyed his jokes and occasional songs.

Tough and sinewy was not an apt description for the nag that was transporting Elvin and Uzmir. In the mountains, for their own protection, they had dismounted from the beast and had been leading it up and down the tortuous ascents and descents of the rocky mountain paths. Sometimes the path was very narrow with an unguarded, dizzy precipice to one side of them with, perhaps, a raging torrent, which could be heard below, and a dark and mysterious drop to certain death.

It was at such a place, under the shadow of the highest peak in the range, where they began descending towards the plain on the other side, that the accident happened. They were following, more or less, the route of the River Genil, which would eventually bring them down to the city of Granada.

Suddenly part way down the descent their beast stumbled and totally missed its footing. Within a second it had disappeared over the mountainside. It was a matter of extremely good fortune that it had not taken Uzmir with it. With his wits about him he had been able to disentangle himself before the beast had fallen over the precipice and crashed to its death somewhere below.

The rest of the way they were obliged to go on foot and with what food and water the muleteers were prepared to share with them. Their water bottles and all their equipment had been attached to the horse's saddle and had crashed with it down into the valley below.

Fortunately the merchants were familiar with the location of an occasional spring. They would stop and then bend to lift a rock and the water would shoot into the air. All of them could quench their thirst and partake of a refreshing, cooling wash before proceeding on their way.

From time to time, whilst traversing wild passes on their slow descent, they caught sight of walled, fortified towns and villages, perched on the rocky crags. They were aware that they were being watched but nobody challenged them. Whether it was out of fear of strangers or because the muleteers were well known in the region they did not know.

And then, before them, on the third day, they spied the great walled city of Granada in the distance, dominated by the imposing fortress of the Kadima.

The mule caravan made its way now along the banks of the river until they reached the confluence of the Genil and another river, the Darro.

They turned away from the River Genil and followed the Darro, right under the cliffs of the hill upon which city and fortress lay. The walls that overhung the river were embedded with iron bars to stop any attempt to gain entry to the city by that route.

The thick, grey, buttressed walls of the city seemed to Elvin to be immensely impressive and capable of withstanding many a siege. Glancing up from time to time he could see the houses spilling down from the fortress on the summit intermingled with the square towered minarets of the mosques dotted about, here and there, and decorated with intricate, embossed, geometrical patterns on the stonework and multi-coloured tiles.

Crossing a bridge they approached one of the main gates into the city manned by the Governor's guards. Protracted arguments and negotiations now took place between the muleteer merchants and the guards on the extent of the tax to be charged to enter the city.

The guards questioned Uzmir closely as to where he had come from and they seemed to accept his story, both about himself and Elvin. They were ushered through, and after pausing to thank the leader of the mule train, started to make their way slowly up the steep slopes of the city towards their goal.

The city was a labyrinth of narrow alleyways descending down from the fortress at the top of the hill. They were crowded with people, for large numbers of refugees from besieged areas to the North had settled in the city over recent years. Many of the houses were quite small but the one in which Uzmir's family resided was of the size which befitted his father's rank.

The exterior frontage of the house was a blank wall built of layers of dried clay. A single entrance pierced it, above which had been constructed a brick relieving arch. A heavy, studded, wooden gate with a single iron grill filled the entrance.

Uzmir hammered on the gate and the iron grill was opened and two piercing eyes stared out.

"What is your business?" came the inevitable question from the guard on the gate.

"It is I, Uzmir, the eldest son of Aderbal, the Governor's physician, returned from Africa. Please tell my father I am here."

The grill was shut and there was a wait for a while. Then there was the sound of the drawing of bolts and the turning of heavy iron keys and the gate creaked open. They passed through into an entrance hall, each side of which a guard stood. In these days of uncertainty it was obvious that all court officials were well guarded. A white turbaned young man, dressed in the red flowing robes, received them.

"This is Yusuf, my father's assistant," said Uzmir.

Yusuf led them along the entrance hall and then through an intricately designed wrought iron gate and out into the sunlight again. They crossed a courtyard of the most staggering beauty. In the centre was a fountain with a lotus shaped basin set on a column, from which a continuous stream of water was ejected into the air to fall again, filling the basin and trickling down over the edge into a larger pool at its base. The air was clear and the sound projected a sense of great calm.

Purple coloured bougainvillea cascaded down the outer walls. Orange and lemon trees in full fruit gave welcome shade from the heat.

The floor was covered with cool, dark green and beige marble tiles arranged in a diamond pattern. Around the far end of the courtyard stretched a colonnaded gallery the lower part of whose walls were decorated with embossed, patterned green tiles.

Yusuf led them through to the back of the main house and into a room that seemed like a laboratory. There were bubbling jars everywhere. Phials of all kinds of substances lined shelves along one wall. The person, who Elvin took to be the father of Uzmir, was stood at a bench mixing some concoction. He was dressed in a simple white robe over which he wore a waistcoat of blue brocade. A plain white turban completed his dress along with the Persian style slippers.

"Welcome, my son," he said. " I never thought I would cast my eyes upon you again. You cannot imagine what a great day this is for your mother and I. I will be with you in just one minute. I just have to finish the mixture of this medicament for a member of the court and I will be with you."

Elvin was surprised at the fragrance of the ointment the physician was making up. It was so different to any ointment, with which he might be familiar. He asked Uzmir about what constituents made it so fragrant.

"It is only rose jam with spiced cream to thicken it and give it its fragrance," he explained.

"It seems a lot more pleasant than the foul smelling ointments used in my country. There they use cat's grease and stewed slugs as a thickener for the ointment. It's a most offensive odour," said Elvin.

"I'm not surprised," commented Uzmir.

Aderbal finished what he was doing, wiped his hands on a cloth and then embraced his son. They spoke a little in Berber and then Uzmir introduced Elvin.

Aderbal grasped Elvin's hand firmly, looked him straight in the eyes and said in good French:

"I understand that you are a Christian from a land to the North, my friend, but you are most welcome in my house. There was a time when Christian, Jew and Muslim lived in great harmony in this land but now we live in much more uncertain times and even some of us of the faith of Islam have to be careful about what we are saying and doing. But any friend of my son is a friend of mine and Allah's blessing be upon you," he said.

"Now I have a number of things to do here. I will leave you in the capable hands of Yusuf to show you to your quarters and we will speak later."

"The best rooms of the house are on the floor above," Uzmir explained and gestured towards an imposing marble staircase, which led to the upper storeys. "In the heat of the summer, however, we live on the ground floor where it is much cooler."

Elvin was impressed by the contrast between this seemingly luxurious house and his father's gloomy castle in Cornwall. It seemed to perpetuate the heritage of the Roman villa but was made even more colourful by the proliferation of Islamic styles of decoration and design, which were most pleasing to the eye.

There appeared to be no strict rules and the house had been designed to enhance plays of light and shadow and to show off intricate decorative effects. The whole feeling was of coolness, peace and tranquillity. He liked, particularly, the central courtyard with its fountain and the calming influence of its cascading waters. Heaven itself, he thought, could hardly provide a much better place to live.

Later Uzmir and Elvin visited a nearby bathhouse. This was yet another new experience for Elvin. He was aware from their travels in North Africa that the Romans had been fond of these but he had not realised that the people of Al Andalus still made use of them.

In Cornwall Elvin had seen little need to bathe that often. Nor was it the custom amongst his equals.

Each man changed into a kind of chequered loincloth and wooden clogs. They were given a box of cleansing materials in an ornate copper box and ushered into a large room dominated by a forest of columns bedecked with horseshoe arches. All around were braziers full of burning charcoal. Above was a domed ceiling with a large number of apertures built into it, each fitted with a small bottle glass window. Each small window directed pinpoints of sunlight downwards.

A number of men sat around on marble benches conversing and socializing with one another whilst slaves poured water onto the braziers to create steam. When the steam got too oppressive a slave would be asked to open some of the apertures in the ceiling to let out the excess.

Elvin was soon sweating profusely and frequently wiping his brow. "It is good to sweat," whispered Uzmir. "It opens the pores to let out bad humours and is good for the health."

After a while he motioned to Elvin to follow him and they went to a side room to descend into a sunken bath of cold water. The coldness came as shock to Elvin but, once having got used to it, he began to feel refreshed and renewed. Slaves poured water over them using copper bowls. Then they climbed out of the bath and the slaves supplied them with highly decorated towels to dry themselves.

Then they went to yet another area where there were a number of marble benches. Laid out naked on the benches with just the loincloth covering them for modesty, they were vigorously massaged with a rough glove by slaves to remove all the dead skin. Soothing oils were then applied to their bodies and massaged gently in. Such was the relaxing nature of this treatment that Elvin almost fell asleep. All the weariness of their travel across North Africa and Spain seemed to disappear in a moment and he felt like a new man.

Later that evening the men of the household gathered in one of the rooms to dine. The floor was covered with a large red Persian carpet of a complex design and scattered with colourful silk-covered cushions. Wall hangings also adorned all sides of the room and there was a large mirror at one end.

"How do you get the metal of the mirror to shine in such a way?" asked Elvin of Uzmir.

"It is not metal," replied Uzmir. "It is made of glass."

Elvin stared in amazement at the clear reflections coming from the mirror. He had never heard of a mirror being made with glass before and he had never seen its like in England.

There was little other furniture in the room and the men sat round the edge of the carpet. As well as Aderbal and Uzmir, Aderbal's two younger sons, Meddur and Iddir, had joined them. They appeared to be somewhat more suspicious of Elvin than their father but were polite enough.

All were formally dressed in loose fitting robes with long full sleeves. They had goatskin slippers on their feet and a small curved dagger at the waist. Each wore a large turban.

The women of the household served a meal. Aderbal's wife supervised everything and was assisted by her two daughters-in-law and her daughter. Each wore a hood and was veiled. Under the hood each wore a headband, from which were suspended large gold discs like coins. They were swathed in colourful robes with lace covers over their skirts. They also wore waistcoats, which were trimmed with gold glitter thread and spangles. Elvin noticed that all the women's feet were hennaed too. The picture conjured up a mixture of modesty and allure.

The meal consisted of a lamb stew full of the most intriguing herbs and spices as well fruit. Elvin asked Uzmir about the ingredients.

"There are many ingredients," he said, "including cinnamon, cloves, nutmeg, apricots and sultanas." Elvin shrugged, for he had not heard of any of these. There were also bowls of rice, with which Elvin was familiar, but this rice was of a yellow hue.

There were no implements used to eat with as was common amongst the Muslims. Elvin had learned from Uzmir long before never to eat with his left hand, only the right. After their long travels he was now used to dipping his fingers into the hot stew and not immediately withdrawing them because of the shock of the heat.

None of the women looked at Elvin as they served the food except one. A short glance from behind the veil came his way and he was entranced. It was just a fluttering glance from two of the most attractive bluey green eyes he had ever seen and he had a feeling that somewhere under the veil was just the glimpse of a flirtatious smile. As soon as she had looked up, she had looked down again and the moment was past. Elvin knew this to be Tayri, Uzmir's sister.

After the women had gone Elvin asked Uzmir: "Are the women always adorned by veils?"

"No," he replied. "In our tribe the women enjoy greater freedom than is general in Muslim society. The veil is not always worn. It is because you are here this evening and they do not yet know you well that they wear the veil."

Another thing, which Elvin noticed, which he had not experienced in the North of Africa on their journey, was that the women had served wine to the men. It was a rich, fruity wine, which brought a glow to the cheeks and heightened the conversation.

The men tried their best to be polite to Elvin, urging him to partake of one morsel or another, but it was clear that the younger men at least, Uzmir's two brothers, were slightly embarrassed by his presence. From the snatches of conversation he could understand – and he was now picking up some of the Berber language – the subject of the conversation was the reverses being experienced by the people of Al Andalus at the hands of the Christian forces to the North and they were trying to update Uzmir on the situation.

"These are dark days for us in Al Andalus," Aderbal told his son. "The Christians make continual forays into our territory and frequently kidnap our citizens for slaves or ransom. They are now raiding well into territories that surround us. There have been many problems in the years since the last great defeat. Al Andalus seems in political chaos with one faction or other betraying the others. Our Governor, Idris, is also Governor of Cordova and, I think, a very ambitious man, who would be Caliph if the chance were ever to arise."

"I do not know why we do not try to get revenge on those Christian b...," said Meddur and then he stopped himself short, conscious of the presence of Elvin. "The Berbers must be amongst the best raiders in the world," he continued. "They have been raiding one another for centuries." There were nods and chuckles of amused agreement.

"There does not seem to be the same will for a fight," said his father. "We have suffered badly at the hands of the Christian Kings and their well-equipped armies. They know how to use their siege engines to the greatest effect in bringing down the walls and destroying our cities and fortresses alike. Our leaders would rather pay tribute to them, nowadays, to avoid it ever getting to such a point."

"Then it will only be a matter of time before they lose their kingdoms altogether," observed Uzmir.

"Then we must pray that we can all live in harmony once more when that happens," said his father.

"What think you, my friend?" said Aderbal changing to French and explaining the essence of the discussion to Elvin.

"I must say that there was a time when I would have gladly seen the whole of Islam swept into the sea," Elvin replied. Meddur and Iddir frowned at this.

"But now that I know more about your people and have met your son, Uzmir, and, indeed, all of your family, I find I am changing my opinion greatly. Those, whom I believed to be barbarians, I find to be sophisticated and cultured. In so many ways you appear to have a superior style of life to those of us from the North of Europe. I see wonderful architecture, advances in medicine and science, amazing developments in farming, great libraries and literature and a genuine attempt, at times, to be tolerant of the beliefs of others. I wish I could say that those who attack your borders now could promise the same. It makes me wonder upon whom God really looks with favour."

"You speak very generously of us, my friend," said Aderbal. "You will find that not all here would accept you as we do and it would do to tread carefully always. Heed the advice of my son in all things. As a friend he has your welfare at heart. You are welcome to stay here as long as you need."

Elvin slept well that night. For the first time in his life he felt that he was somewhere where he could be truly happy.

He awoke in the early hours of the morning, however. Happy as he was, in his heart of hearts, there was a growing feeling that he would have to return to Cornwall. One day he would have to succeed his father. There was also the blossoming of a thought in his mind that had been germinated in the caverns of the monastery in the mountains of Aragon. Joseph of Arimathea had brought the Holy Grail to Glaston. Why was it then in a monastery in Aragon? The more he thought about it, the more he was convinced that it had been stolen and that it was his duty to return to its rightful place.

Later in the morning he wandered into the central courtyard to enjoy the tranquillity. It was a bright sunny day and the heat was quite intense. The reassuring play of the fountain was pleasing to the ear. There was a heady smell of fruit and blossom. He sat upon a marble bench under the colonnade and just breathed in the enjoyment of the relaxing atmosphere.

He might have dozed slightly but all of a sudden he became conscious of being watched. He opened his eyes and, there, on the other side of the courtyard stood Tayri regarding him intently.

She was unveiled and for the first time he cast eyes upon her countenance. He took a sharp intake of breath. She had beautiful reddish brown hair that sat above an oval face with soft, dark skin of a nut-brown hue. Her lips were full and rosebud red and she had a long slender neck. But it was to her eyes, set above a trim nose, that he was drawn.

They were of an intense aquamarine colour, quite unlike anything he had seen before.

Their eyes met. Her face burst into a radiant smile. Then, perhaps feeling she should not have been there, she raised her veil to her face, turned swiftly and disappeared.

Elvin called after her but she was gone. For him she had been a vision of exquisite beauty and he knew that he must be alone with her again.

The next day Elvin awoke from a pleasant dream. He could not get the image of Tayri out of his mind. The incredible eyes and the ravishing smile had captured his heart. He could not wait to see her again.

He wandered the marble tiled hallways of the house half hoping he would meet her again but it was not to be.

He came upon Aderbal's study-come-laboratory and the door stood open. Aderbal was working away at his bench crushing what seemed like flowers in a bowl preparing yet another medicine for a patient.

Elvin had grown to like Aderbal. He had a gentle, fatherly manner and inspired confidence in his wisdom. Elvin's own father was a harsh, brutal man with few endearing qualities. Aderbal seemed to have accepted Elvin and treated him like one of his own sons. He made nothing of the fact that Elvin was a Christian and, therefore, technically an enemy. He had welcomed him into his house and the mere fact that he was a trusted friend of his son had been enough for Aderbal.

Elvin knocked on the door and Aderbal looked up.

"Come in, my son," he said. "I trust you have slept well this night."

Elvin nodded.

"What can I do for you?" asked Aderbal

"I wondered if I might watch you in your work for a while. I find it fascinating how you mix all these different potions to help your patients. How have you learned all these different recipes?"

"Well. We physicians in Al Andalus have to spend many years studying before we can practice our profession. We have to know about science, mathematics and philosophy as well as medicine. There is much to learn and you can see from all the books up there that there is much to read from the works of eminent physicians from the past."

Elvin looked up at the many shelves laden with leather bound volumes that adorned the far wall of the room. In his own home there were few volumes of this sort except the Bible.

"Over time I have learned about many drugs and their use in medicine."

"What do you mean by a drug?" enquired Elvin.

"We use the word to describe a chemical substance, which is given to a patient to prevent or cure a disease or to enhance their welfare in some way," explained Aderbal.

"For example, at the moment, I am making up a drug to use in an operation that I am going to perform on one of the Governor's staff, who has seriously damaged his hand. Unfortunately I am going to have to remove several fingers and this drug will put him to sleep for the period of the operation and he will feel nothing."

Elvin stared at Aderbal almost in disbelief. He had never heard of such a thing. He could only remember the agonized screams of wounded soldiers taken from the battlefield, who had festering limbs severed with the Infirmarer's saw without such pain relieving aids.

"How do you make such a potion?" he asked.

"There are many plants and seeds which can be used for all kinds of purposes in medicine," said Aderbal. "I grow some of them in a small garden at the back of the house. I am making up my sleeping drug from the juice of poppies that I grow in the garden. I extract the juice and thicken it and then I add other ingredients like mulberry juice, hemlock juice and lettuce seeds. I place a new sponge into the liquid and boil it all up until the sponge has absorbed all the liquid. I apply the sponge to the nostrils of my patient and he falls asleep. I can then perform the operation without pain to my patient. We call it the sleeping sponge."

"It is surely wondrous. I have so much to learn about your world," said Elvin. "Would you teach me some of your knowledge?"

"If that is what you will," replied Aderbal, realising that Elvin was genuinely interested. "But first you must read." He took down some volumes from the shelves. "These are written in the Latin tongue. Are you able to read these?"

"Yes," replied Elvin, now hungry for knowledge. He had been taught Latin as part of his studies as a boy.

"For most of the books you will have to read Arabic. So a first step will be for you to learn that tongue as well. I will ask Yusuf to teach you."

"I am most grateful to you, sir. I did not know there was so much to learn in the world."

"I wish you well in your studies, my boy. Education and knowledge are wondrous things and make you just as much a man as do the sword and the lance."

Elvin left Aderbal and wandered down into the courtyard again. It was bathed in bright sunshine. He found a sheltered spot under a tree and sat down to pour over his books. There was so much to learn.

After a while he felt once more that someone was watching him and he looked up. Tayri was standing in the same place as before staring at him. He stood up and she made to leave.

"No, no," he cried beckoning to her. "Don't leave."

She hesitated and drew her veil up closer round her face.

Her eyes were captivating and Elvin approached her slowly not wishing to frighten her away. He felt frustrated at his lack of Berber.

"I am Elvin," he said, pointing at himself, although he knew full well she knew his name.

"I am Tayri," she replied in the same manner.

"Please sit," he asked her, pointing to the bench

She hesitated and looked round. Seeing no one about she sat down on the bench beside him.

"Your father has given me books to read," he said trying, as far as he was able, to make conversation.

She nodded and he felt she was smiling under her veil.

"Why are you smiling?" he asked.

"You have a funny accent," she replied.

"You - very beautiful," he said pointing to her and unable to resist the temptation to tell her any longer. Again she appeared to smile.

He became bolder. "Such a beautiful face - no cover with veil."

"It is not fitting for a young woman to show her face to a stranger," she replied in a low voice, her eyes averted from his for a moment.

"But I do not feel a stranger," he said somewhat frustrated and struggling with the language. "Your family welcome me to your house. Your father is kind to me and your brother, Uzmir, is friend. And you forget," he added, "I have already seen the beauty of your smile."

"How is that?" she asked.

"Yesterday," he said. "You were unveiled the first time that we encountered one another."

"That was so," she said. "It should not have been."

"It is not right that such a beautiful face should be hidden - especially from one who would be your friend," Elvin said looking at her intently.

"It is our custom," she said.

"Will you not give me just a little glance?" Elvin said with a pleading, boyish grin, looking at her with his head on one side.

She hesitated for a moment. Then her hand slowly moved upwards and she drew back the veil to reveal her face.

Again Elvin almost gasped at the beautiful creature before him. Her smile was like a hundred bright spring days, lighting up all around. And his eyes were drawn to her eyes – of such a blue green hue. He could not remember if he had ever seen a woman with such a colour of eyes and these were more colourful than the Mediterranean Sea itself.

"From which land do you come?" Tayri asked him.

"I come from a land called Cornwall, which is many leagues across the sea to the North of here," he replied.

"I have not heard of such a land," she said.

"It is part of the island of Britain," he explained.

"Oh, yes," she said, perhaps not a great deal wiser.

"How old are you, Tayri?" he enquired.

"I am of seventeen summers," she replied.

"Have you ever been away from Granada?" he asked.

"No, I have not ventured far from the city. I sometimes think I would like to see other lands like I am sure you have. But, alas, that is not to be my lot," she sighed.

"You do not know," he said becoming more confident in the language, "one of these days you may travel to far off lands. We do not know what God has in store for us."

"That is true," she said.

"You may marry a man who is an ambassador to some foreign clime and you will find yourself spirited away to some exotic land across the sea," Elvin said.

She gave a fetching little chuckle. "To Corn…wall, perhaps," she said with a cheeky smile and hesitating slightly over the pronunciation.

"Perhaps so," laughed Elvin.

"Do you have a wife?" she asked.

"No, I do not," he replied

"Are you poor?" she asked.

"No, why?"

"Here a man is only without a wife if he is poor."

"Then he is doubly sad. Not only is he poor but also he has no one to care for him and bear his children," mused Elvin.

Just then Tayri's brother, Meddur, appeared in the courtyard. Tayri turned away from him quickly and recovered her face with the veil.

"Good day to you Elvin," he said. "I trust you are well. I see my father has provided you with plenty of reading."

"Yes, it will keep me occupied for some time," replied Elvin.

"Tayri," said Meddur, "I think it would be wise to join your mother now."

With that Tayri scampered off towards a corner of the courtyard and disappeared inside.

Elvin and Meddur continued to converse for a while and then Meddur left.

Elvin felt elated at his contact with Tayri, yet empty and alone now she had gone. He could not stop thinking about her. He had never felt this way about a woman before. Always in the past the maids of the village had been there for the taking if he had wished. The women of his own rank in Cornwall he had found singularly unattractive on the whole and he had certainly not liked the woman chosen for him by his father, who had later become his stepmother.

The whole of the next day Elvin kept an eye on the courtyard hoping to catch a glimpse of Tayri, but she did not appear. He found himself desperately disappointed. He liked being with her. He liked talking to her and her playful, flirtatious manner made him yearn to be with her. He had felt that there was a mutual attraction between them and yet, when she did not appear the next day, he felt somehow let down.

Several days went by and still there was no sign of her. Elvin sank into a bout of depression but consoled himself with his books and started lessons in Arabic with Aderbal's assistant, Yusuf.

One morning, feeling somewhat down, Elvin wandered into the courtyard with the intention of sitting quietly in the sunshine and reflecting. There on the seat under the tree sat Tayri without her veil.

She smiled as he approached seemingly as pleased to see him, as he was to see her.

He greeted her and said, "I have missed you these last few days. I hope you have not been unwell."

"No, no," she said, "I have had to help my mother and my sisters-in-law prepare things for a feast that we are to have tomorrow. The son of the Governor's personal secretary, who is a man of great importance, is visiting us from Cordova. It is a great honour for us to receive him."

"Does this happen very often?" enquired Elvin.

"No. He is coming to talk business with my father." She avoided his look at this statement and Elvin was not sure why this was so. "We will all have to dress in our finest robes."

"I am sure you will look as beautiful as you always do," said Elvin.

"Please do not tease me," she said, feigning hurt. "I know you are only saying that because you think it is polite to do so to the daughter of your host."

"No, not at all," he said. "To me you are amongst the most entrancing of women. Whoever gains your hand will be the luckiest of men."

She smiled and yet there was a trace of sadness about her eyes. They continued to talk about their families, about their hopes for the future, about the birds and about the flowers. They felt at perfect ease with one another and Tayri gently helped Elvin when he struggled for words.

Then he said: "When you are married, what sort of man would you hope for?"

"A strong, brave, and handsome man," she said, "a man who will respect me for who I am, a man who will not treat me as a chattel, a man who will talk to me – just as you are talking to me now."

Their eyes met and they smiled.

"Alas," she said, "we have to accept whoever is chosen by our fathers. That is the way."

"It is the same in my land," said Elvin, thoughtfully, and then he found himself pouring out the story he had related to Uzmir about his father's choice of Alis de Trevarno and the events that had unfolded thereafter.

She listened intently, not interrupting, and said: "It is an unhappy story. And now you find yourself far from home. Do you miss your land across the sea?"

"Of course," he replied. "What person would not think of the land where he was born? Sometimes I feel weary of battles, of the blood and the gore. Sometimes I feel weary of having to pretend to the outside world here that I am someone I am not. But then sometimes there are things which make up for all that."

"What things?" she asked.

"I would never have been talking here with a creature with such a beautiful smile," he said.

She touched and patted his hand gently and looked straight at him. She appeared to be thinking deeply but uttered no word. After a pause she said:

"I must go now. My mother will wonder where I am."

"Will I see you again soon?" he asked.

"Perhaps," she said and was gone.

Later that evening Elvin was passing Aderbal's study, when the old man beckoned him in.

"We have an important guest from Cordova visiting us tomorrow," he said. "I would like you to be present at our deliberations but clearly there are still problems. There are still those who would not understand your presence here. You will obviously have to maintain your identity as the refugee from the horrors of Doumyat. We will find some appropriate robes for you"

Then Aderbal gave him news, which took him aback somewhat.

"Our guest is Muhammad ibn Mustapha al-Avokato, the son of the secretary to the Governor of Cordova and Granada, and a very important man indeed. He is coming to enter into negotiations for his marriage to my daughter, Tayri."

Aderbal went on talking but Elvin was not listening. The air seemed to be full of fuzzy sounds and he was not paying attention at all but to one fact. Tayri was to marry. He ought not to have been surprised and yet somehow it had struck him like a thunderbolt. He knew he did not want this to happen and yet he was probably powerless to do anything about it.

Elvin went away in the depths of despair. He could not get Tayri out of his mind. He told himself that it was insane. He had only talked to the girl on two occasions and yet he was smitten. He had never before felt like this about anyone. The thought of losing her distressed him.

The next evening all the guests gathered. Muhammad obviously came from a very wealthy family as was witnessed by the manner of his dress and the number of retainers who accompanied him. The women of the household including Tayri served a sumptuous meal. Their eyes met once or twice and he tried to communicate his concern to her but she just smiled to fuel his growing jealousy still further.

When the meal was over the men continued to drink wine and Elvin presumed the negotiations were underway. His knowledge of Berber or Arabic, or whatever language, in which the business was being conducted, was insufficient to keep up with the details.

Whether it was the meal or the wine, which accompanied it, Elvin did not know, but the discussions between the men folk of the family and Muhammad began to disintegrate into a meaningless burble and his mind began to wander. Perhaps he had begun to drowse a little, for, suddenly, he was conscious of all in the room staring at him.

"And what does our friend in the corner think? He has said very little."

Elvin made to reply, feeling that he had to confess that he did not fully understand what was going on. Then he remembered, just in time, that he was supposed to have been struck dumb by the traumatic events relating to the siege of Damietta.

"Er…" he mumbled, but was immediately rescued by Uzmir.

"I'm afraid our friend is unable to speak because of the terrible things that happened in Doumyat," said Uzmir using the Arabic name for Damietta. "He lost all of his family there and has been unable to recover from the shock since."

Muhammad shrugged his shoulders and moved his attention elsewhere, much to the relief of Elvin. He wondered how much longer he could get away with the deception. He had been very lucky so far.

After some time hands were shaken and presumably some agreement had been reached. Aderbal clapped his hands and more wine was brought. Then the evening was crowned by what seemed to be the grand passions of Al Andalus – singing, dancing and lute music. Tayri appeared before the assembled host and entertained them with a song and dance. Elvin was entranced. The music of her song was beautiful and mysterious, the like of which he had never heard before. It made the hairs on his back bristle with excitement.

Then she began to dance before the assembled host. It was a highly sensual dance with a sinuous twisting of her body in time to the beating drum and a voluptuous rotating of her hips as the drum beat faster and faster. The men began to clap their hands in time to the rhythm and Tayri danced faster and faster until she collapsed exhausted in a heap before them. The other women picked her up and escorted her away.

Muhammad, leering, appeared to make some comment, which Elvin was unable to catch. His only thought was that he did not want this man to have her as his wife. Elvin had never felt this way about any woman before but he was utterly captivated. The men continued to talk and drink until late into the night. When the party broke up he felt utterly dejected and depressed.

He had taken an instant dislike to Muhammad, who appeared to be a boorish, degenerate man in spite of, or maybe, because of his education and wealth. But Elvin fully understood the role of dynastic marriages, for much the same thing occurred in society back in England.

Muhammad and his retinue returned to Cordova the next day. Elvin comforted himself with his books and continued with his lessons in Arabic with Yusuf.

It was another two days before he saw Tayri again in the courtyard. She was standing by a lemon tree admiring the fruit. He greeted her and she smiled.

"Would you sit with me for a while," he asked. Nothing was said for a moment or two.

"I enjoyed your singing and dancing the other evening," he said.

"You have a voice like a songbird rejoicing in the sunshine after a shower of rain." He was not sure whether she understood this compliment but from her look it appeared that she had.

"And you dance in a most alluring way," he continued. "It would make any man want to sweep you off your feet."

She chuckled. "Would you want to sweep me off my feet?" she enquired flirtatiously lowering and then slowly raising her eyelids to look him straight in the eye, her top lip slightly curled in a coquettish smile.

"You must know by now that I surely would," he exclaimed and then with a degree of frustration he blurted out: "Do you really want to marry that man?"

She lowered her eyes and murmured: " No, not really. It is my father's wish and I must obey." He detected a slight tear in the corner of her eye.

For the first time he took hold of her hand and held it gently in his for a short while, massaging and turning it in an attempt to comfort her. Nothing further was said but it must have been clear to Tayri that he harboured great concern for her and, like her, did not really relish the idea of her impending marriage.

CHAPTER FOURTEEN

A Letter From America

It was several weeks before Peter was able to leave hospital. He had fractured a couple of ribs as well as a leg and was quite badly bruised. The main problem had been the leg and he had had to go on traction and to have the shaft of his femur pinned.

Mary picked him up from the hospital and took him to the house in Marshallswick. He had been supplied with a single crutch, which he had now become quite adept at using.

When he opened the front door there was a pile of post on the doormat. A large proportion of it was junk mail. There were some bills and a letter from the USA, which caught his eye.

The previous week he had been informed by Bernard Harper that the dig at Tremennek Bay had been abandoned as it was felt that the team had retrieved enough in the way of artefacts and other materials there to prove their point that a castle had been sited on the headland during the Middle Ages.

It was thought that the next stage would be to conclude the work at the site in Granada and to do further investigative work on why there were no records of the castle at Tremennek Bay.

Peter did not open the post until the next day and the letter from America contained a surprise. The letter read as follows:

"Dear Dr. Verity,
I understand from an article I have read in the Chicago Sun that you and a team have been carrying out archaeological work on the site of a medieval castle at Tremennek in Cornwall, England."

"Hmm," thought Peter, "some people I know won't like Cornwall being described as being in England, but there you go."

The letter continued:

"I have a document in my possession that was bought, I believe, by my grandfather, at an auction in the nineteen twenties in New York. The document in is Latin and appears to be the grant of some land to one William Le Gard by King Richard in 1194 and giving permission for the construction of a castle. The location is described as being at Tremennek and on land formerly held by the Bishop of Exeter.

Peter gasped. This was just the kind of documentary evidence of the mystery castle that they were seeking.

The letter went on:

"If it would aid your work in any way I would be happy to send you a copy of it for you to examine to see if this document relates to the castle you are currently investigating.
Yours sincerely,
Daniel Hoffer"

Peter replied immediately:

"Dear Mr. Hoffer,
I was most interested to receive your letter and would certainly welcome sight of a copy of your document, which sounds very pertinent to our current dig in Cornwall.
I look forward to hearing from you soon.
Sincerely,
Peter Verity."

About a week later an envelope arrived from the US containing a good quality copy of the document, the original of which was clearly in a state of some disrepair. Most of the Latin text was decipherable, however, and the signature of the King, Richard the Lionheart, was clear for all to see along with his seal.

Peter consulted with Bernard Harper as soon as possible. Both agreed that the document represented a useful addition to the overall picture and appeared to grant permission for the building of a castle at Tremennek.

"I wonder where Hoffer's grandfather bought it and who the owner was before," Bernard queried.

Peter telephoned Daniel Hoffer and had quite a lengthy conversation with him. It turned out that he still had the original documentation relating to the purchase. It had been made at the specialist auction house of Hollander and Benson in New York City in 1925. Apparently the previous owner had been one Miguel Guardia, who had claimed to be a direct descendent of William Le Gard, and who had been of Spanish nationality.

"We would certainly like to have a look at the original to authenticate its age and to assure ourselves it isn't a fake," said Peter.

"Well, I can understand that although the supporting documentation would seem to indicate that it is the genuine article. Look, my friend, this is really of limited interest to me. I would certainly be prepared to make a gift of the document to your University for research purposes in exchange for some kind of recognition, of course. That is, if you thought that would be appropriate."

"That would be a most generous act," said Peter. "I am sure the University could come to some arrangement with you. I think, honestly, the document needs to be in professional hands if it is to be preserved. It looks to be in a bit of a state from the copy you sent."

"It's actually not too bad. It is a bit tatty round the edges but otherwise in reasonable condition. I've had advice from a guy at the National Archives and Records Administration about its preservation."

In due course the University received the donation of the original and Peter and Bernard were given access to it. The document had, in fact, been fairly expertly preserved to minimize physical and chemical deterioration. Somebody relatively early in its history had seen the importance of preserving it. It was yellow and frayed around the edges but most of Latin script was there along with the signature and seal of King Richard.

One person who was very excited about the document was the local historian in Cornwall, John Trehane.

"There seems to be no doubt, now, that a castle did exist on the headland at Tremennek Bay," he commented. "And the connection with the grave in Spain seems to have been reinforced by your discovery of the identity of the owner previous to Daniel Hoffer."

"Yes, I don't have much doubt now that the Le Gard, who had his castle destroyed, probably escaped and returned to Andalusia with his Saracen bride. But he must have upset some important people for his castle to be razed to the ground and for all trace of him to be expunged from the records. I wonder if we will ever know the full story?"

CHAPTER FIFTEEN

The Knight's Dilemma

It was Uzmir who first brought up the matter.

It had been a beautiful, sunny day and Elvin had been sitting in the courtyard. The sky above was cloudless and of the brightest blue. He was sheltered from the intensity of the sun by the design of the courtyard, which was always the coolest place in the house, to which to retreat.

The waters of the fountain danced and played and the babbling sound of their trickle over the edge of the basin into the pool below gave a therapeutic calmness to the place. The water's descent threw up a fine mist, which was occasionally caught by the rays of the sun, creating a rainbow like effect.

Elvin was reading. He was struggling with the Arabic in a volume by a writer called az-Zahrawi, a renowned physician who had died at the beginning of the eleventh century. The book was one of some thirty volumes by this man held by Aderbal in his library. Aderbal had told him that he was one of the most important pioneers of medicine to have been produced in Al Andalus. In the book there were copious instructions on how to carry out surgical operations. There were lots of fascinating diagrams and details of how to prepare the "sleep sponges" that Aderbal frequently used. Elvin found the going hard but his Arabic was beginning to improve under the conscientious tutelage of Yusuf.

Suddenly Elvin was conscious that Uzmir was standing by him.

"I'm sorry I did not notice you there," said Elvin

"Yes, you seem very bound up in your reading, my friend. What is it that you study so diligently?"

Elvin told him and Uzmir remarked "Ah, yes, he was a very famous physician who has passed much great knowledge down to us today. There are many such volumes in my father's library, as you know. I am glad you find interest in their contents – and your Arabic seems to be improving no end according to Yusuf. Indeed, so is your colloquial

Berber. I am amazed at what strides you have made since you have been our guest."

"It is kind of you to say so," said Elvin.

"I suspect there might be an ulterior motive in your learning our language so well," remarked Uzmir.

Elvin looked at him a shade quizzically.

"Is it not that you wish to converse more effectively with my sister? It has not gone unnoticed that you pay quite some attention to her."

"It is true that I find your sister very easy to talk to and I am improving my knowledge of your language a great deal by doing so. She has a very engaging personality and is a creature of great beauty. I enjoy our conversations together very much," Elvin said hesitantly.

"This is what I wish to talk to you about, my friend. In fact, my father has asked me to talk you, as your friend, on this subject.

"The family has noticed your attentions to my sister. It cannot be allowed to continue. You are aware that she is betrothed to Muhammad ibn Mustapha al Advokato, the son of the secretary to the Governor of Cordova and Granada? This marriage will be a very important one to our family and my father will gain considerable kudos from the fact that his daughter will be married to a person of such high esteem. In any event, no matter how highly we think of you, and we do, there is no way that a non-Muslim man can marry a Muslim girl in our society. A Muslim man can marry a non-Muslim girl but not the other way round," said Uzmir emphatically.

"And what is the logic behind that?" Elvin asked somewhat testily.

"Islam considers the husband to be the head of the family and, therefore, a Muslim woman cannot marry a non-Muslim because she would be under the control of someone outside of our Faith. That man may prevent her from practising her religion and their children may well be brought up as non-Muslims. That is why the Prophet has forbidden it. There are no conditions mentioned in the holy books where this would be permitted," Uzmir attempted to explain.

Elvin looked disappointed. " I feel that she enjoys my company and I must confess I have a growing liking for her," he muttered, "but do you not think that you are drawing certain conclusions from this that are somewhat exaggerated?"

"My friend, we do not think so," said Uzmir. "We have noticed certain changes in her since you arrived. There is no doubt that she finds you interesting and attractive. She is but a slip of a girl in many ways. She is a little flirtatious and obviously meeting with someone from another land has been different and intriguing for her. She has to learn a little more about her duty in life and not to be too wilful with regard to the wishes of her family. Her father wishes her to marry Muhammad and that is where her duty lies."

Elvin remained silent.

"Come, my friend, there are surely many other women of your own religion who would be honoured to be betrothed to such a warrior as yourself. Tayri is not for you. If it is a question of your carnal instincts coming to the fore after all this time, I will ask Naima to visit you in your room tonight."

Naima was one of the slave girls attached to the household. She was from a Berber tribe far to the south in Morocco, which had been in conflict with the union of tribes that made up the ruling dynasty that had conquered most of North Africa and Al Andalus. She had been captured as a child during one of the raids on her tribe and had been sold into slavery in Al Andalus. She was a pretty girl but Elvin knew this was no answer to the problem of the growing feelings for Tayri, which were raging in his mind. He had no real desire to make use of a young woman who may have been used regularly by the rest of the men in the household. But he said nothing for fear of offending Uzmir.

After Uzmir had departed Elvin felt somewhat depressed. He did not know how he felt really. He had not yet contemplated marriage with Tayri. He had just enjoyed the company of a very attractive female, with whom he felt totally at ease. True, he had felt more than a touch of jealousy when Muhammad had visited the house and had been rather disappointed to hear of Tayri's betrothal to him. He knew that she did not like this man and probably did not want to marry him. But she did not wish to offend her father.

Elvin did not know what he thought really and all sorts of emotions were battling against one another in his mind. Did he feel more for this young woman than he thought? She was certainly a most attractive and innocent creature – perhaps the most beautiful young woman he had ever encountered. But was it just a little innocent dalliance with which he had become involved whilst he was a guest of the family in their house? He was far from sure and he was not happy at the way he felt. He knew there was the potential for offending the family, which had sheltered him so kindly for all this time and, yet, he felt strangely drawn to her.

Elvin did not sleep well that night. He felt hot and tossed and turned and could not really settle. Part way during the night he was conscious of somebody being in the room. He awoke with a start and once his eyes had become accustomed to the darkness he was aware that Naima was standing by his bed.

She was certainly a handsome young girl. Her skin was dark, almost chocolate in complexion. She had full red lips and eyes as black as jet. She held a candle and the flickering flame enhanced her seductive charms in a way, which could hardly be imagined. She muttered soothing and sensuous words in a Berber dialect that Elvin could not understand but whose meaning could not be mistaken. Her eyelids were heavily covered in blue make-up. Dark eyes stared down at him from under thick lashes in an unmistakably enticing way.

In an instant, the robe, that she was wearing, had fallen to her waist and Elvin was left to gaze upon the fullest, firmest pair of dark breasts he had seen for a long time, encircled by aureoles of the darkest brown, from which projected black nipples, erect and straining towards the stars.

Elvin was conscious of a warm feeling creeping into his loins but he knew this was not really what he wanted.

"You like me?" asked Naima in Berber that Elvin could understand.

"Yes, I like you very much," said Elvin. "You are a very pretty girl. But you must go. I have no need of you this night."

"You would like me to send Abdullah to you?" she asked puzzled. Abdullah was one of the male slaves attached to the household.

"No, no, no," cried Elvin. "I have no need of anybody. Please go. I am tired and wish to sleep.

"But my master will be offended that I have not brought you pleasure," she said with a worried look on her countenance.

"Do not worry," said Elvin. "I will explain to him and you will not get into trouble."

With that, Naima, looking almost relieved, made herself decent and scuttled off into the night. Elvin sighed, chuckled to himself, and turned over and sank into a deep sleep.

The next morning Elvin was passing the door to Aderbal's laboratory when a voice called to him.

"Elvin, my son, can I have a word with you?" It was Aderbal.

Elvin entered and Aderbal asked politely, "Did you sleep well the past night?" There was the faintest glimmer of a smile on Aderbal's face but Elvin revealed nothing.

"Yes, thank you, I slept well," he said.

"I am glad I have seen you," said Aderbal, "for there is a matter I wish to discuss with you. I have a request to make of you."

"Please tell me," replied Elvin. "If there is any way I can repay your kind hospitality, I would be most willing to help."

"It concerns Tayri," said Aderbal and Elvin's heart sank for a moment. "I am sure my son has spoken to you of this matter. You will be aware that the marriage of Tayri to Muhammad is of great importance to my family and I wish nothing to spoil the occasion."

Elvin wondered whether this was a veiled hint to him to cool his attentions to Tayri and not to do anything, which would disrupt the marriage plans. But the request was, perhaps, much simpler that that.

"In just over a week's time," said Aderbal, "my daughter, with wedding gifts from our family and her personal belongings, will be travelling to Cordova to join the family of Muhammad in preparation for her marriage to him."

The thought that Tayri was to depart and that he might never see her again did not lighten Elvin's depression regarding the matter.

"I understood that might be the case in the not too distant future," was his mumbled comment.

"My problem is that the journey to Cordova is fraught with danger in these uncertain days. The forces of the Christian Kings are making frequent incursions into our territory and sometimes attacking caravans and stealing horses, booty and women. Recently they have been striking at caravans well inside our territory and isolated bands have even been reported as far south as the main route to Cordova. I have been informed that a small Christian force arrived in an area half way between Granada and that place only some two weeks ago. It is a matter that troubles me somewhat."

"What do you propose to do?" enquired Elvin.

"We may well have to take an alternative, but longer, route through the mountains to try to get behind them. My daughter will have to be accompanied by a strong escort to protect her on this potentially perilous journey. All my sons will be accompanying her together with a contingent of the Governor's guard from the Kadima. Fortunately Muhammad, her betrothed, has agreed to meet us with a force of his men at a castle half way between here and Cordova. He will take her on from there."

"I am sure she will be in good hands," remarked Elvin, hating the very thought of Tayri being anywhere near Muhammad.

"This is where I have my request of you," said Aderbal. "With all your experience and training as a Templar knight you would be of invaluable aid to my sons in their endeavour. I would deem it a great favour if you would accompany them on their journey."

Elvin had to think carefully. He reflected upon all that had happened since he had left Egypt and knew he would be in even deeper trouble with the Templar Order if he took up arms against Christian knights. So regretfully there was no hesitation in his reply to Aderbal's request:

"Please do not ask me to do this thing, sir. Uzmir and I went through many adventures together after we escaped from our prison in Egypt but I have never taken up arms against my Christian brothers. You must know that I am under oath not so to do. I am sure you can appreciate my position."

"Surely I can," replied Aderbal. "It had occurred to me that it might be something you would wish to do but I understand your position and the importance of any oath. We will talk no more of the matter."

Then a thought occurred to Elvin. Whether it was profound disappointment with regard to the betrothal of Tayri or just the onset of homesickness after so many years away, he suddenly felt perhaps the time had come to leave this family and embark on the long journey back to Cornwall.

"There is one way, maybe, that I can help," he said. "I feel the time has come, perhaps, to leave your household, sir. I have appreciated very much your family's great kindness towards me. I have been thinking for some time," he lied, "that I ought to return to my home across the sea. I would be happy to escort your daughter on, at least, part of her journey. But I must state two conditions.

"Firstly I would request that I be permitted to leave the caravan at an appropriate point and be given assistance in slipping across the Christian lines so that I can commence my journey home. Secondly, it should be understood by all that I cannot, on account of my oath to the Templar Order, fight against any Christian knights, who may attack.

But I will defend Tayri to the death against bandits, thieves or anybody else who might attack us."

"I understand what you are saying, my son. We will all be very sorry to see you go — not least Uzmir. But I can appreciate how your native land is drawing you back to her shores. Perhaps you are right in wishing to return there. Your help on the journey, however modest, would be much appreciated and we will, of course, render you every assistance in leaving Al Andalus safely. I feel that I will be losing not only a daughter, but also someone I have come to regard as an adopted son. It will be a sad day."

Elvin was much touched by this warm statement from Aderbal. He made his excuses quickly and returned to his room. There was a small tear in the corner of his eye, but he sniffed and told himself this was very unworthy of a warrior knight and that, perhaps, he was getting soft from his stay with this family.

He had to admit to himself, though, that he would miss them. They had been at such pains to make him welcome and he thought it would be very unlikely that he would ever see them again.

It was a deeply depressing thought in many ways. He would particularly feel the loss of the fatherly advice and guidance of the old man, who had done much to broaden his education and make him think in a different way about other races and creeds. It would, indeed, be a sad day when he had to leave.

On the due day an enormous throng of relatives and well-wishers gathered to say farewell to the bride-to-be in the courtyard of the house. There was a great deal of hustle and bustle as people kept on appearing with gifts for the bride and groom, which even included various sorts of livestock like sheep and goats. Musicians had gathered to accompany the prayers and blessings to be uttered before the departure.

As is usual on these occasions Tayri's mother and sisters-in-law and several female relatives were in tears at the prospect of her leaving. There was a distinct possibility that they might never see her again especially in the dangerous days, in which they were living.

Elvin, like the other men who were to escort Tayri was dressed in a smart white turban and full length, loose robe of the same colour, impeccably bleached. Elvin remained unobtrusive whilst all the relatives said their farewells.

Tayri was a picture of stunning beauty. She was wearing a long loose indigo caftan. A multi-coloured piece of fabric of bright pastel colours, perhaps five metres long and two wide, was wound round her body several times. Both the front and back portions of the cloth were secured at each turn at the collarbones with a decorative brooch. The last two metres had been left unwound to be pulled up and draped over her headdress if necessary.

The headdress was also of many beautiful colours and went on top of the hood of the caftan. Braided plaits hung down on each side of her head and fell almost to her waist. The front of the headdress was decorated with silver coins, turquoise, coral and mother of pearl ornaments attached to a leather band.

Henna swirls had been painstakingly painted onto her hands and feet and there was just the trace of the intricately patterned make-up that adorned her face, visible above her veil. A sandy, bronze coloured make-up on her eyelids and the blackened eyelashes only served to enhance the beauty of her incredible blue green eyes.

Round her neck she wore a magnificent necklace of filigree silver ornaments, which covered her neck and hung down over her chest.

The slow beat of a drum heralded the time for departure and prayers and blessings were accompanied by music and dance.

The men of the family escorted Tayri to the gate of the house.

Outside was assembled a caravan of horses to transport the wedding gifts and the people who were to embark on the journey. A special detachment of the Governor's Mauritanian Guard, black warriors, renowned for their bravery, drew up alongside.

Tayri was assisted up onto a magnificent white horse of obviously good stock. Everybody else mounted and the last gestures of goodbye were made.

At a command from Aderbal the caravan set off and picked its way down through the steep, rocky streets of the area of Granada, which was later to be known as the Albaicin.

As they clattered down over the cobbles the narrow streets were crowded with refugees and several times Aderbal had to cry out:

"Make way, make way for the bride!" The crowd would then draw back at further urging from the Mauritanian guards and the horses would struggle through in single file.

They rode out through the same gate, by which Elvin and Uzmir had entered the city many months before. They reached the river Darro at the foot of the hill and crossed it by the same old, humped back, bridge. They then turned out onto the track, which led them away from the city and northwards towards Cordova.

It was on the second day that the attack came. It was swift and totally unexpected for they considered themselves to be well within Moorish territory.

The caravan had been making steady progress with a strong sun beating down from a totally cloudless sky.

Suddenly round a bend came a woman and two young boys running at full speed towards them.

"Help us, in the name of Allah, help us," the woman cried desperately. "The Christians are coming."

"Form up around the Lady Tayri," barked Aderbal to the Mauritanians. "Elvin, dismount and find cover quickly. This fight is not for you! The rest of you without arms find cover as well! Iddur," he instructed his youngest son, "ride with all due haste and warn Muhammad that we are under attack and beg him to come to our aid."

Elvin ran along a rock-strewn path and scrambled up a small embankment covered with large boulders. He took cover behind these and had a good view of the surrounding area.

The woman and the children were still trying desperately to make the safety of the caravan. Almost immediately Elvin heard the sound of the pursuing horses. Round the bend, riding at full rein, galloped a sizeable group of Christian knights, swords drawn and ready for slaughter. The woman stopped, out of breath and the two little boys turned and urged her desperately to keep running:

"Come on, Mummy, don't stop now. We are almost there."

Almost as it was said, the horses were upon her and a burly knight lent down and grabbed her by the waist to lift her onto his horse. The horses trampled the two screaming young boys into the ground before the knights realised the presence of the halted caravan. The horses drew up some paces distant. There was a rapid exchange of words between the leading knights, who now realised what a prize they had chanced upon. The horses neighed and bucked and then charged forward again towards the richly laden caravan.

From his hiding place Elvin could see most of what was going on. He wanted desperately to help out but he dare not for fear of discovery of his identity. The sight of several white smocks adorned with red crosses further convinced him of the wisdom of staying out of sight.

A blood-curdling scene began to unfold before him. The Christian knights, seated high on their prancing chargers, launched themselves into the crowd dealing out death with their sharply honed broadswords. The Mauritanian Guards fought bravely to defend the caravan but were heavily outnumbered by the Christian troop.

Elvin felt numbed as he watched, seemingly helpless to prevent what was turning into a disastrous rout. He was in two minds. He was very conscious of his own precarious position, if discovered, but, at the same time, he felt he could not stand by and see people he had grown to accept as a surrogate family slaughtered before his eyes.

Elvin was left in no further doubt when the knights beat down the last of the Mauritanians to gain the reins of Tayri's horse. Aderbal and Meddur already thrown from their mounts were fighting desperately on foot to get to her. Elvin was already half way down the path towards the melee. Tayri was screaming and sobbing, her panic stricken cries to her father to free her getting more and more hysterical.

Meddur was the first to get to Tayri but was sliced near in half as a Templar brought down his sword with full force onto his shoulder, shattering his collarbone. It was a deep cutting blow only halted eventually by Meddur's breastbone. Aderbal followed him and was immediately struck down with another blow.

As Elvin arrived upon the scene, Tayri's horse had been turned and was being led off at full gallop by a few of the knights. The others, dragging the booty-laden packhorses behind them, quickly followed them.

Elvin quickly leapt onto a stray mount and set off in pursuit with no thought of the foolhardiness of his action. He had but one thought – the rescue of Tayri, the one thing in his life that he was now convinced was most important to him. He had no idea how he was going to achieve this. He was lone figure pursuing a large group of well armed knights who would make short work of any effort he made to get anywhere near the girl.

If the Templars abided by their vows it was possible they might not harm her, although their general attitude towards those they regarded as non-believers did not fill Elvin with any great confidence about this.

He was still within sight of the escaping horde but was, by this time, beginning to have second thoughts. It was probable that, when they found out who she was, they would demand a ransom and, therefore, she might not come to too much harm. In the meantime the family might be able to gather together some reinforcements and make a bid to rescue her. He had slowed to a canter now and was still turning over the problem in his mind when one of the Templar knights stopped and wheeled round to face him and then began advancing towards him in a threatening manner. As he approached Elvin was convinced he knew the face and the battle scar that marked it. Straining to get a better view he suddenly gasped. There, confronting him some eighty paces distant was Enrique de Larraga, his captor at the monastery in Aragon and the person responsible for his torture and eventual initiation into the Templar Order.

Elvin knew well that this was not the time to renew the acquaintance. He turned tail and fled, very conscious of the mocking laughter and the obscene shouts and gestures that followed his retreat.

CHAPTER SIXTEEN

More Mysteries Unfold

A couple of months after Peter's accident he was invited to a meeting in London attended by Bernard Harper, John Trehane and several other leading personalities from the dig in Cornwall.

After re-acquainting themselves with one another and catching up on all the gossip Bernard Harper drew the meeting to order and introduced the matters to be discussed.

"Well," he said, "I think you can gather why we are all here. It's been established quite clearly that there was once a medieval castle on the headland above Tremennek Bay and, indeed, we are now in possession of the authenticated original document, signed and sealed by Richard the Lionheart, giving permission for its construction. However, it still remains a mystery to us as to why it was attacked and razed to the ground in the manner that it was and why there are no other apparent records of it as far as we know.

"I think the next stage in our work will be to flush out any other records there might be on the subject and to try to discover why it was thought necessary to expunge all traces of the existence of the castle from the records."

"That's going to be a pretty tall order I would think," remarked John Trehane.

"You can say that again," said Harper, "but I feel it's got to be done before we close the book on this one."

"Well, where do we start?" asked Peter.

Harper thought for a moment and said, "I think that we have to get down to some pretty smart detective work and look at all the possible sources of information that might be available to us. That's the only way we are going to get even the remotest clue as to what happened. So, we've got to dig out what we can of property records for Cornwall, records of the County Sheriff, records of the Bishop of Exeter and any other ecclesiastical records we can get our hands on. This may even mean a trip to Rome for someone. There is also some connection with the Templars, which needs to be followed up. Legend suggests that our

Le Gard may have been excommunicated and also expelled by the Templar Order. So what had he been up to? We need all the pieces of the jig-saw to start to assemble the overall picture."

Tasks were assigned and then everybody returned home.

When Peter got back to Marshallswick he picked up a message from his mother on the answer phone.

She had not been well herself in recent weeks and was rather concerned that he had not been to visit her. It had not seemed to occur to her that he had been recovering from a rather serious accident himself and had not been able to drive.

But that was how it had been, increasingly, since the passing of his father. His mother had turned in on herself and had become more and more self-centred. Peter had found it difficult to avoid having rows with her and had tended to rely too much on Mary to calm things and take a more diplomatic approach. He smiled to himself, as his mind had tended to be full of rather negative thoughts about Mary of late. However, he had to admit to himself that this was something she had been rather good at and he was going to miss her rescuing him from his mother's sometimes barbed tongue.

Peter called his mother and immediately made the mistake of asking her how she was. She went through the usual ritual of outlining just about every ache and pain known to man before saying:

"I was wondering when you were going to come up to see me. I haven't seen you for months."

"Mum, I was there only ten days ago. If you remember I was hobbling around on a crutch."

"Oh, yes," she said, and then as an afterthought, "How are you?"

"I am a lot better now," he replied, "but I'm terribly busy at the moment. I can't always get away just like that."

"I've had terrible pains in my stomach lately," she said, "and I wanted to talk to you about something really important."

Peter put his hand on his brow and sighed to himself.

"Mum," he said, "if you have these pains you must go to the doctor."

"Oh, they're no good," she said dismissing the whole medical profession out of hand.

"What is it you want to talk to me about?" he asked. "Is it so important that it won't wait for a day or two?"

"Well. I don't know. The point is I don't want to discuss it over the telephone. Are you sure you can't come up to Kenilworth next weekend?"

"Mum, I can't promise. I've just got too much work on at the moment. But I'll let you know."

"I bet you've got enough time to swan off down to Cornwall sunning yourself," his mother remarked. It was intended, he thought, as some kind of emotional blackmail and completely ignored the fact that it was his work that had taken him to Cornwall. He found it really annoying that she thought any visit to Cornwall must be for a holiday and did not consider archaeology as a serious means of employment at all.

"Look, Mum, I've got to go now. I'll call you during the week." He put the phone down and found himself wondering what on earth it could be that she wished to talk to him about. He shrugged his shoulders and then forgot all about it. It was not that he was unfeeling or unsympathetic towards his mother's ills. It was just that she had cried wolf on many occasions before.

The following week T6 (as Bernard Harper referred to them in e-mails - i.e. the Tremennek Six) met for a progress meeting. The minute of the meeting read as follows:

"Extensive researches have taken place amongst manorial records, court records, records of inquests or inquisitions, entries in the Fine Rolls (records of fines) and other records relating to property. These researches failed to reveal anything in addition to the evidence of the grant of land to William Le Gard by Richard the Lionheart in 1194, which was obtained thanks to the good offices of Mr. Daniel Hoffer of Chicago, USA.

There appears to be a wealth of documents relating to the later medieval period in Cornwall but few have survived from the thirteenth century and the majority of those that have, are in poor condition.

Records of oaths, taxation and wills produced no further evidence nor did the records of the criminal courts.

The one authoritative book on thirteenth century Cornwall makes no mention of the castle but strangely does mention one William Le Gard of Tremennek as a trader in tin ore at the time we are investigating. This information was apparently gleaned from the records of the Cornish Stannary Parliament, the body responsible for the regulation of the tin mining industry from 1198 during the reign of Richard the First.

This progress was disappointing but not wholly surprising. It is left to the committee to investigate ecclesiastical and possibly Templar sources to see if further light can be shed on what happened at Tremennek.

Peter Verity agreed to take on the task of investigating any ecclesiastical records and John Trehane agreed to follow up Templar sources. Peter Verity agreed to undertake his role so long as he was not called away to Granada for further investigations on the site there, in which case Bernard Harper agreed to act as his reserve."

Peter rang his mother again during the week. She seemed depressed and a little despondent but this was not an unusual state of affairs. He tried his best to raise her spirits but she stressed again that she needed to see him fairly urgently and that the matter could not be discussed over the telephone. He again re-iterated that he had a lot of work at the moment but that he would to get to see her as soon as he could.

Peter did not really know where to begin with his investigation of ecclesiastical records. After all it was not really his field. However, he had one contact, which he thought might be useful.

Among the members of his local tennis club in St. Albans, where he played on a somewhat irregular basis, he remembered a Paul Sweeney, who was the Education Officer for the local Catholic diocese. He was sure that he could be helpful.

Peter telephoned Sweeney and explained his problem and they arranged to meet a couple days later in a local hostelry.

For convenience sake they met in a well-known pub on the edge of St.Albans, where Peter put Sweeney fully in the picture.

"Hmm," said Sweeney, "this is a difficult one. You must realise that once Roman Catholicism became disestablished in Britain any records would have been in great peril. The dissolution of the monasteries in the time of Henry VIII did not help in any way and many records were lost during that time. That is the reason why ordinary citizens, trying to trace their family history, have so many problems before 1601.

"I suspect from what you tell me of this case that the details would have been placed in a secret diocesan archive anyway and during the dissolution of the monasteries many records of this sort would have been destroyed even if they had survived."

"Why do you say it would have been kept in a secret archive?" asked

Peter.

"Because, if you say he was married to a Saracen woman and was also excommunicated, it was probably a case of heresy. The Church would simply not tolerate any challenge to its authority in those days or, indeed, any intellectual arguments that sought to challenge the truth of the Christian religion. Islamic sympathies would have been highly suspect during the Crusades and not something that the Church would have liked the ordinary folk to have any knowledge of. Details of the case would have been kept in a secret archive most likely, which, in all probability, is no longer available to us."

"Right," said Peter, "so where does that leave us?"

"I think if you say that your knight was possibly excommunicated and, indeed, also expelled from the Order of the Temple, then it is quite likely that it was reported to Rome. If this was the case the record is possibly stored in the Vatican Archives and possibly even in their Secret Archives and that will mean seeking permission to access those archives, permission for which is not lightly given."

"Not even for an excommunication that took place nearly eight hundred years ago?" Peter asked with an air of incredulity.

"I'm afraid not, if it is judged not to be in the interests of our Holy Mother Church," was the answer.

"So to whom do I apply?" asked Peter.

"You will need to get in contact with the Cardinal, who is responsible for the Secret Archives, and apply for permission from the Holy Father himself."

"What are these Secret Archives?" asked Peter.

"Well, I don't know a lot about them," said Sweeney, "but I understand that there are some thirty miles of shelving housing records of scandals, secrets, and revelations of the sort that the Church would not want to be made public, extending from the very earliest times of Christianity. For example, you would find there details of Henry VIII's whole quarrel with the Church and his subsequent break with it and the establishment of the Church of England. It is quite possible that your friend's transgressions were such that they might have been reported to Rome and could have ended up in the Secret Archives, I really don't know."

"Right, well, I am very grateful to you. It is obvious I have to get in touch with Rome and have to try and get permission to examine the

Secret Archives in the Vatican. What would be the correct protocol?"

"Well, I would suggest that you send a letter outlining your request to the Archbishop of Westminster in the first instance," Sweeney replied. "He is not only the Head of the Catholic Church in Britain, but St. Albans lies within the Diocese of Westminster, for which, as Cardinal Archbishop, he is personally responsible. He is also my boss. You can mention that you have spoken to me, if you like."

"OK. Look, thank you very much. You really have been helpful"

"I wish you luck, anyway," said Sweeney in a way that did not suggest that he was overconfident about the ultimate success of this venture.

In due course Peter wrote to the Archbishop, addressing the letter to his Private Secretary, and awaited a reply. When it came it was very disappointing. The letter merely read:

"Thank you for your request, the nature of which has been drawn to the attention of His Grace the Cardinal Archbishop. I am instructed to inform you that the Secret Archives at the Vatican, to which you refer, are not normally open to other than a very limited number of approved scholars with specific purposes of interest to the Church and with the permission of the Holy Father himself. Regretfully His Grace does not feel that, with the present information before him, there would be any purpose served in supporting an application on your behalf to the Holy Father."

Peter took this news to the next meeting of T6. The committee was obviously very disappointed.

"It's like trying to get information out of the Kremlin during the Cold War," remarked John Trehane.

"Yes, it does seem difficult," said Bernard Harper. "What we've got to do is to ask ourselves as a committee what information we really do need. We don't need the Vatican to tell us there was a castle at Tremennek. We have enough evidence for that already. We don't need them to tell us that the castle was razed to the ground in the thirteenth century. What we do need, at the very least, is confirmation that a file exists on our knight and for them to give us his name and to tell us whether he was excommunicated or not. That would be a start. Access to the actual file could come later, perhaps"

"OK. I'll try the Archbishop's Office on that one," said Peter.

"Now," said Harper, "how have you got on, John"?

"Well, I managed to get hold of a guy, who has written extensively on the Templar Order and he was most helpful. Apparently there's no central core of documents because the Ottoman Turks probably destroyed the main archive of the Templars in the East in the sixteenth century. As a result we are left with a whole host of individual documents covering a variety of periods.

"If our friend did offend against the Templar Order then it would have been an offence or offences against the Templar Rule, which was almost, like the Army's Queen's Regulations for the Templar Order. It is relatively easy to consult this and find out about the system of penalties imposed. The Rule is in French rather than Latin because many of the brethren had only limited Latin. One thing that it does do, in explaining the penalties, is to illustrate them with actual incidents, which took place within the Order. Nowadays it has been translated into English, of course. So I'm sifting through it to see what I can come up with from that point of view.

"Written documents are the main source of information but there are a lot of gaps for various reasons. Since there seems to be a connection with Granada in Spain I am seriously looking at Spanish Templar records, which, I have been advised, are more extensive than those of some other parts of Europe."

"Fine," said Bernard, "carry on the good work and we'll meet again in a month's time."

Peter got into contact with the Diocese once again. There was initial scepticism about his second, somewhat scaled down, request but promises were made to look into the matter. During the course of the next three weeks he made several telephone calls to check on progress but nothing had been heard. The next meeting of T6 was fast approaching and he was getting a little frustrated when he received a further short letter, which provided the following information:

"You will be interested to note that it has been confirmed by the Cardinal in charge of the Vatican Archives that a document does exist relating to one Sir Elvin le Gard, Lord of the Manor of Tremennek in the County of Cornwall in England, the bull for whose excommunication was issued in the year 1227."

"Bingo," thought Peter.
The letter continued:

"This document is currently housed in the Secret Archives and access to it can only be gained with the permission of the Holy Father himself. The document is in a perilous state and it would seem unlikely that permission would be granted from this point of view alone."

"Well, at least we now know the guy's name and we have a date to work with," said Bernard Harper at the next meeting. "The destruction of the castle would have taken place some time after the issue of the bull. But it does seem to have been an extreme penalty. He must have been a very bad boy. I wonder what chance there would be of getting a site of this document?"

"It doesn't sound very promising, but we can keep trying," said Peter.

Peter was not the only person to report good news at the meeting. John Trehane had also made progress.

"Our investigation of Spanish Templar documents has also come up with the same name," he explained. "Dr. Anya Naziri has been most helpful in assisting with our enquiries on this one. She gave us a whole list of primary documentary Templar sources in Spain and a number of important secondary sources as well. It took a lot of hard work but one document produced a mention of a Le Gard. This document was entitled 'La Crónica de Enrique de Larraga', The Chronicle of Enrique de Larraga, which is a record of the exploits of a Templar knight from Aragon, who took part in the Crusades of the thirteenth century and, in particular, in the Reconquest of Spain from the Moors. He mentions an Elvin Le Gard, who was a Templar knight from Cornwall in England, who fought in Spain and Egypt, and was later expelled from the Order on the grounds of desertion and apostasy, or the abandonment of religious faith, and other heinous crimes."

"Well done, both of you," said Bernard Harper, "we now seem to be making some good progress. They certainly must have been heinous crimes for them to burn his castle down and to try to destroy all record of him. I certainly have never come across such a state of affairs before. I wonder if we shall ever know?"

"Well, we've not made bad progress so far," said Peter. "It would be nice to have a look at that Vatican file."

"Exactly," said Bernard.

The next day Peter had a call from Anya in Granada.

"Hi," said Peter, "John Trehane has been telling us how helpful you've been in digging out Templar documents over there. One, in particular, has been very useful."

"Larraga's Chronicle, yes," she said.

"Look, Peter, we've made another important discovery. It's not strictly to do with your field of medieval armour but I feel somebody from the English end of things should be here. It's that important. Personally I would prefer it if it was you. Do you think you can arrange it?"

"Yes, we've been half expecting something like this so I've been delegated to come in any event."

"Oh, good," she replied. "How soon can you get here?"

"I'll book a flight as soon as I can," he said. "I should be in Granada in a day or two. What is it that you have got?"

"I would prefer not to say over the phone," said Anya, "and I think it would be better if even your committee did not know at the moment. Suffice to say that it a find of some importance and somewhat controversial. I think you are going to be absolutely stunned by it."

CHAPTER SEVENTEEN

Kidnap, Ransom And Rescue

Elvin galloped back to the caravan. All across the trail were strewn the bodies of the dead and wounded. The attack had not lasted much longer than ten minutes but had brought devastation to the caravan. The Christians had only been interested in the booty and capturing prisoners, for whom there might be a potential ransom.

Uzmir was desperately trying to do what he could for the wounded.

"Elvin," he cried. "Thanks be to Allah that you are back. With all your reading about medical matters you must be able to help to some degree. Don't bother with those that are close to death, but see what you can do for the others."

"Elvin," came a cry from not far away. It was Aderbal. He had an awful, gaping wound in his upper chest.

Elvin approached him and crouched down by him. "Oh, my God, what can I do?"

"Do not panic, my son. Now is the time to put to the test some of which you have learned," croaked Aderbal. He had extreme difficulties in breathing but managed to gasp out:

"My horse is over there. In the saddlebags you will find my medical pouch. Bring it over here and I will guide you." He winced with pain for a moment.

Elvin sought the saddlebags and eventually found the leather medical pouch.

"You must clean the wound first. Find a water bottle and some clean cloth and begin to bathe the wound."

Elvin followed Aderbal's instructions to the letter.

"Now," Aderbal directed, "there is a bottle in the pouch labelled 'purified alcohol'." Pour some of this liquid onto a cloth and bathe the wound with that. It will hurt but do not worry. I can bear it."

Aderbal grimaced as Elvin applied the alcohol.

"What is this liquid for?" enquired Elvin.

"It is an antiseptic," replied Aderbal still in great pain. " It will help to prevent the wound from festering."

"Should the wound not be cauterised?" asked Elvin, referring to the usual way the knights were treated in the field.

"No, this is a more effective way. You are going to sew the wound up. In the pouch you will find some material like the thread used by women in their needlework. It is made from catgut."

"Made from what?" cried Elvin.

"From catgut. It's a thread made from the intestines of animals. It is the only really effective way of dealing with wounds. You can sew together the wound with this thread and it has no adverse reaction. Come on, please find a needle and start sewing the edges of the wound together. It will hurt but give me a piece of leather to bite on and I will get through it."

Elvin was very nervous. Needlework was not something that a warrior knight from England was usually called upon to employ. He had watched women doing it, when he had been a young boy and he now wished he had paid more attention. It was not seen as a manly occupation at all amongst his fellow knights.

After the first few attempts at sewing the wound together he began to become more proficient and could gradually see the sides of the wound being drawn together. Aderbal was in obvious pain and was biting hard into the leather strap, which Elvin had given him.

When Elvin had completed the sewing up of the wound Aderbal said:

"Good work, my son. You have learned well. Bind up my wound with some clean cloth." Elvin set about this task equally conscientiously.

"Now take the pouch and see if you can help some of the others," Aderbal said in a state of complete exhaustion.

Elvin and Uzmir helped those that they could and then the survivors, that were able, set about the grim task of burying the dead.

"What are we going to do now?" asked Elvin.

"We will wait for Muhammad and then we are going to have to get the wounded back to Granada, so that they can be properly cared for. Then we will have to plan a further course of action."

"We've got to rescue Tayri," Elvin blurted out in desperation. "God only knows what some of them might do to her."

"In due course my friend," said Uzmir. "We don't know where they are going or where they have come from. There are a couple of wounded Christians. I thought of slaying them but we will take them with us as well. They may be able to give us some information."

Muhammad and his men joined them the next day and they agreed that Aderbal's family would have to return to Granada. Muhammad demanded that he be included in any rescue attempt and Iddur promised to inform him of any developments.

The journey back to Granada was slow and painstaking. Some of the wounded died on the way. Aderbal was breathing badly but surviving. He looked ill and grim for he had now learned that his son Meddur had been killed as well as having lost his daughter to the kidnappers.

The two Christian prisoners were taken to the Kadima fortress where they were later interrogated. It seemed, from what they were able to tell their interrogators, that a ransom demand was almost certain and that they only had to wait.

Sure enough a few days later a messenger came running up to the house from the main gate down by the river.

"Master," he said to Uzmir, "there are six Christian knights, carrying a white flag, at the main gate saying that they wish to speak to Aderbal, the Governor's physician."

"I will go," said Uzmir. "Elvin, you come with me but keep yourself out of sight. See if you can identify anyone."

They made their way down the hill to the gate. Elvin remained at a viewing point on the walls whilst Uzmir went down to talk, at a guarded distance, to the leader of the delegation. The knights had been ordered to remain at the far end of the humped back bridge by the Governor's guards. Elvin had no trouble in recognising Enrique de Larraga.

"What is it that you want?" asked Uzmir.

"We wish to talk to Aderbal, the Governor's physician. Clearly you are not he," said de Larraga.

"Aderbal is gravely wounded and unable to come here. I am his son."

"Tell him that we hold his daughter, Tayri, whom we will not harm if we can exchange her for fifty Christian prisoners from the Kadima dungeons, whose names we have here." He held up a scroll with the names on it.

"How do we know that you do, indeed, hold my sister?"

Enrique then held up the magnificent necklace of filigree silver ornaments that Tayri had been wearing when the caravan had been attacked.

"I will have to consult my father," said Uzmir.

"Do not take long, my friend," said Enrique. "Our patience is very limited."

"Guards," said Uzmir, "make sure they have water for themselves and their horses. I will return shortly."

Uzmir and Elvin met back together again and returned to the house with the list of prisoners' names. They went to see Aderbal. He looked a very sick man. He had considerable difficulty in breathing and struggled to speak with them.

"Fifty prisoners seems a lot to exchange for one young girl even though she is the betrothed of a person of status. They may not even know of the marriage," whispered Aderbal. "Do you know any of the people on the list, either of you?"

"Well," said Uzmir, "they have obviously listed their best knights, whom they want returned to them."

"You must negotiate with them. We don't want to be taken for fools even though we dearly want Tayri returned to us," Aderbal said. "Do what you can to reduce the number," he instructed Uzmir.

Uzmir returned to the gate with Elvin looking on from the battlements.

"You know full well that fifty prisoners is out of the question," Uzmir said.

"Hah," said Enrique, "you Moors love to haggle. It is never a straight bargain for you people."

"But it is always an honest bargain," Uzmir replied. "That I cannot often say of you Christian dogs."

"Be careful how you talk, Moor, or your sister is a dead woman," threatened Enrique.

"If there is no bargain, none of you will leave these gates alive," retorted Uzmir.

"What are you offering for this woman, then?" asked Enrique.

"We will return to you the two wounded men that we have tended since you attacked us," replied Elvin.

"And that's it? Do not jest Moor. We are not in the mood. Your threats will do you no good. Kill us and thousands of Crusaders will attack your city and raze it to the ground," threatened Enrique.

"You know that that is an idle threat," said Uzmir. "This city and its fortress is the most impregnable in the whole of Al Andalus. Reduce your demands and we can make a bargain."

"Thirty prisoners, then," said Enrique.

"We will give you five," said Uzmir.

"No," shouted Enrique wheeling on his horse. "I say twenty prisoners and that's my last offer."

"We will give you ten and you can choose the names of the ones who are most valuable to you," said Uzmir as he stood his ground.

Enrique shrugged his shoulders and looked frustrated but then turned to have a whispered conversation with his colleagues.

"It is agreed. Ten prisoners of our choosing." The two men shook hands on this.

"I will send a messenger soon telling you where to bring the prisoners and there we will exchange your sister for them," was Enrique's final word.

That evening Aderbal called for Elvin to visit him at his sickbed. He looked worse and his face was ashen and haggard.

"I have called you here, Elvin, because I fear my life is draining away," he whispered.

"No, that can't be so," said Elvin with a note of extreme concern. "Is there nothing that can be done?"

"No, my son. I fear I am destined to journey to Paradise."

"My efforts to sew up your wound must have been too unskilled. I plead for your forgiveness," said Elvin with a depressed look upon his face.

"No, my son. It is not your fault. The sword that tore into my chest must have pierced a lung. I am not long for this world."

"I do not want you to leave us, sir. You have taught me so much and treated me with the greatest kindness," Elvin said, struggling to hold back the tears.

"Do not distress, yourself, Elvin. You are a fine young man. You are intelligent and more open-minded than many of your faith. You are willing to learn and I have no doubt that, in time, and, should you wish it, you could become a very good physician. I am proud that you are Uzmir's friend. Promise me one thing before I die?"

"I will – anything," replied Elvin.

"Promise me that you will rescue Tayri. I know that you feel deeply for her and I am honoured that such a worthy person as yourself has found favour in my daughter. I know that it is deeply disappointing to you that she is betrothed to another. But you know that you cannot marry her. Our religious law may be difficult for you to comprehend but it is the way of our people. In spite of all that I am relying upon you, my friend, to assist my sons, in every way, in rescuing her from the clutches of those evil men so that she can be married according to my wishes. Will you promise me that?"

"I promise, I promise," said Elvin and left Aderbal to sleep.

During the night Elvin awoke to hear the wailing of the women and he knew then that Aderbal had passed on from the world. He was buried with due ceremony the next day.

The messenger appeared at the city gate two days later. Uzmir was instructed to bring the ten named prisoners to a mountainous region to the north of Granada, and to meet Enrique de Larraga before the Muslim held castle there in a week's time.

The arrangements were accordingly made for the release of the prisoners into the care of Uzmir and he was given a further detachment of the Mauritanian Guard after the Deputy Governor had granted his permission.

Uzmir and Elvin arrived at the castle in good time. Iddur had gone on in advance to inform Muhammad in Cordova. They were expected to arrive within a day or two. Everybody was edgy because this was a front line border region subject to frequent incursions by the Christians. There were many fortifications and they frequently changed hands. This castle had remained unscathed however. It was perched on a rocky peak in a very mountainous area and its towers and walled areas were all at different levels, which made it extremely difficult to attack. There was a good view of the landscape all around and its Moorish occupants were continually at the ready.

Elvin became rapidly aware of the heady scent of the pines and the sound of the rushing rivers, which criss-crossed the area. There was much wildlife and there was reputed to be good hunting around the castle with stags and wild boar in abundance. But they had no time for that. That evening Iddur and Muhammad arrived with a detachment of men.

The next day the guards on watch summoned them to the walls. The six knights had appeared with a white flag below the castle calling for

Uzmir.

"Have you brought my sister," Uzmir yelled down to them.

"Have you brought the prisoners?" Enrique yelled back.

"Yes we have," cried Uzmir and he had the prisoners brought to the battlements so that Enrique could see them.

"Then we have your sister," Enrique shouted. "Bring them down to the foot of the castle and let them walk towards us. As soon as you let them go, we will release your sister and we will give her a horse, as befits her rank, so that she can ride in the opposite direction."

It took a while for them to shepherd the prisoners down the tortuous, sloping paths, which ran around the castle. They eventually arrived at the bottom and halted. Nothing happened at first as each party stood about two hundred paces apart eyeballing one another suspiciously.

Enrique brought Tayri to the front mounted on a brown nag. She was still in her heavy wedding caftan and wearing the multi-coloured headdress that Elvin remembered from the day of their departure but there was no sign of the jewelled attachments. Elvin wondered what had happened to the beautiful white horse on which she had been mounted when they had been attacked.

"Let the prisoners go," shouted Enrique. Muhammad said little but his hand was on his sword at all times and he looked grim faced.

The prisoners were untied and released and began walking towards the Christians. At the same time Enrique smacked the rump of Tayri's horse and it trotted slowly off towards the castle. Elvin became a bit worried as Tayri looked very unsteady on its back.

The horse passed the prisoners, who had started out walking but were now beginning to run in the opposite direction. Tayri did, indeed, look unsteady and about fifty paces before reaching them she fell off the horse.

"Tayri, are you all right?" shouted Uzmir and they all began to run towards her. When they got to her she was face down in the sandy dust. Elvin got there first, just in front of Muhammad and turned her over. Two glazed black eyes stared up at him.

"It's not Tayri," Muhammad shouted. "The bastards have tricked us."

Uzmir looked at the woman's face and drew back her veil. He was staring down at the face of the mother of the two little boys, whom the knights had been pursuing before they attacked the caravan. She was dead.

The knights, along with their returned colleagues, had quickly disappeared into the trees.

Uzmir and Muhammad both panicked and began shouting up to the castle to send down their horses and giving orders to the Mauritanian Guard to pursue the fleeing Christians. It was Iddur, Aderbal's youngest son, who counselled caution.

"Steady, steady," he cried, "Much as I love my sister, panicking is not the answer. Enrique obviously carefully planned this. They must have had horses hidden in the trees. They will be well away by now and don't forget that they have the advantage of knowing the area much better than we do."

"Yes, you are quite right, my brother," said Uzmir. "We must think carefully — and seek help from the locals. Everybody back up to the castle," he ordered.

They held an immediate council of war to try and decide how they would put right the catastrophe, which had occurred. The castle was in the temporary hands of Mahmud al-Askari, a mercenary chieftain, who had fought in Palestine. There had been many skirmishes in the area and the border territories of Al Andalus appeared to be in complete chaos.

"We have seen these knights in this area before so I don't think they are too far away. They could be planning an attack upon the castle anyway. In which case you may find there are more of them than you would wish. I personally would advise that you do not risk confrontation with them," said Mahmud.

"We have to rescue Tayri. Any other proposal is out of the question," Uzmir interjected. Everybody nodded his head in agreement.

"You are fools but I understand your desire to rescue your kin. We have a couple of tracker scouts who know the territory very well. I will lend them to you but I cannot release any soldiers. You will have to use your Mauritanians."

"We are grateful to you for your help and hospitality," said Uzmir.

They loaded up with provisions and water and set out a few hours later. The trackers were soon able to pick up the trail of fleeing horses.

Uzmir was not totally happy about the Mauritanians. These were soldiers who were used to fighting on sun-baked, sandy plains. They had no experience of crawling around unobserved in forested regions.

But at least they were known to be dependable and he knew that they would fight to the last man if called upon. Muhammad's contingent would be useful as well.

They made slow progress as the trackers went about their work examining the ground, and the bushes and trees around, for any sign of the fleeing band. Occasionally they would disappear ahead, scouting the trail before them and making sure there were no surprises in store for them. They rode in single file, observing complete silence unless absolutely necessary.

The trail ran through pinewoods dotted with rocky outcrops. They crossed the infant river Gualdalquivir, the longest river in Al Andalus, which had its source not far away. They began descending down a wide trail covered with twigs and fallen branches as well as a thick carpet of pine needles. To the left of them was a steep drop to the valley floor. They crossed the stream various times along the valley floor. Occasionally a refreshingly beautiful cascade poured down the mountainside. There were a variety of different trees lower down in the valley including willows and there was also a heady scent of aromatic plants like lavender and oregano.

At one point the trackers motioned them to stop and were listening hard for a sound. Then they all smiled as they recognised the grunts and snorts of a group of wild boar foraging in a copse ahead of them. Normally these would have been regarded as a good hunting prize but they had other objectives on their minds and passed round them.

They camped for the night in a clearing dominated by a craggy rock on which they stationed lookouts.

The trackers disappeared during the night and, at first, Uzmir thought that they had deserted them. But very early in the morning they returned.

"We have found them," said one of them who was called Asafu. "They are resting up in some abandoned buildings not too far from here."

"Well done," said Uzmir. "How many of them are there?"

"There are the six knights and the prisoners you exchanged plus the knights that attacked you – about thirty in all."

"There was no woman with them?" enquired Uzmir.

"Not as far as I we could see," said Asafu.

They moved out the next morning very early. They rode up over the pine-clad hill ahead of them. The trees all around were tall and sturdy and Elvin thought to himself how useful they would be for the masts of ships. They slipped over the crest of the mountain in a disciplined silence. Then the two trackers drew them to a halt.

Down in the valley below them were two stone buildings, which might have been abandoned. But smoke rose from the chimney of one of them and horses were tethered all around. They all dismounted and surveyed the scene. The sun was just on the point of rising.

A figure came out of one of the buildings and stretched and yawned. He picked up a bucket and went to a well to fill it. He paused to cough and then ejected a large globule of spit onto the ground. He then disappeared back inside.

Two other men came outside and stretched and shook themselves in the misty, early morning air. There was no doubt that this was the party that had attacked the caravan and it looked as if there might have been more of them than anticipated.

"Get the others," whispered Uzmir. "We're going to attack."

Iddur disappeared and returned shortly afterwards with the others, including the somewhat apprehensive Mauritanians, who were unused to the landscape. Uzmir had encouraged and cajoled them in such a manner, however, since the departure from the castle, that they were now feeling very much more at ease.

They attacked on two sides with their full force. They had the advantage of complete surprise. They advanced silently down the hill, the hooves of their horses covered in sacking to deaden the noise.

As they reached the bottom of the hill another knight came out of the building and realised the danger. He sounded the alarm but it was too late. The group was upon them before they had time to recover their wits. Sleepy, half conscious knights were no matches for their vengeful foes.

They cut down those knights who were awake enough and stupid enough to venture outside and then they dismounted and fought their way into the buildings, showing no mercy to the rest of the half sleeping squadron.

Elvin fought his way into one building and then the other with one thing on his mind — to find Tayri. He had become quite adept at wielding the curved broadsword and used it with clinical skill.

As Elvin entered the second building the first person he was to confront was the sergeant, Pablo, who had tortured him at the monastery. It was instant recognition on Elvin's part but the sergeant probably did not recognise Elvin in his Moorish costume. He had no time to think, in any case, because Elvin was the quicker. The last thing that the sergeant would have seen was the determined look on Elvin's face as he brought the curved sword down, with both hands, onto the unfortunate man's skull. It split clean in two. The sergeant ran around for short second or two in a blind panic. His hands rose to his blood-soaked head, before he collapsed in a heap near the doorway. Elvin ran him through with a dagger to make sure and then stepped over the body into the building.

"Tayri," he cried out. "Where are you? It is I, Elvin. We have come for you. If you can hear me, yell out."

He heard a faint voice. From where it was coming none of them was quite sure. It was now obvious that they had gained the upper hand but they knew the Templars were unlikely to surrender.

Leaving the Mauritanians to finish the job, Uzmir and Elvin began searching for the location of the voice.

Suddenly Elvin noticed a trap door in the floor of the building and he bent down immediately to open it. Down in the darkness below he sensed there were people. He called for a burning torch and descended into the hellish hole.

"Tayri," he cried out, "where are you?"

"I am over here. Allah be praised that you have found us." She was shackled to the wall and was dirty and half naked.

Elvin leapt towards her and clasped her in his arms.

"Thank God you are alive," he said. "Keep calm and we will soon release you."

Elvin and Uzmir searched around amongst the dead bodies and eventually found the key on the unfortunate Pablo.

Elvin released Tayri from her shackles and she collapsed sobbing into his arms.

"I knew you would come," she whispered, sniffing and sobbing. "I knew you would come," she repeated. "You have no idea what we have been through," she said tearfully.

Elvin hugged her tightly, gently kissing her forehead and stroking the back of her head and neck. He whispered comforting words to her as she sobbed and sobbed into his shoulder.

"They raped all of the women," she confessed to him.

"Come on, don't talk about it now," he urged her but she continued.

"No man will take me for a wife now," she sobbed.

"Come on, don't distress yourself. I will look after you, never fear," Elvin whispered into her ear.

She went quiet and just clung to him. Elvin unwound his turban because he was so hot. As he swung round with Tayri in his arms he spied Muhammad looking at him very intently. He knew that Muhammad had heard him speak to Tayri and now could see him unmasked without his turban. Muhammad's look of disbelief and growing suspicion was clear.

"It appears, that the dumb one from Doumyat has found his voice again," he sneered. "…And a foreign voice at that! I don't like the look of this and I don't like the way he has got his arms all over the woman, to whom I am betrothed. I suspect we have a stray dog within our midst, who is not all that he pretends to be." Muhammad's hand was already on the hilt of his half-drawn sword.

As he began removing his sword from its scabbard, Elvin drew his sword, but immediately Tayri jumped in front of Elvin, her palms raised towards Muhammad.

"No, no. You don't understand. He is Uzmir's closest friend and a friend of the whole family including me. I will not see you harm him. You will have to slay me first," she said emphatically.

"Hah! So the dumb one also hides behind the skirts of a woman. I suspect that we have a cowardly, foreign impostor amongst us and it would not surprise me if he turned out to be an infidel as well. He certainly does not have the look of a Berber. Maybe he is a spy. Out of my way, woman!" Muhammad's sword was now fully drawn and ready for attack.

"Muhammad," came a sharp voice from behind. "Put down your sword." It was Uzmir and his own sword was at Muhammad's throat.

Muhammad sought to give an order to his retainers but Uzmir glowered at them.

"Don't you dare move," Uzmir ordered. "Disarm them," he barked to the Mauritanian Guard. Muhammad dropped his sword.

"You are going to sorely regret this, Uzmir. Nobody raises a sword to me or any of my clan," said Muhammad.

"Do not over react, Muhammad," said Uzmir. "You have raised a sword not only to my sister, to whom you are betrothed, but also to one whom I would regard as my brother. Yes, he is from another land, but I would trust him with my life. I think most sane men would think me justified."

"And most sane men would think me justified in calling off my impending wedding to your sister," said Muhammad. "I am told the infidels raped her and now I find another foreigner with his hands all over her. She is spoiled merchandise, my friend, and there is no question of my marrying her. We will be departing for Cordova immediately."

It was all Uzmir could do to control himself such was his anger but he knew the wisdom of containing his rage.

"Such is your choice," he mumbled. "I thank you for your aid in rescuing my sister." Muhammad shrugged his shoulders in a dismissive manner, gathered up his men and mounted up.

"I hope our paths do not cross again," said Muhammad, "for surely next time I will kill you."

After Muhammad and his men had gone, those remaining made sure all was clear before they, in turn, departed. One or two of the Christian knights had escaped and Enrique de Larraga must have been one of them for there was no sign of him. They made a fairly speedy departure. They did not wish to risk a larger force of Christians happening onto the scene, which was quite possible in this volatile border area.

The element of surprise meant that they left the forest clearing with few of their number badly wounded.

They rode back to the castle in silence. Both Elvin and Uzmir had grim looks on their faces. Elvin had really thought that the Templars would not have allowed anything to happen to the women. How wrong he had been. But then again, should he have been surprised where Enrique de Larraga was concerned? He also felt extremely guilty about having carelessly revealed himself to Muhammad and about the subsequent events.

"Uzmir," he said after a while, " I am so sorry about what happened back there. I was careless because I was so anxious to see your sister safe. I feel I have let Aderbal down, God rest his soul, and I feel I have let the rest of the family down. Can you ever forgive me?"

"Do not distress yourself, my friend," said Uzmir. "I know what it took for you to come to our aid in this mission and how you have compromised your oath to the Templars. I am grateful for that help and so is Tayri as well. As far as revealing your identity was concerned, it was, perhaps, bound to happen at some time or other. It is amazing that you have got away with it for so long. Do not worry about Muhammad. He is all talk and bravado most of the time. He may come round when he has had time to think."

Later they returned to Granada.

* * *

"Who was it that raped you?" Elvin felt able to ask a few days later in the presence of Uzmir and Iddur. Understandably Tayri was reluctant to talk about it and had to be cajoled into doing so by her brothers.

"I don't know," Tayri said. "He was the one in charge. I think his name was Anreeker."

"Enrique?" Elvin asked.

"Yes, that was it," she said. "He said he was going to keep me as his personal slave and would look after me. He tried several times to force himself upon me. He beat me and I was unable to resist," she said, as she dissolved into sobs again.

Elvin sought to comfort the distressed Tayri.

"Now I'm afraid," she continued, the tears welling up in her eyes again.

"There's no need to be afraid now. You are in safe hands," said Uzmir.

"No, no," she said frowning and nervously moving her hands in and out of one another. "I'm afraid that no one will wish to marry me. No man will be interested if they know a Christian has despoiled me in such a way." She held her head in her hands, her shoulders shaking with her distress.

Elvin spoke to Uzmir the next day about how Tayri was feeling. Uzmir revealed to him the problem.

"I have not told her yet," he said, "but her fears are justified. It is a great dishonour for a woman in our society. Certainly Muhammad declared clearly how he felt about it and I have since had an official message from Cordova to say that the wedding is off. His exact words were that he did not wish to continue with the marriage to a woman who has been taken by the Christians and despoiled by them. Nor did he wish to marry a woman from a family, which appeared to be hiding an infidel within their house. He indicated that the Governor might well be asking serious questions on that subject. I fear that you must hasten your plans to leave us and return to your land. It is only a matter of time before they come seeking you."

"Please do not judge all Christians by the standards of those evil men," said Elvin. "On his deathbed your father asked me to protect your sister. And so I will. What has happened is not her fault. You know how I have grown to feel about her. I have had women before, of course, but it has always been a purely physical experience and I have never forced my desires upon anyone. I have grown to enjoy the company of your sister and talking to her. And I think she likes being with me. I am sure there is a mutual attraction between us."

"I know there is," said Uzmir. "We, in the family, were well aware of this before we started for Cordova. Indeed she told us so. She did not want to marry Muhammad at all. I remember my father had to speak to her quite sternly and remind her of her position. You must appreciate that the marriage to Muhammad would have been a great honour for her and the whole family and there was a large dowry involved. It was not only the marriage of two people, but of two Berber clans. Do you not have arranged marriages in your country too?"

"Of course we do," replied Elvin. "It is exactly the same. But somehow I feel there should be something more. There is something that beats inside me and says that we should be together. I don't know why this is and she probably doesn't know why."

"Are you saying that you wish to marry Tayri?" Uzmir enquired.

"Perhaps so," replied Elvin. "When she was kidnapped and we did not know if we would ever see her again, I felt desperately lost. I knew then that I loved her but I appreciated that this was impossible. Now the situation is different. It is untrue to say that no man would marry her. For, in truth, if there was some way it could be arranged, I would marry her myself, if she would have me."

"I appreciate what you are saying but I must counsel you carefully my friend. You remember that I spoke to you of the situation between Christian men and Muslim women? Islam recognises Abraham, Moses and Jesus but it credits Mohammed for reintroducing the true religion without contamination. My tribe believe, however, that the rejection of any one of the prophets and saints is the rejection of the essential truth behind them – the one God or Allah. That is why we are very tolerant of other religions, which believe in the one God. That's providing they are not attacking us, of course. We may be very much involved in the role of the inner self and our personal relationship to Allah but we have to live in the outer Islamic world and abide by its laws and customs. Otherwise we would not be tolerated ourselves. One thing is clear. There is no way that in our society in Al Andalus a Christian man can marry a Muslim woman. If you wish to marry my sister, you will have to think long and hard, for you will have to convert to Islam."

"And if I took her with me back to my land and married her there?" Elvin asked.

"Her Faith forbids that she marry a Christian man. It is as simple as that. She would have to convert to your Faith."

"And what would you think about that?"

"I am not sure that I have a right to an opinion," said Uzmir. "I converted to Christianity, albeit by force and out of cowardice. Members of my tribe find their own way to Allah and I have always been happy in my own mind that whatever people demanded of me on the outside, I would always be a Muslim on the inside. I feel you are a good man. My father certainly thought so. For his sake I am sure you would always treat her in a way that would not conflict with Islamic principles."

"I cannot promise any less," said Elvin.

"Then both of you have much to think about. In principle, as the head of the family now, I am not against the two of you familiarising yourselves sincerely with one another within the bounds of good morals," said Uzmir as a final word. "You will have to let me know what you decide. But you cannot afford to delay. It is only a matter of time before Muhammad will come seeking you out."

It took a while for Tayri to recover enough from her ordeal to be alone with a man again. But gradually Elvin began to re-establish her trust in him and they began to spend more and more time together. They instinctively knew that they were destined to be with one another. The vexed question of who was going to convert to which faith was bound to crop up eventually and it was not long before they were discussing this.

"I am prepared to convert to Islam if that is what I have to do, for I know now that I truly love you," Elvin declared. "The thought of losing you when you were kidnapped was unbearable for me even though I could not have married you then. But things have changed now and Uzmir has given me his blessing, providing you are willing and that one of us converts to the other's faith. That alone will not be without its problems. I am a sworn Templar knight, sworn to Christianity. I have already broken many of my vows, albeit under mitigating circumstances. I would be in real trouble back in my own country if I arrived there having become a Muslim."

"Then why return there at all?" she asked.

"Because I am the heir to a castle and many lands in my own country. Here I have nothing. I cannot even provide you with a dowry. Besides that, I have recently been drawn to my native land. I miss my Cornish home. They say that anybody born there always craves to return home. I told your father this before he died and our journey to Cordova was to be my last before I returned home. But much has happened since then."

"Would you rather return to your native land than to take me for a wife?" she asked.

"No, of course, not. If you really wish it I will remain here and become a Muslim, if that is what you really want," he replied.

" I do want to be married to you, Elvin, and all I wish is that I can make you happy, bear your family in time and be honest and loyal towards you," said Tayri seriously. "I have no objection to travelling to see other lands and how other people live. After my experience with Enrique I have a reluctance to stay here anyway. If I can honour you as my husband by becoming a Christian then so be it. I am prepared to do that for our love."

They came together and hugged one another closely. It was not a sexual thing but a union of two hearts set on the same path.

That night it was very hot. Elvin moved his mattress to the very top of the building where there was an open terrace. He felt he had much to think about. During the night he was awakened by a rustling sound close to him and he realised that he was not alone.

"Go away, Naima," he whispered, "I have no need of you."

"It is not Naima. It is I, Tayri. Can I lie beside you for a while?"

She lay down beside him with her back to him and motioned to him to put his arms around her.

How long they lay like that he did not know but he awoke and felt aroused by her presence and he began to move his hands up over the front of her body. It had been a long time since he had had a woman.

Awakened Tayri turned to him and whispered:

"Please, Elvin. I am not ready yet. Be patient with me. My experience with Enrique has left me scarred. Let us wait until we are truly one."

He gently kissed her on the forehead and drew her to him, cuddling her affectionately. In a little while Elvin whispered to her:

"I think you had better return to your bedchamber now, my love. I have promised Uzmir that we will observe good morals before we are married. I will not betray his trust. I am sorry that I was so unthinking."

She placed two fingers on his lips motioning him to be silent. She gave him a smile and a final peck on the cheek and disappeared into the night.

Elvin fell into a deep sleep again. It was a sleep of disjointed dreams. He dreamed of the rescue of Tayri and of holding her close. Then he saw the face of Aderbal smiling and then the sneering face of Muhammad. He dreamed of the dramatic cliffs of Cornwall and thunderous waves below them and finally he dreamed that he was standing amongst the bright yellow gorse on a Cornish hilltop holding the Sacred Chalice of the Last Supper. He awoke with a start and knew then precisely what he had to do before he returned to Cornwall.

CHAPTER EIGHTEEN

The Chalice

Peter took a cheap flight from London Stansted to Malaga and then went by bus up to Granada. He booked into a small hotel facing the River Genil a few hundred yards from a major congress hall.

Anya had invited him to stay with her, but Peter had politely declined, not wishing to stir up any resentment that might still be lurking in the mind of Yuba. But he did agree to meet them for a drink on the first evening.

He met them outside a popular ice cream parlour in the centre of the city at about ten in the evening. Anya looked as immaculate as ever and Peter was reminded of why he had found her so attractive in the first place.

They decided to go and have a drink in a small tapas bar just round the corner from the post office.

The streets were very busy and it was difficult to find a seat in the bar. But they got one eventually and tried to converse amongst the general hubbub that was to be expected in such a place.

Peter felt sure that the Spanish could never hold a quiet conversation with one another and he never failed to be amazed at the way the locals shouted and gesticulated at one another — all apparently in good heart. In spite of all this he felt at home there somehow.

He spoke good Spanish, having got an A-level in it at school, and had frequently practised it with Anya. He seemed to have a good ear for the language and he put this down to the fact that his mother had been a modern languages teacher, when she had been working, with her major language being Spanish. He reminded himself that he ought to ring her to see how she was.

Peter had a glass of wine but both Anya and Yuba had soft drinks and they nibbled at the small plate of sliced aubergines in batter, which accompanied the drinks.

They conversed in general terms for a while, enquiring about one another's families. Anya expressed her sorrow that Peter and Mary had separated but said that she did not find it altogether surprising. Peter told her that he thought that his relations with Mary had, perhaps, improved since his accident, probably because he, himself, was becoming more accustomed to the reality of the situation. Yuba listened with an ill-disguised indifference.

"So, what have you brought me over to see?" asked Peter eventually.

"We'll show you tomorrow," Anya said. "I can't stress enough that this has to be kept under wraps for the moment. It's a major find. I suggest that you come up to the site first thing and we can have a look before the students arrive."

"OK, I'll see you tomorrow then," he said shrugging his shoulders. He wished Yuba a good night and received a rather disdainful wave good-bye back.

"Bastard," he thought.

He decided to walk back to the hotel. The streets were full of the usual evening promenaders and he thought to himself how refreshingly different was the atmosphere from a city of equivalent size in Britain when one bore in mind it was close to midnight. Here there were no drunken brawlers, bouncers on bar doors or foul-mouthed 'ladettes'. There was a pleasant family atmosphere and maybe the British had a lot to learn from the Spanish about how to enjoy life without gallons of alcoholic sustenance.

"Stop it," he said to himself, "You are beginning to sound holier than thou. You've sunk a few pints in your time along with the rest of them." But, nevertheless, life did appear to be different in Spain although, to be fair, the authorities, even here, were beginning to witness problems of alcoholism and drugs amongst young people. It was to be hoped that the 'Anglo-Saxon problem', as some Spaniards described it, did not spread too quickly or too far.

Crossing a main square he noticed a crowd had gathered and heard the music of a guitar strumming a haunting sevillana. To the uneducated ear it sounded much like flamenco, but to the Granadinos there was a world of difference.

A young gypsy girl, no more than fifteen or sixteen, was dancing the intricate steps and twirls. With her arms raised in the air and her hands dancing to the music as well, she interpreted the dance throughout her whole lithe young body in a way that non-Spaniards would find almost impossible to imitate. Her body spoke a language refined over many centuries from the gypsies' own Indian influenced culture combined with Moorish and Andalusian folklore. An expression of all the sorrows and joys of life poured out of her.

Peter stood entranced. He had a strange feeling of déjà vu. He felt somehow he had been in this situation before but he did not know where or when. He remained captivated for some five or ten minutes until the young girl had exhausted herself and began wandering through the crowd with a small cup seeking pecuniary appreciation for her efforts.

Peter threw in a few coins and then went on his way. He stopped for one final drink in a small bar off the Calle de Alhamar unable to get over the strange feeling he had inside.

At last he shrugged this off and returned to the hotel.

The next day he took a bus up to the old part of the city and sought out the site where Anya and her team were working. Only Anya and a rather pretty young woman were there at that time. She introduced the young woman as Cristina, her assistant, and a research student. She was short, slim and dark and spoke English with an Australian accent.

"It was Cristina who first set us on to our find," she said. "It's all yours, Cristina."

Cristina began to explain. "It was obvious that these two bodies had not been buried in a traditional Islamic graveyard nor in the usual Islamic style. The only Islamic characteristic was that both bodies were facing towards Mecca. The existence of grave goods was a distinctly non-Islamic trait. Since we know that this was an urban area in the thirteenth century and we have found no other bodies we came to the conclusion that they must have been buried, perhaps, in the garden of a house or something of that sort.

"We decided to open another trench further away from the graves where we thought the original house might have been. After a while we began coming across scattered pieces of masonry and decorative tiles and we came to the conclusion that we had discovered the traditional Moorish courtyard attached to the house.

"When we began piecing a few bits of the broken up masonry together we discovered that we had parts of the original fountain in the courtyard. There appeared to have been a lotus shaped basin set on a column covered with inscriptions. The basin had been designed to be continually full to the brim so that the water trickled between the petals of the lotus flower shape to fall onto some smooth stones in a larger pool below. This had been enclosed by a hexagonal shaped retaining wall, which had been intricately tiled on the outside.

"On the central column there were traditional inscriptions in Arabic like 'How beauteous this place where the flowers of earth joust with the stars of heaven' or more religious ones like 'No one conquers but Allah'. The whole column was covered with them and this would not have been unusual. What was unusual, however, was that amongst them was another inscription, which, at first, looked a bit like the others. But we realised that it was not Arabic script at all. It was, in fact, in Latin and had been added later. It read: *Ex substructio fontis medici Aderbali donum beatum surgit.*

"We took that to mean, "From the foot of the fountain of the physician Aderbal surges the blessed gift of the Lord." Naturally, at first, we thought this was just referring to the water itself.

"It would have not been unusual for the inhabitants of sun-baked Andalusia, increasingly influenced by their conquerors from Saharan North Africa, to treat water with a great deal of respect and we know that an immense restraint was used in the design of fountains for the courtyards of Moorish houses. There were no great jets of water flying high into the air but an economy of water designed to trickle gently over basins into calm pools below.

"In the process of trying to assemble the various bits of the fountain scattered about we found one piece of the lower retaining wall of the pool, which appeared to have a hollow compartment set into it. Originally, of course, this compartment would have been covered by tiles and, therefore, hidden. There appeared to be no real reason for it to be there unless it was the hiding place for something."

"So did you discover your find there?" enquired Peter.

"Yes, we didn't have to look very far. For, there, lying inside, where it had been hidden for centuries, was an article wrapped in what remained of the strangest of materials – sailcloth. This was a material you would not normally find in inland Andalusia and, stranger still, it was of a type usually only found in Northern Europe.

"Anyhow, what had been originally wrapped in the sailcloth was this." Cristina leant down and picked up an item wrapped carefully and stored in a wooden box. As she unwrapped the artefact Peter gasped.

"Oh, my God," he said.

There before them was the most beautiful chalice he had ever seen.

It was a proper cup, semi-spherical in shape, of a sort of reddish/green hue and probably about nine or ten centimetres in diameter. To this had been added a gold structure composed of a centred hexagonal column with a round nut in the middle. An upper gold plate held the cup whilst a lower gold plate supported the base structure, which was made of the same material as the cup. The base had a garniture of gold and was set with pea-sized pearls and other jewels. There were also two lateral, snake shaped handles, hexagonally carved. The whole thing was no more than seventeen or eighteen centimetres high.

"You were quite right," Peter said to Anya. "This is an absolutely stunning find and it's quite heavy isn't it? Lord knows how much it is worth, for a start, in terms of the gold alone."

"I thought you would be impressed," said Anya. "It's full marks to Cristina really. She found it."

Cristina was grinning proudly.

"Yes, really well done, Cristina," Peter added. "Now can I look at the central column of the fountain again?"

They took him over to the particular piece of the fountain that he wanted to examine. He looked at it closely for a while and then said:

"Yes, it's much as I thought. I've seen an inscription written in the same Celtic kind of script before. I'm prepared to bet a pound to a penny or, if you like a euro to a cent, that they were done by the same person. It's almost identical in style to the inscription I saw on the wall of the tunnel leading down from the headland at Tremennek. We'd have to get photographs, of course, and compare them but I suspect our friend, Sir Elvin Le Gard, had something to do with all this. I'm convinced of it."

"Hmm, I think you're right," said Anya.

"Have you had the chalice dated?" asked Peter.

"No, we haven't," replied Anya. "We've kept this whole discovery under wraps for the moment. We don't want the press crawling all over the site."

"I can understand that," said Peter. "But you're going to have to do it, aren't you?"

"Well, I do have a colleague at the University, who should have all the equipment to be able to put a date on it. We'll make an appointment and go and see him as soon as possible. I presume you would like to come along with us, Peter?"

"I certainly would," said Peter.

Two days later they were ushered into the office of Professor Jaime Gonzalez at the University of Granada and lost no time in showing him the chalice.

"Well, well, well. What have we got here?" he exclaimed. "What a beautiful article."

"Do you think you are able to date it?" Anya asked.

"Well, it will be difficult. It's not possible to date gold correctly in the same way as other metals. The usual methods we use to test objects of antiquity wouldn't be any good. This chalice has a substantial amount of gold in it, so we will have to try and identify the style rather than anything else. We can check for an electrical charge because gold, along with amber and shale, gives off a charge, which can be measured. But essentially we will need to go to the books and look for the closest similarities in style. It's funny, though. I've got a feeling I've seen something like this before."

"Really?" exclaimed Anya.

"Yes, I can't think, for the moment, where. But I'm sure I have," he said slowly still trying to wrestle with the thought in his mind.

They agreed to meet up again in two days.

Two days later they met again in Professor Gonzalez's office.

"Welcome back, friends," he said. "Some interesting things have developed from this since I saw you last. First of all, archaeological investigations that we have made show that the chalice is of some antiquity. We believe that the cup itself was made in a workshop in Palestine or Egypt somewhere between the fourth century BC and the first century AD."

"It's not medieval then?" exclaimed Anya.

"Well, yes. We are pretty certain that the cup and the base are of the Roman period," said Professor Gonzalez, "but the gold framework of the chalice and the jewels were added at a much later period – probably in the thirteenth or fourteenth centuries.

"The cup and the base are both made from red agate. The framework is made of solid gold. The base is set with twenty-eight pea-sized pearls, two rubies and two emeralds. It really is a lovely piece of work. We also took a forensic swab of the cup and found that it had been used for drinking wine. It goes without saying that the chalice is of enormous financial value, almost priceless."

"Well, what sort of sum are we talking about," enquired Peter.

"I would not be surprised if were not worth something in the region of three hundred and fifty to four hundred thousand euros or over a quarter of a million of your English pounds," came the reply.

There were gasps of amazement from Peter, Anya and Cristina.

"However, there is another matter, which could pose a problem," the Professor continued. "You remember that I mentioned to you that I felt I had seen something similar to this before. I was right. It was a relic held in the Cathedral at Valencia."

"What sort of relic?" enquired Anya.

"It is reputed to be the Sacred Chalice of the Last Supper and is greatly revered by the hierarchy of our Holy Mother Church. Indeed, Pope John Paul II used it during a Mass celebrated in Valencia in 1992."

"What's the story behind the Chalice in Valencia?" asked Peter.

"Well, apparently, the official story goes like this. After the Last Supper the Sacred Cup stayed in the hands of the disciples, Peter and Mark, who took it to Rome where it remained for two centuries.

"During a violent repression of the Christians by the Emperor Valerian, Pope Sixtus II entrusted the Cup to his deacon, Lawrence, who sent it to Huesca, his native city in Aragon, somewhere between 258 and 261 AD. Following the invasion of the Moors in 713 the Bishop of Huesca, Audeberto, abandoned his episcopal seat and journeyed into the Pyrenees, taking the Cup with him. He lived in some caves near to the spot where, later, the now famous Monastery of San Juan de La Peña was founded. There the Cup remained until 1399 when the King of Aragon, Martin the First, transferred it to the Palacio de la Aljafería in Saragossa.

"Finally, in 1437, during the reign of Alfonso the Fifth, it went to the Royal Palace in Valencia and then to the Cathedral for safekeeping."

"So what's the similarity between our chalice and the one in Valencia Cathedral?" enquired Peter.

"By the look of the photo in the book of reference they are not identical but they are very, very similar," was the reply. "The obvious thing to do is to get permission to have a look at them both together and examine them carefully to see what are the major differences. You were right to keep this discovery quiet for the moment. Our findings could be sensational.

"I have a colleague at the University of Valencia who is very close to the Curia or Council of Valencia Cathedral. I'll seek his advice and see if we can proceed from there. We can meet up again in a day or two's time."

A few days later they all met again.

Professor Gonzalez brought them up to date. "I contacted my friend in Valencia and he advised me to write to the Curia to ask for permission to examine the Sacred Chalice. Almost by return of post I received a letter turning down my request and explaining that it was not their policy to allow anyone other than Vatican approved academics to have access to their treasured relics. I telephoned and asked how one became a Vatican approved academic and really did not get very far. The answers were evasive to say the least.

"Then I spoke again to my colleague and he said that the Chapel that housed the Sacred Chalice at the Cathedral had been closed indefinitely for 'restorative repairs'. He also told me that, soon after they had received my letter, a special meeting was held involving Vatican officials, Cathedral officials and a number of academics, all of which were probably Vatican approved. So it certainly looks as if we've stirred something up. I don't know where it leaves us, but I'll continue to do what I can to work for a proper scientific study of the two chalices to be undertaken."

It was the following day when the news broke. Anya rang Peter on his mobile and asked him to meet her as soon as possible at the Alhambra. She explained that the hordes of tourists there might shield them for a while from too many prying eyes and awkward questions.

"What's the problem?" Peter had asked.

"The inevitable has happened," said Anya. "Have you seen the front page of Sur this morning?" Sur was a local daily newspaper in Andalusia.

"No," replied Peter.

"You'd better have a look," said Anya.

Peter bought a copy as quickly as he could and there, emblazoned across the front page, was the headline in Spanish: **"Sensational Find By Archaeologists in Granada."**

"Damn it," thought Peter. "The news is out."

CHAPTER NINETEEN

The Search For The Holy Grail

Elvin and Uzmir crept through the thick, almost impenetrable, brush and trees that covered the valley floor. A heavy mist lay over the isolated region and it was damp day.

Elvin climbed a pine tree to see if he could get a better view of the terrain ahead. Higher up, ahead of them, he could just make out the muddy pathway in front of the monastery. He remembered the building well from his first visit there. Built under the overhanging rock face it was almost completely hidden from all but the closest of observers. The reds, greys and blues of the rock face, worn smooth by centuries of weathering, made it an impressive sight. Above the caves into which the monastery had been built the forested slopes and crags of the mountain stretched away in the distance.

One of the horses snorted and Elvin gave a sign to Uzmir to keep them quiet. He remembered full well what had happened on the last occasion he had stumbled through these woods. He climbed down again.

"There don't seem to be many people about," he observed to Uzmir.

"Well, are you going to risk it?" asked Uzmir.

"Of course," said Elvin. "That is why I have come here."

"So, what are you going to do?" enquired Uzmir.

"I am going to walk right up to the walls and ask them to let me in," Elvin replied.

"Do you think they will?"

"I don't know for sure, but there is only one way to find out."

Both of them were wearing the standard woollen clothing that was the feature of the Christian world. They had donned this immediately before slipping across the border into Aragon so that they would not stand out. Elvin touched the St. Piran's Cross, which now had pride of place again around his neck. He would need all the luck he could get.

The plan was simple. Elvin would attempt to get into the monastery by explaining that he had returned from the East, after having been imprisoned in Egypt. He would tell them that he was attempting to rejoin the Templar Order. They were gambling on the fact that many of the knights would be away on the borders of Andalusia taking part in the Reconquest and that news of Elvin's lengthy absence from the Templar Order had not reached this remote region. He would get in, do what he had to do and then disappear again.

"Well, there's no time like the present," Elvin said with a sigh. "Wish me luck."

They embraced one another and then Uzmir said, "I will wait for you for three days only. When you are ready to come out, give me a signal. If after three days I have heard nothing from you I will have to return."

"I will draw a burning torch back and forth across a window five times," said Elvin. "When you observe this, have the horses ready then and I will make my escape. We will have to make a very speedy retreat."

"So be it," said Uzmir. "Take care my friend."

"And you be careful too," said Elvin.

With that Uzmir retired into the trees, taking two of their three horses with him. Elvin was left alone and rode on up the slope towards the monastery gateway.

"Who goes there?" came the challenge in Aragonese from a window above the wooden door.

Elvin replied in the French tongue. "It is I, Brother Elvin Le Gard. I am a Templar Knight, who has been imprisoned in Egypt and am seeking to return to the Order. I seek Brother Enrique de Larraga."

"He is not here. He is away in the South," the soldier shouted down. Elvin knew this, of course, and was relying on there being no one, who had fought with him in Egypt, being present at the monastery.

"I need shelter and food," Elvin pleaded.

"Wait there," said the soldier.

A short while later an older man dressed in a white habit and wearing a white mantle over it with the customary red cross on the left shoulder came to the window.

"What do you want?" he shouted down.

"I need shelter and food," said Elvin. "I have travelled many leagues from the land of Egypt. I was a prisoner of the Saracens there but I managed to escape. I was here in your monastery some years ago. You may remember me. Enrique de Larraga brought my squire and me here and later took us to the castle at Monzon to be enrolled into the Order."

"I do not remember you," said the Templar. "Tell me, what do you know of this place?"

"I know that it houses the Sacred Chalice of the Last Supper and that it is the task of the Templar Order to guard it," replied Elvin.

"Have you seen this Chalice?"

"I have when I was last here."

"Then describe it to me," ordered the Templar.

Elvin described to him the reddish green coloured chalice resting on a golden stem with two snake-like gold handles and a jewelled base.

"Where were you received into the Order," the Templar asked.

"At Monzon," replied Elvin.

"Can you remember the words you were taught to say after you were asked whether you were still willing to join the Order and then brought before the chapter?" he was asked.

"Yes," said Elvin. "I was brought before the Master and had to say: "Sire, I am come before God and before you and before the brothers, and ask and request you, for love of God and Our Lady, to welcome me into your company and the favours of the house, as one who wishes to be a serf and slave of the house for ever." Enrique de Larraga had imprinted it upon his mind.

The Templar seemed satisfied with this and ordered the soldier to let Elvin in. Some minutes later the wooden door opened and Elvin was admitted to the monastery.

The Templar introduced himself as Brother Miguel de Torla and said he was in charge of the detachment left in the monastery. As Elvin had surmised most of the soldiers were away in the South and only a very fragmented guard had been left.

De Torla took Elvin through to the quarters where he could temporarily stay. As they passed through the various parts of the monastery Elvin sought to take in everything he could about the buildings.

He noticed, firstly, that there were about the same number of Benedictine monks present as upon his first visit but the number of soldiers had been drastically reduced. He was able to count only about half dozen men in Templar habits and not more than a dozen others.

The soldiers were a motley bunch being made up of either very young men of twelve to sixteen years of age or older men in the twilight of their soldiering careers. The toughest, fittest, most experienced men were obviously engaged in the actions on the borders of Andalusia.

It could not be said that Elvin was not made welcome, for he enjoyed the same basic accommodation and frugal rations as the others.

Naturally Brother Miguel showed great interest in Elvin's adventures since he had escaped from Egypt and questioned him closely on these matters. Elvin only revealed to him what it was safe for him to know and mentioned nothing of his sojourn in Granada.

In his turn Elvin sought the advice of Brother Miguel on how to join up again with the Templar squadrons and stressed the urgency of doing this.

"I must confess," said Miguel, "that we get little news here. I am not at all sure where they are. The last time we heard they were somewhere around the city of Cuenca on the borders of the Muslim lands."

"They've made much greater progress than that," thought Elvin, thinking of his clash with De Larraga's men in the mountains in Andalusia.

"Tell me," Miguel continued, "Why did you come here? You must have heard that many soldiers are in the South."

"Yes, I did," replied Elvin, "but I mistakenly thought that Enrique de Larraga might still be here. But there I was wrong."

"What then do you plan to do?" asked Miguel.

"My duty is to leave as soon as possible for the South to rejoin my comrades," replied Elvin. "But before I leave I must beg one further request of you."

"If I can help you in any way, I will," said Miguel, without any doubt being more than willing to aid a fellow Brother.

"There was another reason that drew me here," Elvin explained. "Last time I was in the monastery I attended a Mass, at which the Sacred Chalice was paraded. It was a sight of great awe that I have never forgotten and it filled me with the Lord's energy to fight earnestly against the Saracen unbelievers and sustained me during the long days of my miserable imprisonment in Egypt. I wondered if I could be allowed to see once more that glorious relic and to place my hand upon it to ask for Christ's blessing for the perilous journey ahead?"

There was a long pause. Miguel said: "Well, this is a highly unusual request. I will have to consult the other Brothers. I will let you know the result of our deliberations."

Later that evening Miguel spoke to Elvin again and said:

"The Brothers have agreed that, in view of your heroic attempt to join up again with the Brotherhood under such adverse conditions, the least we can do is to accede to your request. Please follow me."

Elvin followed him out of the residential quarters and through the Royal Pantheon where the tombs of several Aragonese kings were stacked. They crossed over into the lower church, hewn straight out of the rock face, and then ascended a staircase to the upper part of the building. There lay a small chapel, outside of which two soldiers were standing on guard.

Miguel entered the chapel and approached a large wooden chest situated at the far end. He felt behind it and produced a large iron key, with which he proceeded to open the chest. He leaned forward and brought out the Chalice.

Once again Elvin thought it was the most magnificent object he had ever seen. The agate cup and base gave off an iridescent glow with reds and greens prominent. The solid gold cage shone and glowed in the light glow of the burning torches. The jewelled base twinkled and sparkled and it almost seemed as if there was a visible aura around the whole Chalice.

Elvin fell to his knees and crossed himself. Miguel presented the Chalice to him and Elvin put his hands on it and bowed his head in prayer.

"I will leave you to pray," said Miguel. He replaced the Chalice in the chest and put back the key.

Elvin continued to appear to be deep in prayer. In reality he was making himself aware of his surroundings. He took note of where the key was deposited and of the exact location of the wooden chest in the same way that he had familiarised himself with the various buildings around the monastery.

"It will have to be tonight," Elvin thought to himself and wondered how Uzmir was out in the damp forest. He prayed that his friend would be safe from harm.

Meanwhile he had a problem. He knew he had to act that night. However, he was sleeping in the residential quarters with the other Templars. This meant that, according to the Templar Rule, he was allowed a mattress, a bolster and a blanket, had to sleep fully clothed and in a room that was fully lit until morning. No Templar was allowed to sleep in the dark.

Elvin had anticipated this state of affairs. He had prepared materials, before departure from Granada, for making a number of Aderbal's sleeping sponges, albeit in a slightly milder form than for a medical operation. He had managed to hide these amongst his personal belongings, with which he had arrived.

On the excuse of checking his horse and equipment in preparation for the following day he would slip out and prepare the sponges for use later in the night. He knew that there would be at least four of the complement of Templars sleeping in the dormitory that night and two soldiers guarding the chapel. He had to be ready to deal with them.

Elvin found it difficult to sleep that night, for he had to feign it. With the room fully lit it was easier to keep an eye on the others to establish when they were all sound asleep. Provided they kept sleeping Elvin would not have to use the sleeping sponges.

Deep in the night Elvin decided that the Templars were fully asleep and made his move. He looked at each in turn to make doubly sure. He had checked the first three when the fourth awoke. Elvin was obliged to move quickly and was upon him before he had gathered his wits. There was a bit of a struggle but Elvin managed to subdue the unfortunate knight with a sleeping sponge ensuring that he would enjoy the deepest of slumbers that night. Fortunately none of the others had awoken.

Elvin slipped out of the dorter and crept silently towards the chapel where the Chalice was kept. He had to dodge stealthily from column to column to avoid being seen. He approached the window from which he had arranged with Uzmir to give his signal. He took a quick look round to check that no one was about and then took down a torch from the wall. He drew it across the window five times as arranged and then replaced the torch. He could only pray that Uzmir was alert and watching out for the signal.

As he approached the entrance to the chapel he could see that there were still two soldiers on guard. He considered his plan of action. He would have to separate them, if he could.

One of the soldiers was a stranger to him but the other had been on guard earlier in the day when he had visited the chapel with Miguel. Elvin thought that he remembered that Miguel had addressed him as Sanchez. Concealing himself well out of sight Elvin whispered as loud as he dare: "Hey, Sanchez!"

"What was that?" said Sanchez.

"I don't know," said the other soldier. "I didn't hear anything."

Elvin tried again.

"There it is again. It's coming from over there," said Sanchez.

"Go and check it out," said the other man. "I'll keep guard here."

Sanchez starting moving in Elvin's direction with his sword drawn. Elvin remained in the shadows hidden behind a column.

"Come on out, whoever you are," Sanchez ordered. Elvin rolled a small pebble along the floor to disorientate Sanchez. Sanchez obliged by turning his back on Elvin and Elvin was upon him before he could react. The sleeping sponge did its work.

Elvin now only had to wait.

The other soldier shouted over: "Sanchez, are you all right?"

Elvin gave a low moaning sound.

"Sanchez?" the soldier called again.

Elvin moaned again and the soldier began moving away from the chapel towards the shadows. It was almost a repeat performance and soon both soldiers were sleeping like babies in a dark recess below the chapel.

Elvin had to work speedily and entered the chapel. He made his way to where the chest was located. He felt around for the key and then panicked slightly because he could not find it. But then he realised that it was kept behind a loose stone in the wall and he lifted it out with a sigh of relief. He opened the chest and there it was – the Sacred Chalice of the Last Supper, the Holy Grail. And he was going to return it to its rightful location, chosen by Joseph of Arimathea, in England.

"What do you think you are doing?" came a voice behind him. Elvin swung round. There, in front of him, was Brother Miguel.

Elvin did not think twice. He had no alternative. He launched himself at Miguel with all his strength. He had the advantage of some twenty years on the elderly Brother, who really was no match for him, but nevertheless he put up an almighty struggle.

Miguel got his hands round Elvin's throat and Elvin felt a rushing in his ears and began to see stars before he was able to extricate himself. He wrestled Miguel down onto the stone floor and began banging his head against the floor. Blood began to flow from a gash in his forehead but still old man was struggling. Then with one final effort Miguel stopped struggling and did not move any more. He was not dead but unconscious. For how long Elvin did not know, so he had to move fast.

Elvin stripped Miguel of his white mantle and wrapped the Chalice in it. Then he rushed out of the chapel and across the cloister to the far wall of the building. Where it was adjacent to another chapel, he clambered over the wall and dropped some six or seven meters down onto the sloping ground below. He rolled over a couple of times, but apart from a few bruises, had not broken anything. He recovered himself swiftly and dashed across the path and down the slope into the trees.

It took a little time for him to become accustomed to the pitch darkness, as there was no moon visible in the sky. He gave a low whistle – an arranged signal yet again but there was no response.

"Damn it, where is he?" thought Elvin, stumbling on through the trees.

He gave the whistle again. This time there was a reply and suddenly Uzmir appeared with the two horses.

"Thank God, for that," said Elvin. "I thought you had gone."

"No, my friend, I saw your signal. Were you successful?"

"Yes, I have got what I came for," replied Elvin.

"Good, then we must depart with all haste."

They mounted the horses, whirled them around and lost no time in disappearing into the forest.

CHAPTER TWENTY

Problems With Relations

Peter was awoken by the sound of his mobile ringing. He shot off the bed and picked it up from the bedside cabinet. He'd been taking a quick nap in the hotel before going down to dinner in the busy restaurant.

"It's Cristina," came the excited voice. "Turn on your television, quickly. Anya is being interviewed."

Peter turned on the television and, sure enough, there was Anya engaged in an interview on a daily chat show.

"What is the significance of this find?" the interviewer was asking her.

"Well, we are not quite sure," said Anya. "Our experts have told us that the agate cup part of the chalice is of some antiquity, probably of the Roman period, produced in Egypt or Palestine. The rest of it is medieval. It is remarkably similar to the Chalice on display, at present, in the Chapel of the Holy Chalice in Valencia Cathedral. We would very much like to compare them but are unable to get permission at present."

"Are you suggesting that the one in the Cathedral is a medieval fake and yours is the real Chalice," asked the interviewer.

"Careful," thought Peter.

"No, no," replied Anya. "We are just surprised that there appear to be two chalices, which seem to be about the same age and very, very similar in appearance."

"Do you think one is a copy of the other?"

"Possibly, but which is which would be pure surmise. It just seems strange that two different agate cups from the Middle East have been brought to Europe and enclosed in two different gold cages and appear so similar."

The interviewer then turned to a gentleman who was sitting opposite to Anya.

"Professor Pedro Velasquez, you are a spokesman for the Curia at

Valencia Cathedral?"

"That is correct," replied the Professor. "There are, in fact, a number of people who are interested in the preservation of the relic."

"Why is the Cathedral refusing access to the Holy Chalice to the archaeologists from Granada?"

"We have to remember that the Chalice is of great antiquity. It is not in our interest to be constantly allowing academics to handle and examine it. This would only lead to the danger of it being damaged or disfigured in some way. It has a large crack in it already, which came about when a priest dropped it in the eighteenth century and we have no wish for further damage to take place. An exhaustive study of the relic was carried out in 1960 by an eminent archaeologist who confirmed its historical authenticity and we see no reason for further examinations of it."

"But surely," said the interviewer, "this must be a special case. This discovery appears to be of similar antiquity and there is something to be said for comparing the two."

Professor Velasquez continued: "I have no doubt that the discovery in Granada is of immense archaeological significance and I must congratulate the archaeologists there on their find. But to challenge the authenticity of the Holy Chalice in Valencia would be wrong. Everyone in Spain believes it is the Holy Chalice of the Last Supper and we have thousands of pilgrims coming to view it every year."

"But surely when a similar chalice is discovered elsewhere, it is worthy of note," persisted the interviewer.

"Of course, it is. But chalices of various sorts have turned up throughout history. To be honest, no reliable information has come down to us regarding the vessel used by Christ.

"Many centuries ago pilgrims to Jerusalem thought that the chalice was in the Holy Sepulchre there. The Sacro Catino at Genoa is equally venerated as the Holy Chalice of the Last Supper and that is not a cup at all but a dish made of a green glass-like material, possibly from a large emerald, and of almost priceless value. The British Museum in London holds several chalices, all of great antiquity.

"I think we are missing the point to some degree. The value of the Chalice in Valencia is not in any scientific investigation, which has been applied to it, even if archaeology itself has shown it to be reasonably authentic. Nor is it in the thousands of euros that people may think it is worth. Its value lies in its role as a sign of the institution of the Eucharist in our Holy Mother Church.

"It reminds people of the greatest story ever told – that of the life of Our Lord and his death upon the Cross – and of the importance of Holy Communion in the services of the Church."

"Dr. Naziri, Professor Velasquez, thank you," said the interviewer winding up the interview.

Hardly had the programme finished when Peter's mobile rang again.

It was Cristina: "Well, what did you think of that?" she asked.

"It doesn't look as if they are going to relent, does it?" said Peter. "I don't think they have any intention of our getting our hands on the Valencia Chalice."

"No, it's a pity really," Cristina said. "I can't help feeling there's another agenda, perhaps.

"Look," said Peter suddenly, "do you fancy going for a drink after dinner? We could chat about it a bit more."

There was a slight hesitation from Cristina before she agreed to meet him at a bar in the centre of the city.

When he arrived at the bar she was standing outside it, as it was very crowded. He asked one of the barmen about a table and he directed Peter downstairs where there were a number of vacant tables.

The waiter brought two glasses of red wine and a simple plate of green olives.

"Well, it's nice to talk to you outside of work for a change," said Peter.

"I didn't know really whether to come," said Cristina failing to look him straight in the eye.

"Why was that?" asked Peter.

"Well, you are a married man," she replied.

"What difference should that make?" asked Peter. "We're only a couple of colleagues having a quiet drink together."

"Yes, I suppose you're right," Cristina replied.

"Look, I don't know whether you are married or not," said Peter. "It shows how little I know about you, really, considering we work together. Tell me about yourself."

"OK, what do you want to know?"

"Well, first of all, you speak Spanish like a native but you speak perfect English albeit with an Ozzie accent."

"Well, my parents emigrated from Spain to Australia in the 1960s. I was born in 1968 and brought up as an Australian. My father retired five years ago and they decided to return to Spain. I came back with them because I wanted to do archaeological work here. I got married in Oz but it didn't work out so I wanted a new start."

"Have you got any children?" asked Peter.

"Yes, one little boy," she replied. "I have to speak to him every evening before he goes to bed."

"You don't live in Granada then?"

"No," she replied, "we live in Saragossa but this was the nearest job I could get. I manage to get home every two or three weeks. My mother is very good and looks after my little boy. And what about you?"

"Well, I expect Anya has told you that I am separated. It just didn't work out either. I have two kids, Emma and Martha, who live with their mother. I suppose my wife, Mary, has never appreciated the work that I do and it has been the cause of some arguments because of the poor salary."

"My husband was a little bit the same," said Cristina. "He was an engineer and found archaeology a bit of a - what shall I say - trivial occupation. 'You're stuck in the past,' he used to say, 'Get a job that matters, if you're going to work.' I found it all a bit irritating at times."

"Yes, I know what you mean," Peter said sympathetically.

They got on very well and carried on talking about this and that through several more rounds of drinks.

"Well, I suppose I'd better get back to my hotel," Cristina said eventually.

"Whereabouts is it?" Peter inquired.

"It's in the main street not far from here," she replied.

"I'm not far away either," he said. "We'll have one more and then I'll walk you through to your hotel."

They were walking through the back streets towards Cristina's hotel when Peter suddenly said: "Look, why don't you come back and have a drink at my hotel. I've got a very nice bottle of malt whisky that I bought on the plane coming over and it's such an interesting place. It's an old monastery and I know you'll love it. And then I'll walk you back to your place. It's not far."

Cristina did not look too sure about his invitation, at first, but she had enjoyed his company and he looked at her with such boyish appeal that she saw no harm in going there for a quick nightcap.

They reached the hotel and slipped past the office, which was off to the side at the entrance. Little attention was paid to who was coming or going. They walked around a large open cloister, in which lemon and orange trees were growing. The floors were beautifully tiled in the Moorish style, as were the lower parts of the walls. They took the lift up to the first floor and Peter showed her into his room.

There was only one chair and Cristina said she would sit on the bed. Peter poured two large glasses of a twelve-year-old malt.

Peter took the chair and sat opposite her.

"I've enjoyed this evening," he said.

"So have I," Cristina said, this time looking him straight in the eye.

"I suppose some people, especially my wife, would not really understand what we are doing having a drink together in a hotel bedroom like this," he said.

There was a slight pause and Cristina said, her speech now a little bit slurred: "What the eye doesn't see, the heart won't grieve about, I suppose. Can I have another drink?"

"Of course, you can," said Peter and poured her another large malt. Instead of returning to his chair he joined her on the bed, sitting down next to her and chinking his glass against hers. She smiled.

"You know, you're really a very pretty girl, especially when you smile like that," Peter found himself saying.

She collapsed back on the bed laughing, almost spilling her whisky.

"Oh, Peter, that is so corny. I've been brought up as an Australian. We have a reputation for not beating about the bush. Do you want to make love to me?"

Peter was rather taken aback by this and stunned into silence for a moment. It had been a long time.

He put his whisky down and took hers and put it on the bedside cabinet. As he turned round again she was standing in front of him. He put his arms round her and their lips joined in an alcohol-fuelled passion. They fell back onto the bed and began stripping one another in a sexual frenzy. One thing led to another and, as they were in the throws of a passionate embrace, Cristina began moaning and writhing in a way, which could only serve to encourage him further.

Then, as suddenly as they had begun, the moaning and hip movements stopped and were replaced by light snoring. Cristina had fallen asleep.

"Shit," Peter thought. "Just my luck. Oh, well, maybe it's inevitable. It might have been a messy situation anyway."

Peter wondered what to do next. Cristina was well away and obviously not fit to return to her hotel. He quietly undressed her down to her bra and pants and placed her into the bed. It was a large double and there was plenty of room. He undressed himself, got in and turned out the light.

He awoke the next morning and she had gone. She had obviously slipped out in the early hours. She had left a note on the writing desk saying:

"Dear Peter, It was a very enjoyable evening, but I'm sure you'll appreciate that, given your circumstances, it was a one off and should not be repeated. Thanks for the whiskies. Luv C."

"Hmm, I wonder what she thinks happened," thought Peter. "I bet she's got a thick head this morning."

The next day the Granada team met again to assess progress.

Cristina said a cursory 'Good Morning' to Peter along with the other members of the team and then proceeded to avoid his gaze for the rest of the meeting.

Professor Gonzalez chaired the meeting and updated everybody on the situation to date.

"At the moment," he said, "it looks extremely unlikely that we will be given permission to examine the Holy Chalice in Valencia. However, my contact at the University is saying that the Curia does not like the publicity being given to the matter at all and it is possible that they may relent to a limited degree. But in what way he is not at all sure. There are people within the Church, some of them very senior, who are very much against any acceptance of there being a chalice which could, in any way, rival the one in the Cathedral at Valencia He said he would contact me again later in the afternoon. I would suggest we adjourn for an extended lunch and meet up again about five o'clock."

With that everybody got up to leave and Cristina was unusually quick to depart. Peter chased after her down the corridor and shouted " Cristina, wait a moment."

She stopped, shrugged her shoulders and turned to address him:

"Look, Peter, I hope you don't think that what happened last night is going to happen again. I got a little drunk. I am not usually that easy."

"I know you're not, Cristina. Last night is precisely what I want to talk to you about. Look can we go for a coffee somewhere?"

She did not look at all sure, but in the end said: "Well, yes, but I haven't got a lot of time. It will have to be quick."

They found a small bar close by and ordered a couple of 'manchados', the local version of a caffe latte. They settled themselves down at a table by the window and Peter said:

"Look, Cristina, I don't want you to get the wrong idea about what happened last night. We both had more to drink than we should have done but I can assure you nothing happened."

Cristina gave him a knowing look. "Oh, yes, I'm sure it didn't," she said sarcastically.

"It's true," protested Peter. "You fell asleep on me and it was I who put to you to bed because you were well away. Nothing happened, believe me."

"Well, I'm not sure I do believe you," she said.

"For heavens sake," said Peter, "you are an extremely attractive girl and there was no doubt that had circumstances been different then things might have happened. But I can tell you there is nothing so much calculated to be a turnoff as your partner falling asleep on you. And even I am not such a bastard as to take advantage of that situation. Nothing happened, I can assure you."

Cristina thought for a moment and then managed a half smile. "Well, if you say so, I believe you. Oh, God, I feel such a fool," she said putting her head in her hands.

"No worries," said Peter. "Are we still friends?" he said offering out his hand.

"Yes, of course," she said and leaned over and kissed him lightly on the cheek. "Thanks for putting me to bed," she said. "I must have been in a bit of a state."

"I expect it was a combination of the alcohol and tiredness," said Peter. "Perhaps we can meet again and have dinner and not so much to drink?" he asked.

"Well, maybe," she said, "But, I'd rather it was not such an intimate affair next time. Perhaps we could have a meal with another couple or something like that?"

"OK, just a thought," said Peter. "We'll have to see what can be done."

As they left the bar, Peter did not notice that they were being watched. Two men sat in a black Seat Alhambra studying their movements as they walked up the street. The car moved slowly forward, tracking their every step.

At five o'clock they returned to the University. Professor Gonzalez looked pleased with himself and lost no time in reporting the latest development:

"My contact phoned during the afternoon and advised me to ring the Cathedral which I did. I was informed that the Cathedral did not wish to be difficult with regard to the Chalice and that it is very aware of the "unhealthy" public interest, as they put it, in our discovery and the similarities between the two chalices.

"They have, therefore, decided to allow us to examine their Chalice in the presence of several interested parties representing the Cathedral authorities.

"This is on the understanding that we will not be able to do any more than handle it under close supervision. We will not be able to carry out any testing on any part of it. No use of carbon dating, x-rays or any other technique will be permitted. Finally they have demanded that these investigations be undertaken in absolute secrecy and that there should be no publicity whatsoever. As long as we understand that situation then they will make arrangements for us to view it.

"I don't think, personally, we are going to get a much better offer. I've got the feeling the Church is very nervous about the whole thing and there are probably those who are dead against any comparisons being made at all. Any challenge to the status quo is viewed by some quite high up in the Church as almost akin to heresy."

"The news is disappointing but hardly unexpected," said Anya. "I think we might as well take advantage of their offer. There is no other way we are going to get a close enough look. How do the rest of you feel?"

The others all agreed and it was left to the Professor to make the arrangements.

Peter returned to the hotel, had a meal and retired early. He had not been asleep very long when the sound of his mobile ringing awakened him. He noticed the call was from his mother. "What does she want to moan about now?" was his immediate thought. He glanced at his watch and saw that it was three o'clock in the morning.

"Mother," he said, "it's three o'clock in the morning here. What do you want?"

"Peter, can you come up to Kenilworth? I've got awful pains in my stomach and I really don't know what to do," she replied.

"Mum, I told you last weekend. I'm in Spain working. I can't just drop everything like that!"

"I don't know what to do," his mother continued. "The pain is awful"

"Call an ambulance if it's that bad, mother," said the frustrated Peter, well aware that his mother had cried wolf on several occasions before.

"Peter, can't you come up?"

"No, I can't," snapped Peter. "You know I can't. I'm coming back to the U.K. in a day or two. I'll try and come up and see you then. But, at the moment, I can't get away. Look, I'll give you a ring tomorrow. Try and get some sleep now."

Peter felt a little uncomfortable. His mother had the habit of creating anxiety and guilt in him, from time to time, and it seemed to have got worse lately. He groaned, gave a shrug, switched off his mobile and fell into a deep sleep.

The next morning Peter noticed he had missed a call from a number he did not recognise. He called it and discovered that it was his cousin, Bill Carter, from Kenilworth.

"I've got some bad news for you, old chap," said Bill. "Your mother has died. She had a stroke and the ambulance men discovered her collapsed behind the kitchen door at home. She had managed to telephone an ambulance, but she died soon after reaching the hospital. I'm so sorry. She was no age really."

Peter was almost too shocked to reply.

"Thanks for letting me know, Bill," he mumbled. "Where is she at the moment?"

"In the chapel of rest at the hospital," replied his cousin.

"Tell them to keep her there, will you? I'll get the earliest available flight and come straight up. I'll sort things out then."

Peter put his mobile down and flopped into a chair. No tears came to him. He just felt numb. He sat for a while not knowing how he felt. After a couple of hours he rang Anya but there was no reply. So he rang Cristina.

"I've had some awful news," he told her. "My mother has died in England. Can we meet for a coffee or something? I just need to talk to somebody."

"Oh Peter," replied Cristina. "I am so sorry. Yes, of course we can meet."

They met in a coffee bar in the centre of the city. Cristina was very sympathetic and listened to him as he poured out all his feelings of guilt at not listening more carefully to his mother's pleas for help.

"You mustn't reproach yourself," Cristina said with her arm round him. "From what you say she did cry wolf on occasions and it is no small wonder you were reluctant to drop everything just like that when there had been a number of false alarms before. You mustn't feel guilty. There is no way you could have got to the hospital in time."

Cristina tightened her arm round his shoulder and clutched one of his hands as the tears welled up in his eyes.

"This is silly," he said, wiping his eyes with a handkerchief. "This must be so embarrassing for you. Please forgive me."

"Don't be silly," she said. "I'm glad you called me."

"Will you tell the others what's happened? Obviously I am going to have to be away for a few days."

"Of course," Cristina said.

* * *

Peter flew to London Stansted the next day and was picked up by his cousin, Bill Carter. They drove straight to the hospital in Coventry.

The hospital was a huge factory typical of the modern National Health Service and they had some difficulty in finding a place to park.

The ward, where his mother had spent her last hours, was on one of the upper floors. Peter spoke to the sister-in-charge and was assured that his mother had not recovered from her stroke and had not suffered. The Chapel of Rest was just down the corridor from the ward.

Bill left him alone with his mother and Peter sat in a chair next to her body, reflecting on their life together. She looked rather serene now although her last years had not been years of content. He remembered her as being very difficult, at times, in recent years, but all that was forgotten now, as he preferred to remember their years together when he was a boy.

For some reason he remembered bus trips that they used to take together when he was about six. They would play a game where they would get off one bus and get on the next whatever its destination.

"Well, Mum, your troubles are over now," he whispered. "God bless." He leaned forward and kissed her on the forehead and left.

* * *

Peter's mother's funeral took place just over a week later. Peter was quite surprised as to how many people attended the service and he was pleased to see that Mary had bothered to attend. The breakdown in their marriage was irretrievable, but relations between them were less strained.

After the service Peter did his duty at the church door and thanked various people, who had come to the service, for their attendance. Most of them he knew but one obviously foreign gentleman he did not. The man grasped his hand very firmly and said it had been an honour to attend.

Apparently he had been a student friend of his mother's when she had been undertaking her year's study in Spain whilst she was preparing for her language degree many years before. Peter invited him to come round with the others to Bill's house, where refreshments had been laid on, but the man had said that he had to return to London right away. Sadly Peter had not even caught his name.

Peter had been quite surprised by this incident, as he had not been aware that his mother had maintained any contact with former student friends in Spain.

"It just goes to show," he thought to himself, "that you don't know everything about your parents you thought you did."

CHAPTER TWENTY-ONE

The Return Of The Knight

The ship dropped anchor on the western side of the Mount of St. Michael well away from the treacherous rocks, which lurked below the water

Elvin and Tayri stood on the fo'c'sle head gazing at the land ahead of them.

"It is so green," she said.

"It is a pleasant land," he assured her. "They say that it is blessed by dews distilled from Heaven, which is what keeps the fields always green. It is a land of perpetual spring compared to the dry lands of Al Andalus."

Elvin gazed around. It had been a long time since he had set sight on the land of Cornwall, his birthplace.

One could not fail to notice the monastery on top of the Mount of St. Michael, which dominated the whole area from the promontory, which projected into the sea from the small town of Marhas-gow, or Market Jew as it was known in English.

It was said that, once upon a time, the monastery had been six miles inland and surrounded by forest but that a great flood had covered the lower land and placed it out to sea.

Above the town stretched forested hills extending as far as the eye could see. He tried to make out the narrow path that stretched up from the town to the main roadway, which ran along the ridge towards Breage. He wondered what they would find when they arrived back at the castle and how his father would react.

"It's time to disembark," said the captain. They made their way to the ship's ladder which fell sharply down into the boat below which was being tossed about on the gentle swell.

Tayri looked petrified. She had not travelled well on the sea.

"I will descend first and help you down," said Elvin and swung his leg over the side. The rope ladder, held taut by a seaman below, was nevertheless a fearsome experience for anyone not used to seafaring ways. Elvin went down a short way and then beckoned to Tayri to come over the side. It was a very slow process because she was absolutely quaking.

"Don't look down," he said. "Just put your foot down and I will place it on the next rung."

Eventually she reached the bottom of the ladder and was assisted into the boat by the sailor holding it.

It was as well that it was not too far to the shore because the motion of the sea in the small boat was making Tayri look decidedly pale. She had not proved a good sailor throughout the voyage and this final short journey was proving no different. They arrived at the beach where the boat deposited them. They waded through swirling water to dry land. Their baggage was deposited on the sand.

A horse, which Elvin had brought with him was winched down into the sea and prodded and pushed towards the shore. It was a magnificent milk white beast, which had been given to him by Uzmir as a parting present. It was of the finest stock in all Al Andalus and had been the beast on which Tayri was being carried when she had been kidnapped and which they had managed to recapture.

The boat returned to the ship ready to unload its cargo of silks, brocades and spices from the Orient.

A small boy approached them and asked if he could assist with the baggage. Elvin told him he could and that he could escort them to an inn nearby, which turned out to have one room left. The many ships in Mounts Bay were testament to the number of traders staying in the town.

Market Jew was a busy place and Elvin was conscious of how people were staring at Tayri. Although he had obtained suitable clothing for her in France, people were aware of her reddish brown hair, dark skin and lustrous aquamarine eyes and just stared. But she just smiled and they were won over. It was strange, indeed, because sailors and traders with dark skins could be seen every so often in Market Jew from the ships trading for tin. Many Bretons and Cornishmen also had quite swarthy complexions. But it was the fact that she was a woman with unusual, amazing coloured eyes combined with the coffee coloured skin and reddish brown hair, that seemed to captivate people.

Before the boy left Elvin said to him: "Boy, do you know the village of Tremennek?"

"Yes, I do, my lord."

"I want you to go there and seek out a man called Yestin Kyger. Tell him that Sir Elvin has returned from the East and asks him to bring horses, one for the lady to ride, and some packhorses, with all haste tomorrow morning. Here is a silver coin for you and, if you persuade him to come, there is another in it for you."

The boy departed immediately for Tremennek.

The next morning Yestin arrived. The moment the two boyhood friends saw one another they rushed forward and wrapped their arms about one another.

"I never thought to see you alive again, my lord," said Yestin.

"How is my father?" asked Elvin.

"You have not heard?" said Yestin. "Your father died some three years ago. You are now the Lord of Tremennek and truly my liege lord. Your stepmother rules the roost in the castle now and has been seeking for a long time to have you declared dead so that she can inherit your father's wealth.

"She is worse than your father. She had old Jago's eyes put out for just leering at a lady, who was staying at the castle. He was making lewd signs behind her back. There are murmurings that she poisoned your father but nobody dare come out and say it directly."

"That accursed witch! It was her lies that were the cause of my being sent on the pilgrimage. A plague on her! Does she have a child"?

"No, she is childless. That is why she could not inherit your father's wealth and why she has been relying on your being declared dead."

"She will be mighty pleased to see me, then," said Elvin sarcastically.

"How fared you in Santiago, my liege?" asked Yestin.

"I never arrived there. T'is a long story but I have been to the Crusades. I will tell you about it before long."

They loaded the horses. Elvin had brought many books from Al Andalus and jars of all kinds of dried herbs and powders. He was also carrying bales of brocade and rich silks, which had been given to him by Aderbal's family.

One particular bale he handled very carefully himself and would not let anybody touch. Inside, although others could not see it, was a small article wrapped in a Templar's mantle.

Then Elvin turned towards Tayri who was lurking in the background.

"This is Tayri, my betrothed, whom I will marry soon in

Tremennek."

Yestin looked vaguely surprised but tried not to betray it. He smiled at Tayri and said:

"You are most welcome to our land, my lady."

Tayri nodded, still having some trouble with the language.

They set off, riding up the steep track through the woods to the top road, which led to Breage and Hellyston. Several other travellers, who sought to take advantage of their protection on the route, joined them. Most of them were pilgrims on their way to Fowey.

The road was muddy because of recent rains and the sight of so much water, just lying about, and the greenness of the land fascinated Tayri.

Some peasants in a field looked up as they passed by, staring at Elvin's magnificent white horse, and then at the dark skinned lady accompanying him. They leaned on the handles of their scythes for a moment gazing intently at them before returning to their work after they had passed.

A few miles to the east of Market Jew they turned once more down towards the sea and descended a horrendously steep and windy track towards the village of Tremennek. They had to dismount to negotiate the slippery path and make their way down through the valley floor, which was choked with undergrowth, and was a bit swampy.

A narrow path led to the village where there was a church, a water mill and a number of cottages, which lay along a stream running down to the sea. Because of the rain the stream was full and running quite fast. A heron drifted down looking for a place to nest.

And there on a headland, above the sandy bay, the castle was situated. They approached the edge of the village and passed the mill worked by Piran. Piran was outside carrying out some minor repairs to the water wheel and glanced up as they passed.

"All right, are ee, Piran?" asked Yestin in Cornish.

"Right on," replied Piran, straining nosily to see if he recognised the well-dressed stranger and his dusky consort.

"Sir Elvin has returned," shouted Yestin, knowing that the news would be all round the village by eventide and that there would be considerable speculation as to the kind of reception Elvin would get at the castle.

They turned right and began to make their way across the boggy ground towards the higher, better-drained land that led up to the approaches to the castle. It was not really a castle but a solid manor house, but it was the biggest and strongest house in the area and very well fortified.

The land rose sharply as they approached the headland. A deep ditch and a curtain wall of thick stone surrounded the castle. Notched battlements topped the stone wall and there was a wooden drawbridge, which gave access to the gatehouse. The round tower attached to the main stone building inside the walls was visible to them as it was several stories high.

The drawbridge was raised as they approached the gatehouse. Guards were posted on top, looking out over the crenellations.

"Halt, who goes there?" one of the soldiers shouted down.

"Oh, come on, you know me," shouted Yestin, "it is I, Yestin Kyger, the son of the butcher."

"Aye, I know you, but who are the strangers who accompany you?"

Elvin interrupted rather testily, "Open the drawbridge, man. It is I, Sir Elvin Le Gard, the lord of this domain, returned from the East."

The two guards were thrown into some confusion. They spoke to one another and then shouted down to them to wait.

After a while the guard returned to the gatehouse and shouted down to them again.

"I am ordered to forbid your entry. The Lady Alis says that Sir Elvin is dead and, therefore, you must be an impostor. She bids you go on your way from this place."

"I order you, as your liege lord, to open the drawbridge, man, if you value your future," said Elvin firmly.

"Sir, I cannot," cried the soldier, "I suggest you ride on your way."

"On your head be it," replied Elvin. Then turning to Yestin he said, "We are going to have to find a way to make the bitch let us in."

"I will fetch Father Trystan. He will be able to vouch for you and she will have to let you in."

Yestin returned about an hour later with Father Trystan. The priest hobbled along behind Yestin aided by a staff. He was dressed in what resembled a monk's habit. His awkward gait was caused by a malformed foot, which had resulted from an injury when he had fallen out of a tree as a child. He had a pasty complexion and a certain lack of personal charisma but to underestimate him would have been a grievous mistake as the occasional villager had discovered to his cost.

"My lord," he said gazing up at Elvin on his magnificent white palfrey, "we thought you were long dead." At the same time he gave a shifty sidelong glance at Tayri and could not betray the frown that appeared on his face when he saw her coffee coloured skin and foreign appearance.

"Well, you all thought wrong," said Elvin. "I am in rude health and have come to claim my rightful inheritance after carrying the Cross to the East. I want you to explain to that baggage in there where her duty now lies and demand that she grants entry to my betrothed and I or, by Our Lady, I'll not be responsible for what follows."

"There is no need to blaspheme, my lord. I am sure we can resolve the problem given good will. Your stepmother has been doing all in her power to maintain the manor in your absence."

"With the idea of taking over the domain if I should be declared dead, no doubt," said Elvin bitterly.

"That would have been her right had you not, by God's good grace, been returned to us safe and sound," said the priest. "Now let us be sensible." He approached the gatehouse and asked the guard to fetch the Lady Alis.

After a while Alis de Trevarno appeared at the top of the gatehouse with the guard.

Elvin remembered her reasonable good looks but she had aged considerably and still bore the poisonous personality that he knew from days gone by. He loathed her then and he loathed her now.

"Good day, my lady," said the priest in a somewhat obsequious fashion. "As you can see Sir Elvin has been miraculously restored to us and is here to claim his inheritance. He would expect that you would see it in your mind to give him entry to the castle, now rightfully his property."

"This man is an impostor," Alis shouted down, "who comes to steal these lands away from me, lands promised to me by my poor departed husband. I knew it as soon as the news was brought to me. And who is that Saracen whore with him?"

"News has travelled fast," thought Elvin. He was about to shout back but the priest urged calm and said: "It is not an impostor, my lady. I can vouch for that and the lady, who accompanies him, he says, is his betrothed. I urge you to let them in"

"Never," shrieked Alis. "I will never let him in. Tell him to depart and take his vile foreign whore with him."

"But it is the law, my lady. Do you want him to have to resort to legal means to enforce this? You know what that will mean. You will be thrown out of the castle."

"He can do what he likes," she shouted back.

The priest was quickly becoming exasperated by the situation and beginning to lose his patience. Normally he would hesitate to act counter to the wishes of someone superior to him in the village but the legal situation was clear. He shifted awkwardly on his crippled foot, which was beginning to pain him somewhat. Then he shouted up to the guard:

"You know the law, my man. This is your liege lord. Open the drawbridge!"

"You do nothing of the sort," ordered Alis sharply.

"You had better open up, my man, or live with the consequences," shouted Elvin with some conviction.

"Come on, man. Lower the drawbridge. You know the penalties for disloyalty to your liege lord," urged the priest.

This had the desired effect as the guards began to lower the drawbridge despite the stream of obscenities coming from Alis. She struggled to prevent them carrying out their orders and had to be forcibly restrained.

"Put her in the dungeon to cool off," Elvin ordered as their horses' hooves clattered across the drawbridge and under the now raised portcullis. The guards dragged Alis off kicking and screaming.

They rode across the bailey towards the stables in one corner where they dismounted. A groom took charge of the horses and several servants appeared to unload the baggage.

Opposite, on the seaward side, stood the main stone building consisting of the great hall with private quarters at each end of it. In the other corner, at the same end of the bailey as the stables, was the round, or rather hexagonal, keep, the last refuge in case of a siege of any sort. It was connected to the main hall by an enclosed passageway, but it could also be entered by its own doorway leading from the bailey. All these stone buildings were covered in a spectacular white lime wash. All the other buildings were of wooden construction.

Smoke rose from a chimney in the middle of the roof of the great hall, which was little more than a hole with a specially constructed raised cowl over the top of it. The windows were small and there was very little glass on account of its expense. Most of them just had iron bars and wooden shutters.

"It's good to be back," said Elvin stretching himself. "I have to thank you, Father, for assisting us," he said addressing Father Trystan. "I trust you will join us for dinner this evening."

"I would be most honoured, my lord," replied the priest.

Later that evening they sat at the long table in the great hall with a huge log fire burning in the centre of it. They dined on roast goose and a venison pie accompanied by good red wine. The priest munched noisily as he ate, which brought the occasional frown from Elvin who did not approve of bad table manners, although, to be truthful, his father had never been one for fine etiquette at the table.

"Is the Lady Alis not to join us, my lord?" enquired the priest, whilst tearing a piece of flesh from the goose and not yet having finished the previous mouthful.

"No," said Elvin. " I have judged it best to leave her to reflect upon her situation for a day or two. I am sure she will come to her senses. It must have been a surprise to her that I have returned unscathed."

"Quite so," commented the priest.

"But I have a much more important matter to discuss." said Elvin changing the subject. "It is the question of my marriage to the Lady Tayri, which I wish you to undertake with all due haste."

"Mmmm," mumbled Father Trystan feeling decidedly uncomfortable. "She is clearly not of our land and she does not appear to speak very much of our language. From where does she come?"

"She is from Spain and of Berber origin," said Elvin truthfully although it seemed evident that the priest had little knowledge of exactly what that implied.

"Is she of the True Faith?" asked Father Trystan.

"If you mean by the True Faith - that of Our Lord Jesus Christ and the blessed Trinity - the answer is no. She has been raised in the Islamic Faith. But she would be willing to convert to Christianity," replied Elvin emphatically.

"With the greatest respect, my lord, there appear to be several difficulties. Firstly this is a time of great conflict between Christian and Mohammedan. The Lady Tayri is a heathen and technically an enemy of the True Faith. Secondly she appears to speak little of our language and one wonders whether she would be able to make the great strides necessary to totally understand all the implications of converting to our Faith."

"I can explain much of what you may require of her to her. I have a certain knowledge of her language," explained Elvin.

"I am a bit uncertain about the whole business," said the priest. "I may well have to refer the matter to the Bishop in Exeter."

"So be it," said Elvin. "But whilst you are doing that perhaps you would mention to him that I have in my possession an article of great significance to our Faith. I have brought it with me from across the water and I intend to restore to its rightful place at Glaston."

"Mmmm, and what might that be?" enquired the priest.

"Nothing less than the Holy Grail itself," declared Elvin proudly, "stolen from our land and now rightfully returned to it."

"Is it possible that I might see this — er — Holy Grail?" asked Father Trystan, a trifle sceptically.

"Perhaps," said Elvin, "when the moment is right."

Father Trystan took this to mean that he was not going to be privileged to view the relic on that particular evening and conversation passed to other things. Father Trystan was already thinking about how he would word his letter to the Bishop.

Several weeks later Father Trystan was summoned to St. Germans to meet with a Canon, Robert de Lynton, delegated by the Bishop of Exeter, to discuss the matter of Sir Elvin's marriage.

"We read your letter with great interest," said Canon Robert when their conversation began. "You seem to have some reservations about this marriage."

"Yes, I do," replied Father Trystan. "Sir Elvin's betrothed is a Saracen lady whom he has claimed to have brought to our country from the land of Spain. She is, as you would guess of the Islamic Faith — a faith that would not be acceptable for a Christian to marry in these troublesome times."

"Well, certainly not, unless she is prepared to convert to the True Faith. Is there any possibility of that?" asked Canon Robert.

"Sir Elvin claims so but her knowledge of English, French or Latin is almost non-existent. In my humble opinion she would be incapable, as yet, of understanding any question put to her."

"It is vitally important that she understands the significance of the incarnation of God as Jesus, and its importance to Our Faith, and of the salvation of the Trinity," Canon Robert said with emphasis. "If she is to marry a knight of our realm she will be required to renounce her infidel beliefs."

"I agree," said Father Trystan. "Belief in an untrue god and acceptance of the promiscuous ways of the Mohammedans is not permissible. Do you know that they permit the marriage of a man to more than one wife?"

"Yes, indeed," said the Canon. "It is a scandalous situation. What has Sir Elvin had to say about their beliefs?"

"He seems deluded into thinking that all religions are fundamentally the same, that they all preach love and tolerance, condemn violence and follow the same basic set of morals. He has even told me that he thinks Islam is a peaceful religion."

"You must dissuade him from such views," urged Canon Robert. "They could be extremely dangerous. Unfortunately there are a few misguided creatures, who have come back from the East with such unworthy views. I only wish that the Saracen Saladin had followed a course of peaceful non-violence after the Battle of Hattin and not beheaded absolutely every Templar and Hospitaller that had been captured. You must warn Sir Elvin that he is sailing close to the wind in pronouncing such views about Mohammedanism. They could be construed by some as heresy."

The Canon sat thinking for a short while. Then he said: "At the moment there appears to be no way we could publish a wedding notice or declare the banns in church for such a marriage. You will have to inform Sir Elvin of that. I will ask the Bishop to send a letter to that effect as well. We must both pray for a change in the circumstances that will return Sir Elvin properly to our Faith and introduce his betrothed to the True Faith as well."

"There is another thing," said Father Trystan. "Sir Elvin claims that he has brought the Holy Grail back to our shores and seems to be offering this as a means of expediting his marriage."

"The Holy Grail?" said the Canon. "What do you mean, the Holy Grail? Have you seen it?"

"No." replied Father Trystan. "As yet he has refused to show it to me."

"The Church's attitude to the legends regarding the Holy Grail is clear," said Canon de Lynton. "They are the stuff of troubadours and poets provided for the entertainment of princes. If Sir Elvin has a true relic of some kind and wishes to bestow it upon our Holy Mother Church then well and good. But we need to know rather more about it and it will have to be authenticated. You will need to discuss this with him."

"I will return post haste and see what I can establish," said Father Trystan.

"Good. Let me know what develops and how he reacts to our decision with regard to this marriage," was the Canon's final word.

Father Trystan returned to Tremennek. As he approached the village the sky turned dark and a strong wind got up. The weather became most inclement. It began to rain hard and, from time to time, showers of large hailstones fell upon the drenched priest nearly knocking him from his mule. He took temporary shelter in the church seeking in vain to dry himself off.

When the showers had subsided he made his way up the slope towards the castle with the aim of informing Sir Elvin of the result of his meeting with the Bishop's envoy. As he approached the gatehouse there was a tremendous commotion coming from inside.

Suddenly the drawbridge was lowered and the gates opened. The astonished priest witnessed the indignant and screaming Lady Alis being ejected from the castle. She had been placed on a scrawny packhorse and was accompanied by two others loaded with her personal belongings. Two of the Sir Elvin's retainers were prodding and pushing the horses across the drawbridge. In the damp and wet she looked a bedraggled sight and the priest was rather concerned at the treatment being meted out to her.

When Lady Alis spotted Father Trystan she yelled furiously at him: "Look, Father, at how this bastard has treated his own stepmother. He has expelled me from my rightful property and slandered me as a poisoner of his father. A thousand curses on him and on his Saracen whore and all their issue!"

"Get moving," growled one of the soldiers and gave her horse an almighty rap on the rump. It carried her off at a gallop down the slope towards the village.

"Is there any need to treat the Lady Alis so?" asked Father Trystan, somewhat concerned.

"We have our orders, Father," replied the soldiers. "Sir Elvin has accused her of poisoning his father in order to try to unlawfully inherit his domain. Her lady-in-waiting has confessed to assisting her. She is lucky that she has not suffered death for such a murder. Sir Elvin has decided to outlaw her from his domain instead."

"That I have," came a voice behind them. It was Elvin mounted on his white horse. "I am glad to see the back of that bitch. You men, return to your posts."

When the soldiers had gone Elvin invited the priest into the castle to dry himself before the great log fire in the great hall and offered sustenance of a mug of ale and some cold roast chicken.

"What news do you bring me, Father?" asked Elvin at last. Father Trystan explained the situation and it was clear that Elvin was not best pleased.

"Did you tell the Canon what I have brought back with me?" he asked

"I did, my lord," replied Father Trystan. "I must confess, however, that I was not able to tell him very much as I, myself, have not seen the Grail, as you call it."

"Then I will show you now," said Elvin and bade the priest follow him. They left the hall via a long stone passageway, which led them under the solar or private living room of the castle and into the hexagonal keep. At the top of the keep they entered a room the like of which the priest had never ever seen in his life.

The walls were hung with carpets of the most intricate designs and a similar rug covered the floor in the centre of the room.

One wall was lined with shelves upon which rested many leather bound volumes. A table stood below, upon which lay an open book and Father Trystan stole a glance at the highly decorated tome. He was one of the very few people in the village who could read and write but he was unable to make any sense of the hand in which the book was written. The script seemed to be made up of a collection of strange squiggles and loops the like of which the Father had never seen before. What he could make out on the page, however, were drawings of parts of the human body, which somewhat disturbed him.

On another wall were ranged a variety of jars and phials of all sorts of sizes containing liquids, powders and other concoctions of many different colours.

In the fireplace which lay against an external wall of the keep strange looking liquids bubbled in a couple of metal pots, which were suspended over the burning logs.

For Elvin the scene conjured up fond memories of Aderbal's laboratory and study back in Granada. For Father Trystan it conjured up his worst nightmares of a sorcerer's den.

CHAPTER TWENTY-TWO

Shock And Confusion

After the funeral Peter returned to his mother's house. He felt rather empty, and a little guilty, at not having had more contact with her.

He felt, in a way, that he had not really got to know as much about her as he could have done and their contact in recent years had been sketchy to say the least. It was true that she could be a difficult woman and this situation had got worse after his father, Brian, had died of cancer in his early seventies about five years previously. She had tended to try and use Peter as a crutch at a time when he was raising his own family and pursuing a career, which often took him away from home. He found life, perhaps, quite stressful himself and was not as sympathetic to her problems as he might have been.

Peter searched around for some whisky, as he knew his mother had liked a tipple. In fact, he had sometimes complained that she tended to drink too much of it. He found a bottle, which was about a quarter full, hidden in the filing cabinet where she kept all her papers. He poured himself a stiff drink and fell asleep not long afterwards.

The next morning Peter pondered on what he should do about his mother's estate. He had a search through the cabinet, where he had found the whisky, and came across a file labelled 'Will'. Peter had been aware that it could be found in the filing cabinet because his mother had advised him of this sometime before, although he had taken little notice at the time.

His mother had named her executors as a firm of solicitors called Ansell & Flower of Kenilworth.

Peter gave the solicitors a ring during the morning and informed them of his mother's death. It was suggested that there should be an initial meeting between a representative of the firm and Peter to run over the arrangements for settling his mother's estate. A meeting with Chris Ansell was set up at his mother's house for the beginning of the following week.

Peter and the solicitor met on the Tuesday of the following week and Chris Ansell ran through the procedure for applying for a Grant of

Probate on his mother's estate and settling her various debts. Peter was the only beneficiary under the will but he was warned that it would take some months before the solicitors would be able to release the bulk of the monies due to him. Most of those monies would relate to the sale of his mother's house and contents.

Chris Ansell advised him to take any small items of sentimental value that he wanted right away as once they had become part of probate they would no longer be available him. Everything would have to be sold.

"Incidentally," Ansell said just before he was about to leave, " your mother instructed us to give you this letter on the occasion of her death." He handed Peter an envelope on which he recognised his mother's spidery writing.

After the solicitor had left Peter opened the envelope. The letter ran as follows:

"My darling Peter,
When you read this letter I will have passed on to another world. I have asked my solicitors to give you the letter because I feel you ought to know what, cowardly as it may seem to you, I have failed to tell you over all these years. In the weeks before I began to feel ill I tried to tell you but felt unable to do so over the telephone. I am sorry that you have had to hear this via a letter and I hope you will find it in your heart to forgive me.

Peter, your father, Brian, was not your real father. He urged me to tell you before he died and I made a promise to him to do so, but somehow I could not bring myself to do it. It's something we should have done years ago.

When I did my year in Spain in the nineteen fifties, I fell in love with a Spanish student at the University of Granada called Juan Antonio Guardia. One thing led to another and I fell pregnant by him in 1960 and you were born when I returned to England in early 1961. Juan Antonio was unable to marry me because he was already betrothed and about to marry another woman, whom he had known since childhood. His family was very old fashioned and just would not have accepted me. We had a tearful parting and I always wondered what happened to him.

I had known Brian since we met at a Sixth Form dance. I met up with him again soon after I returned from Spain and soon we were going out. We got on very well together and he agreed to marry me and bring you up as his own son. He took our secret faithfully to his grave.

After Brian died I wondered about Juan Antonio and what happened to him. I still received the odd New Year's card from students I had known in Granada and I asked one, Luis Fernandez, to find out for me. Luis told me that Juan Antonio had died a few years before but that he had always asked after me and, in particular, you. Apparently they had been very close friends, something of which I had not been aware. The sad thing was that Juan Antonio's marriage had not been a particularly happy one and had remained childless. He and his wife were divorced in 1977.

I am so sorry, my dear, that you had to learn this news in such a way. I hope that it will not come as too much of a shock.

I know you might like to talk to somebody, who knew your real father and Luis Fernandez promised me that, if you wished, you could go and see him in Spain. He is a nice man and I am sure you will like him.

Don't forget in all this that Brian loved you very much as his own son. He was a good man and I grew to love him dearly.

God bless you and keep you well,
Your loving mother, Anne."

Peter sank into a chair. His mind was in a whirl. At first he was angry, very angry. He could not understand how they could have kept the secret from him. Surely they could have told him when he reached an age where he would have been capable of taking it all in. But, perhaps, they were afraid that he would want to seek out his real father, whose family, in turn, may not have known the truth. It might have been embarrassing for all concerned.

He could not really complain. On the whole Brian and his mother had treated him well, given him a good education and brought him up properly. He had good memories of his childhood.

Nevertheless Peter was very tempted to take up the offer contained in the letter. Apparently Luis Fernandez still lived in Granada and Peter would have to return to the city very soon anyway. He could follow the matter up then.

* * *

A few days later Peter returned to Granada. Everybody was very sympathetic regarding his mother's death, particularly Anya. She expressed deep regret that she had been out when he had telephoned.

Discussions had taken place with the Cathedral authorities and, now that Peter was back, arrangements were made to visit the Cathedral in Valencia.

The Cathedral was typical of those of South and Eastern Spain in that it had been originally converted from a mosque and demonstrated a variety of different architectural styles.

After making enquiries they were shown through to the Chapel of the Holy Grail, an old chapter house, which had remained closed since their first dealings with the Curia.

One of the officials of the Cathedral, who introduced himself as Javier Aviles, met them. There were several other persons in attendance. Professor Velasquez, who had appeared on the TV programme with Anya, was also lurking in the background. There was a certain air of unease apparent among some of those present.

The Chalice had been removed from the magnificently rich florid Gothic relief that usually framed it and placed upon a table specially set up for the purpose. At first sight it was amazing how similar it appeared to the chalice, which they had found in Granada. Both were placed side by side and the archaeologists were free to examine both cups provided they wore special white gloves provided for the purpose.

After a while the four archaeologists looked at one another and agreed that the two chalices were virtually identical apart from two things. Firstly there was a large crack in the Valencian Chalice, the result of the accident in the eighteenth century. Secondly and, perhaps more importantly, the Valencian Chalice had an inscription on its foot in what appeared to be Arabic. Although Peter was an expert in medieval armour and had studied some Arabic he could not make head or tail of it.

"Would it be permitted for us to take some photographs?" Peter asked.

The Cathedral officials consulted with one another for a while and it was clear that there was not wholehearted agreement. But eventually permission was given, provided that they promised not to make any photographs available to the Press.

"Make sure you get some good photos of the inscription on the base," whispered Professor Gonzalez to Peter, who had the digital camera. And that was as far as they could go.

They repaired to a small bar not far from the Cathedral to compare notes.

"They certainly seem to be remarkably similar apart from the crack and the inscription," said the Professor. "One must surely be a copy of the other. We know that at least one copy of the Valencian Chalice has been made in modern times so there is really no reason why it should not have happened in earlier times for whatever reason. I'd like to know what the inscription says, though. Any chance of your finding out, Peter?"

"Well, I'll do my best," said Peter, looking at the digital images displayed on the LCD monitor of his camera. "The problem is that Arabic letters and inscriptions are often very elaborate and decorative. This is quite clearly some classic form of Arabic and it has been etched into the stone very faintly. The characters appear to be on the crude side as well. They may be difficult to interpret. I'll see what I can find out. Somebody must have done some work on it."

They left the bar and returned to their hotel, an elegant nineteenth century building not far from the Cathedral. Nobody noticed the ominous black Seat, which was still tracking them.

Later that evening Peter went out to look for a magazine stall where he could purchase something to read. On his way back the skies darkened and he suddenly felt the cold of a solitary raindrop on the top of his forehead, which became two and then three. The drops were slow in their intensity at first, but then suddenly increasing to a downpour.

He ran back as fast as he could to the shelter of the hotel. It had suddenly become quite close and it looked as if they could be in for a stormy night. The neon lights outside twinkled and glimmered from their reflections in the puddles in the street and in the trickling rivulets of water desperately making their way towards the nearest drainage outlets.

Peter read the magazine for a while and then dozed off. An enormous clap of thunder woke him from his slumbers. He had no idea what time it was. He must have dozed for longer than had thought He glanced at his watch and saw that it was half past midnight. Looking out of the window he blinked from time to time as great flashes of lightning, probably far out to sea, illuminated the whole city.

Then he was conscious of some faintish tapping on his door. He peered through the spy hole and observed Anya standing at the door in her dressing gown. As he opened the door there was another huge flash of lightning, followed almost immediately by a clap of thunder, which shook the whole building. Anya literally bolted into the room.

"What's the matter?" cried Peter.

"Can I come in with you?" she said. "I've always been frightened of thunder storms ever since I was a child. I really can't stand them."

"Yes, of course you can," said Peter and motioned her to go inside. "You can sit in the chair over there, if you like, or you can take the other half of the bed." It was a large queen size bed and she chose to lie down on top of the duvet without taking off her dressing gown.

"Do you mind if we keep the lights on," she said. "It frightens me when I see the flashes of lightning. I know, then, that there is going to be a great crash of thunder and I absolutely hate it."

She was visibly shaking and Peter went across to her. He put his arm round her to comfort her.

"Come on," he said, "it's only a bit of thunder and lightning. The chances of anything happening to you are x million to one."

"Oh, I know all that, but I still don't like it."

"Do you want a drink or something?" Peter asked.

"No, no," she said, "I just don't want to be alone."

"OK," he said, "let's try to get some sleep."

He lay down beside her on the ample bed. He thought to himself: "The number of times in the past I wished I could have been in this situation." He smiled to himself. But he knew there had never been any mileage in those kinds of thoughts.

Somewhere about one o'clock the lights went out. The continuing flashes of lightning and claps of thunder woke Anya up again.

"What's happened to the lights," she asked.

"There's been a power cut," Peter explained.

"Oh God," she moaned and felt for him in the dark. He put his arms round her and gently stroked her forehead.

"Come on, try to get some sleep," he said. "It'll soon be over."

And that's how they remained until the storm subsided at about five in the morning.

Peter tapped her on the shoulder to wake her and said: "Come on, you'll be all right now. You'd better go back to your room or else you'll get me talked about."

She smiled sleepily, whispered her thanks and returned to her room.

Peter came down to breakfast early. Cristina was already there and Peter joined her at her table. He detected a somewhat frosty air, which he could not quite put his finger on.

"What an awful night," he said. "It's a long time since I have experienced thunder and lightning like that."

"Yes, it was quite frightening," Cristina replied. After a pause she said: "Did I hear Anya knock on your door last night?"

Peter was a little taken aback at this but knew he could not evade the question.

"Yes, she did," he replied. "She was absolutely petrified. So she came in with me for a bit."

"You two seem to be becoming very friendly," said Cristina, icily.

"Perhaps she's not told you but we've been good friends for a number of years, in fact, very much in a platonic way. She was just frightened and needed a bit of company." Peter sensed that his explanation was not washing somehow with Cristina.

"I think there's rather more in it than that. I've noticed how you attach yourself to her. You always sit next to her at meetings and you seem to be whispering little comments to one another from time to time."

"What's the matter?" asked Peter. "Are you jealous?"

"Don't be ridiculous!" she replied sharply. But Peter felt certain he had struck a chord.

It was Sunday and Peter had planned to visit a friend from England who had just bought a house in Oliva not far down the coast from Valencia. It was a representative from the car hire firm, who interrupted his conversation with Cristina. Peter completed the paperwork and accepted delivery of his vehicle for the day.

He went up to his room to collect his coat. And just as he was leaving a thought occurred to him. He knocked on Anya's door.

She opened it still clad in her dressing gown.

"Look," he said, "I've got a car for the day and I'm going down to Oliva to see a friend. I wondered whether you'd like to come as well."

"Well, I don't know," she said. "I'm not even dressed."

"I can wait. There's no problem. I'll be in the lobby in half an hour."

"But, do you think we really ought to, bearing in mind the past?"

"I don't see why not. The whole thing is entirely innocent as far as Yuba is concerned and I don't owe any obligations to Mary anymore anyway. Do yourself a favour and have a day off."

"OK, then, yes. I'd love to come."

The journey to Oliva was uneventful and the traffic was relatively light. This was fairly unusual as they were travelling down the main coastal highway towards Alicante.

Peter's friend, a university colleague, had bought a two hundred year old house in the old town of Oliva.

The house was a traditional whitewashed building on old Moorish foundations. There appeared to be a mixture of Spanish and English families living in the narrow street and, apparently, more and more English could be heard spoken in the shops and bars round about. In fact, the first person Peter asked for directions, turned out to be English.

They knocked on the front door and it was opened by a tousled haired man of about the same age as Peter, who was dressed in a tee shirt, baggy shorts and sandals. They were ushered into a sitting room and saw that the first floor was built on several levels. White walls, Valencian beams, terracotta tiles and a large wood burning stove helped to maintain the original character of the house, of which Larry, Peter's friend, was immensely proud. He took them through to a large terrace at the back of the building, which looked out over the olive groves, from which the town had got its name. To one side, as well, stretched orange groves almost as far as one could see.

Larry had a cool, refreshing jug of Sangría waiting for them. Unfortunately he had not realised that Anya was teetotal and hurried to get her some fruit juice instead. Whilst they enjoyed their drinks, June, Larry's partner, cooked wonderful 'paella a la Valenciana' on the wood fire, which was burning in the stone barbecue to one side of the terrace.

After their lunch Larry and Peter chatted about their jobs and June showed Anya around the house. It was an enjoyable day and Peter was pleased to see Anya smiling and relaxed.

On their way back Peter said: "I hope it hasn't been too boring for you today."

"Oh, no," Anya replied gently touching his knee, "I've really enjoyed it. It's such a change to go somewhere and feel totally at ease and relaxed. It's not always like that for me."

"I didn't realise that the work got to you like that," said Peter.

"It's not the work. I enjoy that immensely. It's my home life. There's – how do you call it? – an atmosphere."

"What sort of an atmosphere?"

"It's Yuba. He can be very critical of my work and, sometimes, he can fly into the most furious temper over nothing. I sometimes go home and, at first, everything is fine and, then, after a day or two, some silly thing sparks it off.

"Last time it was all about a traditional dish from the south of Morocco, that I had tried to cook for him. He comes from that area and I thought he would be pleased. But he said it was not spiced enough and that his mother would have cooked a much better one. I offered to cook him something else but he said he didn't want anything. I tried to humour him but he began to rant and rage and said the dish had not been fit to eat. To top it all he made a great show of scraping his meal into the dog's bowl and saying that it was only fit for an animal to eat. I was in tears by this time but he was not in any way sympathetic."

"The guy's a bastard," said Peter, "but you know what I think. I don't know why you stay with him. He treats you like a chattel. You don't have to put up with that in this day and age."

"He's not always like that. Sometimes he can be very nice," Anya said.

"I wouldn't have treated you like that," said Peter not quite sure what he was starting. And then it all came out as Peter stared relentlessly at the road ahead of him. He told her again that he had loved her ever since he had first seen her at university all those years before. He told her of his agony when she had been away at the weekends or during vacations. He told her of how he had yearned to be with her all the time and how jealous he was when he had known she was with Yuba. He told her of how he had prayed that something would happen to break up her relationship with Yuba and of his eventual realisation that this was not to be.

"Oh, Peter, I'm so sorry you suffered on my account," Anya said. "But you did find Mary in the end."

"Yes, I did," Peter replied, "and, at first, it was fine but, then, when I kept meeting you at conferences and things, it was all stirred up again. I can understand now why Mary got so jealous. She probably had every right to be."

"I do have strong feelings for you," confessed Anya, "and, but for differences of religion and culture, we might have been lovers. But that can't be and my duty now is with my husband. We are a devout family and to leave him would go very much against our Muslim beliefs. Unlike some of my sisters I don't see the need to wear anything but European dress. But that doesn't mean to say that I do not subscribe seriously to the beliefs of my faith."

"I know," said Peter, in a matter-of-fact way.

They got back to the hotel in Valencia. They declined dinner as they had eaten well at lunchtime and Anya said that she was going to her room to ring Yuba. Peter went to his room for a while and watched television. There was not much on except the usual Sunday bullfight, which was not to his taste at all. He found it difficult to settle and, after a while, he decided to ask Anya if she would like to go for a walk.

He knocked on her door and, at first, there was no reply. Then a weak voice asked who it was and, when he answered, she opened the door. She was in her dressing gown and looked bedraggled and distraught.

She fell into his arms sobbing inconsolably. She explained that she had rung Yuba and, during the course of the conversation, had made the mistake of telling him that she had spent the day with Peter. Yuba had become very angry and had started to call her all sorts of names. He had finished off by saying that he did not care whether she came home again or not and had slammed down the phone.

Peter ushered her into his room. He found some tissues and wiped her eyes.

"C'mon now," he whispered to her. "We can't have tears spoiling those beautiful blue eyes."

She gave him a weak smile and dropped her head onto his shoulder. He held her tightly, stroking her hair and gently massaging the back of her head. Then he drew her head up to look at him.

"You can't go on like this," he said, shaking his head. She shook her head in turn and looked utterly confused.

"I don't know, I don't know," she whispered.

"C'mon, lie down on the bed for a while. Just relax. Get all that garbage out of your mind."

Anya lay down on the bed on her tummy and he began to gently massage the back of her neck and shoulders. He continued doing this for a while. Then thinking she was falling asleep, he said: "I'll leave you for a while. Try to sleep. I won't be too long."

"Don't leave me," she pleaded and offered her hand to him. When he clasped it, she pulled him down beside her.

Anya turned and gazed up at him with all kinds of emotions expressed in her eyes. Her hand gently stroked his cheek. Then she grasped his head gently from behind and pulled it down to hers. Their lips met and they kissed passionately. They undressed one another slowly, each removing a garment in turn. He made love to her in a gentle, unhurried manner. It was as if the nerves in her body were the taut strings of an instrument, from which was being released the haunting tune of some ancient love song. She arched up to receive him and they were one. Later, exhausted, they both fell asleep in one another's arms.

Their slumber was interrupted by the ring tone of Anya's mobile. It was Yuba. He seemed to be apologising and Peter could only hear her answering 'yes' repeatedly to the questions being asked at the other end of the radio waves.

She switched off her mobile and turned to him, clearly annoyed. She looked him straight in the eye and said: "Peter, you've made me do something I was determined not to do - betray my marriage vows. I don't know how I am going to look Yuba in the face again. How could you, you bastard? I hate you."

"But................" Peter protested in vain.

Anya was in no mood to listen. She turned her back on him and dressed hurriedly. She stormed out of his room, slamming the door behind her.

Peter sank back onto the bed with a frustrated shrug.

"One call from that bastard and she's flying back to him," he thought.

"How masochistic can you get? What the fuck have I done? She instigated it. One thing's for sure. I don't think I'll ever understand women."

CHAPTER TWENTY-THREE

The Evil Knight

Father Trystan stood in wonderment at the relic before his gaze. He had not known what to expect when Elvin had unwrapped it from the Templar mantle, in which it was concealed. It was a chalice of almost indefinable beauty.

"It is truly magnificent. From where did you obtain it, my son, and why do you say it is the Holy Grail?"

"This is the Sacred Chalice of the Last Supper of Our Lord," explained Elvin, "brought to this land by Joseph of Arimathea after the Passion of Our Lord. He filled it with the blessed blood of Christ and took it to Glaston where he buried it to preserve it from those who would steal it. But stolen it was and, somehow, it came into the hands of the Kings of Aragon. I have won it back and am offering to return it to its rightful resting place in Glaston, provided, of course, that a change to a much more favourable view regarding my marriage to the Lady Tayri is made."

"I am not sure that you can bargain with our Holy Mother Church in such a fashion," replied the priest. "We are not common peddlers, with whom one can haggle at will. We are here to do the work of the Lord and to preserve God's will. It is true, so I have heard, that there is a legend surrounding the so-called Holy Grail at Glaston. No one has ever discovered the Grail in Glaston in spite of many efforts to find it," said the Father.

"Well now you know the reason," said Elvin.

"Well that be as it may," replied Father Trystan. "The point is that, if you have a relic, which you wish to bestow upon the Church, you will have to hand it over to me to be properly authenticated."

"I am not handing over anything to you, at the moment, Father," said Elvin emphatically. "A Holy Mother Church that refuses to marry one of its sons, who has carried the Cross in Spain and Egypt, has no right to such a relic."

The priest frowned. "You are fully aware, my son, as to why you cannot marry this woman, at present," he said.

Just at that moment their conversation was interrupted by the sound of a liquid boiling over in the fireplace. There was a curious egg-shaped copper pot there with a large spout on it. The steaming liquid shot out of this container straight into another placed in front of the fire.

"Damn it," said Elvin, retrieving the pot from the fireplace.

"What is it you are preparing with such care?" enquired Father Trystan, straining to see what was in the pot.

"I am exploring the various methods of producing alcohol," Elvin explained.

"Well, I look forward to sampling the product," said the priest.

"I am afraid it is not for that purpose, Father. It is for use as an antiseptic."

"I am afraid I do not understand," said the puzzled priest.

"It's for treating wounds of all sorts," explained Elvin. "If you apply it soon enough it will prevent the wound festering and may well save lives."

"And where did you learn that from? From your strange foreign books?"

"Yes, I did. I think we have a lot to learn from others."

"It is, perhaps, not wise to meddle with the will of God," said Father Trystan. "If it's God's will that someone dies of a wound, then so be it."

"I believe that I am carrying out the will of God and that He is guiding me in my endeavours to heal the sick," said Elvin with zealot-like belief in his calling.

"Be careful, my son, that you are not perceived as dabbling in sorcery and alchemy," said Father Trystan in an almost threatening tone of voice.

"I think you had better leave now," urged Elvin. "I hope to see you again when your mind is more open to the things we can learn from others."

And so the Father left.

* * *

Two or three days later Father Trystan had a visitor. It was Sir Richard Godrevy, an elderly uncle of Alis de Trevarno.

"I am much concerned for the welfare of my niece," said Sir Richard. "Are you aware that she has been expelled from the estate of her late husband in the most pitiless way?"

"Yes, I am," replied Father Trystan. "I must say I was far from happy about the circumstances. I felt that she had done a lot to maintain the Le Gard domain, whilst Sir Elvin was away in the East."

"That surely was so," said Sir Richard. "Many rumours, too, have come to my ear regarding the strange antics of this knight. I have heard tell that he is practising magic and sorcery up at the castle and casting spells from books he had brought with him from the East."

"That would appear to be so," said the priest. "He is certainly meddling in things that may be contrary to the will of God and I fear very much for his soul."

"So what is to be done with this festering boil in our midst?"

"I will have further discussions with the Bishop of Exeter. But it is clear that Sir Elvin is under the influence of the heretical practices of the East and of the woman that he would have as his wife."

"Quite so. My niece, the Lady Alis, is convinced that she is a witch and has the evil eye. I really think that some action should be taken against the two of them."

"Leave it with me, my lord," said Father Trystan. "I will keep a close watch on events at the castle and, if I feel that the Anti-Christ is at work, then I will not hesitate to do God's bidding."

* * *

A week later Father Trystan was sitting in the confessional in Tremennek Church. It was his custom to take confessions at dusk when the villagers were returning from the fields. The church was ill lit and gloomy. The flames from the braziers cast weird shadows and the figures on the painted columns almost seemed to be moving. The priest gave a little shudder and uttered a short prayer, as he was wont to do on such occasions. He was never one hundred per cent happy in the church on his own in the darkness of the evening.

Father Trystan started as the great wooden door to the church clanked open. He had great difficulty in making out the figure that had walked quickly through the church and slipped into the confessional.

He peered through the grill as the figure sat down. The absence of one of the person's hands identified the confessor. It was Myghal, the blacksmith.

Father Trystan remembered that Myghal had lost a hand when Elvin's father had cut it off in a fit of temper after the smithy had made a bad shoe and caused the elder Le Gard to fall from his horse. Myghal was the source for most of the gossip in the village, especially since he had trained up his son to take over most of the heavy work and Myghal had much less to do. It was not for nothing that the other villagers had nicknamed him 'bucket mouth' behind his back.

The blacksmith crossed himself and said: "Bless me Father, for I 'ave sinned. It 'as been seventeen days since I made my last confession and these are my sins. I 'ave taken the name of the Lord in vain on more than one occasion and I 'ave had lustful thoughts 'bout a maid from the fields. More 'n that, I 'ave had thoughts of murder. For these and all my sins, I am truly sorry."

Father Trystan gave mild penances for the first two sins but was truly shocked by the confession of murderous thoughts.

"What were these thoughts of murder, my son?"

"Sir Elvin came to the forge the other day to 'ave a horse shoed. As he were standin' there with 'is back to me, I put my hand on a hammer and thought to bring it down on his 'ead," confessed Myghal to the priest.

"Why would you want to do that, my son?" asked Father Trystan.

"Because I 'ate his whole family. T'was his father who chopped off my 'and and nearly killed me them years ago. He destroyed my livin' and I cannot scourge myself of the hate that I feel for all on 'em," Myghal explained.

"Remember, the sins of the father should not be visited upon his children," said the priest.

"But this one is just as bad," said Myghal desperately. "They do say he do practise sorcery up there at the castle. On some nights we can see the flames from his evil fires in the windows of the tower where he d' be. The Lord knows what he be doin'."

"Precisely," said Father Trystan. "Only the Lord does know. Until there is any proof of such a thing, you must put all thoughts of this out of your mind. To kill another person is the most terrible sin.

"Remember, too, that Sir Elvin is your liege lord, to whom you owe obedience in all things upon peril of your life. Your penance for this will be to attend the church every day for a week to think about what you might have done and to pray for the forgiveness of Our Lord. Now make an act of contrition." The priest guided Myghal through the prayer and then said the prayer of absolution.

"Right, my son, your sins are forgiven," said the priest afterwards, "Go in peace."

After Myghal had gone, Father Trystan was left deep in disturbed thought. The visit of Sir Richard and the confession of Myghal had set him thinking. He, too, thought that all was not well up at the castle. Since Sir Elvin had returned, a number of things had disturbed him.

Who really was this strange foreign woman of an ungodly faith whom Sir Elvin had brought back with him from the East? What were the mysterious experiments, which Sir Elvin was carrying out at the castle? What was this golden chalice that he had in his possession, which he claimed to be sacred, and how had he come by it? Father Trystan was wrestling with his conscience as to what should be done. He stayed longer than usual in prayer that evening.

* * *

Whilst Father Trystan was hearing the confession of Myghal, Elvin was finishing off an experiment to turn tin into gold.

He had carefully followed the instructions in one of his Arabic volumes on alchemy and from a mixture of mercury and a small amount of gold had managed to produce a material, with which he could cover tin plate to make it look like gold and to give it added strength. He could see a use for this in improving the appearance of tableware or of jewellery to give it a more luxurious appearance. He felt very pleased with himself although he regarded the experiment as a sideline from his main interest in medical science.

He descended from the keep and made his way along to the great hall to join Tayri for their evening meal. When he arrived she was already sitting on a bench gazing into the huge log fire.

They greeted one another with a kiss on the cheek. "How fared the day, my lady?" asked Elvin in French.

"The day fared well, my lord," she responded in perfect French with a beaming smile.

"Good," he replied. "You are making good progress."

When Elvin had expelled Alis de Trevarno from the castle, he had also expelled her personal servants as well. It had meant he had had to start again. He had managed to persuade a friendly nobleman, who had also been to the Crusades, to help him. He held land on the other side of Hellyston and had agreed to let his youngest daughter come to the castle at Tremennek as lady-in-waiting to Tayri. The lass had taken to her duties very well and had begun to teach Tayri snippets of basic French, English and Cornish. Elvin had encouraged this, for, after they had been wed, Tayri would have to undertake some of the duties, at least, of managing the household.

As they were eating their meal Tayri suddenly said, "Do you think I will ever see my family again?"

"That I cannot say, my love," said Elvin. "One day, perhaps, it may be possible. Are you feeling homesick?"

"Just a little," she replied. "I cannot help but think of my family from time to time. It does not mean that I do not want to be with you. Sometimes, though, I feel the people of this land do not like me. They look at me strangely, especially the blacksmith."

"Oh well, he is a strange one anyway. They look at you strangely because they are not used to foreigners and because of your stunning beauty, too. I know because I cannot take my eyes off you whenever I am in your presence," Elvin said taking her hand. "There is not a day goes by that I do not love you more and more and I have loved you since that first day I saw you in the courtyard in Granada."

Tayri smiled and squeezed his hand. Her beauty had always enchanted Elvin, but it was not just her beauty. He had a feeling, somehow, that they were kindred spirits in spite of the difference in race and religion between them. It seemed to have been an eternity since that first time he had seen her without her veil in the courtyard. He was besotted then and he was besotted now. Her good humour and her infectious laughter always brightened his day.

It was true that she was young and immature in some ways and almost child-like in her naivety at times. But the journey out of her native Al Andalus, all the way across Spain and France, and then by sea to Cornwall, had opened her eyes to another world. Elvin liked the idea of being her mentor and her guide on this journey of discovery. The differences between them – he, the seasoned warrior, who had been all over Europe and North Africa, and, she, the innocent young girl, who had known little outside Granada – could not have been more obvious.

Perhaps, Elvin had found something that had been missing from his childhood when his mother had died so young. Though, to be fair, Tryfena Kyger, who had raised him in his early years, had always commanded a great deal of respect from him.

It was understandable that Tayri would feel homesick. She was frustrated by her inability to communicate and was a long way from her native land. Not everybody had been as welcoming as they could have been.

Her beauty and her fun-loving ways charmed some people like Tryfena. She had commented on her beauty and on her likeable nature. Elvin felt that Tryfena would have liked to have taken Tayri under her wing if only they had been able to communicate better.

Others, like Myghal, the blacksmith, appeared to be suspicious and unfriendly towards her and quite incapable of seeing any good side to someone they regarded, for some reason only known to themselves, as a foreign witch. Elvin was very concerned about this attitude.

He thought to himself that, after they were married, and, if it were safe to do so, he might return with her to Al Andalus to visit her family. He longed to renew his acquaintance with Uzmir again. Little was he to know how soon that would be.

CHAPTER TWENTY-FOUR
The Desire For Retribution

A bedraggled, bloodied and haggard man, with his hands and ankles in chains, was dragged forward and thrown roughly onto the floor in front of the dais.

Jaime the First, King of Aragon, Count of Barcelona and Lord of Montpellier, stared down at the pathetic figure sprawled before him.

"So this is the piece of excrement responsible for our problem," he scoffed.

Before him lay Miguel de Torla. The veteran Templar was paying for his negligence in failing to prevent the theft of the Holy Chalice of the Last Supper from the monastery in the Pyrenees.

"Do you know what you have done?" asked the King.

There was no response from de Torla. A knight stepped forward. Enrique de Larraga pulled Brother Miguel's head up by his hair so that he could face the fierce gaze of the King.

"You have allowed a priceless relic, the Chalice, in which the blood of Christ was borne by Joseph of Arimathea and, which was used by Our Lord at the Last Supper, to be stolen from our Kingdom, where it has resided since the time of our forebear, Ramiro the First. It was the Chalice, which it was your sworn duty to protect upon your life. Have you nothing to say?"

Miguel mumbled something but truly he was not in any state to say anything to anybody.

Enrique de Larraga prodded him with his sword and said: "Say something you dog!" But there was no reply.

"The wretch appears to have lost his tongue," said the King. "That will not be the only thing he will lose before we are finished with him. Get him out of our sight!"

Larraga ordered a couple of soldiers to take the wretched Miguel away.

"Do you know who is responsible for this crime?" asked King Jaime.

"We do, Your Majesty. De Torla has told us that a knight from

England called Sir Elvin Le Gard came to the Monastery of San Juan de La Peña a little while back.

"He claimed that he had taken part in the Crusade to Egypt, had been captured by the Egyptians, and then escaped. He had, somehow, made his way back to Spain and turned up at the Monastery claiming he was looking for me in order to rejoin the Order.

"Whilst he was at the Monastery he made a request to see the relic once more so that he could touch it and gain protection in his efforts to rejoin us. Foolishly Brother Miguel acceded to his request. And it appeared that it was an elaborate trick in order to steal the Chalice."

"Do you know this man?"

"Yes, I do, Your Majesty. I enrolled him into the Order at Monzon after he had turned up at the Monastery on a previous occasion."

"Were you suspicious at the time?"

"We were, Your Majesty. We interrogated both him and his squire under torture and became convinced that they were what they claimed to be, that is pilgrims on the way to Santiago who had got lost.

"Huh!" sneered the King.

"To be fair he fought well for us and distinguished himself in a number of battles in Spain and in Egypt but he was captured in Egypt. We believe that, after this, he contravened a number of the Rules of the Order and may have even gone across to the Saracens. We are actively seeking him ourselves."

"Well, we hope you capture him and we will take a close personal interest in his fate. But the loss of the Chalice puts us in an embarrassing position. We simply cannot tolerate some foreign knight entering our realm and stealing royal relics at will, especially one of the significance of the Chalice. People will come to wonder whether we are in control of our own kingdom. So far we have managed to keep the theft secret but there will come a time when one of my royal visitors from abroad will ask to see the Chalice and we will not be able to display it to them. We will then lose face and we are not prepared to do that. We are holding the Templar Order responsible for this. What is the Order going to do to rectify the matter?"

"We have discussed the matter fully, Your Majesty. Our Grand Master, Peter de Montaigu, has instructed me to assure you that all efforts will be made to capture this man and to make him pay for his heinous crimes. In addition to this the Grand Master has asked me to inform Your Majesty that the Order has made arrangements to commission a copy of the Chalice, to be made at the expense of the Order as a matter of goodwill. All efforts will be made, in the meantime, to track down the original."

"We hope sincerely they will. Our patience is wearing thin. The Order has been found severely wanting in its duty and it may be that we will be forced to review some of our grants of land and property to the Order in future."

Enrique de Larraga was only too aware of the implications of what the King was saying. He withdrew from the audience feeling decidedly uncomfortable. A number of courtiers and advisers had been present but he had also noticed, scattered amongst them, knights, with whom he had fought in the Reconquest, who were members of other military orders. He had caught a glimpse of the mantles of the Calatrava and the Knights of Santiago and he knew full well that these Orders were cultivating improved relationships with the monarchy and would not be at all unhappy if the Templar Order fell out of favour. They would stand to gain much from it. De Larraga was not a happy man.

* * *

In due course the Grand Master convened a meeting of the senior members of the Templar Order to advise him on what should be done.

"What charges can be laid against this man, Brother Elvin?" enquired Peter de Montaigu.

"It is a question, Grand Master, of where one chooses to begin," said de Larraga. "Of the nine things, for which a Brother of a House may be expelled from the Order for ever under our Rule I would suspect Elvin Le Gard of being guilty of at least seven of them.

"I would charge him with deserting the banner in Egypt as a result of a cowardly fear of the Saracens and allowing himself to be captured by them, instead of fighting to the death.

"Our spies have informed us that he was imprisoned in Damietta and was then moved down river towards Cairo. At some time on the journey he escaped along with a Morisco scout called Uzmir ibn Aderbal, who came from the Moorish territory of Andalusia.

"Both these men made no attempt to return to our squadrons at all and, in all probability, joined up with the Saracens. Some time later, probably still together, they reached Andalusia.

"Le Gard was recognised by one of our men as part of a band of Moors who attacked us close to a castle to the north of Granada. Most of our Christian number there was killed and it is believed that Le Gard had a hand in some of those killings. Having joined up with the Moors there must be more than a suspicion that he has been guilty of heresy and apostasy. He may well have compromised the secrecy of his chapter as well.

"On his return to the Monastery of San Juan de La Peña in the Pyrenees he committed the theft of the Chalice and escaped from the fortified Monastery without trace.

"There are probably a whole host of other minor offences under our Rule, which he will have committed as well, which would mean, at the very least, he would forfeit his right to wear the Templar habit. But what he has done overall is much more serious than those minor misdemeanours.

"I submit, Grand Master that Brother Elvin should be brought before a chapter meeting at the Castle of Monzon. There he should held to account for his crimes and, if found guilty by his Brothers, be expelled from the Order and committed to the dungeons of the Chateau Pèlerin in the Kingdom of Jerusalem, as is our custom, for the rest of his natural life as God wills. I think the Brothers will find that there is little doubt as to his guilt."

"You have the appropriate documentation and witnesses to this?" enquired de Montaigu.

"We do, Grand Master."

"Where do you consider this man is now?"

"We believe he will make efforts to return to his native territory in Cornwall in England to claim the inheritance of his deceased father's castle there. I have sent a message to the Grand Preceptor of the Templars in England seeking information on the whereabouts of our Brother, Sir Elvin Le Gard, and stating that he is wanted for questioning on serious offences before his chapter in Monzon."

"Who is going to England to bring our Brother back?"

"I feel duty bound, Grand Master, to deal with the matter personally," replied de Larraga. "It was I who enrolled him into the Order, if you remember, after he and his squire first turned up at San Juan de La Peña."

"Yes, I do remember. It appears to have been a grave mistake. Now you will have to rectify it. We will issue a warrant for his detention and appearance before his chapter to answer for those things, of which he is accused. Please keep me informed of all developments and let me know when the chapter meeting will be taking place and I will endeavour to attend. I will also send a letter to the Pope with regard to the conduct of Sir Elvin, for it would seem to me to me that excommunication may well have to be considered, if what you tell me turns out to be proved."

"I would agree, Grand Master. As soon as I receive confirmation of where Brother Elvin can be found, I will travel there with all due haste."

"Then I wish you God's speed and fortune in your endeavours."

CHAPTER TWENTY-FIVE
A Problem Of Two Chalices

Peter sat in a pavement café in Valencia watching the world go by. He felt depressed and low. He should have been getting on with the task of investigating the inscription on the Cathedral Chalice but he did not feel like it at that particular moment.

He sipped his coffee and pondered on the progress of his life to that point. The incident with Anya had left him feeling decidedly dejected. He was angry, too. Anya had stormed out of his room at the hotel, very much acting the injured party. She had obviously been racked with guilt. But he did not feel that it had been he, who had initiated the moves that had led to their lovemaking.

There had been no sign of her that morning and he had no idea where she had gone. He thought back over the number of years he had known her.

He had always lived with the vain hope that, somehow, the situation between Yuba and Anya would take a downturn and that Anya would be thrown suddenly into his arms as if by some heavenly miracle. For a moment he had been deceived into thinking that, at last, it had happened. But it was only a passing moment. In truth Anya would never abandon her husband, her faith or her culture. It was too ingrained in her.

Perhaps he had treated Mary badly by continuing his close relationship with Anya, however platonic? But he thought Mary had been almost insanely jealous about it and had never accepted their friendship for what it actually was.

Peter felt annoyed. He felt, perhaps, that he had been used in some way over the years. Anya had always claimed that she would not have been able to complete her course at university without his help. Perhaps this situation had just extended itself over the years? Perhaps, all the time, he had just been there as a shoulder to cry on when Yuba was playing up?

Peter felt that he was unable to understand women. They seemed to have this kind of masochistic streak in them, some of them, which kept them in relationships with men, who treated them like absolute dirt, or, even worse, were sometimes violent towards them, either physically or mentally. But still these women, frequently as not, claimed they loved their men.

As for himself, where had the relationship got him? He had a broken marriage and an inability to make any very long-lasting relationships. The prospect of a pretty lonely rest-of his-life loomed. For the first time Peter felt that he really ought to do something about this obsession he had with Anya. He had to transform their relationship into a purely professional one with only very occasional meetings. He had, simply to get on with his life.

The thought occurred to him that he could develop a relationship with Cristina, but he was not sure about that. She had, obviously, been rather bruised by her marriage and did not seem over keen on embarking on another long-term relationship with anybody. But he had detected a hint of jealousy in her on the Sunday morning. So he could never be absolutely sure.

He paid the bill and stood up in a determined fashion. He felt, somehow, he was about to embark on a new phase of his life, but he was probably only kidding himself, and it would not have been the first time as far as Anya was concerned. Somehow, however, he knew that this time it had got to be.

He made his way back to the hotel to collect his briefcase and then set about the task of trying to find out more about the inscription.

Peter considered carefully who could help. He remembered that a neighbour in St. Albans had once brought him some hammered silver coins with Arabic script on them. The neighbour knew that he had contacts in the archaeological world and wondered whether he could get the script deciphered. Peter found that the Arabic was beyond him and so he had contacted a former student friend, who had been a colleague at London University's School of Oriental Studies. His friend had been able to identify the coins, as coming from nineteenth century Afghanistan and Peter had been grateful for his help. Now he wondered whether Tim Merriman could help once again.

Tim asked Peter to send him an enlarged scan of the photograph of the inscription and said he would do what he could.

The next evening Merriman contacted Peter on his mobile.

"I've not got very far, I'm afraid," he said. "The inscription is very faint and, obviously, the swirls and decorative flourishes of the script make it quite difficult to decipher. All I can say is that it is very old and probably some form of Cuficus Arabic. This is a form of classical Arabic, which could have still been in use in medieval times for certain purposes. Have you asked the authorities at Valencia Cathedral about it?"

"Well, no," said Peter. "I wasn't sure how co-operative they would be."

"I can't see any reason why they wouldn't share their knowledge with you. It's no skin off their noses, surely. If they'd had that much in the way of objections I doubt they would have let you examine the Chalice in the first place."

"True," said Peter. He thanked Tim for trying and immediately got in touch with Javier Aviles to see what information he could glean from him. Aviles was, in fact, more than helpful.

"The interpretation of the inscription has been a problem ever since it was discovered it in the nineteen sixties," he said. "It looks like Arabic script using Cufic characters but the inscription, as you know, is very faint. That's probably why nobody noticed it before. The characters are also very crude. A number of people have analysed the script since then but there has been no agreement as to what it means. It was thought that it either meant 'For who flourishes (shines)' or 'For who is the flowering'. Some experts leaned towards the latter interpretation and speculated that the base had been made in Cordova, which, in medieval times, had been known by the Moors as 'the flowering town.' It was possible that the base had been a replacement for an earlier one and that this had been done whilst the Chalice was at the Monastery in the Pyrenees.

"Another expert in the nineteen eighties transcribed the inscription as ALBST SLJS, which he took to mean 'Al-labsit As-Silis,' which may have had its origins in the Latin 'lapis exilis' or 'marvellous stone.' This was one of the names for the Holy Grail in medieval times.

"In the nineteen nineties the inscription was sent to experts in Jerusalem who concluded it was an ancient Arabian script and could be interpreted as 'The Merciful', a Muslim epithet for God.

"So, you see, there is no concrete agreement at all. You can find discussions on the various interpretations on the internet, in fact, so I would suggest you have a look there."

Peter thanked Aviles for his help and decided to follow his advice.

Walking back to the hotel Peter decided that, after he had looked at the Internet on his laptop, he was going to have an early night as Professor Gonzalez had called a final breakfast meeting for the next morning. The aim was to tie things up in Valencia and let everybody get back to Granada.

Peter failed, once again, to notice the two men hanging around on the corner of the street, keeping an eye on who entered or left the hotel.

* * *

At precisely that moment a group of strangely dressed men was meeting in an old monastery on the outskirts of Valencia.

The members of the Order of the Ancient Knights of Aragon were ranged round a table located deep in the crypt area of the building. All were distinguished by the habits that they wore, which were embroidered with a variety of heraldic emblems.

Professor Pedro Velasquez, the spokesman for the Curia of Valencia Cathedral, who had been interviewed on television along with Anya Naziri, was chairing the meeting.

"I think we are all agreed that the situation which has developed in Valencia should not be permitted to continue. I think it is regrettable that the Curia has given in under pressure from the publicity generated by the actions of the archaeologists from Granada.

"I know they have insisted that it was all conducted in secret but I have doubts as to their ability to prevent news leaking out.

"I tried to play down the significance of the Granada Chalice in my television interview the other day but there is no doubt that there is a great danger that the authenticity of the Holy Chalice at the Cathedral will come into question and that the real truth will be discovered."

The Order of the Ancient Knights of Aragon was a secret order run upon military lines in the style of the Christian militias of medieval times. Its aims were to combat the spread of Islam, to root out heretics and to halt what it termed as the dilution of the Faith.

Its methods were militant and direct and it was no secret that the security services were interested in its activities but had made little progress in finding out who was involved or where they met and organised their activities.

An inner cell, known as the Warriors of God, undertook the direct action. Their leader was an ex-army officer called Julio Larraga. He was a direct descendant of Enrique de Larraga, the medieval Templar knight, from whose chronicle the Tremennek team had gathered information about Sir Elvin Le Gard. Julio was a forthright individual with strong views, who was not afraid of becoming involved in the 'dirty work' that defending the Order's cause might involve.

"I think it is disgusting," Larraga remarked. "I can't imagine what the officials at the Cathedral were thinking that they were doing in pandering to these people – and one of them a Muslim woman at that! I wouldn't have even allowed her inside the Cathedral, let alone anything else. There were nods of agreement from several members sitting around the table."

"I certainly think it was ill advised of them to even countenance any idea publicly that there might be a similarity between the two chalices," continued Professor Velasquez.

"I must say that I was very reluctant to be interviewed on television. I did not think that it was in the interests of our Holy Mother Church for the validity of the Holy Chalice to be questioned at all. But the publicity surrounding the Granada Chalice was such that the Curia had to respond. I tried as well as I could to emphasize the importance of the Holy Chalice in Valencia to our Faith."

"Well maybe you didn't try hard enough," grunted Larraga.

"I know, I know," admitted Velasquez in a somewhat dispirited fashion.

"Well, what are we going to do about it?" asked Larraga.

"Well, to be sure, the Church is too vulnerable these days to be further discredited in such a way. Everybody in Spain believes the Valencia Chalice to be the Chalice used at the Last Supper. The Pope has even used it at a Mass in the Cathedral. If the real truth got out, the discovery of centuries of deception would simply mean another victory for the atheists and unbelievers who seek to destroy the very existence of the Church. We are beset enough by the moral decay and the advance of secular societies all around us without the growing threat from Islam. A decline in the role of the Church would be immensely damaging to the world. The truth must not get out. I wish to God that the Granada Chalice would just go away."

"That could be arranged," Larraga commented in a matter of fact fashion. "My view is," he continued, "that arrangements should be made to relieve the Granadinos of their Chalice by whatever means are necessary. It will create a bit of publicity at first but the longer the true Chalice is out of the picture the more chance there is that the press will lose interest and it will eventually be forgotten. My men have already been keeping a watch on the movements of the Granadinos. We could strike at any time."

"And what do you propose to do with the Chalice once you've got hold of it?" enquired Velasquez.

"We shall return it to its rightful home in the Pyrenees. My ancestor in the thirteenth century, Enrique de Larraga, was responsible for the protection of the Holy Chalice. He promised King Jaime that he would track down the thief and return the Chalice to the Monastery. In that he failed and we know that the Templars provided the King with a copy at the expense of the Order so that they could retain the King's favour.

"I feel it is my duty to complete the task on behalf of my ancestor. We cannot any longer deal with the treacherous thief who absconded to join the Moors in Granada all those centuries ago but we can return the Chalice. There would no longer be two chalices and the integrity of the Holy Chalice in Valencia would be upheld whilst the original would be returned to the monastery and hidden there forever."

"This does sound like a solution to our problem," commented Velasquez. "How will you achieve this noble objective?"

"I think, for security reasons, the actual arrangements should be known only to a few," said Larraga. "I am asking for the wholehearted support of the Knights in using the Warriors to serve the cause of our Holy Mother Church and, at the same time, to re-establish my family name in the annals of Aragonese history."

"All right. Is everybody happy to support this venture under the command of Colonel Larraga and to allow him free and unquestioned rein to carry out the operation as he sees fit?"

What the assembled company did not know was that Colonel Larraga had already put the wheels in motion to retrieve the Chalice. Nevertheless the Knights enthusiastically signalled their approval in the traditional fashion. Their unanimous cry was the same as the Templars had used all those centuries before:

"Deus le volt!" ("God wills it!")

* * *

Professor Gonzalez, Anya, Cristina and Peter met again at breakfast the next morning. Apart from a cursory reply to his general 'good morning' Anya totally ignored Peter. He sat down next to Cristina.

"I thought I would sit next to you this morning," he whispered to her with a cheeky grin on his face. She smiled in return but said nothing.

Professor Gonzalez asked Peter to report on his findings with regard to the inscription. After he had outlined the details Professor Gonzalez said:

"Thanks very much for that, Peter. Unfortunately it doesn't seem to have got us a whole lot further forward. We seem to have two chalices, very similar to one another. One may be a copy of the other but which is which? Have you got any view yourself, Peter?"

"Well, I must say I am rather drawn to the Cordova connection and the fact that the inscription may have been placed on the Valencia Chalice whilst it was still at San Juan de la Peña in the Pyrenees. Now, why was it necessary to make repairs to the Chalice? Had it been damaged? Did they decide to have a copy made of it and, if so, why? I don't suppose we shall ever know for sure. Unfortunately we are now wandering into the realms of speculation rather than hard scientific facts, but there you are."

"Yes, I tend to agree with that," said Professor Gonzalez. "I think we have completed all the work we can do here. I am sorry I could not be of any greater help but I wish you good fortune in your researches. I would suggest that we wind things up here now and return to Granada.

"One more thing," continued the Professor, "has anybody noticed the two men hanging around the entrance to the hotel lately?"

The others shook their heads.

"There has also been a black Seat Alhambra, which, surprisingly, always seems to be close to where we are at any moment. I must say I'm not completely happy. The Chalice is a valuable item. I think our security should be increased. I don't think you would be wise to continue to carry it around in a simple metal case any longer especially with all the publicity, which has surrounded its existence."

He was alluding to the fact that Anya had transported the Chalice to Valencia in a lockable metal case only.

"My advice would be to attach the case to your arm by means of a handcuff and a metal chain and also to employ some security to escort us back to Granada. I can recommend a firm that the University frequently uses."

"Well, if you think it is necessary," said Anya, " I will contact my Head of Department and get him to arrange it."

"Yes, I do," said Professor Gonzalez firmly, "and I think that would be a wise move."

* * *

They set out the next day for Granada in the Professor's car, for it was he who had brought them to Valencia in the first place. Only Anya was not with them for she was riding in a security van with the Chalice and accompanied by two armed guards. The journey back went without incident and the Chalice was duly deposited in the University's safe in Granada. Anya had very little to say to Peter and spoke only to the group as a whole who were obviously pleased that the Chalice had been returned safely.

Anya made an excuse to depart quickly and did. She shook hands with everybody and disappeared.

Peter walked through the back alleys with Cristina to her hotel.

"Well, it's been a very interesting time in more senses that one," he said. "I was pleased to be able to see your fabulous discovery. I was very pleased to meet you too, Cristina. I do hope we can keep in contact and, maybe, meet up again in the not too distant future."

"I'm afraid I've got some bad news for you on that front," said Cristina quite seriously. "I enjoyed your company as well, Peter, but I've had to do some deep thinking."

"Don't do too much of that. You might strain yourself," Peter said jokingly.

"No, no, I'm being serious," said Cristina. "I've decided to take my son back to Australia and to attempt to repair the damage with my ex. I had a long telephone conversation with him last night and that is the decision we have both come to."

Peter was silent for a moment.

"Well, I won't deny that I'll miss you," he said.

"You'll be all right. But you'll have to sort out your relationship with Anya. You can't go on trying to court a married woman from a different culture. There's an awful lot against you."

"I know, I know," Peter said with a slight air of desperation.

"I can tell you one thing though. She likes you – a lot. Take it from me. I'm a woman. I know.

Peter shrugged. He did not really know what to say.

"Anyhow, I wish you all the best," he said.

They exchanged addresses and telephone numbers and parted with traditional kisses on the cheek.

He walked back to his own hotel. He felt at once up and again down. He felt that he and Cristina could have been good friends and, in time, who could say where their relationship might have gone. But that was life.

At the same time he was disappointed at Anya's reaction to their brief moment of bliss and her subsequent snubbing of him. They had known one another too long for their relationship to end in such a fashion. He determined to call her at the University the following day and try to put things right.

As he entered the hotel lobby the receptionist caught his eye and said:

"Dr.Verity, a friend has been enquiring after you."

"A friend, what friend?" was Peter's reply.

"He did not leave a name, sir. He said he had come from Valencia to see you on a matter of great importance. He said he would come back later."

"Right, thank you," replied Peter, somewhat mystified.

He took the lift up and took out his key card. He opened the door. The room was in darkness, as expected, but something was not quite right. As he turned to put the key card in the slot to put on the lights, what felt like a hood was thrown over his head and his arms were held behind his back and tied together.

At first he panicked. He had never liked his face covered in such away and he felt he could not breathe. Besides that he had no idea what was happening to him.

"Stop struggling," said a voice in Spanish behind him. Something resembling a gun was prodded into his back and he was pushed forward towards a chair. But Peter refused to stay seated

"Who are you? What the devil is going on? How did you get into my room? Release me, this moment!" commanded Peter. At that Peter received a hard slap across the face.

"Sit down, Dr Verity," said a voice in English in front of him. It was also clear that there were two intruders in the room – one behind him with a gun in his back and the other in front.

"What do you want? I keep no money or valuables here," cried Peter desperately.

"Calm down and shut up!" said the stranger. Peter was shoved roughly back into the chair.

"Who we are is of no importance. We are here because you are going to make a phone call for us."

"A phone call?" said Peter. "A phone call to whom?"

"To Dr. Naziri," replied the voice.

"To Anya?" said Peter. "What for?"

"Never mind what for," said the stranger. "We want you to get her to come to this room in the hotel – at once!"

"And what if I refuse?"

"Then, my friend, behind you, will put a bullet into a part of your body of his choice and will do so on each occasion that you refuse to co-operate. Do I make myself clear?" said the voice with menace.

"Don't be so ridiculous," said Peter. "How do I really know he's got a gun?"

"Hernando," instructed the stranger. Peter felt the hood being lifted and a piece of sticky tape being placed across his mouth. Then his hands were stretched out behind him. He heard the short shrill whistle of the silencer muffled shot and then felt a searing pain as the bullet ripped through the flesh, gristle and bone of his left hand. Peter cried out in pain and horror but nobody could hear him.

"Perhaps that will persuade you," said the stranger.

"Oh My God," mumbled Peter, head and back arched back in pain. "Why did they have to do that?" he thought.

"Now, you are going to make that telephone call for us, aren't you?" the stranger said.

"Oh no I'm bloody not," Peter mumbled through the sticky tape.

The stranger must have understood him and Peter could almost see him nodding to Hernando. Again a muffled shot and Peter felt the pain as the bullet ripped through his right arm.

The sticky tape silenced his scream but then it was sharply removed once more.

"Don't be a fool, Verity, things can only get worse," the stranger warned.

"Who the hell are you?" asked Peter as best he could in his agony.

"That doesn't matter," came the voice. "All you need to do is to telephone Dr. Naziri and get her to come to us here. Are you going to do that or not?"

"You must think I'm a fool. I'm not going to do that," said Peter.

"Oh yes you are, if you want a body left."

"Go to hell," said Peter.

The sticky tape was replaced and Peter knew what was going to happen. He braced himself. The next bullet ripped through the calf of his right leg. Peter had never experienced such excruciating pain.

"Are you going to co-operate, Dr. Verity?"

Peter nodded. The sticky tape was removed.

"That's better," said the stranger. "I'm glad you're beginning to see our point of view."

"I want you to say that you have to see her urgently with regard to the Chalice," continued the stranger. "Get her to come round here as soon as possible."

"She won't do that," said Peter.

"It's up to you to persuade her."

"OK, give me the phone."

"Tell me the number first," instructed the voice.

Peter heard the number being dialled and then a mobile was thrust into his hand.

"No wrong moves or Hernando has instructions to blow your brains out."

Peter heard the number ringing and it was obvious that the mobile had been put on loudspeaker so that the others could hear the conversation.

"Dr. Naziri," came the reply.

"Anya, it's Peter" he struggled to say in his pain. "I wonder if you can come round to the hotel. Something's cropped up regarding the Chalice and it's rather urgent."

" What do you mean? You sound very shaky. Are you O.K, Peter?" asked Anya.

Peter felt the gun pushed against his head.

"Yes, yes, of course. I'm a bit tired. That's all. Look, I can't talk about it over the phone. Please get here as soon as you can."

Anya said that she would come right away and the phone was taken from Peter.

"That was very good, Verity. I'm glad you made the sensible decision."

"If you harm a hair of that girl's head, I shan't be responsible for what I do," said Peter.

"You are hardly in a position to do anything, are you?" came the reply. "You just do as you're told and she will not get hurt and you can spare yourself further pain."

Anya took about half an hour to get to the hotel. She knocked cautiously on the door and the stranger checked that it was, indeed, her and then let her in.

She received the same treatment as Peter had done. A hood was quickly thrown over her head and she was led struggling to the bed.

"Oh, my God, what is going on? Peter, where are you?"

"Anya, I'm over............" Peter cried out but a hand was placed over his mouth right away.

"Dr. Naziri," said the stranger in a quiet but matter of fact way, "in a moment I am going to take off your hood and allow you to look at your colleague. If, at any time you look at anybody else in the room, I will shoot Dr. Verity dead. Do I make myself clear?"

"Who are you? What do you want?" Anya appealed to her tormentors.

"Do I make myself clear?" emphasised the stranger.

"Yes, yes," she replied and her hood was removed.

"Oh, my God, Peter. What have they done to you?" she gasped and rushed over to where Peter sat. He had obviously been shot several times. The perpetrator had done his work very efficiently, for there was little blood to be seen – just a series of angry looking entry and exit wounds. But it was clear that much damage must have been done internally. Peter looked gravely wounded and in great pain.

"Dr. Verity has been very co-operative with us and I want you to be the same," said the stranger.

"Oh, please don't hurt him any more," pleaded Anya.

"If you are co-operative with us, that will not be necessary."

"What have I got to do?"

"I will accompany you to the University, where you will obtain the key to the safe. You will open the safe and hand over the Chalice to me. I will then ring my colleague here in the hotel and he will leave the hotel, freeing you to make arrangements for Dr. Verity to be taken to hospital."

"That is ridiculous. I can't do that. And, anyhow, you will never be able to get rid of the Chalice unless you melt it down and what would be the point of that?" said Anya.

"We do not wish to get rid of it," came the reply. "We are going to return it to the place, from where it was stolen centuries ago by an English heretic. In this way we will also protect the integrity of the Valencia Chalice for the True Faith."

"You are mad," said Anya. "Everybody knows the Monastery in the Pyrenees, from where it was probably stolen any way."

"Believe me, Dr. Naziri, it will be well hidden. But, enough of this," snapped the stranger, "we seek your co-operation. If you do not co-operate with us, I will give orders to Hernando here to continue to shoot Dr. Verity in the same manner as he has done so far. It will take him a long time to die. I will then let him loose on you and, believe me, he is just waiting to get his hands on a pretty Muslima, whom he regards as an enemy of the True Faith. He will dispose of you in a most unpleasant way, I can assure you."

"All right, all right! I will co-operate," said Anya.

"Good, that's what I was hoping to hear."

Peter had heard everything but was unable to say anything. Hernando had stuck the tape firmly back over his mouth.

Eventually he heard the stranger and Anya apparently get up to leave. The door slammed shut and he was left under guard with the sadistic Hernando.

CHAPTER TWENTY-SIX

Knight Errant

Tayri descended from the private living rooms in the castle and went out into the pleasant spring sunshine. She walked across the bailey to a garden area next to the keep where Elvin was giving directions to two men who were planting seeds in the ground.

"I do not want the seeds broadcast just anywhere. I wish you to plant them an inch or two into the soil about six inches apart and then, when you have finished, to rake the soil carefully over them." Elvin was instructing the men based on principles that had been explained to him by Aderbal.

Then Elvin noticed Tayri approaching. "Good day, my lady," Elvin greeted her. "What a wonderful morning it is."

"Yes, it is," she replied. "What are you doing in your little garden?"

"I am getting the men to plant seeds that I brought with me from Granada. There are poppy seeds, hemlock, deadly nightshade and lettuce seeds, all of which I am growing for the purpose of making a mixture for putting people to sleep, before they have operations on serious injuries to them. Your father taught me all about this when I was in Granada. It is so much pleasanter for patients than just stupefying them with alcohol."

Tayri smiled. "You really seemed to have learned a lot from my father," she said. "It is a pity that his death was so untimely."

"Yes, it was," he replied. "There are so many questions I would have liked to have asked him, God rest his soul. My thirst for knowledge was almost unquenchable."

"Is it your wish to be able to become a physician?"

"Yes, I have been thinking about that. I feel this is the way I can truly serve God. It is almost as if He is calling upon me to do this."

Whilst Tayri and Elvin were in conversation the two men doing the planting were whispering to one another.

"What in 'ell's name is he up to?" said one to the other.

"I'm buggered if I d' know," said the other. "What's he doin' plantin' poisonous things like deadly nightshade? He d'seem t'ave some strange habits. Some d'reckon he's a bit of a sorcerer."

"Mebbe he is at that!"

"Stop whispering you two and get on with the job," Elvin shouted at them.

Just then a soldier arrived from the gatehouse.

"There is a party of men at the gatehouse wishing to see you, my liege."

"Who are they?"

"It's the priest and some monks, my liege," replied the soldier.

"Hmm. I don't know what they want," said Elvin. "Let them in and escort them to the Hall," he instructed the man as he took his leave of Tayri.

When he arrived at the Hall, Father Trystan and another man were warming themselves by the big log fire. The monks were arrayed in the habits of the Benedictine Order. The one sitting with Father Trystan appeared prosperous and well fed. He wore a habit of obvious good quality and sported a bejewelled cross around his neck.

Two monks sat at the long table with scrolls of parchment in front of them together with a large wooden chest.

"Good day to you, Father," said Elvin. "What can I do for you?"

"May I present to you, Sir Elvin, the Reverend Father Robert of Bath, the Abbot of Glaston," said the priest. Elvin acknowledged the Abbott with a nod.

"To what do I owe this honour?" queried Elvin.

"You will be aware, Sir Elvin," said the Abbott, "that the Abbey Church at Glaston was disastrously destroyed in 1184. Since that time my predecessors and I have been travelling the south west of England, from time to time, in an endeavour to raise funds to rebuild what is undoubtedly one of the most important churches in our Christian Faith. It is a very slow process. We have come here today to ask you to support our cause."

"I am surprised that you lack funds, Reverend Father. Is it not said that, if the Abbot of Glaston married the Abbess of Shaston, they would possess more lands than the King himself?"

By Shaston Elvin was referring to the nunnery in Dorset at what was later to be called Shaftesbury. It was clear from the Abbott's expression that he did not find this in any way amusing.

"Our Order has always abided by all its vows including that of poverty," he replied rather sourly.

"Hmm," thought Elvin to himself, "you don't look that poor to me."

"What land and wealth the Order possesses," continued the Abbott, "is put to the pursuit of charitable work amongst our fellow men and the praise of Our Lord and Father in Heaven. We wish to rebuild the Abbey Church at Glaston to provide a glorious place for the worship of Our Lord, which people will be able to see from far around and which will remind them of their obligations to Our Holy Mother Church."

"I fear, Reverend Father," said Elvin, " that we have little here that could assist you in your project. We grow enough to provide for ourselves and our wealth is mainly held in the form of this castle and the lands that surround it. We earn some income from the sale of tin ore but little else."

"Father Trystan has told me that you possess a relic, which may be of interest to the Order at Glaston."

"It is true that I have retrieved the Holy Grail and brought it back to these shores, from whence it was stolen some centuries ago," said Elvin.

"What form does this Holy Grail take?" asked the Abbott.

"It is the Holy Chalice of the Last Supper of Our Lord, which Joseph of Arimathea filled with the blood of Our Lord after the Crucifixion and brought to Glaston. It is a Chalice, which is believed to have magical powers and brings good fortune to all who possess it."

"One should not be bewitched by the myth of the Holy Grail, Sir Elvin," said the Abbott. "That is something which has been conjured up by minstrels and poets. Any powers granted by God reside in our Holy Mother Church alone. If you possess a relic of Our Lord, Sir Elvin, it must be authenticated. If it belongs to Glaston then it must be returned from whence it came."

"I fully intend that this should happen," said Elvin "but there is the little matter of my marriage to my betrothed, the Lady Tayri."

"Yes, I am aware of this. Father Trystan has already spoken to me upon the subject. In the present circumstances you know full well that your marriage to an infidel is totally out of the question."

"But she is prepared to convert to Christianity," protested Elvin.

"That is something that simply cannot be entertained at present. In time, maybe."

"Then, in time, I may see fit to bestow the Chalice upon Our Holy Mother Church, but not before," said Elvin tartly.

The Abbott looked at Elvin very deliberately. "You would do well, Sir Elvin, to consider your position very carefully. Not only have you consorted with the enemies of our blessed Faith, but also there are accusations that sorcery and witchcraft are being practised in this castle and I do not have to remind you of the penalties faced by you and your infidel lover were such offences to be proved."

"Do not threaten me in my own castle, Reverend Father. You might live to regret it," warned Elvin.

"I would give you notice, Sir Elvin," said the Abbott with a face black with rage, "that you are perilously close to excommunication. I would consider very carefully how you proceed from now on if what I hear from Father Trystan is correct."

"Oh," said Elvin, " I thought it might be him. I had an idea he was in league with that vindictive bitch of a stepmother of mine." He glared at Father Trystan. "You poxy little toad," he uttered with venom.

Father Trystan cowered behind the Abbott. The two monks, sitting at the table, suddenly rose sensing a serious altercation was about to take place.

"Guards," cried Elvin. Two soldiers appeared. "Escort these gentlemen from my lands and see that they don't come back!"

Father Trystan at last found a bit of courage. "Listen to the foul-mouthed ravings of a sorcerer and unbeliever, Reverend Father," he cried to the Abbott.

With that something snapped in Elvin's brain. He took hold of the priest and shook him violently, throwing him to the ground.

"I don't want to see you here ever again, you odious little scab," cried Elvin, aiming a kick at the prostrate priest. "Get them out of here!" he barked to the soldiers.

The priest and the three monks were bundled roughly out of the door of the Hall bound for an unceremonious exit through the gatehouse.

Elvin sank into a chair pondering upon the immensity of what he had just done. Just then Tayri arrived.

"I heard people shouting," she said, looking concerned. "What is happening?"

"Do not concern yourself too much, my love," said Elvin, putting his arm around her. "I have had an argument with some visiting clerics. It seems that we are not to be allowed to marry in my village church, as I would have wished. Indeed it now seems highly likely that I will not receive permission to marry you at all. But do not worry because I have another plan.

There is a church some miles away on the moors near Bodmin, which I have visited before. It is no ordinary church for is attached to an abbey belonging to the Knights Templar. It does not, therefore, come under the rule of the local dioceses. In consequence the priest there is able to marry men and women without banns or license. People from all over Cornwall get married there without the need of permission from their local priest. We will be married there."

* * *

A few days later Father Trystan and the Abbott took their complaint to William Bruere, the Bishop of Exeter.

"I understand," said the Bishop, "that you wish to make a plea for the excommunication of one of the parishioners of the parish of Tremennek in the County of Cornwall."

"That is so, Your Excellency," replied Father Trystan.

"Who is the person involved and upon what grounds do you make the plea?" enquired the Bishop.

"The person involved is Sir Elvin Le Gard, the Lord of the Manor of Tremennek."

"Is this the man who has requested to marry a woman not of our Faith?"

"It is, Your Excellency."

"He seems to be somewhat of a problem to Our Holy Mother Church."

"He is, Your Excellency. He seldom attends his local church, preferring instead," continued Father Trystan, " to carry out all manner of diabolical experiments in the keep of his castle. We suspect that he is indulging in acts of sorcery and witchcraft, the spells for which he draws from various books in a foreign hand that he has brought back with him from the East. I have personally seen diagrams of disembowelled bodies in one of his books, which were disgusting beyond belief. Further to this he continues to consort with the infidel woman and insists that the Church should marry them in spite of the fact that he shows little enthusiasm for the Faith into which he was born. In fact, we suspect that he may well have deserted the True Faith altogether."

"Indeed, this is most serious." commented the Bishop.

"But, Your Excellency, it is even worse than that. A few days ago the Abbot and I visited Sir Elvin to ask for contribution towards the rebuilding of the Abbey Church of Glaston. Sir Elvin has in his possession a jewelled chalice housed in a solid gold cage, which he brought back with him from the East. He claims that it is the Holy Chalice of the Last Supper of Our Lord that was stolen from Glaston some centuries ago. From whence he obtained it, we do not know. He refuses to hand it over to the Church for authentification unless the Church gives its consent to his marriage to this Muslim woman.

"When we said this would be impossible, he became extremely angry and attacked us both physically. He managed to knock me to the ground and aimed vicious kicks at me before ordering his soldiers to throw us out of the castle."

"To physically attack gentlemen of the cloth is scandalous beyond belief," said the Bishop. "Do you have the names of witnesses that can support the various accusations that you make?"

"We do, Your Excellency."

"Good. In that case I have no hesitation in placing a request before the Archbishop, and then before the Curia itself in Rome, for Sir Elvin to make answer with regard to your complaints. I have no doubt that a Papal Bull will be issued in due course and Sir Elvin will be called upon to answer for his sins. Leave the matter in my hands."

* * *

It was not very long afterwards that Elvin and Tayri and small party of guests rode up the gnarled slopes of the Temple Moors near Bodmin bound for the little church where they were to be married. It was the lambing season and the little lambs, skipping across their path, fascinated Tayri, who shrieked with delight. It was a bright, sunny day and the slopes were clad in huge clumps of yellow ling, and Tayri knew then why Cornwall was sometimes described as the Land of Yellow Ling.

The little church was set in a tiny hollow in a forested valley surrounded by steep, wooded hills.

It was unusual for a marriage to be based on true love like that of

Elvin and Tayri and, indeed, for the bride and groom to have met before. But the priest, whose name was Father Martin, had not seemed particularly concerned about that.

"What will happen when we get to the church?" Tayri asked Elvin.

"Well, my love, it is our custom that the ceremony takes place, first of all, outside the church door. Only after we have answered two important questions do we enter the church for the nuptial mass. The church doorway will be decorated with flowers and bits of greenery. For the purposes of the ceremony in front of the church door I will stand on your right side and we shall both face the church door. The reason for this is that woman was formed from a rib on the left side of Adam and, therefore, the bride always stands on the left side of the groom."

"What are the questions that the priest will ask?" Tayri asked.

"He will commence the ceremony by asking us both whether we know of any reasons why we should not be married," explained Elvin.

"Are there any?" asked Tayri, looking a bit concerned.

"No, of course not," replied Elvin.

They were still a mile or so away from the church. Elvin turned to Yestin Kyger, who was riding just behind them. "Yestin, ride on in advance and see that everything is ready for us."

Yestin galloped off towards the church in the hollow.

"I am glad it is such a lovely day for our marriage," Elvin said to Tayri. "It must be blessed by God."

It was not long before Yestin appeared again, galloping towards them.

"I think you should turn back quickly, my liege. There are Templar soldiers everywhere. I don't like the look of things."

"Take the Lady Tayri back and wait for us by the river crossing in the valley," Elvin ordered their escort. "We will go and investigate what is taking place."

Elvin accompanied Yestin back towards a position, hidden in the trees on a slope, overlooking the church. They kept themselves well out of sight.

There was a line of mounted Templar knights stretched out in front of the church and a number of foot soldiers as well. The priest was nowhere to be seen. The Templars seemed to be waiting for someone and their leader was pacing up and down outside the door of the church. As he turned round, Elvin strained to get a glimpse of the Templar leader's face. There was no mistaking the battle-hardened, dark skinned man with the huge scar running down the right side of his face.

"Damn it," said Elvin. It was Enrique de Larraga.

CHAPTER TWENTY-SEVEN

The Theft Of the Chalice

Colonel Larraga held Anya at gunpoint whilst they were driven in the Seat Alhambra to the University Archaeology Department's campus on the outskirts of the city. As the car was parked Larraga said:

"Now, Dr. Naziri I want you to listen to me very carefully. In a moment I am going to remove your hood and untie your hands. At no time must you look at my face or you will surely be a dead woman. You are going to take me into the University and you are going to take me to the office where the safe is. You will sign me in as Dr. Jimenez of the University of Salamanca. You are going to open the safe and give me the Chalice. One wrong move and it will be the last one you make. Do you understand?"

Anya was in a daze. The sweat was dripping from her palms and she was shaking with fear. She was also desperately worried about what might be happening to Peter.

"Do you understand?" snapped Larraga.

"Yes, Yes."

"Good. If everything goes smoothly, then I will walk out of the University with the Chalice in its case and leave you free in the office. You must wait there for one hour. On no account must you call the police or contact anybody. After that hour I will call Hernando and ask him to free Dr. Verity. Is that clear?" concluded Larraga.

Anya nodded her agreement. The hood was removed and her hands were untied. She was ushered out of the Alhambra with Larraga in close attendance. She was very conscious of the gun still in the small of her back

They approached the entrance and were greeted by the porter on duty.

"Good evening, Dr. Naziri. One visitor?"

"Good evening, Bernardo," Anya replied. "Yes, that's right. This is……………." For a moment she panicked and thought she had forgotten the name. She felt the gun being shoved further into her back, gulped and suddenly remembered. "This is Dr. Jimenez from the

University of Salamanca."

Still averting her eyes from Larraga's face she signed the visitor's book and the Colonel was given a badge to wear.

They made their way to the office. Anya opened a key cupboard with a key on a chain, which she carried on her person. She then took out a card on which the combination to the safe was written.

Anya nervously started to turn the dial. Her fingers felt numb and she felt nauseous with terror. Her legs were shaking and she found it difficult to concentrate on the task in hand.

"Hurry yourself, Doctor. We haven't got all night."

At last there was a click and the safe was unlocked. Anya opened the door and took out a metal case.

"Open it up," said Larraga. Anya opened the case and there was the Chalice. Larraga gazed down at it and gasped at the sheer beauty of it. As he was doing this Anya was able to snatch a surreptitious glance at his face and it remained etched in her memory.

"Right," said the Colonel, "remember, one hour." And with that he strode purposefully out of the room with the case.

* * *

In the hotel Peter was still sitting in the chair with his hands behind his back and with the hood over his face. He had got over the initial panic of having the hood placed over his head and was breathing fairly steadily bearing in mind the pain he was feeling from his wounds.

Hernando was watching television and was laughing at some cartoon or other. Peter could also smell the smoke of a cigarette.

What Hernando did not know was that Peter had managed to slip one hand free of his bonds and was now deciding what his next course of action was going to be.

His biggest worry would be his inability to move about much because of his wounds. However, knowing the layout of the room, he was pretty sure that Hernando was not too far away from him.

It was just possible he could launch himself onto Hernando if he had the element of surprise. He strained to make out where Hernando was. The hood was made of a hessian like material, through which, because of its weave, it was possible to make out odd shapes around the room.

Peter was pretty sure that Hernando was sitting on a chair in front of the television, which was on the end of the desk that ran along the far wall. This meant that he had his back to Peter.

But Peter knew that just launching himself at the, hopefully, unsuspecting Hernando was unlikely to achieve much in the way of success. Hernando was more than fully fit and Peter was full of gunshot wounds.

If Peter could free his other hand and get the hood off without Hernando realising — and it was a big 'if'— he would have to have something with which to attack Hernando. Peter remembered that, at his end of the desk, close by where he was sitting, there was a heavy lamp made of some bronze material. If he could grab that and direct a carefully aimed blow to Hernando's head, he had a good chance of knocking him out.

Peter worked carefully with his free hand to loosen the bonds securing his other hand. It took what seemed like an eternity as he was in considerable pain. But at last he had done it.

Just as he was about to lift his hands to deal with the hood Hernando appeared to stand up. Peter could make out his form searching the pockets of his jacket, which had been slung on the bed. Peter suspected he was after another cigarette. He heard the striking of the match as Hernando lit it and then Peter heard him sit down again.

Peter knew that the element of surprise was vital. Fortunately the hood had not been secured very tightly. Consequently he was able to remove it relatively easily. The brightness of the lighting in the room temporarily blinded him but he had soon adjusted to it and his eyes searched for the lamp on the desk. Unfortunately it was plugged into a socket on the wall. He would have to be extremely careful.

Peter leant slowly towards the desk trying to make as little noise as possible. Just as he was reaching to remove the plug from its socket Hernando turned round.

Peter could not afford to delay and wrenched the plug out of its socket and grabbed the lamp. As he raised his hand to bring down a blow on Hernando's head, Hernando grabbed his gun and loosed off a round, which caught Peter between the fourth and fifth rib on his left hand side. Peter winced and was knocked slightly off balance but was not about to stop what he had set out to do. He brought the heavy lamp down hard, first on the gun hand, forcing Hernando to drop the pistol onto the floor and then he hit Hernando with full force across the face, knocking him backwards against the far wall.

Peter just had time to grab the gun as Hernando, with bloodstained forehead, launched himself with all his might straight at him.

Peter was no expert in the use of firearms and the kickback from the revolver surprised him as he did the only thing that occurred to him in the situation. He fired straight at the charging Hernando.

Hernando landed right on top of him, knocking him to the floor. Hernando made a last feeble attempt to throttle him but it was clear the sadistic monster was dead before his fingers could ever reach Peter's throat.

It was then that Peter passed out.

* * *

Anya waited no longer than twenty minutes. She was very concerned for Peter's safety as much as anything else.

With grim determination she marched out of the office to find Bernardo. Bernardo was lying on the floor in front of the porter's office in a pool of blood. He had been shot right through the temple.

"Oh, My God," she thought, "Why did he have to kill him?"

She grabbed the phone and rang the police immediately.

Because of the high profile of the Chalice it did not take the police long to arrive in a fleet of cars all with wailing sirens and flashing blue lights.

Amid the chaos Anya tried to explain what had happened and stressed the urgency of assuring Peter's safety at the hotel.

Inspector Garcia dealt with matters at his own pace and wished to get more of a picture of what had occurred before charging off back into the city.

By this time Anya was in tears. She struggled to leave the scene but was restrained by several officers, seeking to calm her down.

"They will kill him for sure, if you don't do something," she sobbed.

"OK. Where is he staying and what is the room number?" Garcia asked. Anya told him.

Garcia barked out some orders to his men to secure the crime scene and beckoned to Anya to come with him.

They drove to the hotel, which was already surrounded by police, crouching behind cars in anticipation of a possible hostage situation.

It was an eerie scene with the flashing lights of the police cars reflecting off the waters of the river, next to which the hotel was situated.

Garcia checked with his men and established that there had been no sign of Hernando or Peter. He gave orders for the deployment of his men at both the front and back of the old monastery building, which made up the hotel. He made his way towards the front entrance.

"Please let me come with you," said Anya, but the Inspector was having none of it.

"It could be very dangerous in there. I want you to stay in the car."

He beckoned to a woman police officer and asked her to look after Anya. He then strode purposefully towards the entrance of the hotel with several of his men and disappeared inside.

What was occurring inside Anya did not know but it seemed like an eternity before anything happened. The policewoman sought to calm her anxiety as best she could but Anya was very agitated and worried about what had happened to Peter.

Eventually a wailing siren heralded the arrival of an ambulance and Anya's anxiety increased.

The ambulance men went inside and it was not long before they were rushing out of the hotel with a stretcher, upon which a blood-soaked body lay attached to all manner of drips and tubes.

Anya was out of the car before the policewoman could restrain her and ran across to the ambulance.

She was immediately relieved to see that it was Peter, but he looked in a very sorry state.

"Oh, My God, is he going to be all right?"

"He'll be OK. You leave things to us," she was assured, as the policewoman led her back to the car.

The stretcher was pushed up into the ambulance and the door was closed. As it screamed off towards the nearest emergency hospital Anya did not know when she had ever felt in such a depressed state.

* * *

Peter was taken to a large hospital complex not far from the University. The Accident and Emergency Department was housed in a basement in the main building on the site.

Anya made her way independently to the hospital. She was very anxious about Peter's state.

She went immediately to the reception desk and said:

"I'm enquiring about Peter Verity who has been admitted to the hospital with serious gunshot wounds. Is there any news on him?"

The receptionist lifted a phone, held a short conversation with the staff involved, and put the phone down again.

"Are you his wife," asked the receptionist.

"No, no, his wife lives in England and he is separated from her in any case. I am a very close friend."

The receptionist was unsure how to react but said in a vaguely officious tone:

"Well, I am sure you must appreciate that Dr.Verity is in a very critical condition. At the moment he is undergoing surgery. Only next of kin would be allowed to see him when he is out of theatre."

"But I have told you, he is separated from his wife and she is in England. I am a close friend and working colleague and the only person he knows well here in Spain at the moment," added Anya.

"I'm sorry. I have my instructions. And, in any case the police have ruled that no visitors be permitted at the moment. They have imposed high security around Dr. Verity because they wish to question him as soon as he is well enough – and that could be several days. You are obviously free to telephone us for updates on his condition."

Anya shook her head in frustration. She was desperately worried about Peter and yet she could do nothing. She would probably learn very little until the police interviewed her as well. There was nothing to do but return home.

* * *

Inspector Garcia asked to see Anya the next day.

"I'm sorry to call you in so soon," he said, "but, as you can appreciate, I am under some pressure from various authorities including the University to retrieve the Chalice and bring this case to a successful conclusion. We've got two killings and an attempted murder as well as a priceless missing Chalice. All in all it's a very high profile case and I need all the help I can get.

"At the moment there is little chance that I shall be able to interview

Dr. Verity in the very near future, so you are my only major witness. I want you to tell me as much as you can about what happened the other night. Don't leave out anything no matter how insignificant it appears."

Anya told the Inspector all she could remember of the events that had taken place. She described the telephone call she had received from Peter, her visit to the hotel, the threats to Peter's life and his tortured state and how she had agreed to co-operate with the thieves. She explained that, as a Muslim, she had felt particularly threatened by these men – more so than normally would have been the case.

"Did you get any sense of what the motive was for the theft?" asked Garcia. "The Chalice would be immensely difficult to sell on."

"Yes, I did question that," Anya replied. "I was told that they wanted to protect the integrity of the Chalice in Valencia Cathedral and to return the other Chalice to what they described as its rightful place in the Pyrenees."

"Hmmm, that's interesting. So you think that greed was not the motive?"

"No, it didn't sound like it," Anya agreed. "It appeared to be more of a religious issue."

"That gives me an idea. There is a bunch of Christian fanatics that might be involved in this. We know a lot about Islamic terrorist organizations but very little about Christian ones. The one I have in mind is a very shadowy organization indeed. The Church is very worried about their activities and so are we.

"Look, I would like you to have a glance at some photos. You say you got a sight of one of them. Perhaps you might recognise him. That would be a start."

"OK, I'll do what I can," said Anya.

Anya looked at literally hundreds of 'mug shots' but failed to pick out anybody, who was remotely like the person who had accompanied her to the Archaeology Department.

Then Inspector Garcia disappeared and came back with a separate file with just one or two photos in it.

"That's him," cried Anya pointing at one photo.

"Hmmm," said Garcia. " Are you absolutely sure that's him"

"Absolutely," said Anya, visibly shuddering at the memory of what had happened.

"OK. Thanks very much. You've been very helpful"

After Anya had left the Inspector picked up the telephone. He rang a number.

"You'd better make yourself scarce," he said, shredding the photo as he was saying it.

"She's picked out your photo."

CHAPTER TWENTY-EIGHT

The Marriage

William Bruere, the Bishop of Exeter, was in his study in the Bishop's Palace in Paignton when the emissary from the Archbishop of Canterbury arrived. A number of scrolls were handed to the Bishop, who recognised the seals immediately. The heads of the apostles Peter and Paul on one side and the name 'Honorius III' on the other showed that they were communications from the Curia in Rome and, therefore, from the Holy Father himself.

The Bishop dismissed the emissary, who was invited to partake of a meal, a night's lodging and a change of horse before embarking on his journey back to Kent.

One document was addressed to the Bishop himself and the others were copies for the various parties involved. The document was a Papal Bull for the excommunication of one Sir Elvin Le Gard, Lord of the Manor of Tremennek in the County of Cornwall.

The Bull listed the accusations made against Sir Elvin, which included assault upon a priest and an abbot of the Holy Roman Church and invited Elvin to 'make answer' as to why he should not be excommunicated within forty four days of receipt of the Bull. It was pointed out that he could be absolved of his sins if he was prepared to confess them to the Bishop of Exeter himself, to ask for absolution and to undergo such penances as the Bishop might require of him.

The Bishop called for a messenger to carry the Bull to Cornwall to Father Trystan, the priest in the parish of Tremennek. The Bishop's accompanying letter instructed Father Trystan that, in the event of Sir Elvin not "making answer" in the allotted time, the bells of Tremennek Church should sound the funeral toll to indicate that a member of the flock had been lost to the Church and consequently deemed to have been excommunicated.

It was not long after that that the Grand Master of the Templar Order, Peter de Montaigu, got in contact with the Bishop through his intermediary, the Grand Preceptor in England, regarding the charges that the Templar Order required Elvin to answer. It was agreed that both the cases, with regard to Sir Elvin, should be put before the King's representative, the Sheriff of Cornwall, Henry de Bodrugan, with a view to co-ordinating efforts to bring the wayward knight to task.

The Sheriff agreed that, if Sir Elvin was unwilling to surrender himself of his own volition, a joint effort should be made to obtain his arrest to answer for his various crimes. If Sir Elvin resisted arrest then every effort was to be made to take him alive. It was noted that it was the wish of the Curia that, if Sir Elvin was found guilty of the charges laid against him, his castle should be razed to the ground and all details of his titles expunged from the record. The appropriate warrants were issued and plans put into motion to seek to apprehend the malefactor.

* * *

On the day of the planned arrest of Elvin at St. Catherine's Church on the Temple Moors he had been fortunate indeed that he had decided to send Yestin in advance to check that everything was in order for the marriage service. Yestin's cautious approach to what was happening at the church had enabled him, more by luck than judgment, to discover what was afoot and to fall back to warn the wedding party of the danger. Yestin's quick action enabled Elvin to find out what was going on and to get a considerable head start in his retreat back to Tremennek. The presence of Enrique de Larraga at the church had not been a welcome sight at all.

Elvin had been aware of the issue of the Papal Bull against him because an emissary from the Bishop of Exeter, accompanied by Father Trystan, had delivered it to him a couple of months before. He had given both persons scant respect and decided to ignore the mostly unfounded allegations against him. He was well aware, however, that, at some juncture, attempts would be made to remove him from the castle.

Tayri had been distraught about the wedding.

"What kind of land have you brought me to?" she had cried angrily at Elvin. "What sort of people prevent others from worshiping their God in one of your holy churches? What sort of people deny the right of genuine believers to convert to their religion? What sort of people deny loving couples the right to marry one another and bear children? What sort of people hate others just because they are from a foreign land and speak a different language? I hate this land. I hate the people and they hate me. I don't know why I came to this country forsaken by Allah. It is all your fault. You will never marry me, I know."

Elvin had not really known what to say. "The people don't' hate you," he had mumbled but in his heart of hearts he knew it to be true of some ignorant souls. "I will marry you, never fear." But again he had not been sure how he would be able to bring this about and Tayri had stormed out of the room unimpressed.

Elvin was at very low ebb. He sought the advice of Tryfena Kyger, whom he regarded as almost like his own mother.

"She will calm down," Tryfena said. "Remember, she is a long way from home in a strange land, my lord. It has not been easy for her. She is a good woman, who will make you an excellent wife, when the opportunity arises. I, for one, do not hate her at all and never have and I am sure that I am not alone in this. Sure, the language is difficult for her, but she is kindly, beautiful, and intelligent and very quick to learn. She knows her own mind without being overbearing and she will make an ideal Lady of the Manor."

"Unfortunately I don't think that is going to happen," said Elvin and he explained to Tryfena his fears about the future.

"I want you to promise me that, if anything happens to me, you will do your best to protect her," urged Elvin. "There are those in the village and elsewhere who would do her harm if they got the chance."

"Of course I will," promised Tryfena, "and so will Yestin. Keep your faith in God and everything will turn out right, my lord."

"I hope your optimism proves justified," Elvin said.

Elvin knew that it was imperative that he found some means to wed Tayri and he felt that this needed to be done with all due haste because of the threat hanging over him. He would know then that his objective in returning to Cornwall with Tayri had been fulfilled. It was Yestin who came up with the answer.

"I have heard, my liege, that some couples, when the Church refuses to marry them or there is no priest available, tie the knot at a place they call Pen Kerensa, the Hill of Love. It is a very ancient place in the woods on the other side of Tregonning Hill. It is supposed to have been a sacred site in days gone by. I can take you there, if you like."

Elvin became more and more attracted to this idea and decided that, if the Church authorities were refusing to marry them, then he would have to find an alternative way. He asked Yestin to make the arrangements.

One night, not long after, Tayri was asleep in her bedchamber when Elvin awakened her. He was fully dressed.

"Shsh, don't make a sound," he said. "Get dressed. We are going somewhere special."

"In the middle of the night?" protested Tayri

"Yes, you will see."

He took her down to the stables where Yestin was waiting for them with the horses. Elvin lifted Tayri onto a mount and then jumped up behind her.

"Why are you not riding your white horse?" Tayri asked.

"Because we do not wish to stand out in the dark. Where we are going is to be our special secret."

On the way to their destination Elvin told Tayri how much he loved her and how sorry he had been that she felt so unhappy. He told her that he was determined that they should be married in spite of the opposition of the Church. He explained to her that he had found a way they could be joined in marriage following the customs of ancient times in Cornwall. She smiled and that delicious radiance, which so drew him to her, returned to her face.

It was a night of a full moon and they were fearful that they might be seen. But no incident took place and they travelled in safety across the moors to Pen Kerensa. When they arrived Yestin gave a low whistle and an old man appeared as if from nowhere. He was dressed in the manner of a druid and carried a long wooden staff. He had beautiful, silken white hair and a certain serenity about his being. He beckoned them to follow and led them up the hill. Part way up he stopped and parted the undergrowth. Buried in the side of the hill was a granite well and the well was filled from a spring, which ran down the hillside.

"This is a place of great sacredness from the old times," the old man said in Cornish. "You d'only come' ere, if you d' truly love one another and wish to be joined for ever."

"Yes, we do," said Elvin.

The old man drew a large circle with his staff in the dirt in front of the sacred well. He muttered some words to himself as if consecrating the circle and then he motioned Elvin to step into the circle.

Then the old man addressed the bridal couple on the bond, into which they were about to enter. He warned that marriage was not something to consider lightly and that it would have its ups and downs just like any other aspect of life.

After that the old man addressed Tayri and said: "Do you come 'ere of your own free will?" Elvin translated for her.

She replied: "Yes I do."

The old man then asked: "With whom do ee come to Pen Kerensa?"

"She comes with me," replied Yestin, "and I d' know her to 'ave the blessings of her family 'cross the sea."

"Please enter the circle and join 'ands with your betrothed," the old man instructed Tayri.

Yestin ushered Tayri forward into the circle.

The old man then addressed Elvin and Tayri together. He asked them to join hands and then placed his hand over theirs and said:

"Your love for one another should be as solid as the granite on the carn and as constant as the stars in the sky. Let the power of your love bind you together and make you 'appy and strong in your life to come and 'elp you overcome the trials and tribulations that will sometimes be your lot. Just as in nature storms will come but they will pass. Always love and respect one another."

Then he turned to Elvin and asked: "Do you wish to be bound to this woman?"

"Yes, I do," replied Elvin.

"Then place the ring upon her finger."

Elvin placed the ring upon her finger and she gave him a glorious smile, which somehow the moonlight enhanced.

Elvin was then asked to repeat his wedding vows after the old priest. Then Tayri placed a ring, given to her by Yestin, upon Elvin's finger and repeated her vows as best she could, given her limitations in the language.

The old man next produced a white cloth and wound it round both their wrists as a symbol of their being bound to one another. The priest produced a small cup with two handles, which he filled at the well. He handed the cup to Elvin and said:

"You are now husband and wife. May you drink from this cup of love and may your love endure till the end of your days."

Elvin held the cup for Tayri to take a sip and then indicated that she should do the same for him and then they embraced one another as man and wife and stepped out of the circle. And as quickly as he had appeared the old priest suddenly disappeared.

They returned to the castle and Elvin made love to Tayri gently and with respect. The horror of her time with Enrique de Larraga began to disappear into the mists of time. Exhausted and satiated they fell asleep in one another's arms, happy for the moment, but knowing full well that the storms, which the old priest had warned about, were beginning to brew.

CHAPTER TWENTY-NINE

Serious Injuries

It took several days before Anya was able to get permission to see Peter. The hospital authorities relented at last but the police proved more difficult. They wanted to be the first to talk to him, when and if he recovered from his ordeal at the hotel. They were also of the opinion that there could still be some danger to both of them.

Inspector Garcia met Anya at the entrance to the Intensive Care Unit and said:

"We can only allow you a short time with him. He is not conscious anyway. But if he shows any sign of coming round, we will have to ask you to leave."

Inside the Intensive Care Unit the sister in charge directed her towards a basin to wash her hands and gave her a green smock to wear.

"He is not conscious," she explained, "but you can talk to him. In fact, we would encourage you to do so. There is a strong belief that people do hear what you say even if they do not appear to be conscious. The more encouragement to him to pull himself round, the more chance there will be of a recovery"

Peter looked a mess. He was attached to all kinds of drips. A ventilator was undertaking his breathing for him. He was surrounded by all kinds of monitors beeping away and spewing out green digital readouts every few seconds.

Anya sat down beside him and wiped away a tear. She took hold of his hand and began to massage it gently.

"Hello, Peter. It's Anya," she said tentatively. "This is a fine state of affairs, isn't it?" There was a pause from her for a moment.

"We all want you to come back to us, Peter. We miss you. I miss you," she added with a slight break in her voice.

"I need you, Peter. I don't want to lose you. I am so sorry about what happened between us. It wasn't entirely your fault. I was foolish and should have been a bit more responsible. I've got to live with the consequences if I am true to my Faith. It's very difficult, though, because I have very strong feelings for you. I didn't really realise until I saw you in the hotel like that. I knew then that I couldn't lose you. I knew at that moment that that night had been special to us and that I loved you, even though I am married to Yuba.

"I don't know what is going to happen. All I know is that I don't want you to leave me like this. Please, please hang on, Peter, please, for my sake. If you truly love me, come back to me, Peter."

At that point Anya thought she felt a slight movement in Peter's hand, but nothing more.

Then the sister came in and told Anya she would have to leave.

"What's the chance of his recovery?" Anya asked.

"I would think he has a reasonable chance," said the sister. "The weapon used was of relatively low velocity, so the internal damage is not so great as it might have been. These sorts of wound don't appear to be much externally but they can do a lot of damage internally. He's had surgery to repair damaged veins and nerves as well as broken and fractured bones.

"The damage to his ribs was extensive. He had one broken one and several fractured ones. The broken one was dangerous because there was the threat of the lungs or heart being punctured. He was extremely lucky because the bullet hit the rib, broke it but the impact caused the bullet to change trajectory and exit without doing any further damage. The fractures were caused when the other man fell on him.

"The shot in the leg was probably the worst. He appears to have broken it fairly recently anyway."

"Yes," Anya volunteered, "he had a nasty accident not so long ago in Cornwall."

"Anyhow," the sister continued, "they've managed to save it, but it is unlikely he'll be able to bear much weight on it again.

"All in all he's not a well man and it will take some time for him to recover. He will be in a lot of pain. There will have to be a lot of careful drug management and physiotherapy before he's really well again. That's given there are no complications."

"What will happen to him when he comes round," Anya asked.

"He'll be returned to the U.K. as soon as he is well enough," the sister answered.

Anya tried not to betray her disappointment.

"Thanks for explaining everything," said Anya.

As she left, she hesitated a moment, turned and gave a lingering farewell wave to Peter even though he could not see her.

Anya remained deep in thought as she found her way to the hospital exit. She was very worried about Peter's condition and nobody could be any doubt as to her concern for him.

CHAPTER THIRTY

Excommunication

On the forty-fifth day after the delivery of the Bull, the church at Tremennek sounded the funeral toll. This caused quite a stir amongst the villagers in the fields for they had not been aware that anybody had died. They dropped their tools and began to gather outside the church. Eventually Father Trystan hobbled into the church doorway.

"Do not be alarmed, my children. No one has died within the village. The toll indicates that our Holy Mother Church has excommunicated a member of our flock, Sir Elvin Le Gard, and I am, henceforth, prohibited from giving'n communion. He has many charges to answer and, as I told ee in church last Sunday, he now has the status of an outlaw. Nobody must render aid to'n. Go back to the fields and forget'n and his Saracen whore. They will be taken away in due course."

The villagers straggled back to the fields gossiping with one another about the events which were unfolding.

Elvin appeared to be relatively unperturbed about what was happening. He continued with his experiments in his laboratory in the keep.

However, he was worried. He knew full well that, at some time in the near future, a party would arrive at the castle gate with a view to his arrest. He had already asked Yestin, who had been his steward since the departure of Alis de Trevarno, to inspect the defences in order to make sure that they were not taken by surprise and to put the guard on twenty-four hour watch in the gatehouse and on the watchtowers.

Elvin had tried to keep Tayri unaware of the imminent danger that they faced, but it was difficult. He had not even told her the true reason why they had not originally been married at the church on the Temple Moors. But she was as intelligent as she was beautiful and the activities around the castle had led her to ask all kinds of searching questions. In the end he had to tell her the full story.

The mention of the name of Enrique de Larraga had shocked and terrified her and brought back the nightmare of her capture and de

Larraga's sickening rape of her. She begged Elvin to protect her from a man she clearly regarded as a monster.

Elvin had no liking at all for the vicious brute, who had raped the woman who was now his wife and who was pursuing him so relentlessly. He wondered what right de Larraga had to question him over charges of breaking his Templar vows. Elvin knew that there were some Templars who did not keep to the vows and de Larraga was one. He was a drunkard and a fornicator and was engaged in hypocrisy of the first order in pursuing Elvin.

Elvin felt that he had every right to call de Larraga to answer before the chapter in Monzon himself, but he did not think he would get very far. Elvin knew that de Larraga had the ear of some very important people including the Grand Master of the Order and the King of Aragon.

"Never fear. I will protect you, my love," he assured Tayri. "Now, what I want you to do is to begin to pack the bare essentials for a long journey by sea and land."

"Why is this?" she asked. "Where are we going?"

"It is possible we may have to flee the castle," said Elvin. "There was a Moorish ship in Mounts Bay last month purchasing tin ore. I made contact with its captain who agreed to take a message to Uzmir. He agreed to pass it on to a muleteer going to Granada as soon as he arrived in his homeport of Seville. I wrote to Uzmir of our problems and told him we would have to avail ourselves of his promise to give us shelter if we were ever in trouble in England."

"But Enrique de Larraga will never allow us to escape," cried Tayri desperately, tears welling up in her eyes.

"He won't necessarily know that we have gone. Come with me, my love. I want to show you something."

He took Tayri by the hand and led her towards the keep. As they entered the keep Elvin took a burning torch down from the wall and led her towards the stairs to the upper floors. About three stairs up Elvin moved a stone in the outer wall and then, to the amazement of Tayri, began to push the step in front of them. That part of the stairway swung round on some kind of axle to reveal an opening with some steps leading downwards. Elvin led Tayri down the steps. She giggled with delight at the revelation of this secret.

"My father had it constructed when the castle was built," Elvin explained.

"But, won't people know of its existence?" asked Tayri.

"They will guess that there is probably some kind of bolt hole, because most castles have them. My father was a ruthless man, however, and had the men, who constructed it, killed afterwards so that it would remain a secret. Also this is better than the usual escape route as you will see."

He led her a short way along what was obviously the inside of the outer wall. Then they came to a halt because the way ahead was barred to them by solid rock. Elvin felt within the leather jerkin he was wearing and produced a large iron key. He bent down and began brushing away the earth on the floor of the passageway to reveal a wooden trapdoor with a keyhole in it. He then opened the trapdoor and they found themselves looking down what looked, at first sight, like a well but with a wooden ladder down to its bottom. Elvin helped Tayri down the ladder and, to her surprise, at the bottom, there was a passageway that led off in a slow descent.

"Where is it leading to?" Tayri asked.

"You will see," said Elvin.

After a short while Tayri could hear the roar of the sea and knew that they must be descending down through the headland to the sea itself and, sure enough, they soon arrived at the cave opening on the rocks below the headland. Just within the mouth of the cave lay a boat, which had obviously been well maintained and prepared for a quick departure. It was equipped with two sets of oars and a small sail.

"Oh dear!" cried Tayri. "We will not be able to go far in such a little boat."

"We will not have to go too far," Elvin explained. "Yestin and I are experienced sailors, never fear. When it comes to the time, we will sail with all due haste around the head to Mounts Bay and board the ship, which I have chartered, which will be awaiting us there. We will make passage to Bordeaux and then make our way to Granada. We found our way here in the first place. We ought to be able to find our way back. Smile, my love, you are going home."

Tayri did, indeed, smile but it did not prevent her from feeling a great deal of apprehension about what the following days would bring.

CHAPTER THIRTY-ONE

Surprises, Fact And Speculation

Anya continued to visit Peter in hospital all the time he was in the Intensive Care Unit. Yuba exhibited his usual fits of jealousy on the subject but Anya dismissed these by saying:

"Don't be so silly. Other people are visiting him as well and, anyhow, I feel duty bound to do so, since he was injured as a result of my inviting him over here to help out with our investigations."

One day Anya made her way to the Intensive Care Unit but Peter wasn't there. She found the sister in charge and enquired as to what had happened to Peter.

"He has been transferred to a general ward and is looking much better. It won't be long before he will be able to travel back to the U.K.," she was informed.

Anya made her way to the ward where Peter was located and asked a nurse where Peter was.

"He's over there, by the window," she was told.

Anya looked across at the beds and could see nobody she could recognise. But then she realised that Peter was not in bed, but, to her surprise, standing by the window supported by crutches.

She almost ran across to him.

"Peter, she cried, almost weeping, "I'm so glad you're better." She gave him a huge hug, forcing him to say to her:

"Steady, on. You'll knock me off my feet."

"I'm so glad you're all right. I was so worried about you," Anya said.

"I'm still feeling a bit groggy but I think I'm on the mend. I shan't be what I was before but at least I'm alive. Anya, I really want to thank you because I understand you've visited me almost every day. I'm very grateful for that although I was out for the count."

Anya wondered to herself whether Peter had heard some of the things that she had said to him to encourage him to cling on to life. She felt slightly embarrassed about it.

"We didn't want to lose you. I didn't want to lose you," she ventured. "You mean an awful lot to me, Peter. You should know that."

"I know and I am sorry I upset you," he said.

"Forget it. I was just as much to blame as you were. I suppose I had a very guilty conscience."

"How's Yuba?" Peter asked.

She hesitated a little and said; "Yuba's the same as he always is. He doesn't like the attention I pay to you. But there's nothing new there. I have something to tell him that will make him very pleased, I'm sure."

"And what's that"?

"I went for a pregnancy test this morning. Yuba's going to be a father. I hope it's going to be all right this time and I don't miscarry."

"I'm sure it will be. Listen carefully to what the doctors say. What will he want? A boy or a girl?" Peter asked.

"Oh, almost certainly a boy."

"Well, I hope everything goes all right this time. Take care, won't you?. I'm sure you will make a wonderful mother."

Peter grabbed hold of Anya and gave her a most affectionate hug. As he released her he fancied he spied just the slightest trace of a tear in her eye. It took him back years to when they were at University and had said good-bye to one another at the completion of their course.

"I'm told that, for insurance purposes, I have to go home in a few days time. I'm not sure that I want to go, but I have no choice."

"Well, I'll really miss you," said Anya. "I hope you stay in touch."

"Of course I will," said Peter. "I want to come back to Granada anyway. I have to seek out an old friend of my mother, Luis Fernandez.

I can't remember whether I told you or not before I was injured. You know my mother died? I discovered from my mother's effects that my father was not my true father. It was a shock I can tell you. But an even bigger shock was that my real father was Spanish and lived here in Granada. Unfortunately he is dead now but Luis Fernandez was his best friend and can probably tell me quite a lot about him. Do you think you can trace him and tell him that I will be over to see him as soon as I can?"

"Yes, of course, I will," promised Anya.

At that moment Peter suddenly went very grey and collapsed on the nearest bed.

A nurse came rushing over.

"I think you had better leave now," she said to Anya. "He's probably done too much today considering the state of his health."

"OK, I'm going now," said Anya. "I'll do that for you, Peter. And I'll look forward to meeting up with you again when you come back to Granada. God bless, darling. Please take care."

She gave Peter a gentle kiss on the cheek and left, as he was being tucked back into bed.

* * *

Peter was flown back to the U.K. a few days later to continue his postoperative care and rehabilitation. In between various sessions of physiotherapy and the like, he was able to call in at the School of Oriental Studies and update everybody on what had happened to him in Southern Spain.

Some weeks after he arrived back he attended a meeting of T6 in London.

Bernard Harper welcomed Peter back and offered him the committee's condolences with regard to his mother's death and its regret with regard to his experiences in Granada. He was assured that all the committee members wished him a speedy recovery from his various injuries.

Bernard invited him to report on his visit to Granada and Valencia, provided he felt up to doing so, leaving out, of course, the more sensational events, which had taken place.

"Well, even without those, it was a very intriguing visit," Peter started. "The object that Dr. Naziri wished me to see was a chalice of the most indescribable beauty that the Granada team had discovered on their site, concealed in the base of a medieval Moorish fountain.

"You have probably all seen the press on the discovery by now. Evidence suggests that our friend from Cornwall, Sir Elvin Le Gard, had hidden it there probably after he had returned to Granada following the destruction of his castle at Tremennek. The strange thing was that it appeared to be very closely similar to the Holy Chalice kept amongst the treasures of Valencia Cathedral. The Valencia Chalice is reputed to have found its way there from a monastery in the High Pyrenees, where it is supposed to have been kept from the beginning of the eighth century to about 1399 when it was moved. It was brought to Valencia in 1437.

"With the permission of the Cathedral authorities we were able to examine both chalices in close proximity. They were remarkably similar leading us to believe that one was, indeed, a copy of the other. But which was which was the problem. I think we were really unable to resolve this."

"It's possible that we can perhaps shed some light on that," said Bernard Harper. "In the absence of Peter, I continued to work on trying to find any ecclesiastical records relating to our case. I was unsuccessful in that but a colleague, after hearing about the discovery of the chalice in Granada and its possible connection with the one in Valencia, pointed me in another direction.

"He remembered looking at an ancient collection of account documents in Arabic relating to bills of work done for purchasers in Cordova in the thirteenth century. They had been in a remarkable state of preservation. The item, that he was able to pinpoint, was an invoice from a leather bound account book, which was for the production of a solid gold, jewelled chalice for the King of Aragon in the Arabic equivalent to the year 1224. One Enrique de Larraga, a Brother in the Templar Order, had signed the order for the work. The price quoted was considerable by the standards of the day and one could not help wondering why the Templar Order had invested such monies in a gift of this sort to the monarch.

"The other intriguing thing was that Enrique de Larraga had given his location as the same monastery, to which Peter has referred."

"That is interesting," said Peter, "although I am not sure it takes us much further. It does prove that a chalice was made in Cordova. It seems a bit strange because Cordova, at the time, was part of Moorish Al Andalus and we were right in the middle of the Reconquest."

"It would not have been totally unusual," said Bernard Harper. "There have been many instances in history of trade going on even though the participants were technically at war with one another. Napoleon's army was famously kitted out with British boots, for example, whilst we were at war with the French in the early nineteenth century."

"The whole point is," said Peter, "that we still do not know whether this was the Holy Chalice that now lies in the Cathedral at Valencia or a copy being made for the King of Aragon."

"We can only really guess at that one," said John Trehane. "If it is a copy, why did the King want one?"

"My own personal view, for what it is worth," said Peter, "was that, possibly, the original, which belonged to the King of Aragon and was under guard with the Templars at the monastery because of the fighting with the Moors, had somehow got lost or even stolen. The loss of face for the King would have been immense and hence a copy was secretly made at the expense of the Templars."

"But how did it get lost?" asked Harper.

"I suspect that Sir Elvin Le Gard may have purloined it to add to his other indiscretions. We do know from de Larraga's Chronicle that he was familiar with that area of Spain and had served there. The chances of his being connected in some way with that particular monastery, as a Templar Knight, are quite high. It does seem strange that we discover an almost identical copy of the Holy Chalice near to the place where he was buried.

"I am convinced, from the inscription on the fountain and the remains of the sailcloth, in which it had been wrapped, that it was Sir Elvin, who had concealed it there. The only thing we can be sure of is the fact that, if he did steal it and he had also been expelled from the Templar Order as well as being excommunicated by the Church, it goes a long way to explain why everybody was out to get him and why his castle at Tremennek was destroyed in the way it was."

"It certainly does," said Bernard Harper. "It's amazing that they were able to keep the whole thing so secret, but, then the Church did not wish to reveal its dirty washing to the peasants. It was all about power and retaining that power. Any kind of suspected heretical activity was dealt with very severely."

"What I cannot understand about the Chalice," Harper continued, "is why he would want to steal it in the first place. He does not seem to have made any effort to sell it on. So the motive could not have been greed. Perhaps he thought that possession of the Holy Grail would bring him lifelong protection from adversity. If that were the case, then it didn't work very well, did it?"

"There is one other possibility that has occurred to me," said Peter. "Coming from the South West of England he would have been familiar with the legend that Joseph of Arimathea brought the Holy Grail to Glastonbury after the Crucifixion of Christ and that it had mysteriously disappeared. Perhaps, having discovered its whereabouts, he thought it had been stolen from Glastonbury and felt honour bound to return it."

"Then why did he not do that?" enquired Bernard Harper.

"Perhaps his obvious clash with the Church had something to do with it"? said Peter. "Perhaps he was forced to flee from Cornwall before he had been able to return the Chalice? Who knows? That's, again, something we can never be sure about."

"One final question?" asked John Trehane. "If Sir Elvin was expelled from the Templar Order and had received so much grief from them in the end, why was he buried in the manner of a Templar knight in the middle of Muslim Al Andalus? Why did he not receive a standard Muslim burial?"

"A good question," said Peter. "I don't suppose we will ever know the answer to that one either. It may be that he considered that he had not intentionally broken his vows and that he had been somewhat misjudged. Or maybe he knew that it was only a matter of time before the Christians finally defeated the Moors and entered Al Andalus. Perhaps it was a way of raising two fingers to them. Who knows?"

After some further discussion it was agreed that there was little purpose in pursuing their investigations any further. T6 was officially wound up and it was left to Bernard Harper to make the final report to the University.

Peter returned to the house in Marshalswick with a feeling of anticlimax, but at the same time, pride that the investigation into the castle on the headland at Tremennek and its occupier had been as successful as it had been. The investigations had drawn him closer to the character of Sir Elvin and he would have liked to know much more about him. There were some frustrating loose ends.

Peter felt undeniable empathy towards the long gone knight from Cornwall. Sir Elvin, too, had been drawn back to Andalusia. It was an area of Spain, to which Peter was always drawn, almost by a kind of magnetism he could not understand.

Sir Elvin, too, had been bedazzled by the beauty and charms of a young woman of Berber descent. Seemingly things, in terms of relationships, had turned out rather better for him than they had for Peter. Since they had been buried together it appeared that Sir Elvin had got to marry his "Saracen princess" in the end. Peter's relationship seemed always to be destined to be unrequited. The cultural and religious divide remained as wide as ever and a brief one night's fling was all he had got to show for it. It seemed strange that Sir Elvin and his betrothed had managed to overcome the religious divide whereas Peter, some eight centuries later, had failed to do so.

Peter was intrigued by the knight's apparent interest in medical science and he could understand why the Church would not have appreciated his interest at all. To the Church of the day diseases would have been viewed as brought by the will of God and to interfere with this would have invited charges of heresy or whatever else.

Two mysteries remained. One concerned why Sir Elvin had deserted from the Templar Order and had become accused of losing his faith. Looking at the Templar Rule and the various case studies contained within it, those accused of desertion usually fell into the hands of the Saracens and did not return. If they lived, the likelihood of their converting to Islam, whether willingly or not, was quite high. All that was known about Sir Elvin was that he had been in Andalusia and had obviously consorted with members of the Moorish population there and even eventually married one of their numbers.

The other mystery was why he had stolen the Chalice. Peter preferred to stick to his conclusion that maybe Sir Elvin believed that it was the Holy Grail and had planned to return it to Glastonbury, from whence he thought it had been stolen. Somehow that plan had been thwarted.

Whatever the truth, Sir Elvin had certainly been an interesting character and Peter felt disappointed in a way that the project had come to an end.

CHAPTER THIRTY-TWO

The Attack On The Castle

It was not long after the expiry of the time for making answer to the Papal Bull that the envoy from the Sheriff of Cornwall, accompanied by half a dozen soldiers, appeared before the gatehouse. The guards notified Elvin immediately of their presence.

"We seek Sir Elvin Le Gard, the one time lord of this domain," the envoy shouted up to the guards.

When Elvin heard this, he was incensed and shouted down:

"Who seeks Sir Elvin, for I am he?"

"I am Henry de Ploërmel, a knight envoy of the Sheriff of Cornwall, and I am charged with bringing you before the Bishop of Exeter at the castle of Restormel to answer the allegations that have been laid against you by the Holy Father himself. I am then charged with handing you over to Brother Enrique de Larraga to be transported under guard to Aragon to answer charges laid against you by your chapter of the Templar Order at Monzon. Open the gates, sir knight. You are no longer lord of this domain and your lands have become the property of the Bishop of Exeter."

"The hell they have," Elvin shouted down. "You can take yourself off and take your poxy excuses for soldiers with you."

"I must warn you, Sir Elvin, that failure to co-operate with me may mean an attack upon your castle with a very much larger force. It will mean the forcible seizure of all your assets as well as the slaughter of all those who assist you," said the envoy.

"A pox on you, you witless turd. Crawl back to your master and tell him we are ready to fight and will not answer to unfounded charges," shouted Elvin.

"I warn you, Sir Elvin…" Sir Henry began, but, by this time, Elvin had ordered his retainers to pelt the soldiers below with the contents of a row of pails of manure that they had ready for the purpose.

"On your head be it," shouted the envoy and he turned tail and made to leave.

"And on your head be this," shouted Elvin aiming a large lump of foul smelling, squelchy manure at Sir Henry. It couldn't have been a better shot if he had tried. It hit Sir Henry smack on his helmet and the watery excrement began slowly making its way down his back accompanied by jeering and laughter from the battlements.

* * *

Some hours later Sir Elvin gathered all his servants and retainers together in the great hall and addressed them thus:

"You will all now be well aware that this castle is under imminent threat of attack. According to the law you no longer owe me any allegiance and I release you from any oath that you made before me. You have been warned that anyone who assists me will be slaughtered. That I do not wish to see. The women and children should leave as soon as they will and I thank you all for the service you have rendered me. My steward will distribute a side of salt bacon and a sack of flour to each family. Of the men I can only say that any help you can give me in the coming battle would be much appreciated. I will pay four silver pennies a day to any man that stays. But if you see fit to leave with the women and children, no dishonour will be attached to it."

Most chose to leave but a small handful of retainers stood their ground, for Elvin had not been the severe taskmaster that his father, and then his stepmother, had been. Some had genuinely liked him. To be honest, too, they were very unsure of what their fate would be if they left and, at least, the money seemed an attractive recompense.

It was during the night that they came. Elvin descended from the top of the keep where he had been observing events with Yestin and gently woke Tayri.

"They are here, my love," he whispered.

Those men that were left Elvin stationed at various points around the walls. It was a bright moonlit night and it was easy to spot the large troupe of knights and foot soldiers advancing up the hill towards them. They were moving in complete silence. Elvin felt a sense of complete foreboding and this was unusual for him. The knowledge that he had a means of escape calmed his fears to some degree. The thought of losing his castle and lands, where he had been born, brought only depression.

In the moonlight he was able make out some Templar mantles amongst the mixed body of knights. It was obvious that the Templars and the Sheriff's men had joined forces for the operation and he searched for a glimpse of Enrique de Larraga without success. His hand lingered on the cross of St. Piran around his neck. It had protected him thus far. He could only pray that it would protect him in the trying days ahead.

The sight of some soldiers dragging a wooden battering ram up the hill as well as a couple of supply wagons carrying ladders gave indication of the determination of the attackers.

Elvin had taken the precaution of getting the ditch around the castle filled with sharpened wooden stakes and then water. He knew it would only be a matter of time before the enemy would drain the ditch, hoping to fill it with brushwood and earth so that they could lay boards across. They could then wheel up the battering ram. He was hoping that the stakes would delay this a bit longer and keep the horsemen at bay for a while.

Elvin's men possessed two crossbows only and a number of light ordinary bows. They had spent days gathering boulders from the beach below to drop down onto their attackers and had several long poles which they would use to push the enemy's ladders away from the walls. Elvin wished he had paid more attention to how the Saracen's Greek Fire had been produced whilst he had been in Egypt. It would have been very useful in this situation.

Elvin expressed his concern to Yestin about the battering ram.

"Is there any way we can get somebody down there to set it alight?" he asked.

"Well, we can try, my liege, but it will be covered with wet hides and, unless we can get some good shots into the lower part of the wooden frame, it will be very difficult to set it on fire. They are also bringing up some parts for a siege engine, which they are obviously going to assemble in front of the castle. It would be useful if we can destroy that before they get it up. Otherwise we're going to be in real trouble."

"Who are your best archers?" inquired Elvin.

"I will send Tom and Wella down to see what they can do," promised Yestin. "They are our two best marksmen. There is a small door at the side. We'll let them out of there and they can swim across. Hopefully they can do some damage before the enemy realise."

Elvin and Yestin kept watch from one of the towers but Tom and

Wella never reappeared below them.

"They must have been slain. Damn it!" uttered Yestin.

In the meantime fires had been lit on the other side of the ditch. This was not just to provide light to assist in the siege of the castle. The enemy's plan was now becoming clear. The vulnerability of the wooden buildings within the castle was clear for all to see. It would not be long before flaming arrows and other blazing missiles would be flying over the walls. At the same time the ditch would be drained so that the battering ran could be brought up whilst other experts would make a start on undermining the walls.

It did not take long to drain the ditch. As soon as it was dry enemy soldiers began racing towards the walls with their ladders. Elvin's men fired a salvo of arrows down into their midst. The crossbows, in particular, began to wreak havoc amongst the first attackers because they had little in the way of protection as they clambered onto the ladders.

Other men were desperately trying to limit the use of the very lowest arrow loops by thrusting long lances through them to clear them of anybody with a bow.

The noise, occasioned by the first attack, was deafening and in direct contrast to the silent approach their assailants had originally made. Now there was mayhem. The screams of the wounded shattered the still night air as they were pierced by arrows or pushed off ladders. But, as one ladder fell, another replaced it and as one soldier fell, another replaced him. The pressure on the walls seemed never ending as the determined attackers came again and again.

The brushwood and earth were being laid in the drained ditch now and Elvin's men were desperately trying to set light to it without any success.

"Three of you men, over here!" ordered Yestin for he had spotted men digging at the foot of the walls. They hurled an avalanche of boulders down onto the diggers, followed by boiling water, and this met with some degree of success. As the enemy ran back to avoid the boulders a crossbowman could pick them off almost at will. That was until a further group of archers appeared on the scene to provide covering fire for the diggers. It was not long before some of the diggers had disappeared below the wall. The sign of smoke billowing out from the tunnel told Yestin the inevitable had happened. Fires had been lit with the object of bringing down the timbers that supported the floor above and thus the walls above.

The sling of a trebuchet was now in action and burning bundles of oil soaked rags were being hurled over the walls aimed at the buildings and parts of buildings constructed of timber. Tayri, and what women had elected to stay, formed a chain with pails of water in a desperate attempt to put out the blaze, which was beginning to get out of hand.

There was a huge crash as a section of the outer wall collapsed where it had been undermined and the attackers began pouring through the gap.

Yestin shouted the order for every man to save himself as best he could and then rushed up to where Elvin and Tayri stood in the watchtower on top of the keep.

"Time to go, my liege," urged Yestin. "The enemy is within."

CHAPTER THIRTY-THREE

A Twist In The Tale

It took some months for Peter to be well enough to return to Spain and Anya met him at Malaga Airport.

He had aged a bit and was walking with the aid of a stick. But, apart from that, looked somewhat better than the last time she had seen him.

She, in turn, was now showing definite signs of her pregnancy and looked very well on it. Thankfully there had been no complications.

They drove up to Granada and Peter made arrangements to see Luis Fernandez the next day. Anya invited him to stay with her and Yuba but Peter thought it ill advised. He booked into a hotel in the centre of the city, but not the one that held such grave memories for him.

Luis Fernandez lived in a small apartment next to a baker's shop. In fact, it was not far from the tapas bar, which Peter had visited, on a number of occasions when he had been staying in the city.

As soon as Luis Fernandez opened the door, Peter recognised him. He was the man who had attended the funeral in Kenilworth and disappeared so quickly. Once again Luis shook Peter's hand warmly and made him feel very welcome.

They talked for what seemed like hours about his father's student days and how happy he had been with Anne, Peter's mother.

"It was a shame that they could not have married because, even after a very short time, they seemed completely devoted to one another," Luis explained. "But, in those days, the family was everything and you didn't go against their wishes."

Apparently Juan Antonio had studied pharmacology at university and had run a successful pharmacy in Granada until a few months before he died. He had always shown a great deal of interest in medicine but did not have the preliminary qualifications to pursue medicine as a career.

He had frequently asked about his son in England because he knew that Luis was in contact with Anne. It was his big regret that his marriage was childless and he regarded Peter as the last in a long and distinguished line. He could apparently trace his ancestors back to medieval times but unfortunately had little left to prove it because his grandfather had sold off some important papers in the nineteen twenties. He had resisted the temptation to contact either Anne or his son, not wishing to upset Anne's marriage to Brian, or, indeed, to rock the boat in his own household, whilst he was still married. After he divorced he had thought about it, but Luis had counselled him strongly against it.

As Peter was about to leave Luis asked him to wait a minute and disappeared into another room. He came back carrying a wooden box, which was quite old and carried an intricate Islamic design.

"Your father asked me, before he died, to give you this, as his only son and heir, at a time when it might be appropriate. I think we've reached that time, don't you? The box contains some family heirlooms, which have been in the Guardia family for many generations and have, apparently, been handed down from father to son. He always wanted you to have them."

Peter did not really know what to say. He was greatly moved and there was the trace of a tear in his eye. He bade farewell to Luis, thanked him, and agreed to keep in contact.

He returned to his hotel. He rang Anya and told her all about the visit. She explained that Yuba was away at the moment and that they could meet up.

"Meet me at the hotel first and then I'll stand you dinner," Peter said. "There's something I want you to see first of all."

Anya came over to the hotel soon after.

"What's the box?" she enquired. Peter explained how he had come by it.

"Oh, let's have a look inside," Anya said excitedly.

Peter opened the box. Inside was a collection of bits of jewellery, an antique watch or two and various other artefacts. They examined them one by one and decided that perhaps they ought to be valued for insurance purposes.

Then they noticed off to the side at the bottom of the box was a special compartment. Peter opened it up and found a further artefact wrapped in some kind of specialised paper. On the outside was what appeared to be a note, which had been affixed to it relatively recently. It was written in Spanish and Anya was able to help with the more difficult bits of translation. It read:

"My son,

What is contained here has been in our family for hundreds of years. Fortunately my grandfather knew about such things and had some kind of preservative coating applied to the metal otherwise it might well not have survived at all. An English knight from Cornwall, who came to Granada many hundreds of years ago, originally owned it. We are all descended from him

Guard it well and, like other members of our illustrious family, pass it on to your eldest son.

May God protect you always.
Your father,
Juan Antonio Guardia"

"Well, I'm damned. I can't believe it!" Peter was clearly shocked and collapsed onto the bed for a moment. "After all we've been through. I'm a descendant. This must be a joke. Le Gard – Guardia – a corruption of Le Gard? It's too much of a coincidence."

"But it has a certain air of inevitability about, doesn't it?" observed Anya.

"Did you not have any inkling?" she asked

"No, of course not," said Peter. "I didn't know until I read my mother's letter that Brian was not my true father. The only thing I can say is that, occasionally, when I come to Granada, I have a strong feeling that I belong. But I've never been able to explain exactly why."

"Well, there you are. It must be in the genes," said Anya.

"Well, I'm sorry to have to disappoint the old boy and let the family heritage down and all that. His request doesn't look as if it's going to be fulfilled because I don't have any sons," observed Peter. "Anyhow, let's see what it is, shall we?"

He took the artefact out of its wrapping and gave a gasp. It was the remains of an encircled crucifix of Celtic design but clearly very, very old. Though it had suffered the ravages of time, Peter and Anya could still make out the intricate swirls of the Celtic knots on it and in the middle, within a smaller circle, was what appeared to be the most beautiful black opal. As he turned the item backwards and forwards it was still capable of reflecting many different colours. It was simple yet a work of great beauty.

"It's lovely," said Anya. "Do you know what it is?"

"No, I don't know exactly. I've seen religious artefacts of a similar nature before but not as beautiful as this. I imagine that this one is extremely old, probably medieval."

"It does show one thing, though," said Anya. "Our friend or, perhaps, I've got to say now, your ancestor, must have escaped from Tremennek and returned to Granada. Indeed, he must have lived out the rest of his life here with his Saracen princess. What that life would have been like, one can only guess at."

"Yes, I think you're right. And who knows what further adventures he went through before he ended up in that grave," said Peter, deep in thought. "I doubt if we will ever know."

CHAPTER THIRTY-FOUR

The Escape

Elvin and Yestin descended from the top of the keep with all haste.

Elvin awoke the drowsy Tayri and urged her to gather together some basic belongings as speedily as she could.

"The time has come to go, my love," Elvin said. "You are going home. But you must hurry. They are in the castle already."

He asked Tryfena to assist her. Tryfena was one of the few castle servants who had remained. She was now a widow and Elvin had asked her to come with them, but the prospect of a voyage to foreign climes had not appealed to her at all.

"This is my home," she had said. "I have never known anywhere else. What would I do in a far land across the sea, where no one would even understand Cornish?" She was a brave woman, for she understood full well what would happen to her when the authorities captured her.

Tryfena fussed over and mothered Tayri, talking to her the whole time to keep her spirits up and encouraging her to hurry. There was probably not a lot of what she was saying that Tayri actually understood. But, in spite of this, they had always taken to one another and Tayri appeared to respect the old woman's intentions.

Little encouragement to hurry was necessary, for the hubbub all around outside was clear for anyone to hear and see. There were fierce yells and shrieks as the Templars poured through the narrow gap in the walls into the bailey. They advanced at speed, swords held high, slashing at anything or anybody that got in their way. Even though there were few soldiers left to defend the castle, the slaughter was horrific. The harrowing cries of the dying and desperately wounded could clearly be heard inside.

Dust, flames and smoke swirled around everywhere as the wooden buildings were put to the torch.

A last ditch stand was being made around the keep in a vain attempt to keep the perpetrators of the onslaught out.

At the bottom of the keep Elvin urged Tayri and Yestin to grab torches and then moved the stone in the outer wall. He leant across and pressed the third step up forward and part of the whole stairway to the upper floors swung open to reveal steps leading downwards.

Elvin ushered Tayri through the opening and down the steps. Yestin came through and then swung the open stairway back on its axle so that it closed fast.

The flames of the torches cast eerie shadows in the flickering light.

They followed the outer wall for a short distance until they reached solid rock, blocking their way. Elvin bent down, brushed away some earth and revealed the trapdoor they were seeking. He inserted the key in the lock and pulled open the trapdoor.

They descended one by one down the wooden ladder with Yestin coming last after he had pulled the trapdoor back down.

They made their way down the passageway towards the sea.

Then Elvin said, "Wait a moment. I want to scrawl a message to any one who may want to know what happened to us in the years to come. I am sure those bastards will claim that they have killed us. This will show that they were unsuccessful."

"My liege, we have no time to delay," urged Yestin. "We must hurry."

"This will take but a moment," said Elvin as he took a sharp stone and carved his message in Latin on the cave wall.

The roar of the sea could clearly be heard at the cave entrance as they approached it, although the breakers crashing in were relatively small. It was a calm night and beyond the shore the sea was as smooth as a millpond.

"We will have to row," observed Yestin, with a worried frown.

They threw their gear into the boat and clambered on board.

Elvin clutched his St. Piran Cross as they pulled away from the cave entrance. Both the men were rowing as hard as they could. Yestin had fixed up the sail and, with what little breeze there was, they managed to make reasonable speed.

As they pulled out from under the cliff, they became aware of the swirling smoke and flames coming from what was left of the castle. The noise of the slaughter seemed to have stopped but the crackling of the flames and the crash of falling timbers continued.

The attackers were yelling in communication with one another as they sought the prisoners they prized.

Elvin smiled to himself as he imagined their annoyance at not being able to find them.

Suddenly, however, he spied a group of soldiers on the cliff top. They were carrying torches, inspecting the cliff face and looking down at the open sea. In the bright moonlight he realised, at once, that they had been spotted. Frantic efforts to loose arrows at them were made but the escapees were now out of their range. The soldiers immediately turned tail and ran back into the castle to report what they had seen.

As Elvin and Yestin rowed further out to sea, they could see what was happening at the castle and beyond. A group of horsemen was already leaving the castle in the hope of, perhaps, cutting off their escape somewhere.

As they made further progress St. Michael's Mount came into view and they knew they had to be wary of the vagaries of the currents, the submerged rocks and the petrified forest that lay below the waves. Sailing in the darkness made things doubly dangerous.

Looking up beyond the village of Tremennek, Elvin could just make out the torches of the horsemen galloping at all speed along the ridge way towards Market Jew.

Elvin's objective was a ship, which was anchored on the other side of the Mount and they still had some way to go. His one hope was that the captain, who was expecting them some time that week, had someone on lookout for them. His one fear was that the ship might not be there at all.

The monastery on the top of St. Michael's Mount presented an eerie sight in to the moonlight. As they approached they could now spy the light breakers crashing onto the rocks at the foot of the Mount.

As they got nearer they realised that the one thing, that they had not wanted, had happened. It was low tide and the causeway across to the Mount from Market Jew was clear of the water.

As they approached the port side of the Mount they heard the clatter of hooves as the knights crossed the causeway and began ascending towards the monastery.

"Faster," urged Elvin. "We've got to get round the Mount before they get to the top."

If they could gain the far side of the Mount from the shore, he knew they would be relatively safe. The cliffs there were very steep and there would be no chance that a boat could be launched to pursue them.

As they made the far side, they could see the knights on the top desperately looking for a vantage point to aim arrows at them or to throw various other projectiles down onto them to hamper their progress or sink them.

They pulled further out from the island in an effort to avoid this and, at last, it seemed as if they been successful in evading capture.

Elvin breathed a sigh of relief as the ship, that he was seeking, came into view, anchored in Mount's Bay.

They made for the vessel as quickly as they could.

"Ahoy, there," Elvin shouted as they approached. "It is I, Sir Elvin Le Gard. We are coming aboard."

Immediately a ladder was thrown down to them and the captain shouted down: "Come aboard, Sir Elvin, as quickly as you can. We are about to weigh anchor."

They rested the boat next to ship's ladder and Elvin pushed Tayri up it. As it was not secured to the side of the ship, so it did sway about quite a bit and Tayri took a lot of persuading to continue upwards towards the waiting assistance of a seaman leaning over the side. Yestin did what he could to hold the ladder straight so that Tayri and Elvin could make the top.

Just then, fast approaching in the darkness, came a rowing boat full of soldiers. It came as a surprise as it had obviously set out from the shoreward side of the Mount where the water would be quite shallow because of the low tide. It was coming at full speed making straight for them.

"Hurry, Yestin. They're coming," yelled Elvin. Yestin threw up the rest of the baggage and clambered onto the ladder. The ship was now moving as the captain had given orders to weigh anchor and set sail.

The ladder, with Yestin attached to it, was now swaying precariously.

Suddenly a salvo of arrows whooshed through the air from the rowing boat. Several embedded themselves in the side of the vessel but one found its mark.

Yestin gave a shriek of pain and fell off the ladder into the water.

"Yestin," cried Elvin, "Yestin," he cried again, as Yestin thrashed around desperately in the water with the distance between him and the ship getting greater by the second.

"Do something," yelled Elvin at the captain. "We can't leave him here."

"There's nothing we can do, my lord," said the captain as the rowing boat reached Yestin. As they hauled him aboard Yestin was already dead.

Elvin's face sank into his hands, as the last he saw of his boyhood friend was his body lying outstretched between soldiers in the rowing boat.

"Oh, God, I never wanted this to happen," he said as Tayri put her arm around him to comfort him.

As the ship sailed out of Mounts Bay, that was the last anybody in Cornwall ever saw of Sir Elvin Le Gard and his Saracen bride.

CHAPTER THIRTY-FIVE

Trials And Tribulations

Peter cursed himself as soon as he had opened the magazine. He had not had the foresight to see what was going to happen.

The discovery of the Chalice in Granada and the controversy surrounding its similarity to the Sacred Chalice at Valencia had been news enough originally.

Its subsequent theft from the University had been an added bonus to journalists. All the stories surrounding that theft and the investigation into it, kept them happy for several weeks. But now there was an added factor.

Peter had not really been thinking when he made a chance remark to a small professional, archaeological magazine in the UK that he believed he was a descendant of Sir Elvin Le Gard, the Templar, who was suspected of having been responsible for the original theft of the Chalice from the monastery in the Pyrenees in medieval times.

An alert journalist, working for the Spanish News Agency in London, had picked up the story and wired it to several magazines.

The headlines leapt off the page at him, as soon as Peter had opened the magazine.

"Chalice Archaeologist Discovers Roots in Granada."

There was an old photograph of him, taken at some conference somewhere, and the whole story was there for the entire world to read about.

Peter was not a happy person. There was something vaguely unprofessional about it all, in his opinion, and he felt this sort of sensationalist press attention would make it difficult for him to be taken seriously as far as his work was concerned.

* * *

The effect on Peter's work was the least of his worries, however.

Somebody else had also seen the article and was paying close attention to it.

Colonel Julio Larraga was sitting in his parked car on a motorway rest area. He was reading the same magazine.

He was on his way to the Monastery in the High Pyrenees to meet a fellow member of the Order of the Ancient Knights of Aragon. Between them they were going to set about the business of concealing the Chalice in a secret hiding place amongst the tombs of the Aragonese kings. Nobody would ever find it again.

As he read the details of the article the Colonel began considering what his next steps should be after he had rendered the Chalice safe and secure.

There was no doubt in his mind what he had to do. The Muslim woman had to be removed from the scene, as it appeared that she had been able to identify him to Inspector Garcia. She could not be permitted to live.

He would, also, take great pleasure in dealing with the Englishman. As a descendant of Enrique de Larraga nothing would give him greater satisfaction than avenging his noble ancestor. The Englishman would pay for his ancestor's heresy and theft and for killing Hernando.

* * *

Later during that week Inspector Garcia telephoned Peter at his hotel and said he would like to interview both Anya and Peter again to clear up a few final details.

They both met outside Police Headquarters and were soon shown into Garcia's office.

"I'm pleased to see that you are both looking so well in the circumstances," the policeman observed.

"Have you made any progress on the case?" asked Peter.

"Not a great deal," replied Garcia. "We've been able to identify the man who shot you, Dr. Verity. He has been known by several aliases but we know him best as Hernando Alonzo, a former sergeant in the army, who, since his discharge, has been working as a bodyguard for several well-known people mainly in the business of entertainment. We have suspected for some time that he might have been engaged in some criminal activities like kidnap and ransom but we have been unable to get enough on him to charge him. Thanks to you, Dr, Verity, we don't have to worry about him any longer.

The other person in the hotel room remains a mystery to us."

"But I thought that I had possibly identified him," said Anya.

"Yes, so did I," said Garcia. "That person, however, turned out to have died last year, so it couldn't have possibly been him. So we're back to square one, really.

Now, all I want you to do is to go back over your statements to make sure that we haven't missed anything and then you can go."

"Well. I don't think there is anymore that I can add," said Peter. "What about you Anya?"

"No, I don't think so," said Anya.

"Please, go through them anyway," insisted the Inspector.

They checked through the statements and then they were allowed to go.

As they left Garcia picked up the telephone and dialled a number.

"They've just left," he said and put the telephone down again.

* * *

Peter and Anya left the Police Headquarters and crossed a small square opposite and entered a warren of small streets, which would take them back into the centre of the city.

As they turned down a narrow street they failed to notice the MPV with the blacked out windows, which was trailing them. As it approached them, it sounded its horn and, naturally, both of them stepped back to make room for it. The vehicle was large enough to fill the breadth of the street. As it drew level with them, two of its nearside doors opened trapping them in between.

Before either Peter or Anya could yell out, they found themselves bundled roughly into the vehicle, which then took off at high speed. They had parcel tape hastily stuck across their mouths, hoods placed over their heads and their hands were tied behind their backs.

Peter could hear the sound of the traffic outside for a while and the vehicle stopped and started as if it were negotiating the normal daily build-up in the city. After a while the traffic noise was reduced and they made speedier progress as if they had reached the outskirts of the city and were gradually leaving it behind.

On one occasion they stopped to pick up another passenger.

Soon they appeared to be driving on a trunk road or motorway and continued in this fashion for a considerable number of miles.

To Peter it felt as if every bone in his body was aching and he was, particularly uncomfortable with his arms tied behind his back.

He was very worried about Anya and her condition and hoped that their assailants were not handling her too roughly or doing anything, which would endanger the baby.

At last it felt that they had reached a town again and Peter fancied he caught the sound of waves crashing onto the shore. He was certain they had driven to the coast.

Then they stopped and he heard the sound of iron gates being opened and the MPV presumably moving forward into the property, to which they were being taken. They proceeded along a gravel drive and then came to a halt.

They were bundled out of the vehicle and taken into a building. They were placed in a room and left to wait.

After a while the door opened again and a voice said:

"Dr. Verity and Dr. Naziri, I am going to remove your hoods, provided that I have a promise from you that you will behave yourselves and not attempt to try and do anything to attract attention. It will be pretty fruitless anyway because we are some way from the main road and nobody will hear you. Nod your heads if you agree to co-operate."

Peter fancied he recognised the voice. He nodded his head and felt his hood being removed. There was a sharp stab of pain to the mouth as the parcel tape was unceremoniously drawn back to allow him to talk.

He was pleased to see that Anya was in the same room and now had had her hood and tape removed.

Before them stood a tall, smartly dressed man armed with a revolver.

"What the devil is going on?" asked Peter desperately.

"You will find out soon enough," said the man and now Peter knew who it was. It was the man who had ordered his torture in the hotel room all those months before.

"You are the person who stole the Granada Chalice," said Peter.

The man smiled and said: "I would prefer to say that I have returned it to its rightful home."

"And where would that be?" asked Peter.

"That's nothing for you to worry about," came the reply.

The man then proceeded towards the door.

"What is going to happen to us?" asked Anya, as he was about to leave.

"You will be brought before the Knights for judgment later," he replied.

"Judgment? Judgment for what?" cried Peter, but the man had already left.

Peter and Anya looked at one another.

"Are you all right?" he asked Anya.

"I'm all right at the moment," she said, though she looked a little pale.

"How do you feel?" she asked Peter.

"A little achy," he replied, "but not too bad."

"I wonder what's going on," said Anya.

Peter shook his head.

* * *

The Mercedes swept through the iron gates and glided up the driveway to the Villa De Las Rosas.

After it had parked up a somewhat harassed looking Professor Velasquez emerged and approached the building. Colonel Larraga met him on the steps to the front entrance.

"What is so important that you bring me all the way down here?" asked the Professor rather irritably.

"I have summoned a meeting of the Knights on a matter of great importance," replied Larraga. "I thought it wise, in view of all the publicity, to hold it well away from things."

"What is this matter of such great importance? I have a lot of meetings to attend."

"Suffice to say, at the moment, we have in our custody the Englishman, Verity, and the Muslim woman, Naziri," said Larraga. "Follow me!"

* * *

Peter and Anya both jumped as the door to where they were being kept opened suddenly and two men came in. They were roughly bundled out of the room and along a corridor.

At the end they were ushered into a large room and pushed into chairs, which were set upon a platform looking down into the rest of the room.

Before them, to their surprise, seated round a conference table, were ranged a number of strangely garbed persons. All were dressed in long robes with intricate heraldic designs embossed on them and each wore a hood to conceal his or her identity. It was an extremely unnerving sight.

At the far end of the table sat one of their number, with gavel in hand, who was obviously going to preside over whatever event was to take place.

It did not take long for Peter and Anya to learn the nature of their attendance before these people.

The presiding officer banged his gavel three times on the table.

"Dr. Peter Verity and Dr. Anya Naziri," he began, "you have been brought before this summary court of the Military Council of the Order of the Ancient Knights of Aragon to answer for crimes against the Order."

"Crimes, what crimes?" Peter asked. Immediately he was slapped hard across the face by one of the thugs standing behind him.

"Dr, Verity, I would ask you to remain silent. This is a summary trial not a discussion," said the voice. "You will get an opportunity to make a short statement in your defence. If you do not co-operate, I will ask for your mouth to be gagged. Do I make myself clear?"

Anya froze. She recognised, at once, the voice of the person presiding over the so-called trial. It was the man who had escorted her to the University and stolen the Granada Chalice and the smartly dressed gentleman, who had spoken to them briefly earlier.

Peter nodded and Larraga continued:

"Peter Verity," he continued, "you have been charged with the crime of murder of a Knight of our Order in that you did murder one, Hernando Alonzo, in Granada on the ninth day of May of this year. It is the sentence of this court that you suffer death by shooting. Have you anything to say in your defence?"

Peter could hardly believe what he was hearing. It was a complete travesty of any trial by anybody's standards. It appeared to have been a completely arbitrary decision by bunch of complete madmen.

"This is a complete farce," said Peter. "I have been sentenced without any form of defence by a so-called court made up of complete lunatics. I presume that the Hernando Alonzo, to whom you refer, is the Hernando who tortured me in my hotel and then tried to kill me as I attempted to escape. His death was an accident and no more than the sadistic monster deserved. I protest most vigorously at this assault upon my freedom and demand that you release Dr. Naziri and myself immediately."

"That will not be possible, Dr. Verity," said Larraga. "Sentence will be carried tomorrow at dawn. Take him away!"

Peter's head was in a whirl. He could not believe what was happening. He was taken back to the room where they had been kept, tied up in a chair again, and left to contemplate his fate at the hands of these cranks into whose hands they had fallen.

"Anya Naziri," continued Larraga back in the courtroom, "you have been charged with compromising the integrity of the Sacred Chalice of Valencia by spuriously producing a duplicate chalice, the so-called Granada Chalice. As a result you have thereby threatened the preservation of the Christian Faith. Further to this you have been charged with compromising the security of the Order of the Ancient Knights of Aragon in that you have been able to identify Colonel Julio Larraga to the Police. This presents a dire threat to the existence of our Order, which fights for the preservation of a Faith we regard as under siege from atheists, heretics and other non-believers. As a member of the Islamic Faith you are regarded as a traditional, heretical enemy of the Christian Faith and, therefore, a continuing threat to those who would preserve it.

"It is the sentence of this court that you suffer death by shooting. Have you anything to say in your defence?"

At that moment Anya, who had looked very pale throughout the proceedings, collapsed to the floor in a faint.

"Pick her up again," commanded Larraga.

When Anya had sufficiently recovered, Larraga repeated:

"Have you anything to say in your defence, Dr. Naziri?"

"This is ridiculous," she mumbled, still not feeling at all well. "You must release us both at once. This is complete madness."

"The sentence will be carried out with that of Dr. Verity at dawn tomorrow. Take her away!"

Anya was taken back to join Peter.

"Oh God, Anya, are you all right?" Peter said as she collapsed in her chair. "Look," he said to one of the men who had escorted her back, "if you've an ounce of humanity, get this lady a glass of water."

A few moments later one of the men returned with a jug of water and a glass. He freed one of Anya's hands so that she could take a drink and then disappeared again.

"Are you feeling better," Peter asked.

"Yes, I'm not too bad now," she said. "Peter, what are we going to do? How can we get away from these lunatics?"

"I don't know," said Peter despondently. "All we can do now is to pray."

* * *

During the night both Peter and Anya were awakened by the sound of the door being unlocked and opened. Somebody entered with a torch and approached them.

At first they thought that dawn was approaching and that preparations were being made for their sentences to be carried out. Peter glanced at his watch, however, and found that it was only one thirty.

"Dr. Naziri, Dr Verity," whispered the intruder, "be as quiet as you can. I've ordered the guards outside your door to take a break for a moment, so there is not a lot of time. I am going to release you because I have not been in agreement with what has been going on within the Order for some time.

"What I thought was in the interests of the Christian Faith has become a monstrous aberration and I, personally, want no further part in it. I would have left them a long time ago had not the Civil Guard asked me to remain to provide them with important information.

I am going to untie you and then we will make our way out of the building as quietly as we can. My car is parked just round at the side."

The man swiftly untied them and then led them to the main door. He quietly unlocked it and they all exited as quietly as possible.

Anya was still a little unsteady on her feet and Peter was still not one hundred per cent mobile but they supported one another with the other man's help until they reached his car. In the dim light of the car Anya recognised Professor Velasquez.

Fortunately the gravel driveway ran downhill to the iron gates and Velasquez was able to freewheel, with no lights on, down to the gates, thus keeping the noise down to a minimum. When they arrived at the gates, he started up the engine. With a zapper, stored above the mirror, he pressed a button and the gates slowly swung open.

Whether it was something triggered by the opening of the gates or the sound of the Mercedes starting up but lights came on all over the Villa. There was shouting and the sound of dogs barking. People were running down the drive.

"Get a move on, Professor. They're after us," urged Peter.

The Professor accelerated out of the gates onto the highway. But just as he did there was the ominous sound of shots and bullets starting to ping off the paintwork at an alarming rate.

Peter and Anya kept their heads down as one final bullet smashed through the rear window. Professor Velasquez ducked his head and kept driving.

After a few miles the Professor suddenly slowed down, stopped and slumped over the wheel.

"Professor, what's wrong?" asked Peter anxiously.

"I think the last bullet must have hit me," he said.

Peter got out of the car. Professor Velasquez had a nasty bullet wound in his right shoulder and the blood was just beginning to seep through. Peter helped him into the back of the car and took over the driving himself whilst Anya did what she could to assist the Professor. Fortunately the car carried a first aid kit and she was able to make tentative efforts at patching him up.

"Where are we going to go?" asked Peter. "They're bound to send someone towards the Granada road, thinking we might go that way. They'll probably also have someone else cover the Valencia road just in case we go that way. I think we had better stop and phone Inspector Garcia for help."

"No, no. Don't do that," said the Professor weakly. "He's one of them. That's how you got picked up after you left the Police Headquarters in Granada."

"Good God, what are we going to do, then?" said Peter desperately. "Who the hell can we rely on if the police are in with them?"

"That is the difficulty," said the Professor. "It might be better if we split up and also lost this car for a while. They all know it and will be looking out for it."

They all thought for a moment or two and then the Professor said:

"I've got an idea. I'll give my contact in the Civil Guard a call. I'll tell him what's happened and ask him for advice and help." He made a short call on his mobile and spoke to his contact for a short while. Then he said:

"Right, he agrees that it is wise to split up for the moment. The nearest big city is Malaga. We will go straight to the Civil Guard Headquarters in Malaga and make a full report. He will forewarn the Chief there that we are coming. With a bit of luck I can leave my car with them for a few days. You can get the first bus in the morning to Granada and I'll get a train to Valencia. I can pick the car up again at a later stage."

"What are we going to do to get the lunatic Knights off our backs?" asked Peter.

"My contact says to leave all that to them. They have been watching this group for some time and now is as good a time to act as any. They will probably raid the Villa De Las Rosas sometime before dawn. But it would be wise to be careful for a while until they have all been rounded up."

It was with a sense of immense relief that Peter set off for Malaga.

* * *

Later on the next day Peter and Anya arrived back in Granada. Anya urged Peter to return to England not because she wanted to see the back of him but because she felt he would be safer there. Reluctantly he agreed.

Anya was not looking forward to returning home having been away for a couple of days and unable to contact Yuba. She knew full well he would come to the wrong conclusion and that there would be a row. She was not expecting a great deal of sympathy regarding her plight for a few days at least until things got back to relative normality.

Peter returned to his hotel but, upon arrival, he noticed a police car outside and Inspector Garcia sitting in it.

He was in a bit of a quandary as to what to do. He needed to check out and collect his baggage so that he could return to England. Then he decided to give the Police Headquarters a call from his mobile. He spoke to the desk sergeant and asked for Inspector Garcia.

"He is not here, at the moment," was the reply.

"Would you tell him that Peter Verity called and that I am on my way back to Granada from the coast and wish to see him on a matter of some urgency?"

"Yes, sir, I will give him your message," said the sergeant. "Do you have a contact number?"

"Just tell him that I will come round to Police Headquarters as soon as I have arrived back in about two hours time."

"Right, sir, I will give him your message."

Peter pocketed his mobile and waited for any kind of reaction in the police car. Sure enough, after about ten minutes, the police car moved off and Peter had got his opportunity.

He checked out of the hotel as quickly as he could and took a rather expensive taxi ride to the airport at Malaga. As he could not get a flight until the next day, he stayed the night in a hotel close to the airport.

He checked in next morning and everything passed without incident and he sat in the lounge waiting for the flight. He opened the newspaper he had hurriedly picked up on the way through. There on the front page was the headline:

Chalice Suspect Shot Dead Near Malaga

Following a tip-off Civil Guards yesterday raided a property to the east of Malaga and arrested a number of people implicated in the theft of the Granada Chalice from the University of Granada. During an extensive gunfight Guards shot dead wanted criminal, Julio Larraga. Arrests were also carried out during the day at other locations in Andalusia including that of an Inspector of Police in Granada.

Peter took out his mobile and rang Anya at her office. She answered right away.

"Hi, it's Peter, here," he replied. "I'm just in the lounge at the airport waiting for my flight. Have you seen the paper today?

"Yes, I have," said Anya. "What a relief! They seemed to have got them all. There doesn't seem to have been any sign of the Chalice, though."

"No, I think they have hidden that away in the High Pyrenees and it will be very difficult to find. I've got my doubts whether it will ever be found again. There is too much at stake by all accounts."

"You may be right," Anya said.

"Well, it looks like 'end of story' then," said Peter. "I hope everything goes all right with the baby. How was Yuba, by the way?"

"Oh, OK," she replied without enthusiasm. "He took some convincing that I had not just spent time away with you. There was a bit of an atmosphere for a day or two but he came round in the end."

"No surprises there, then," said Peter rather cynically.

"When are we going to see one another again?" asked Anya.

"I don't know," said Peter. "Probably not for a while, unless some project or conference crops up where we are both involved."

"I shall miss you, Peter," she said. "We've been through a lot together recently, haven't we?

"That's true," he said. "Anyhow, they've just announced my flight, so I've got to go."

"Bye, then," said Anya. "I hope you have a good flight and keep well."

Peter thought he could detect from her a more than usual regret at their parting but thought nothing further of it as he made his way to the departure gate.

CHAPTER THIRTY-SIX

Lost And Found

Peter and Anya were not to meet again for a further three years. The occasion was the funeral of Bernard Harper, who had died after contracting liver cancer only a few months previously.

Bernard had been well respected in his profession and in the community. There was a large turnout at the church and Peter arrived late.

He managed to find a seat at the back and then noticed Mary sitting a couple of rows in front of him. He gave her a wave, as she turned round to look to see who the latecomer was.

Peter's relationship with Mary and Alex had been reasonable enough in recent times and he had even spent Christmas with the two of them and the children on one occasion.

He had had only limited contact with Anya over the time mainly through correspondence relating to archaeological matters and the odd Christmas card.

He had preferred to get on with the business of living his life instead of pursuing an unobtainable dream, but he had failed to establish any other stable relationship.

After the service had ended Peter was invited back to the house with a large number of other people.

As he was helping himself to the extensive buffet, Mary tapped him on the shoulder.

"Hello, Peter," she said, giving him a light peck on the cheek. "How are you keeping?"

"Oh, not so bad," he said. "I'm still hobbling around. I still get the odd aches and pains but nothing I can't live with. How are the children?" he asked.

"They are both well," Mary replied. "Emma will be taking her GCSEs this year."

"And Alex?"

"He's good, too," Mary said. "I'm surprised you haven't sought out Anya."

"How do you mean?" queried Peter.

"Well, she's here somewhere. She's got a lovely little boy."

"Oh, I didn't know she was coming," Peter said. "I'll have to have a chat with her."

Peter found Anya talking to Bernard's widow. When she saw him she detached herself from Mrs. Harper and came up to him. She was holding a little boy by the hand and he was looking a bit miserable and rather fidgety, as if he was bored by the whole occasion.

"Hello, Anya," he said to her. "You are looking well."

"Yes, I suppose so," she said.

"And who is this young man?" Peter asked, bending down on one knee to look at the little boy.

"The gentleman is asking you what your name is," Anya said in Spanish. The little lad struggled to get away from the firm grip that Anya had on him, not seeming to wish to co-operate at all.

"I bet I can guess what your name is," said Peter in Spanish.

The little boy squirmed a little and giggled.

"Is it Jaime?" Peter tried.

The little boy shook his head.

"Is it Justiniano Antonio?" asked Peter.

"No" said the little lad. The length of the name sent the little boy into paroxysms of laughter.

"He is a funny man, isn't he?" said Anya.

"It 's Itri," volunteered the little boy.

"Oh, my goodness, that's a nice name, isn't it?" said Peter.

The little boy beamed and took hold of Peter's hand.

"He seems to have taken to you," said Anya.

Peter laughed and said "How are you, Anya?"

"I'm fine," she said. "I was hoping I would find you here. I haven't heard much from you lately."

"Well, I've been very busy," said Peter.

"Have you recovered fully from your injuries?"

"Oh, yes. Only the odd ache and pain, you know."

There was a pause and then Peter said:

"How's Yuba. Being as difficult as ever?"

Anya looked a bit taken aback, shook her head slightly and said:

"I thought you knew?"

"Knew what?" queried Peter.

"Yuba and I were divorced two years ago."

It was now time for Peter to look taken aback.

"Oh, I'm so sorry. No, I didn't know. I feel a real fool."

"That's all right," Anya said.

"Are you managing all right?" Peter asked.

"Oh, yes, of course I am" replied Anya.

Peter was feeling slightly embarrassed and excused himself.

"I'm just going to get something else from the buffet," he said. "I'll see you again shortly."

He made his way over to the buffet and helped himself to some further titbits.

As he turned to go back Mary was at his side.

"I see you've met up with Anya," she said.

"Yes," said Peter. "I didn't know she was divorced."

"I thought you would be very pleased to hear it," Mary said with a sly smile.

"Now, don't get me riled up again," snapped Peter. "I've moved on from all that."

"I'm not getting you riled up, Peter," continued Mary. "You need taking in hand. You seem to have been wandering around in the wilderness for years. She is the woman you wanted all those years ago. She is free. Go get her."

"Oh, don't be so silly," said Peter. "She won't be interested in me. She'll link up with someone of her own faith, I suspect."

"Not necessarily. You can't just assume that and well, she hasn't done, has she? Why do you think she came to this funeral? In the hope that you would be here, I'm sure."

"Oh, I don't know," said Peter.

At that moment Anya appeared to be leaving. Peter went over. He did not know what to say but gabbled out:

"Its nice to have seen you again, Anya. We mustn't make it so long next time."

"No, of course not," she said.

"Good-bye, funny man," said a little voice in Spanish next to her.

Peter bent down and picked the little lad up.

"Good-bye, little Itri. I hope we meet again soon."

And then they were gone.

Peter went to find himself a drink.

Mary sidled up to him again and said: "Peter Verity, you are a fool."

"Why?" asked Peter.

"Because, why do you think she is now divorced?"

"I don't know. They had a very up and down marriage. He was particularly jealous of me in the same way that you were jealous of Anya."

"And with good reason," said Mary. "Did you look at that little boy?"

"Of course, I did. He was a nice little chap."

"No, you didn't, you idiot. I mean – did you look at him closely?"

"Well, I thought I did," protested Peter.

"You didn't at all. Well, I did. Looking into that young lad's eyes really unnerved me. It took me back to when we were first married. I looked into that kiddie's eyes and I saw you staring back at me. Yuba was never his father and I am sure Yuba knew it. I'm telling you now, Peter Verity, if you don't go after that woman, you'll be the biggest fool in Christendom."

Peter hurried out of the house as quickly as he could. His injuries prevented him from running but he limped along as best as he could.

As he left the house he was just in time to see Anya getting into a taxi with Itri, her little boy. The cab sped up the road leaving Peter totally dejected.

There were one or two of the people who had attended the funeral waiting around outside so he asked a number of them whether they had heard where Anya had asked the taxi to take them.

One woman said: "I think it was the Berkeley Hotel."

Peter gave the surprised woman a huge hug and a kiss on the cheek and went back into the house.

There was little he could do right there and then. He decided to give them time to get back to the hotel, then to ring the hotel and hope that they had not checked out and left for the airport. He realised that he had no idea what their plans were and did not know when their flight back to Spain was, or, indeed, whether they were going straight back to Spain. He felt suddenly that he had really lost touch and the sooner he caught up with Anya again the better.

He rang the hotel later and was told that they had checked out. He felt awful. He felt that he ought to have spent more time talking to Anya and, perhaps, been more informed about her present circumstances. Now he felt he had blown any opportunity to get together with her.

Mary wandered across to him and said:

"You are looking really down, Peter. What's happened?"

Peter quickly explained his predicament.

"How much would you give me, if I told you where they've gone?" teased Mary.

"Oh, don't play about, Mary. Tell me," Peter begged.

"I can't believe, given our past, how I know more about her whereabouts than you do," Mary pointed out.

"I know, I know," said Peter, "but please tell me where I can get in touch with her again."

"She has been telling the little boy all about Cornwall and has decided to take him down there for a few days. Guess where they are going to stay"

"Oh, I don't know," said Peter, "Where?"

"The Tremennek Bay Hotel!" replied Mary.

* * *

The next morning Peter rang the Tremennek Bay Hotel and enquired whether Anya and her son had checked in. This was confirmed and Peter asked to be put through to the room.

"Hello," Anya answered.

"Anya, it's Peter. I am so sorry I missed you at the Harpers' house. Mary told me where you were going. Look, I need to speak to you seriously and it can't be done over the phone. I'd like to come down to Tremennek Bay and join you, if that's all right."

"Well, yes, of course, OK, if that is what you want to do." Anya sounded slightly taken aback but nevertheless pleased that they were going to meet up again.

Peter arrived at the Tremennek Bay Hotel that evening, checked in and then went straight up to Anya's room.

He knocked on the door and heard a shrill little voice, shouting in Spanish:

"Mummy, there's somebody at the door."

"Hold on a moment, darling, I'm just coming."

Then the door was opened.

"Mummy, it's that funny man," cried Itri.

"Hello young man," said Peter. "How do you like it here in Cornwall?"

"It's cool," said Itri. "There's a lovely beach and lots of rock pools and all sorts."

"Hello, Peter," said Anya, embracing him affectionately. "I'm so glad to see you." Anya drew him to one side for a moment.

"Look, I've made arrangements for a babysitter for Itri. I thought we could have dinner and talk about old times together."

"That would be great," said Peter.

They met up a little later and had dinner together in the Hotel dining room. They talked all the way through dinner and then retired to the lounge to talk some more.

Eventually Peter plucked up the courage to say what he had come to say.

"Look, Anya, I had no idea about Itri. I didn't realise. I didn't know you had parted from Yuba. I know now why you brought him down to Cornwall and why I had to be here as well."

"And why is that?" she asked

"Because you wanted to show him his long lost roots and because I wanted to tell you, once again, that I love you and have always loved you. And, on top of that, I was nursing a hope, perhaps forlorn, that, maybe, we could be together at long last" said Peter.

"Anyhow," Peter went on, "I felt I ought to bring this down for Itri."

Peter felt in his pocket and brought out a small box. He opened it and inside was the medieval cross, passed on to Peter by Juan Antonio Guardia.

"I want you to keep this and give it to him when he is eighteen," said Peter. "It's what they call down here, in Cornwall, a Cross of St. Piran, though this is a very, very old and a special one. In all probability, my ancestor, Sir Elvin Le Gard, once wore this. It has always been passed down through the generations to the oldest son – and I know now that it should be passed on to Itri."

Anya was very quiet. There was the hint of a tear in her eye.

"If you love me, Peter, why can't you give it to him, yourself, when he is eighteen? We could watch our son grow up together, if that is what you would really like. I realise I've been a fool for a very long time. Watching you, just clinging to life, in that hospital in Granada I realised then that I didn't want to lose you and that I loved you too. I want us to be together always. I know there will be problems because of our different faiths, but it's something we can work out between us. Nothing is impossible, given the will."

"No, it isn't — and you know it's what I want as well," Peter said.

They took hold of one another's hands and just stayed like that for a while.

The next morning Peter, Anya and Itri went for a walk across the sands at Tremennek Bay. The little boy scampered about with a bucket and spade, digging sandcastles or lingering in a pool, whilst Peter looked for crabs for him.

Peter and Anya strolled hand in hand and, after a while, Itri, a little bit tired, pushed his way in between them and looked up at Peter.

"Are you going to be my daddy? he asked.

Peter's reply was clearly and proudly stated:

"I am your daddy, sunshine. I am your daddy."

As they walked down the beach Peter gazed up at the headland that overlooked the Bay.

There was the odd person walking along the coastal footpath but otherwise it was bare. Peter wondered whether that person had any inkling about what had gone on there.

If the ghost of Sir Elvin Le Gard had really been in the habit of cantering across the land up there, as many villagers traditionally believed, then surely he would be looking down onto the beach, at that moment, with just the trace of a smile on his face.

For there on the sand below the cliff face he would have noticed the happy trio strolling towards the end of the bay – Peter and Anya kept apart so long by dogma and orthodoxy, but having found one another at last and, in between them, little Itri, chattering away to himself, with his feet off the ground, swinging backwards and forwards between the two adults.

Peter was sure that the Knight would have approved.